MW00634123

The Book of Death

978-0-9987836-0-4

The Book of Death

Sidney Berger

The Doe Press
Waban, Massachusetts
2017

For Michele, Rafe, and Aaron.

ONE

The seedy man who brought it to me, along with a dozen or so pieces of trash, called himself Carl Smith, and he asked me to pay him practically nothing for the other things but a great deal for this item. I had been dealing with book scouts for years, but I had never seen this one before.

His approach was typical: "I got some books to sell. Are you buying?"

However seedy he was, I took him seriously. Many of these scouts are quite expert about what they scrounge up. There are the specialists in modern fiction, who can spot true firsts with good dust jackets in a second; they never mistake them for the commoner book club editions. Some scouts can cull a choice paperback from a dozen boxes of paper trash. There are connoisseurs who deliver books on art, history, war, hunting, and cooking, knowing which will bring $25 and which $2500. But this Carl Smith brought me an incunabulum.

Things printed before 1501 are called incunabula, and little Mr. Smith had brought me a dilly.

"What have you got?"

"Some pamphlets. Some are junk, one is expensive. You interested?"

"I don't have a lot of spare cash right now [my usual stance], but let's see what's in the box."

He edged toward the table where I carried out such transactions. His torn tweed blazer smelled slightly of cigarette smoke, slightly of beer. His gray jacket and black slacks were once quite respectable, but they showed the tatters of someone who needed cash. He was nearly bald, with a fringe of gray and reddish stubble around the dome. His pudgy hands, gripping the small carton, were not exactly filthy, but they were unkempt and unhealthy, and not all that steady. His waddle suggested arthritis or rickets or ingrown toenails. He was close enough now for me to get a whiff of his breath. It made me want to make quick work of this transaction with this poor man.

I didn't expect much, and the first few items out of the box didn't disappoint me. A tattered prayer book, mid-twentieth century. Worth a buck. A disbound *Gulliver's Travels*, blue cloth over flexible boards. Worth half the prayer book. "No, thanks." A horribly abused McGuffey's Fifth, lacking a cover here, a fascicle of pages there. "I'll pass on this." Then I saw it, unappealing at first: just a little pamphlet covered in stiff plain paper; no label, no color, no pizzazz. But opening it, I felt as if a light came on. On the title page was a small wood engraving of a skeleton, and above it was the title:

Ein Buchlein
von dem
STERBEN

The last word was in large red letters, and it fairly leapt off the page. DEATH.

"It's really rare. And I want a lot for it."

I pulled my eyes from the title and saw at the bottom of the page "Leipsig :: C. K." There was no date, but I knew it was old. The slightly yellowed laid paper was cockled but lovely; the endsheet had a fleur de lis watermark. I flipped to the back and found a short colophon: C. Kachelofen / (|) (|) L X X X X I I I I. Thank goodness for Mr. McRath, my high school Latin teacher. 1494—MCDLXXXXIIII. (Thanks again to McRath, I knew that an M could be made up of open and close parens, with a straight vertical line between them.) My hands began to quiver, and I'm sure Smith saw it.

"It's worth a lot. How much will you give me for it?"

Smith wasn't too experienced at this game. That was a pathetic approach. "What do you want for it?"

"How much is it worth to you?"

"What's it worth to *you*?"

"Mr. Burgess, I may not look like I know much, but I know what I got here. This book is worth thousands. Look at the page with the big letter at the top."

I had been carefully turning the pages. There were no printed page numbers, but someone had ages ago, in a browning ink, numbered the leaves. The third leaf, which contained the first page of the main part of the text, had a fine majuscule *M* for "Mors." Beneath this were penned-in corrections here and there on the page. Several more appeared throughout the thirty-two pages of the printed text. Someone had marked up this text centuries ago. On the last leaf was a note in German that I couldn't read; it was signed almost illegibly: "Frithof von Escher."

"I'll give you $500 for this one."

"I'll see you later. Gimme my book." He got bristly.

"Wait. I don't know enough about this. I need to do some research."

"Hey, you're the big rare book guy. I want $2,000 for it. Now. Or I take it to Harry Luben."

Oh, shit. Harry Luben seemed to get all the treasures in L.A. He's got the money to buy twenty of these. And he *was* a brilliant bookseller, in many ways. He had once run a business designed for the designers: fancy books for fancy purses. Some people had called him Decorator Harry. He'd sell treasures or trash, but usually to people who wanted to decorate their homes. His customers could brag, "Here's a book we paid $12,000 for. Great pictures!" But it was worthless except for the price tag which made it more desirable. The new owners would invariably leave the penciled-in price on the front endsheet. Guests were impressed. Owners were proud. Luben was rich and he soon graduated into the upper echelons of the book world. He was canny, experienced, and able to buy pretty much what he wanted.

"Let me make a call first."

"Okay, but make it quick. I don't have much time."

What? His chauffeur getting impatient?

I went to the phone at the back of the shop and called Joe Nathan Breeze, one of the best incunabulists in the ABAA. The Antiquarian Booksellers Association of America had plenty of experts, but even they turned to Breeze for advice.

"Joey, this is Elliot. I need some help."

"Not another Wise. I don't need another forgery."

"No, this is the real thing."

"Shoot."

"No author. Title reads '*Ein Buchlein von dem Sterben.*'" I spelled out the words, but I didn't need to. "Simple paper wrapper, no label. No author. Leipzig, 1494. Superb condition. Contemporary annotations throughout. What should I pay for it?"

There was a pause. Joey was leafing through pages of a book. Probably looking through Goff's census of incunabula. I heard humming and mmmmmming. He cleared his throat. "German?"

"Yup."

"You've got something there that there's only one other known copy of, and that one is flawed. It's the first German edition of the Ars Moriendi, the Art of Dying. Lots of Latin versions. This is the only incunabulum of this title in German. Not just scarce. . . . You have an offer of one?"

"Yes."

"What's he want?"

"Won't say. What should I offer?"

"You want to sell it to me?"

"What should I offer?"

"As little as you can. Say $3500. You can make a good profit." Smith had asked only $2000. This sounded promising.

"Thanks. If I do, you've got a dinner. At Mama Leone's." He always mentioned that that was his favorite restaurant. "Lobster fra diavolo. Your favorite."

"You're on."

I turned back to the little scout, but he was at the front door looking out nervously. "Mr. Smith," I called. No response. Louder: "Mr. Smith."

"Oh, yeah?"

"Where did you get this book?"

Hackles up.

"It's mine. I got it in the box you got there. Flea market at Pasadena. If you don't trust me" . . . .

"I was curious. I've never seen this title before. Just wanted to know if you have any more like it."

"Not now. Maybe later. Do you want this one or not?"

"Would you consider $1500?"

"No."

"What's your lowest figure?"

"I told you: two grand. Now."

I paused theatrically. "Will you take a check?"

"Electronic transfer only. And quick. I can find some other buyer."

Another studied hesitation. "I don't know how to do an electronic transfer. What do I do?"

"Call your bank. Tell them to transfer two grand into this account." He handed me a slightly crumpled snippet of paper with the name of a bank and a 23-digit number on it in neat handwriting. Didn't look like the penmanship of someone whose specialty was selling mostly cruddy books. I dialed, spoke to Mildred, read off the number, repeated it, listened to her repeat it, and then hung up. "The money's yours. What about the other books in the box?" I tried to divert his attention from the deal I had just made.

"Keep 'em. Yours." He moved furtively toward the door. My greed got the best of me.

"You said maybe you had others like this?"

"Not now. I'll let you know"

He was out the door faster than his lingering aroma. I grabbed the phone and called Mildred. "Any chance you can put a temporary hold on the transfer?"

"Why would you want that, Mr. Burgess? You sounded like you really wanted this."

"I'll explain later. Can you hold it for, say, a day?"

"Just a minute. Let me find out." Bad music filled my ear, like a Mitch Miller doing a KISS version of the "Sound of Music." I couldn't wait till she got back. "Mr. Burgess? I can put a 24-hour hold on it. Caught it just in time. If I don't hear from you, it goes through at 3:30 tomorrow afternoon."

"Thank you, Mildred. I'll bring you cookies."

"Molasses."

"You're on."

I had to find out where this pamphlet came from. I got onto the Internet and put out messages to the ABAA, to a few of my non-ABAA friends (not all dealers belong to this fraternity), to OUT OF THE LI-BRARY (the bulletin board of rare book librarians), to the chair of the LSL (the Librarians Security List sends out information on books stolen, missing, mutilated, or smeared with peanut butter), and to a few other venues, like the International Database of Important, Old Treasures (a dumb name but an efficient group of people with plenty of clout and a loud and broadly cast voice). I'd need to wait for a reply. I'm in Los Angeles. Many of these folks are asleep: it's already tonight or tomorrow where they are. No matter how marvelous electronic communication is, it still must wait for people to sleep, eat, make love, and perform other bodily functions. Some things do come before the World Wide Web.

My message: "Can anyone tell me anything about the following pamphlet: *Ein Buchlein von dem Sterben* (Leipzig, 1494). Any known copies? Copies missing? From public or private collections? Please contact Elliot Burgess," etc.

I called Breeze back. I had to see if I could find out something about this little gem. "Joe, I heard you riffling through pages when I asked you about this. Was it Goff?"

"Did you get it?"

"Was it Goff?"

"How much did you pay for it?"

"Was it goddam Goff?"

"How much do you want for it? And why do you want to know?"

"I could check my own copy, but it will save me time knowing where you found it."

"Goff."

"Thanks. Call you . . . ."

"Elliot, what do you want for it? Are you gonna sell it?"

Not yet. I wasn't ready to give it up yet. I often needed a settling peri-od, a familiarity period, with a special book, a time to hold and read and savor possession of an item that I would eventually sell. That was part of the pleasure of my trade. I didn't need the money; I needed the thrill.

"I'll let you know later. What other sources can I check? I want to know where this copy came from. There's no sign it was ever in a library. It's clean." I checked for stamps, traces of glue where bookplates might have been, penciled annotations in inner margins, outside labels, and so on. It really was clean. A lovely copy. "I tried Hain. Nothing." Ludwig Hain's *Reportorium Bibliographicum* was another tool of the trade. Old, but reliable.

"Not much else to look into. It doesn't show up in the other guides. I doubt you'll find any other than the NYPL copy that Goff cites. I didn't even bother with Hain. It's a treasure."

"Thanks. What are the chances that this is a stolen copy?"

"If it is, it's from a private library. Institutions would have listed that one somewhere. Are you sure it's genuine?"

"I think so. It looks fine. Paper, typefaces, binding, cover paper, annotations."

Breeze paused. "I'll be in L.A. tomorrow. Can I come by to see it?"

"What time? Can you get here before 3? Earlier is better."

"My flight gets in at 10:30. I'll go straight to your shop. Lunch at Chasen's? On you?"

"Sure." I didn't tell him that Chasen's had closed up and was now an upscale, expensive grocery store. Sushi on Third would be more to my liking. Food there is great, and a third the price of Chasen's. "See you tomorrow."

I felt somewhat queasy about this Little Book of Death. Was it the sad, mysterious man who had so fragrantly sold it to me? the unlikelihood that such a book would waft into my shop on winds of halitosis and b.o.? I had another hour and a half before closing, so I put the book into my vault, locked up, and sat down at my desk. I was working on a catalog of early horticulture and gardening books, but I couldn't get my mind onto it. There was something festering somewhere. Back of my mind? In the safe? On the Web?

The Web. I entered my email. It had been only a half hour since I put out the message, but people surf at all hours. Who knows . . . ? There was one message already, sent from a local university. "I'm in the Comparative Literature Department. Interested in your book. Please contact me at," and there was a name, Terry Luckombe, and a phone number, address, and fax number.

"Oh, Christ. An academic. What hath my message wrought?" I didn't chuck it into the garbage, because it *was*, after all, my first response from the outside world on this book. But I didn't want it in my face. I transferred it to an electronic file folder and forgot about it. I had had it with academics. I had been one myself until I was denied tenure. Botany professors were assholes. I had had a splendid teaching record, plenty of service to the department, school, and community, successful research projects on insect- and blight-resistant fruits, and more publications than any senior colleague at the school. That was my problem. I was canned for some trumped-up charges—like not going to my classes to teach—and I chose not to fight. Bookselling had been in my family for two generations, and I had a large collection of great volumes to start out with. I took the paltry retirement fund that I had accumulated, rented a place, and went into business: Elliot Burgess, Antiquarian and Rare Books, specializing in early printed books and horticulture. No looking back.

One of the great things was that I was now self-employed. No shit colleagues judging my work, exercising their power. My own man. Handling things I loved to handle. Dealing and wheeling. Make a little here, lose a little there. Dad and Uncle Jake as guides. Though they dealt mostly in scholarly books, their stature in the book world was great. With them and my last name, I was able to get good contacts all over the book world. I had good book training, until dad and Jake were killed by a bus in Hoboken on a buying trip. My move into the book world was natural. I was one of the fraternity, and I loved it.

A couple of years ago, after I left the ivory towers, one of my former colleagues, Sam Forester, who had an eye for boys, tried for years to get some of my books from me while we were in the same department. He was an avid collector, and I had what he wanted. I was also the right gender, and in that, too, I had what he wanted. But he was not to my taste. I avoided him and he saw to it that I didn't get promoted. He eventually came into my shop, saw a few of the books he wanted, plucked them off the shelf, and minced over to the counter. I took them from him, hit the keys of the cash register, and said, "$26,550.85." He looked at me blankly.

"They're marked . . . ."

"They're not for sale. I just decided not to part with these. Unless you have $26,550.85."

My grin didn't help either of us. He spun around and strode out, walking as if he was trying to save his socks. I didn't feel good about this. No amount of crap I could pull on him could ever make me feel as if he had been fairly compensated for what he did to me. God, I love vengeance—when I wield it. But it doesn't do any good to let this shit hang on. Get past it. Get past it. Some day. In the meantime, I hope Forester rots before he gets to his grave.

Such images recur periodically, showing me that the wound had not closed yet. But now I've got a book to deal with and a catalog to compile and email to check and . . . . It's time to close. Time flies when you're contemplating revenge.

The phone rang. "Hello."

"Mr. Burgess?"

"Yes."

"My name is Johnson. I would like to see you about a book you have."

"I'll open at ten tomorrow."

"How about in the next half hour?"

"Sorry, I've got a date. I'll be in at ten."

"Ten it is."

I didn't have a date; I just didn't want to stay. I felt funny about *Sterben* and I was truly exhausted. A date? I hadn't had one for four years. It's tough to start dating when you're in your late forties and you haven't gotten over the loss of your true love. Had nothing to do with *Sterben*. My ex walked out one day after what I thought was a wonderful marriage (of two years). She was just what I wanted, but I obviously was not what she wanted. A rich doctor came into her life and she went into his. The details were still too painful to remember. I had had it with women. She was the rock upon which I had built my home. I guess I should have expected some seismic activity: I was, after all, in L.A. Solid today, quakes tomorrow, homeless on Friday. And this *was* Hollywood. Stacy was frankly gone with the wind.

Anyway, the turmoil came when I was transferring from the ivy walls to books. Too much chaos. She couldn't handle it. I barely did.

I went to the parking lot, got into my car, and aimed for home.

I didn't get there.

TWO

Before I had gone one block there was a horrendous noise to my rear and a simultaneous shattering of glass all around me. All I remember was seeing sparkles and feeling pain and hearing screeching and an explosion or was it two and warmth on my face and some serious thoughts ran through my brain about arguing with Stacy. Then I was being pulled by this limb and lifted.

"Mr. Burgess. Mr. Burgess." A pink-clad lady with more adipose tissue than she needed was looking me in the face.

I thought, "Why the hell does she have two chins?" But I didn't say anything.

The adipose tissue disappeared and was soon replaced by a stethoscope dangling from a pimply young face.

"Mr. Burgess, I'm Dr. Nobotny." I'm sure he said something about a lobotomy, and I panicked. "No, Mr. Burgess. Nothing to worry about." Easy for him to say. Here I am being considered for a lobotomy—or have I already had one?—and he says there's nothing to worry about. "Mr. Burgess, can you hear me? If you can hear me, nod your head."

Nod my head? What else is there to nod? Nod my shoulder? Nod my knee? I nodded my head. Pain. Why would this zitty little man ask me to do something that would hurt that much? Friend or enemy? Enemy.

"Mr. Burgess . . . ."

Shit; I know my name. Stop saying my name every time you open your mouth.

". . . you've had an accident." Profound. "You're in Cedars Sinai Hospital. You've been here for two days. Nothing is broken, but you did receive quite a bump." I could feel pain all over: arms, legs, hips, head,

neck, feet, toenails, tongue. That must have been quite a bump. You'd
think a doctor could come up with a more precise term for what I received.

"You will be fine. But we'd like to keep you here for a few more
days for observation." Observation? Like at a zoo? I must look horrible.
Who wants to observe that? "You have a few lacerations and a dislocated shoulder . . . and a . . . a, um wound in your arm."

I finally found my tongue. (Yes, it was really lost for a while.) "A
wound?" My voice didn't sound half bad; but it was only half a voice.
"What kind of a wound?" That sounded better.

"We're not sure, but we believe it was from a bullet." He said this
with the intonation of a question. He paused as if to say, 'Is that okay,
Mr. Burgess?'

I was silent for a moment. Then I asked, "'We believe'?"

"Well, we're not sure. But we have seen such wounds . . . . And the
police said . . . ."

He told me what the police said. They thought it was a DUI until
they found a neat bullet hole in the rear window. I had been hit in
my right arm. The bullet went out through the front windshield and
shattered it. The car went out of control. The right tires rolled up a
driveway. The car flipped over, and a kindly eucalyptus served as brakes.

I had a Godzilla of a headache. Nobotny said I also had a dislocated
shoulder "which will heal just fine in no time," and a wound in my
right arm. I should recover "in no time." What did he mean that I
would heal "in no time"? Nothing happens that fast. Except accidents.

Accidents? Was this an accident? Or was it on purpose? A stray bullet.
Meant for someone else, no doubt. I had no enemies that bloodthirsty.
Even Forester wouldn't pull the trigger, though he must have hated me
as much as I did him. Could it have something to do with books? little
books? little books of death? My head hurt.

They had me walking that morning and talking aplenty that afternoon. An officer named John Coster, tall, polite, soft spoken, with a
slight build, prominent jaw, and graying temples, came to chat. He was
from Homicide? Was I dead? No, just routine when they think someone was the target of someone else's .22.

He asked the standard questions. No, I hadn't been drinking. No, I had no enemies. No, no, no. Then he startled me: "What's this about a book of death?"

My surprise showed. "We did a Web search for your name. It didn't take long to find your recent inquiry."

I told him about Carl Smith. "Are you sure of the name?"

"It's what he told me."

"Carl with a K or a C?"

It had never occurred to me. "I don't know."

"Describe him."

I did. I got no feedback from Officer Coster. No body language. He took notes. I thought that sergeants in movies and on tv were the only ones who took notes on little pads. While he wrote, his eye contact with me was uncanny. It made me nervous. He hardly looked at the pad as he jotted away. Does he want to see a flinch of a muscle here or a clenching of one there?

I told him about the transaction, the transfer of funds, and the furtive way Carl Smith walked out.

"How did you know where to transfer the money to?"

"It was on a little grimy slip of paper he gave me."

"Where's that slip?"

"I don't know." And I didn't. Was it in a pocket? What was I wearing when all that took place? It seemed like weeks ago. Did I leave it on my counter? "You can ask Mildred the account number. She works in the bank I use."

"We know. We have the account number. We want the piece of paper it was written on. Mildred is quite nice." An odd comment.

I had nothing else to tell him. I had seen no one lurking around the store. I hadn't seen anything suspicious or worth noting in my rear mirror. I tried to recount what happened at the moment of the accident, but all I could remember was sound and smell and pain and noise.

"Can you remember the order of the noises?"

"No, only an explosion or two."

"One or two?"

"I think maybe two. Why?"

"One could be a stray bullet; two would be aimed."

"Hey," I said, alarmed. "I don't need to know that someone is shooting at me. Shooting could be dangerous. Especially for the person shot at."

"We are aware of that." He said this straight; no irony. I guess irony is not part of the thinking of someone who must face bloody reality all the time. "You could be in danger. We will give you some protection, but there are things you must do."

This was starting to sound serious. Was it "Hawaii 5-0" that I had seen this plot on? "Mannix"? Not too likely. I hadn't watched tv in thirty years. "Aren't you over-reacting?"

"Possibly. But the title of your book, and the two shots . . . ."

"Two?"

"There were two bullet holes in your rear window."

THREE

"B ut why me?" I thought that dozens of times and said it at least five to Officer Coster during the follow-up interview at my house two days later. I had recovered quickly, as any young man eager to get the hell out of the hospital will, and was back in my little home in Hancock Park, a tiny two-bedroom behind a fine old 1920s stucco house. I had lived there for two and a half years, renting happily from a sweet old couple with the unlikely name of Vacation. Flo and Bob Vacation had owned and lived in the big place for over fifty years, and with the departure of their youngest kid twenty some years ago, they had rented the bungalow to various comers and goers. I liked the small spaces, the cozy feel, and the seclusion, tucked away in the back yard behind the bigger house. I felt my books were pretty safe there, and so was I.

But with Coster sitting across from me asking me questions about enemies and debts and creditors, that feeling was ebbing away.

"As I've said, Mr. Burgess, you could be in danger. This death book may be involved. I'll keep in touch."

When he left I sat gingerly down and ruminated. To begin with, the payment for the damn book went through, so now I was out the money; but I had the book. Also, I missed two appointments. Joe Nathan Breeze and the anonymous caller Johnson probably showed up at my shop the morning after the blast, and I was out. Really out. Who was the caller? What did he want? What could Joe have told me about my Death book?

I grabbed the jingling phone. "Elliot, it's Joe. Where were you?"

"Out." No need to tell him how accurate that word was. "Sorry I missed your visit. I had an accident and I was in no condition to call."

"Nothing serious, I hope. I'll be back in L.A. in a couple of days to wrap up this sale. Shall I visit? Do you still have the book?"

"Sure." But as I said it, I wondered if it was still where I had put it. That little thing made me feel funny from the minute it wafted into the shop. "I'll call you tomorrow and we can make a date."

A few minutes later the phone rang again. "Hello."

"Mr. Burgess?" A soft and gentle voice, but with a firm edge.

"Yes. Who is this?"

"I'm Terry Luckombe. I read in the paper about your accident. I hope you're ok."

"Fine. Who are you?" The name was familiar.

"I emailed you about your book, *Ein Buchlein von dem Sterben*," spoken with a perfect guttural and the right pronunciation on the *shterb*. "I'd like to see it. I am doing a comparative study of various early printed books on dying—the *ars moriendi* tradition, you know" (not spoken as if I Know, but just as a filler), "and I've never seen an early German version."

"What!"

"The book you emailed the list about. Don't you have a copy?" There was a pause. "Oh, I guess I misunderstood your message. It *does* merely ask what people know about it. I guess I figured you had a copy."

I felt funny enough about my death book that I didn't want to say anything to a stranger. I said nothing.

She obviously felt awkward at this point. "Well, I . . . I guess you don't. Have a copy, that is."

"You said you had never seen a German version?"

"Actually, I tried to get the New York Public Library to scan their copy, but they said that it was incomplete and too fragile to copy. I think it might be important for my work. In fact, it might fill in an important gap in my research. But if . . . ."

"What would you say if I told you I have a complete copy?"

"What! Do you?"

"What would you say?" I was intrigued, and I thought also that this Terry might be able to tell me something about the book—something that could be useful.

"I would say that I'd love to see it. That I would be really happy to
see it. And . . . ."

I felt nervous about taking the damn thing from its place of repose.
But I didn't want to let this contact go. "How about meeting me in my
shop tomorrow? Say around noon?"

"I'll be there."

"Got the address?"

"Yes; you're in the book."

Which book? I thought? The book of death? I remember reading a
Nobokov poem about a dying poet in an old hotel finding "both direc-
tories, / The book of heaven and the book of Bell." Any connection to
my experience?

"See you."

Getting down the three stairs from my front door was harder than
getting up them had been. Getting into my rented car (which Coster
said was safe—what did he mean?) was agony. Turning the key and
shifting into drive was torture. But it felt good to be mobile after the
incarceration at Cedars. Was that a car behind me? Oh, yes. Coster
told me about that. Discreet but faithful. Only for a few days, he said.
I waved.

It was already three and I needed some food. The bandage on my
arm was tight; the pain in my head and neck was returning (for which
I took some Advil). And the bumps around the rest of my body made
it painful for me to contemplate eating. But I was hungry, so I decided
to drive over to the shop and eat at the neighborhood café. Betty the
owner was a fine chef; and a good friend. The place, near my shop, had
great food, low prices, and a nice waitress (though sixty or seventy years
older than me).

The food was bearable, though chewing was a chore. It tasted fine,
but swallowing it was no picnic. I guess I got a bump.

My store was only three doors down. I walked toward it hesitantly,
for the first time in my career as a bookseller. Until then I strode toward
it with gusto, loving the place, the thrill it gave me. Somehow that
feeling had been bumped away today. There were no lights inside, as
there shouldn't have been. I opened the door, reached around to flip on

lights, and waited to hear the high-pitched squeal of the alarm. Normally I would swing left, go to a box on the wall behind a protruding bookshelf, open the little door on the wall chest, hit the keypad, and disarm the connection to the local constabulary. This time there was no squeal. I stood there not knowing what to do. The lights illuminated what looked like the normal bookshop of Elliot Burgess, scared purveyor of old books, mostly on gardening. No movement. No sound. No fresh air. I flipped the lights off, backed out, and shut the door. Bud and Lou weren't to be seen. Good tails. I went back into the diner and asked Betty if I could use her phone. My cell had been smashed in the accident. Gotta get a new one.

"Officer Coster, please."

Long wait. "This is Coster."

"Elliot Burgess. I think someone's been in my shop."

"Where are you?" He sounded agitated. "Why aren't you at home where you ought to be?"

"I was hungry. Couldn't cook. And I wanted to look into my shop."

"I told them to call me if you left your home. Where are you calling from?"

"Crocker's Diner."

"I know where it is. Don't move. Have a cup of coffee. I'll see you in minutes."

It was a big cup. Forty-five minutes later he was sitting across from me. "We assumed you'd stay in today. I want to go into your shop with you. Check it out. Look at the book."

"I have lots of books to look at."

"Cute. You know which one."

He was upset, and I guess he should have been. But maybe stray bullets don't strike the same place twice. We went to the shop and I told him about the alarm.

The alarm box seemed fine, but Coster followed the leads to wires outside. They had been rerouted. He showed me how the connection was expertly kept in place with supplementary wires that would instantly make a contact, but while the current which flowed straight to the police station would run, the current no longer ran through the alarm box. Nice clean job. As far as the police were concerned, there was no tampering; as far as I was concerned, there was no alarm.

"Someone's been in here," Coster said. The shop faced out onto the main street, but there was an alleyway behind it and a couple of parking places where I put the car every day. The back door had a heavy metal grate over the small panes of glass. All looked right to me, but Coster pointed out the putty on the pane nearest the door knob. It was white, and all the other putty was weathered and dirty. He pushed on that pane and it moved.

"Whoever installed your alarm should have warned you about the other security flaws in this place." Flaws? Plural?

"I figured the alarms . . . ."

"Alarms like this are cheap and useless. Look at the transom. In a fairly uninhabited alley. And the air conditioning unit on your roof: how big is the air-flow vent? What are the walls made of that separate you from the shops next door? What kind of alarms do you have?"

"Circuit-breaking alarms."

"No heat detectors? movement detectors? sound detectors? surveillance camera? What do you keep here? Used shoes and broken dishes? You need a pro."

This was the first time I had heard him speak forcefully.

A careful search through the shop turned up nothing out of place, or moved, or messy—nothing. In the back was a pile of books with quite a bit of dust on the top one. It was a group I had bought a year earlier on viticulture. "Someone looked at these."

"How can you tell?"

"Easy. You have similar piles of volumes back here. All sizable books. But this pile has little pamphlets in it. And the dust has been disturbed on the top one. When's the last time you touched these?"

"A year ago, probably."

"Was your book of death here?"

"No; it's in my safe."

"Let's see."

But someone had been at the safe, too. When I close the door, I always turn the knob to read 44. The knob was at 57.

"Is the book in there?"

"I guess so."

He gestured, and I started turning the knob. It was there, neatly tucked away on the top shelf where I had left it. This was a big mother of a safe, a good seven feet tall, with two wide, fat doors, safe to hundreds of degrees for four hours of flames. It weighed over 1200 pounds. Nobody was going to walk away with it.

"You feel it's safe here?"

"Well, I think so."

"How about putting it into a safe deposit box at a bank?"

"If you think it'll be safer there," I said.

"And you." What? I should get into a safe deposit box? He saw his ambiguity on my face and said, "The book will be safer in a bank."

"But who is going to know it's in a bank?"

"What other people know is not important. Get it out of the shop and it will be safer than it is if it's here."

Spoken ominously. And whoever it was could have taken tons of other books worth a bundle. But nothing else seemed to be missing. This was a meticulous intruder with only one thing on his mind. And my safe seems to be the only thing that thwarted him. What about next time?

Coster asked me, "What are you going to do with the book?"

"I guess I'll bank it, as you said. But my safe seems safe."

"Your choice."

Coster went back to his station, but Bud and Lou returned fairly conspicuously. I spent the rest of the day sitting in the store thinking, trying to work on the catalog I wanted to send out. More than half my sales come from these catalogs, so they weighed heavily on me. My business was good, but primarily because I kept these things going out.

The phone rang. Shifting around to pick it up sent waves of agony up my arm. I swung around the other way and grabbed it with my left hand. "Hello."

"Mr. Burgess?"

"Yes."

"You missed your appointment two days ago. I'd like to set up another."

"Sorry. Who's calling?"

"I spoke to you about meeting you at your shop. You weren't there."

"Can I have your name, please?"

"Just say that Mr. Smith and I are . . . acquaintances. I'd like to talk to you about a book." The way he dropped his voice and paused, I guess he wanted me to speak at this moment—my turn. But the small shock that went through me made the hairs on my body stir. Silence. "Mr. Burgess? are you there?"

"I'm here. What book?"

"We can discuss it when I see you . . . alone. Is this afternoon ok? Five?"

I couldn't put him off; and I must admit that my curiosity outweighed my fear . . . and my reason. "Five it is."

Even before I could say, "What did you say your name . . .," I heard his click. Sitting here like a duck was stupid. Why had he said "alone"? Should I summon the Mounties? the cavalry? No, they came over the hill when the battle was already raging—or even when it was too late. Where was Coster? Oh, my goodness! It was already four twenty. I was going to see my mystery caller in forty minutes.

I guess the fear was stronger than the curiosity, after all. I reached for the phone with my right hand and stopped abruptly. Not from the pain, but because a crumpled little snippet of paper caught my eye. It had fallen to the floor and was sticking out enough from the pull-out desk platform that I could just make it out. It was Smith's account number. I pulled out Coster's card from my shirt pocket and dialed. He had just left the station and was incommunicado for the rest of the day. I asked if anyone else was familiar with the Elliot Burgess case. Sorry, no one. I asked if there was some way to contact Coster; a pager? a phone number? a fax line? a satellite link? smoke signals? My constabulary interlocutor was not amused. Neither was I, when I got a No to each of my inquiries. The caller said "Alone." Alone it would be. What could he do, anyway? Shoot me?

I stashed the account number into a reference book on my shelves behind my desk, between pages 54 and 55: *The Universal Price Guide*, appropriately enough, now held information about money and a little Mr. Smelly Smith.

My shop was narrow but deep. When someone entered the front door, on the left was a glass and wood counter where I made sales. Half way back in the shop, against the left wall, was my reference desk, behind which was a wall of books marked NFS (I never sold a reference book). The wall at right angles to these books separated the front from the back of the shop, enterable from a small door behind my desk. Back there were the safe, the toilet, and shelves and piles of books waiting for processing or cataloging.

I had drilled two small holes in this back wall, one on the left of the shop and the other on the right, to give me a view of all the activity in the front from the rear. On a couple of occasions I had spotted some not-very-subtle pocketing of books by patrons thinking they were unobserved. The lad I employed part time, Dave Daws, was there to spell me three days a week when I needed to be out. I scheduled my out times when Dave was to be there, and his reliability and good nature with the customers made him the perfect stand-in. He had studied bookkeeping in college, and proved to be an immense help when it came to bills and taxes. But when he wasn't there, I was stuck. Bathroom breaks and quick runs to Crocker's for a phoned-in, take-out sandwich were the only moments that I didn't have the shop covered. Since I had a pretty valuable stock, I usually locked the doors for those few minutes. I had never really felt vulnerable here. It was a good neighborhood, with a decent clientele, and reliable neighbors.

I was turning around from having inserted Smith's account number between pages 54 and 55 when the door opened. It was five to five. For a second I was acutely anxious.

"Mr. Burgess?" The now-familiar voice. I was in the back of the shop. Before facing my adversary, I thought I'd check him out through one of the peep holes.

I could see a distinguished man of rather impressive proportions. His suit didn't hide the muscled torso, slim waist, and powerful legs that he used to stride down to where I was standing. He must have been in his fifties: some gray at the temples, strong smile (or grimace) lines in his face, deep tan, large strong hands (it hurt to shake), and well creased trousers. His "Mr. Burgess" riveted me. His physical presence almost scared me. I stepped to the front of the store to face him.

"That's me."

Pretty meek reply. I somehow felt on the defensive. And I should have had some John-Wayne response like, "That's me, buster. What the hell do you want?" Or, "You don't need to ask. You know who I am. Let's get down to business."

"You know why I'm here, I presume."

"Not really."

"I understand you have a book that I want. I am willing to pay you a good amount for it." His long pause gave me a moment to gather myself for my counter-assault.

"I have plenty of fine books here. Botany, viticulture, citriculture, and a general stock of literature, philosophy, and . . . ."

"I don't need your innocence. I want your book."

Spoken as if there were only a single volume in the entire place. Of course, I knew which book he was talking about. But I didn't want to admit it for a number of reasons. I didn't want him to think that he owned any part of me. I didn't want to let him think that I could be pushed around. If I let him know that his presumption was correct, who knows what other presumptions he would make about me and what powers he had over my life. And I had just gotten my little death book. I hadn't gotten over the thrill of owning it yet.

But the kind of thrill this book presented was possibly more than I had bargained for. Bargain! Was this book a bargain? My physical agony made me think it was a pact with the devil.

"Which book are you referring to?" (I had thought about saying, "To which book are you referring?" but I thought that would be too confrontational. I was not sure he would understand the subtlety of the difference.) This man was civil, professionally attired, and apparently articulate. But his directness, his bearing, his body language almost gave me the fantads. (I know this means some kind of mental disorder, but when Twain used it he meant the runs. I did feel like running.) There was an undercurrent of pent-up power, ready to snap, in this customer. I didn't like it. And my not liking it made me angry, because I hate being pushed—to do anything.

"Mr. Burgess. Mr. Burgess. You recently bought a book from a scout who called himself Carl Smith. It is an incunabulum. It was in excellent condition. And it was—and shall be again—mine." Long pause to let this sink in. "Do you understand?"

Jesus! man. I speak and read and write English. What kind of a dumb question was this? I said to him, "Listen, Mr. I-don't-yet-know-your-name. I speak and read and write English. Of course, I understand. And since I presume your own comprehension of the language is somewhat equivalent to mine, I will tell you that I do not have a book for sale at present that meets the description you just gave. Do you understand?"

Silly of me to say that. It really was mocking, and this man did *not* like to be mocked.

By now it was past five, and there was sure to be no one entering a shop which claimed on its front-door sign to close at five. So I was really in this on my own. Mr. What's-his-name was standing close to me, threateningly, but still contained. I felt rather bold and stupid and defensive and nervous. I was no homunculus, and I could handle myself in a skirmish, if it ever came to that. (The last fight I had had was with Danny Rosenblood when I was about ten, in front of his house. I punched him in the face when he shoved me. He lost. So did I.) The way I was feeling now, I was too weak and sore and drained to have to *think* about a physical encounter. But I refused to step back, as my brain told me to do.

He was silent for a moment, almost menacing. Then in a forced, restrained, soft voice he said, "I would like to purchase the *Buchlein von dem Sterben* from you." Pronunciation inferior to Ms. Luckombe's. He's a collector, not a scholar. Much more dangerous. "You paid $2000 for it. I am willing to give you considerably more."

I paused a second. "You tell me you owned it. Why buy it back? Did you sell it? Who was the real owner before I bought it?"

"Let's just say that it got out of my possession. Mr. Smith wound up with it. Then you wound up with it. I want it back."

"Hold on. Yes, I bought the book. But I want to hold on to it for a while. I'd like to do some research on it. Maybe read it. My German is rusty, but . . . ."

"You don't seem to understand."

I hate that phrase. It sets me off. I am a reasonable person. I have a Ph.D. in botany with a broad background in literature, philosophy, and bibliography. I am not dumb. I understand a shitload more than people like this little fart could ever know.

"Don't patronize me. I *do* understand. I understand! But *you* don't *seem* to understand. It's not for sale yet. Maybe never. Maybe not to you." That didn't help much, but it seemed to make him back off a bit. Maybe some of the tension in his muscles diminished. Maybe not.

More silence. Then I said in a placating way, "I must think it over. I want to keep the book for a while. Give me your name and number. I'll let you know when it's available."

He thought it over, then he fished out a card. Printed on good paper. Engraved. (No thermography for this gent). Edward Myers. Caligula Books (stamped in gold). San Francisco. Phone number. No address. Wasn't Caligula the grand-looking emperor who tyrannized Rome? I seemed to remember, thanks to Mr. McRath, that his name meant Little Boot, but that he booted people around all over the place. Not an inappropriate name for Myers' business. A tough guy, I suppose.

He was finished with words. He spun around and departed, closing the door rather quietly, I thought.

In curiosity, I went outside to see if Bud and Lou were there. Across the street was their car. I ambled over. "Hi, guys."

Bud (or was it Lou) rolled down the window. "Yes, Mr. Burgess?"

"Are you here to protect and serve?"

Not noticing my mild ridicule: "Yes, of course."

"Why didn't you come into the shop when that man came in?"

"Well dressed; wealthy—he was driving a jaguar; no threat."

I guess I was really on my own in this. I felt like giving Lou and Bud a dollar and telling them to run along for some ice cream. Maybe worth discussing with Coster.

Back in the shop I had a notion to open the safe to see if the book was there. But it felt wrong. I didn't want to touch it just now. I walked to the front of the shop, turned from habit to the right to set the alarm, realized the futility of that, and just went out. Didn't turn off the lights either. Seemed symbolic.

FOUR

M r. Smith wound up with it," he had said. What did he mean by
that, Mr. Caligula? If Smith had stolen it, why not go to the police? Why not hunt up Smith and get it back from *him*? How much was
he willing to pay for this book? What was its true worth? How did he
know how much I had paid Smith? Who is Caligula, anyway? Edward
Myers. Does that name mean anything to me? Doesn't ring a bell. Of
course, if I had recognized the name, a bell wouldn't have rung anyway.
Bells don't.

Bells and alarms. The alarm company had come and gone. They fixed
my system. The workman told me that the system I had was state-of-
the-art. What art? Finger painting? Jackson Pollock? Too much ran-
domness for me. I told him to have the owner contact me about additional security for the place. He said he would.

It was ten o'clock the next morning. I was sitting in the shop waiting
for Terry Luckombe to arrive at noon. I figured this was a good time
to check my Web query. I logged on and went to my email. There were
several book orders, a note from my younger brother about his kid's
college graduation and the party he wanted me to attend, and the usual
catalogs and junk mail that came with the technology. There were also
three messages about my *Buchlein*.

The first said, "Is this a joke? Why do you want to know?" It came
from the University of Wisconsin; a professor of German named Hans
Sachsen.

The second was from a bookseller in Pennsylvania who said, "Never
heard of it. Can you describe it for me. I may have a customer for it if it
is in German. What is the price? Standard dealer discount?"

The third was almost a jackpot: it was from Elizabeth Browner, Rare Book Librarian at the New York Public. "Please call me about your inquiry" plus a phone number. Succinct and provocative. The NYPL is where the "only known copy" of *Sterben* is. It's 10:20. 1:20 in NY. "May I please speak to Ms. Browner?" I didn't know her personally, but I did know her from her few but excellent publications and by her good reputation. Solid librarian. No fuss.

"This is Elizabeth Browner."

"Thanks for taking my call. And for getting back to me about my query." I told her who I was and what I had.

She said, "You simply asked what people know about the Kachelofen book. Kachelofen was a Leipzig printer known for about 30 titles. Only two were German, and one was your *Buchlein* of 1494. He also did a Latin version the following year. The German one contains what is apparently a translation, but the actual text differs, so the 'translator' was really an author as well."

"How does it differ?"

"The work is a sample of the *ars moriendi* genre. There are plenty of them, mostly in Latin. They all seem to be derivative from one or two sources. The German one supposedly contains text about means of killing, ways to dispose of bodies, and the corruption of the flesh—both literally and figuratively—that you won't find in any other text. It seems to go back to a version that preceded all other printed ones. It could be in a very early stemma, at the earliest era of the *moriendi* tradition. It is supposed to have some pretty gross passages, along with many rather incendiary ones—ones which show how to kill. But no one really knows what it contains because no full text of the German edition of 1494 survives, and no other edition we know of has the offensive text. It was strongly suppressed after its publication. For our copy to survive at all is practically a miracle. And ours is in quite bad condition. It has none of the offending passages; it lacks pages and passages, torn or sliced out here and there; and it is acephalous, as well."

"What?"

"It lacks its head, its title page. We know its publisher from the colophon and the typefaces."

"Where did you get your copy?"

"It's been in the collection for decades. Came in a purchase of banned books, believe it or not. We're lucky to have it."

"What would a complete copy be worth?"

"I can't appraise. Conflict of interest. But I'd say quite a bit. Though if a complete copy does exist, it's a miracle. The contemporary censors were thorough. I've never heard of another besides ours, and ours is mauled. Quite a victim."

These books seem to surround themselves with victims.

"Anything else you can tell me?"

"Well, one thing. As I said, this Kachelofen piece is reputed to be especially incendiary. Usually these things—especially the German ones—were confiscated and burned, but Kachelofen was additionally imprisoned and tortured, so the story goes. Whatever was in his version must have riled a few people, both in the church and outside."

"Why? What did his version have?"

"No one is sure. We have the only known copy of it, and the missing pages must have been pretty radical for him to have merited such treatment. Only the missing pages can tell us. Nobody has seen them in over 500 years."

"Who knows about this?"

"Just about all incunabulists, especially those who are familiar with German printing. Also, scholars in history, bibliography, and religious studies, since the story is provocative. But it's like seeking a holy grail. Everyone wants to find it, as they wish to find a manuscript copy of one of Shakespeare's plays."

I had handled many an incunabulum, but I was unfamiliar with the story. But what I did know was that such a book would be in demand, half the supply-demand equation for value. My little *Buchlein* was climbing in value before my very eyes.

I asked, "What else can you tell me?"

Elizabeth Browner paused a moment and said, "I can't think of anything more. By the way, why do you want to know? You don't have one, do you?"

"Where do you suppose I'd ever come up with one of those?" One of my college teachers once told me if I didn't want to answer a question, ask another question. Why not?

"Why are you asking about it?" She seemed only mildly curious.

"I have a date with an *ars moriendi* scholar, and I wanted to know all I could about it." Silly answer, but Elizabeth Browner's questions were more perfunctory than out of genuine curiosity, and my answer seemed to satisfy her at the perfunctory level. I thanked her sincerely, for she actually did help me more than I felt like telling her.

So the book was quite rare. And loaded with hot information. And desirable to a scholar. And even more desirable to a collector. Its value had just jumped significantly in the last ten minutes. Maybe Carl Smith didn't have any idea what he was selling. Or maybe he knew and he just wanted to unload it fast. And why did he come to me, of all people? I do advertise in the Yellow Pages and on the Web that I deal in old and rare books, but my specialty is more in the agricultural line than in . . . death. Agriculture. Growing things. Life. Affirmation and hope and rebirth and regeneration. Maybe he came to me because in the cosmos opposites attract. The book was certainly out of my garden.

The door opened and I glanced up. The street went east-west, but the late morning sun beams into the shop from the north sometimes, and for a moment I could not make out who had just entered. The customer moved like a woman, with grace and delicacy, but with a certain firmness of purpose that bespoke the solidity that I heard in the voice of Terry Luckombe. In a moment she was in the shadow of the incandescent lights, and I saw an auburn-waved coif over a classic face over a slender and well-taken-care-of body.

"I'm Terry Luckombe. Are you Mr. Burgess?"

"Yes, Elliot Burgess. Nice to meet you. Have a seat."

I couldn't quite get a grasp on this person. She was both delicate and forceful; firm in her grip (boy, did that hurt, but I hardly felt it), but soft in voice. It was like watching a football player on the verge of tears; or a powerful and positive orator losing his self-confidence. Quite a mixture. And all this in only a few seconds.

"You wanted to know about the *Buchlein von dem Sterben*?" I asked.

"Yes. I've read about this book in various literatures. It is important for a number of reasons."

"Like, how?"

"Its text is notorious. No one knows the full extent of the depredations it describes in its few pages because there are no complete copies anywhere."

"So I've heard. The NYPL copy is defective."

"Oh, you know about that. Yes. I'm going to have to get there to see it some day, but travel funds for young professors are mighty scarce. Also, the book seems to be different from all the others of its genre."

"I heard that too."

"You seem to know quite a lot about it. Are you a scholar?"

"No. I just spoke to the NYPL curator who told me lots. Like it was on the banned books list back in the fifteenth century."

"The infamous *Index prohibitorum*. Well, not exactly. That index was published more like in 1560. But its equivalent existed in the fifteenth century in manuscript. It's not likely that a complete copy of the German *Buchlein* exists. It's a miracle that the defective one at New York survives."

"What is your research?"

She hesitated. "It's pretty complicated. It started out in one direction and then shifted to another." As she spoke about her topic, she got more animated. Her face, with no make-up, was radiant and though not of classic beauty, was mesmerizing to me. It was perfect: medium-sized, perfectly formed lips, smooth complexion over elegantly prominent cheekbones, deep brown eyes with lovely arched brows, long lashes, and a tiny brown freckle (beauty mark, they would have called it, in my mother's day) below her left eye. She was trim and tidy, maybe five foot six. Great ankles showing from her long cream skirt. It was difficult to keep my mind on her talk.

"I was first interested in the *ars moriendi*, but what has taken my brain to new heights is the deviations from it. Not all texts say the same things. Of course, you expect there to be some variation in the texts. But some of them raise issues not to be found in the mainstream tradition. Like Pelagius. He denied original sin and he said that if you die without being given the last rites, it's ok. You don't need the intercessor that the priests said you did. They, of course, were those intercessors, and to deny their required service—you know, last rites and confession, and like that—to deny these meant to deny the necessity of priests."

I was getting in pretty deep, now. I opened a floodgate. But it was coming from such a pleasant source, and I wasn't about to close the gates. "What does this have to do with the *Buchlein von dem Sterben*?"

"Well, I was sort of getting to that. Pelagianism said that each person had free will, and that meant that she or he could *choose* not to sin. This was really not what fifth-century priests wanted to hear. The religion was still pretty young and one didn't fool around with the church."

"So . . . ?"

"So, this is the kind of thing that finds its way into some of the *ars moriendi* texts. It's a heresy. And there is a strong German tradition from the sixteenth century and later that shows such deviations from the standard *moriendi* teachings. And there's more."

Her enthusiasm threatened to turn this into a long seminar session. I suggested that we go eat, and she seemed to snap out of some kind of a trance.

"Oh, I'm sorry. I got carried away." (Like the Sabine women? Not a bad image. I'd like to carry her away.)

"I'm hungry. Let's go to Crocker's."

"Ok. Did you say you had a copy of the German version?"

I could see that this was going to be something of a chore. She seemed to have dying on her mind. I had other things on mine. I set the alarm (a lot of good that did!), put up the "back in an hour" sign, locked the door, and ushered her out. Bud and Lou sat up. I waved.

"You know them?" she asked.

"Old friends."

"What are they doing there?"

"They think they are saving my life."

"What? Are they?"

"No, but maybe you are."

"I don't . . . ."

"Never mind. Just a joke. Let's eat."

FIVE

Crocker's was crowded. It was just after 12:30 and the lunch crowd squeezed in and hummed along, with silverware-hitting-plate sounds and voices blended into one big sine-waving murmur. We waited about twenty five minutes for a table, talking small talk. Terry got her undergraduate degree from the University of North Carolina, with its formidable medieval faculty, and her doctorate at Catholic University, with its rigid curriculum and Robertsonian medievalism—preaching a most Catholic interpretation of literary texts. She came on the job market five years ago, with good credentials in a year when good credentials and five dollars got you a Starbucks and a day-old.

She felt fortunate having landed a job at UCLA, one of the schools that specialized in toying with the lives of junior faculty. She was trying to teach and do university service and public service and publish to get tenure. She had a department enemy, and things didn't look good. She had specialized in medieval literature in her Comp. Lit. program, and she knew codicology (the medieval book) and bibliography in its many manifestations. She knew lots about books, but she never had enough money to buy any except the few she needed for her research that the library didn't own. L.A. was expensive for an assistant prof with no tenure. But her book on the *ars moriendi*, she hoped, would bring her some small cash and—more important—tenure.

"So, do you really have a copy of *Ein Buchlein von dem Sterben*?"

"Let's just say that I know where one is."

"I'd love to see it. Is it where you can put your hands on it?"

"Possibly."

"Who owns it?"

I felt comfortable with Terry Luckombe, but I felt mighty uncomfortable with her knowing that I possessed this death book. I trusted her, but I hardly trusted myself to say that it was mine.

"What if I told you that there's a curse on the book?"

"Silly. Why do you say that?"

"What if I told you that the current owner had an attempt made on his life soon after he acquired the book?"

"That's a *post hoc ergo propter hoc* argument."

This stretched me back again to McRath. But I remembered from a distant logic class that form of fallacy—after the fact, therefore because of the fact. "I believe that there *is* a connection between recent ownership and danger."

She thought for a moment and then said, "You own it. You got it recently. Someone hurt you soon after you bought it. The bandage on your arm and the scrapes I see on your hands and face are the result of some cataclysmic experience. You are reluctant to talk about it because it frightens you and wakens recent memories of pain and your facing your mortality." Then she added, "Mr. Burgess, I am really sorry I brought all this up. I never would have presumed on your time or your physical or psychological feelings if I had known. It's just that I was eager to see the book and surprised to think that there may be a copy so close."

"Well, I do have . . . ."

"Please, let's not talk about it. I will continue to pursue the New York Public Library copy."

The pain must have been showing on my face—and not the pain in my arm. "Listen, Ms. Luckombe . . . ."

"Terry."

"Elliot," I said, pointing at myself. "I don't want to impede your research."

"Please don't do anything you might regret." She said it with sincerity, not with the sarcasm that might have been there with such a trite line.

"Terry, I . . . . Ok. I do own the damn thing." Did I talk about damnation and the book in the same breath? "Someone shot at me, I think." I indicated the arm that I had obviously been favoring and the other marks she had mentioned. "Also, someone has carefully broken into my shop. I think he was deterred for now by my safe. But not for long. I think the book is involved."

I didn't want to tell her about Caligula Myers. Fancy business card. Tough guy who wanted my death book. Should I have thought, 'wanted my death'? I don't know why I am telling her all this. And not all of it. Still uneasy about the whole matter.

She ate her veggieburger and non-fat cottage cheese while I downed a large baked potato smothered in sour cream, butter, cheddar cheese, broccoli, black olives, and diced anchovies. God, Betty was a good cook.

"I feel certain that the book is involved," she muttered. "It's quite rare, and I should think it's quite valuable."

"I suspect so."

After a long courage-building pause, during which I knew from her expression not to say anything, she said cautiously, "Could I see it?" Pause. "The book?"

"I think it's cursed."

"Nonsense! I don't believe in such things, and I'm sure you don't either."

"Hmmm." This was obviously an assent, but I didn't want to encourage her.

"I really need it for my research. It's like a missing link."

"You already know what's in it?"

"Not really. As I told you before, Kachelofen is known to have made significant changes, though I don't know what they all are. Some of the changes are hinted at in the Latin text of about 1495. They are pretty radical and they got him into a passel of trouble."

I thought of Elizabeth Browner's corroborating words.

Terry continued as if gliding into one of her lectures again. "Kachelofen almost lost his life because of this book. The standard *ars moriendi* book is just a good solid religious text, teaching its readers how to prepare one's soul for death. Kachelofen's versions in Latin are traditional texts. But supposedly the German text is loaded with passages that border on heresy. It is speculated that they tell you how to kill. They supposedly describe the decaying flesh of sinners. Whether he was talking metaphorically or not, the text is rumored to be vivid and upsetting—certainly upsetting to the censors of his day. And they probably advocate things that are contrary to the Christianity of his day, of any day. That's why his book, especially the German edition, is so scarce. The church tried its best to suppress it. They were supposed to have burned every copy they could get their self-righteous hands on. No one maybe in the last five hundred years has seen this text."

"You seem to know a lot about this book," I said.

"I should. I have studied the tradition for years. But really, I am not so sure about this very edition. What I tell you is sort of hearsay since people just extrapolate about what the book must have contained from the bitter treatment the printer received."

I remember Elizabeth Browner's words about torture and prison.

Terry was still talking, ". . . and I'd like to be the one to discover a whole copy. It could help my career."

"Want some dessert? Betty bakes great pies." I guess I wasn't in the mood to talk about careers in academia.

"Sure. Apple. I hope it has lots of cinnamon. Anyway, a complete copy of the German edition would bring a fortune."

"What do you call a fortune?"

"For me? Some months that means $75. For the book, thousands. I don't know. But a copy of the more common—and less incendiary—Latin version sold for about $15,000 a couple of years ago."

"How do you know?"

"I moonlighted in an antiquarian bookstore to help pay the rent. God! L.A. is expensive! I read sale catalogs and auction catalogs. Kryss bought a copy of the 1495 for $15,200. It must have been for a customer. Figure a handsome profit on that."

On most books, dealers generally want to pay no more than 30 percent of the retail price of a book. Overhead is enormous in this business. We can hardly make ends meet if we pay over that. On high-priced books for which a bookseller has an immediate sale, a smaller mark-up would be ok. If Kryss had a quick sale at, say, $18,000, he'd have made nearly $3,000 quickly. This would mean that the Latin 1495 would be worth in the $18,000 to $20,000 range, at minimum. My German book was looking better and better all the time. But the more it was worth, the more vulnerable I felt. Would someone kill for a $2,000 book? Maybe. For a $20,000 book? More likely. For my German book? Definitely.

"If what you're saying is true, then I am really in trouble."

She knew instantly what I meant. She asked old Molly, our super-annuated server, if the apple pie had lots of cinnamon. I should have warned her not to engage Molly in any kind of conversation. Molly had a way of answering. No matter how busy the place was, Molly was thorough, and customers were often left waiting long times while Molly answered a customer's simple question. "Excuse me, Ma'am. Do you have the time?" "Of course I do. Can't you see I'm wearing a watch?! Can't you see that clock up there?! Ok, so it's a couple hours off. But it's consistently off. So alls you gotta do is add 2 hours and 15 minutes and you'll get the time. It's 1:37 in the afternoon. P.m., honey. I been telling Betty to fix that damn thing. But all our reg'lars know to add 2 hours and 15 minutes. If we fixed it now, we'd throw 'em all off. Any-way, every damn place has clocks on time. Boring. No imagination. We got one that all our reg'lars can read that makes 'em feel special. Can't fix that clock now. That's what Betty says, and I b'lieve her. Good for business. Makes those in the know feel special. So it's 1:38, honey." Ask Molly a question, you get a dissertation.

Molly said, "What do you mean by 'lots,' honey? It's got enough cinnamon to see and taste. It's got enough to make the apples brown. Not all places makes their pies that away. Sometimes you get a apple pie that's got white apples. No brown in there. No cinnamon. You gotta do lots of cinnamon to get a good apple pie. Betty knows that."

I decided not to cut her off, but to let the storm pass of its own ac-cord. "Betty says, 'You can't put in too much cinnamon.' And I reckon it's true. I eat Betty's pies all the time, and when I get a pow'ful han-kerin' for cinnamon, I get the apple. Best apple pie in the city. Ever try the one at Canter's? Bad pie. Tough crust, practically no cinnamon. No character. The one at Nate and Al's? that's pretty good. But not enough cinnamon."

Customers at neighboring tables were listening to Molly preach. They were rapt. She can bend an ear. Should have been a preacher. Five-hour sermons. That would have cured anyone of any kind of sin. In fact, it wouldn't have left any of the congregation enough time to go out to sin. By the time she was scheduled to finish her apple-pie-cinna-mon sermon, we'd all be hungry enough for dessert.

"Now you can cover the apples with cinnamon, but you gotta mix it with some sugar, the way Betty does. But more than that, you need to put it onto the crust. Yep, a good cinnamony crust makes the pie. Problem is, if you put it on enough, ya can't see the color of the crust, so you don't know when the pie is done. But Betty does. She's got it down pat."

Five minutes later Terry said, "I'll have a piece of apple pie, please."

"Good choice, honey." Molly strutted off smugly, like the used-car salesman who had just unloaded a lemon. But the lemon pie was another ten-minute expatiation.

"Does she always go on like that?" Terry asked incredulously.

"Only when you ask her something. The rule is, if you want to kill a day or two, ask her a question. If you are in a hurry, order your food in simple declarative sentences. She thinks you are in too much of a hurry to receive one of her famous answers. And she goes on like that even if you ask her a question about something she knows nothing about. I once said to her in a sort of rhetorical-question kind of way, 'Did you see that thing about osteoporosis in the paper this morning?' She thought I had really asked her a question, and I got a ten-minute lecture on dinosaurs and how we should leave the poor dead and extinct creatures alone and how they should be left with the simple dignity of their present burial."

Terry's smile got me.

Then she said, "Are you planning to sell your *Buchlein*?"

"I don't know. I don't often get such a treasure. When I do, and I know it's easily salable, I like the thrill of ownership. I hold onto it a while. But I *am* in business. I've gotta eat. Eventually I'll sell it."

"Please, Mr. . . . Elliot, may I see it?"

"I guess so. Maybe you can tell me something about this copy. Sometimes a little tidbit of information could add significantly to the book's value." I still felt queasy about showing the book to anyone. I didn't even know where to do it. I felt the shop was too dangerous. So was my home. Whoever knew where I worked knew where I lived. My address was in the phone book. It was convenient for business to have people know how to contact me when I was away from the shop. And whoever was so meticulous as to have broken cleanly into my shop could be waiting with brass knuckles or a cosh right now behind my front door.

In fact, I didn't feel safe going to the shop to fetch the book. Or even to go to work. This is ridiculous. I should never feel unsafe in my own digs. This was getting me mad. And if there is ever a formidable opponent, it's a mad bookseller. I just didn't know yet what form my formidability would take.

Terry saw the ruminations. She seemed to be inside my head:

"We can take it to my place. It's just a little apartment in Santa Monica. But it's anonymous and unpretentious. No one would know it's there. I even have access to a bank vault, if you'd feel safer. But, I mean, I didn't mean to presume that you'd trust me with such a . . . ."

"Not a bad idea. Maybe I could get a safe deposit box in your bank. But . . . ."

"We could ask the police to accompany you when you get the book out of your shop. And I don't have to be there when you do. I guess it would be dangerous to be seen with the book. But the police would help you, wouldn't they?" She seemed to have a small epiphany. "The guys you waved to. They are there to watch you. They're police, aren't they?"

Fast thinker.

"You said that they think they are saving your life. That was no joke."

"I call them Bud and Lou."

She smiled. Lovely. "Well, maybe Bud and Lou are."

Saving my life?

SIX

I called Coster from the store. Going in made me nervous, but it was broad daylight. Like when I was shot.

Terry had gone away by a different route. Nothing cloak-and-dagger. She had an appointment with one of her grad students. Her car was in the other direction.

Coster wasn't in. So I went out to the curb and hailed a copcar. Bud and Lou cringed, but Bud got out and came over from across the street.

"What is it, Mr. Burgess?"

"I need a lift. I need a police escort. Officer Coster suggested that I put a book into a bank vault. I don't feel comfortable doing it by myself. Can you help me?"

Bud said, "I guess so. Let me call the office."

A few minutes later he said, "Coster's not in. But I can't see anything out of order with that. We were told to keep an eye on you. We can do that from our own vehicle better than trying to follow you in traffic."

"Can you spot it if we are being followed?"

"Getting paranoid, Mr. Burgess?"

"It's ok to be paranoid about someone following you if someone is really following you."

"No problem. Lou and I can spot a tail."

"Did you say 'Lou'?"

"Yes; my partner. Louie Singer."

I was amazed. "And your name is?" I could hardly wait for the answer.

"Jack Neidspondiovanci. It sounds like 'naydspondeeavonchee.' I'm Italian. The Jack is really Jacopo."

"Too bad."

"What's too bad?" He sounded offended.

"Oh, nothing. Mind if I call you Bud?"

He looked shocked. "That's my nickname from childhood. No one has called me that since I was in sixth grade. How did you know?"

"It was obvious."

* * *

Terry had told me the name and location of her bank. Bud and Lou drove me there and waited outside while I stowed my little pamphlet in a small box. In the vault I put the key under the lining of my shoe, at the arch where it wouldn't bother me too much. I felt stupid doing this. More cloak-and-dagger stuff. But shop-breakers are like guys who wear cloaks. And bullets are like daggers.

My chauffeurs got me back to the shop by 3:45. Dave Daws was there. "Are you ok, Mr. Burgess?"

"Sure. I had to go to the bank."

"I read about your accident. I opened up the day after it. My regular time. It was quiet."

"Did anyone come in?"

"Only a scout who wanted to sell you a box of books."

The hairs on my neck stood up. "Which scout?"

"Hans Schrecknagel. The old man with the first editions. He brought in a few nice ones."

"No one else?"

"He was the only one."

Dave's regular time was 10:00 a.m. to 2:00 p.m., Mondays, Wednesdays, and Fridays, and at other times irregularly. We worked out his schedules with mine to give me freedom to move. Today he said he'd stay till 5. At 10:00 a.m. I had gotten a call from someone who identified himself as Mr. Johnson. I told him I would be in at 10:00 the next morning. He said he'd meet me then. If Mr. Johnson hadn't shown up, he must have known that I was in no condition to meet him there. Did he have a .22? Was he Caligula? Did he read about the "accident" in the paper and know not to come in?

I couldn't think this one through. "Phone, Mr. Burgess."

I hadn't heard it. "Hello."

"Elliot?"

That nice voice—firm and soft.

"It's Terry."

"Yes, I know. Finished with your appointment?"

"No, he hasn't shown up yet. Did you go to the bank?"

"Yes. The book's safe."

"Good. When can I see it?"

She sounded almost impatient. I guess the enthusiasm of unbridled scholars pushes them past the point of patient manners. Nice alliteration.

"The bank closes at 6. I can get there just before then and get the book."

"I have a better idea. If someone follows you, he'll see you take the book out. Why not make me a co-signer on your card so that I can get the book out for you. That way, anyone following you will not be around to see me take the book out. I can get it safely to my place. And I can hide it there. There's a place no one will find." I thought of wall safes, loose floorboards, hollowed-out books, under-the-sink-phony-products-with-storage spaces, loose ceiling tiles, and mattresses. I didn't say anything. It made me nervous to be thinking about moving this dangerous little book around in the world. And I felt protective of Terry, for some odd reason. I had met her only once. We barely knew one another.

But she was a young professor, as I had once been, and not too long ago. Would she be pummeled by the system as I had been? Would she get her scars the way I did? Maybe I could shield her from all that.

She said, "Are you still there?"

"I'm here."

"What do you think of my plan?"

"I don't know. If you have a key and know the whereabouts of the book and have access to it, you are vulnerable."

"Who'll know?"

"I don't know. Maybe no one. But . . . ."

"It'll be safe in my place. I promise."

Was she so desperate to see it that she would try to placate me this way? "I don't know."

"How about dinner?"

I hadn't been asked out to dinner my whole life. Least of all by a lady I was thinking about more and more.

"When? Where?"

"My place."

"How about the Captain's Quarters?" It was one of my favorite places. Lots of secluded tables surrounded by fishing nets, corks, stuffed fish (were they real taxidermied buggers or plastic?), and advertising pieces all over the place for passage on old ships long put permanently to berth. "Meet you there at 7:30?"

"Great. See you. Bye."

I called the restaurant and made a reservation.

I turned down a meal at her place. Hmmm. If someone followed me, would he see me there? Link her with me? Put her in jeopardy? Was I afraid of going there for other reasons? Or did I just want a great meal at the Captain's Quarters?

Dave whisked me out of my reverie. "A Mr. Coster called. Here's his number." I didn't need it. I already knew it. I called him back.

"You called for me. Jack tells me you took my advice. The book is in a bank. But why in Santa Monica?"

"It's far enough from my shop to be undetectable."

"Listen, Mr. Burgess. We just found a body of a man who seems to fit the description of your Mr. Carl Smith."

"You need me to identify the guy? What do you mean 'the body'?"

"Pretty bad shape. He's been killed. Beaten to death. But not all at once. Can you meet me some time this afternoon?"

It was already nearing five. Dave was leaving in a few minutes. "This afternoon is almost over. What time?"

"Five thirty?"

That would give me time to see the corpse and get to the restaurant. "Ok. Where is it? How do I get there?"

"The body's in the morgue at Cedars Sinai Hospital." He heard my gasp. "Sorry. If you don't want to go back there, I could bring you pictures. We already have pictures."

I had never been in that damn place until a few days ago. Now it looked as if I was drawn to the place. "I can meet you there."

It was close to my shop and I was there with time to spare. When Coster showed up we went to view the pathetic body. It was Smith, alright. But barely recognizable. Not merely from the pastiness and whiteness of death, but also because his face had been banged around a bunch. And there were cuts on it. Coster had the hospital person (doctor? mortician? orderly?) show me Smith's arms. His wrists had been tied. He had cigarette burns on his arms. I had seen enough.

"There's much more," Coster said.

"You said you wanted me to identify him, not to count his bruises."

"Right."

"Well, it's him."

"Sorry to put you through this. His real name's not Smith."

"I guessed that."

"He was a small-time burglar and hit-man and bad-boy-for-hire. His name is . . . was Rudolf Gens. Many arrests, many convictions, many days in jail."

"Did he ever work on his own?"

"Why do you ask?"

"Because he seemed to be on his own when he brought the book in. He didn't seem to be working for anyone else."

We had walked to the parking structure. We stood there amid the fumes of cars in the enclosed place (the hospital drumming up some business—famous for their pulmonary department).

"Why do you say that?"

"Whom would he be representing? He was selling a box of books, mostly junk, but with one good item in it. Where did he get it?"

"We are working on this, Mr. Burgess. So far no leads. No ideas."

"Officer Coster, who would have killed him? When did he die?"

"He died three days ago. Probably early in the day. We're not sure of the time."

That was the day of my accident. Any relationship? Mr. Edward Myers had known Smith aka Gens. He said that they were acquaintances. I told Coster of that phone call. Coster took out his pad. I felt as if I was in a movie. I remembered Caligula, but not the phone number. It was in my shop. Coster said he'd call the next day to get it. I told Coster that Myers had said the book was his and that he wanted it back. I said that he had offered me a good profit for it. I didn't mention that Myers had said he *would* get his book back. Did I remember that correctly? Am I being paranoid again? I told Coster the rest.

Coster asked, "Do you know what he meant when he said the book got out of his hands?"

"Not a clue. Maybe Smith / Gens stole it from him."

"I don't think so. He would have said, then, that the book was still his. He would have said that it was stolen. He would have filed a police report. That's a valuable book, and he knows it. No. There's more to it."

I said, "When you figure it out, let me know."

He said, "When *you* figure it out, let *me* know."

I said, "So who killed Gens? and why?"

He said, "Murder will out. Be patient."

"And when it will-outs, can I get rid of my shadows?"

"Soon."

I hoped not too soon.

SEVEN

The Captain's Quarters was lively, but its hubbub was subdued by the curtains, carpet, and ambience. Terry was waiting for me at the front door. When we saw each other, I think I smiled. I'm sure she did. Her black knee-length skirt must have been silk, the way it flowed. And her v-necked shirt, gray and white swirls, looking better than JC Penney, not quite Chanel, revealed a warm tan chest and collar bones as prominent as her cheekbones. I wonder what Monet would have done with her. Picasso. Vargas.

We got to our table and ordered. Then we sat there for a while looking at each other. It wasn't awkward, as it could have been. I didn't know what to say, and I was enjoying the scenery. She didn't seem ready to talk. Then the muscles around her mouth tightened a bit, which was a cue for me to wait. Which I did.

"Elliot." It was half question, half statement, half pause. It served 150% of her communication needs. "I'm torn between talking about the book and your life and my problems and . . . ."

"Stop. What problems? You mean getting a copy of the death book?"

"That's only the tip of a large floe."

"Well, let it flow. What're friends for?"

Her smile was gentle and troubled. "I didn't know I had any in L.A. I've been here nearly five years and I still don't see anyone, socially, professionally, or . . . intimately." She said the last word with a touch of embarrassment or hesitation in her voice. I waited. "I mean, I see lots of people. But it's hard to get to know them. I mean, really know them. My colleagues are into their classes, their families, their research, their students."

I grimaced just enough for her to see the implication of that statement.

"You know what I mean!"

"When I was a professor . . . ."

"You were a professor?"

"Botany. Though it became Botanical Political Science. Tenure was always on the other side of the hill. Sisyphus had an easier time to get to the top of his hill."

"At least he got to the top."

"What?" I asked.

"Camus said that at least Sisyphus got to the top. It was a victory. And he could go on to eternity having that little victory."

"Well, I never saw the top of my hill. It's a good thing I could do something else. Anyway, I was saying that when I was a professor, I saw many a colleague into his students."

"How long did you teach?"

"Eight years. The max. Any longer and I'd have had tenure by default. They got me out just in time."

"Why not teach elsewhere?" She really was naive.

"I had too many years of teaching. Anyplace hiring was looking for fresh meat, right out of grad school. No school could afford me. Except those that could, and then they didn't want me. I was tainted. A castoff."

"That's what I'm facing?" She said this as a question, but we both knew it was a declaration.

"Hey, I didn't mean to cut you off back there. You were talking about your problems."

"Same as yours were. I have an enemy in my department and I'm up for tenure this year. I don't stand a chance. The enemy is too powerful and my book isn't near done."

"The one on the art of dying?"

"Yes. It's plenty original, but a dynamite chapter on the first printed German edition would be the thing that sells it to a publisher."

"Tell me again about this edition. What else is there?"

She dug into her caesar salad pensively. Then she put her fork down. Here comes the lecture, but this time I was all ears. Well, not exactly.

"As I told you, there are things in the German edition that are in no other texts. They seem to have been influenced by some contemporary event, in 1494. Maybe a murder. Maybe a major theft. Maybe some kind of heresy. In the preface to another work of the same year, Kachelofen mentions a crime that he says was pretty heinous, so bad that he cannot articulate it. But it may be some kind of court intrigue that, if revealed, would have cost the printer his life. He must have been pretty close to whatever it was."

"Do you have any idea?"

"No. Nobody does. But court intrigues were common. It may have been one of many. What I want to see is the text just after the opening pages—the introductory leaves. From what I know, the NYPL copy lacks those. But on the first page that they do have, according to Steinmetz, who has published a short paper on the German text, there is the last half of a very provocative sentence that goes something like, 'would be death to the one who revealed it, as I have just done.' Here and later the *Buchlein* author alludes to the fact that he is the first to tell the truth. That he is not afraid of the consequences, partly because he seems to have something over the authorities who could have punished him—something else he apparently discussed in the earlier, missing, pages."

"How does that affect the rest of the text—after this introduction?"

"I think it shows that the *ars moriendi* text was a good one to use if you wanted to attack the authorities in any way. Who would suppress what was ostensibly a religious text, one that was designed to prepare people to meet their maker? Kachelofen seems to have embedded into his text some polemic stuff, something of historical and political importance; and the key to it lies in the missing pages. Steinmetz couldn't find it because he lacked the key pages."

Her eggplant parmesan smelled wonderful. My crab loaf with caramelized onions over a bed of garlic potatoes and designer miniature vegetables was delicious. The captain could sure cook.

"So you need to see my copy of the book."

"You did say it was complete?"

"I'm not an expert in *ars moriendi* texts as you are. Nor can I read German as fluently as I once could. And I haven't had time to look into the text at all. I've studied the title page and the colophon. It seems to be all there."

"At least it has a title page. Did you count all the pages? Collate it? See if every leaf is accounted for?"

"Yes; the numbering is continuous."

"From the first printed page—the introduction?"

"I think so."

"Doesn't that sound a bit odd?"

"Well, yes. Now that you mention it." It was more common to have the front matter—title page, introduction, preface, and so on—either unnumbered or in roman numerals and the pages of the text proper numbered from one on. But there were enough variations that the numbering in the Kachelofen pamphlet wasn't unprecedented.

We discussed this and many other things through our dessert (tiramisu for me—with a slightly too tart mascarpone cheese—and creme brulée for Terry).

"When can I see it?" I thought too long without saying anything. "It's not a danger now. No one knows where it is."

"People could know where I am. All they'd have to do is tail Bud and Lou."

"What about my plan? You know: let me get into the safe deposit box when you are nowhere around."

"I can't help thinking that that will put you into danger."

"If someone's watching you, other than Bud and Lou, then he's seen us together. I won't be in any more danger if I have the book than I am now."

That wasn't a comforting thought.

"What's the writing schedule of your book? Are you ready to do a Kachelofen chapter?"

"Any time. I will have about ten chapters. Seven are done. Two are in draft. The last one depends on the *Buchlein*."

"Write chapters eight and nine. We'll work out a plan."

She looked a bit dejected, but not hopeless. "Thank you for dinner. Walk me home?"

Inasmuch as her Santa Monica pad was about twelve miles away, I declined. But I walked her to her car. I faced her somewhat awkwardly and she quickly stepped forward into my space, kissed me on the cheek, and spun around to get into her car.

"Nice evening."

"For me too. Thanks. I'll call you tomorrow. We'll figure out a way to get the book to you." It was already nearing eleven and I was feeling rotten physically, though not bad mentally. I was usually at home reading or cataloging or letting my brain go to mush in front of the computer screen.

She looked at me with one of her stirring smiles. Then just before she swung into her car she said,

"Remember, I have a perfect hiding place."

I didn't know which one she was talking about.

EIGHT

I strolled over to Bud and Lou. They were pretty obvious. Maybe that was the point.

"Don't you guys get time off for behavior?"

"Two others will meet us at your house. Probably already there." Bud seemed unflappable, and he was pretty low-key in his delivery. He must have been bored to sleep.

"Go on home. Or wherever you go to. I'm going straight home myself."

"We'll follow you." And they did.

In front of the big Hancock Park house sat an unmarked police car. How did I know? It had the extra antennas, spotlights on both sides of the windshield, and a uniformed policeman with his butt on the hood, smoking. I pulled into the driveway and stopped near the curb. Marlboro man came over to me, and the wind was just right: I smelled him fifteen feet away. He had crushed his cigarette onto the ground—what a slob. Littering was at least a $500 fine in this neighborhood. I should call a cop. But even with the butt on the ground, I could smell his breath as he approached: stale garbage can smell. I held up my hand as if trying to stop traffic (usurping his job), but he still came on.

"Mr. Burgess? I'm Officer Burns. I'll be outside here all night."

"Alone?"

"No; my partner Officer Steven Gracie is with me. If you need help . . . ."

He didn't finish the sentence. A powerful explosion roared out from behind Flo and Bob's house. Something had happened to my little bungalow.

We raced around to the back to see flames licking up around the front door from inside. Burns screamed to Gracie to call the fire department as he ran to a hose on a reel attached to the back of Flo and Bob's house. It didn't quite reach to my front door, but it was close enough for him to send a stream of water to the door. I ran to the back of the house, from where nothing looked amiss. I pulled out my key, but saw it would have been useless. Someone had broken the glass of the little window and had opened the door easily from outside. I ran in, not thinking that whoever did this might still be there. No one was. But he had been. The place was a mess beyond belief.

I stepped over the piles of stuff on the floor and made my way through the little kitchen to the living room where Coster and I had sat the day I came home from the hospital. There were small flames at the front door, but no great blaze within. There was, however, a stream of water flowing in from outside. I screamed to Burns to shut the water off and I pounded out the flames with a pillow from the couch. Sirens got louder. Firemen were all over the place. They looked very official and concerned, but they had arrived at the ballpark after the last pitch.

"Now, sir; we'll take over. Please step outside. Mr. Scratch will accompany you."

You stupid shithead. I just did your job. I don't need to leave. Even if I wanted to go out, I don't need someone to show me how to get there. "What!" I shouted. I guess I was pretty upset and in some little shock. "I'm not going anywhere."

"Sir. Whoever did this did it with an incendiary device."

A Bomb, you idiot. A Bomb. I guess seven syllables sound more dangerous than one. But that one was onomatopoeic. Bomb. Boom.

"And, sir, there may be another in this dwelling."

House, you moron. It's a house. I live here. I don't goddam dwell here. "What!"

"I can see you are agitated, sir. We can search the dwelling for other such explosive devices. You'll be safer outside."

There was still a good deal of smoke and floating dust in the place. "Listen, if you have to douse any more flames, maybe you could do it in such a way that you use little water. There are many things here that should not encounter water."

"We don't use water on a fire of this kind, sir. We'll take care of it."

"No water. No water!"

Most of my cataloging I did at my shop. But I had some pretty good books here, fortunately most in the second bedroom where I had a computer and desk and office supplies. I did the cataloging of some of my better books here. Safer than leaving them in the shop. Safer? Jesus! I had no safe place left.

Officer Burns stepped into the dwelling from the front door, tracking soot and ashes and muck onto the floor—or rather onto the pile of stuff on the floor. I said, "Please don't step on anything. I've got some valuable books and manuscripts here. You'll ruin them." As if they weren't already ruined by the blast and the deluge and the smoke.

Burns stooped and started to pick up some papers, then let them drop. "Better let the bomb squad check all this out. Let's get out of the house. Unless you think there is a chance that the fire could start up again."

Fireman Fred said, "We have the situation completely in hand. You two gentlemen please step outside."

I was immobile, so Burns grabbed my arm and pulled me out of the house. I was still too stunned to resist.

The rest of the night was some kind of nightmare. At least the first half of it was. I stayed around the place making a pest of myself. Police seemed to be everywhere: in the house, around it, in the front of the Vacations' house, blocking the street. They kept telling me that I should get out of there. But I wanted to stay close. It was my home base, my home. My dwelling. And I had thousands of dollars worth of books and manuscripts there. I wanted to see what had survived. And in what condition.

I was pushed further and further away from the scene. They called it a crime scene. God! My home a crime scene. I didn't know what to do. But Terry's face came back to me again and again, and I got to a phone and called her. I don't know why I called her. Yes I do. I needed comfort and my other friends—acquaintances—were not what I needed.

"Elliot? It's after midnight. What's going on?"

"Have you got a couch?"

"What's happened? Of course I have a couch. It's a bit short, but if you need it . . . ."

I told her quickly and got a warm and concerned invitation. I ran back to the house, fought one fireman and three police folks to get to my clothing and overnight kit, and got out of there. Twenty five minutes later Terry opened the door.

"A bomb? Who would do such a thing? Are you ok? God, Elliot!"

"I was in the street out front talking to my protectors when the thing went off. I don't think it was meant to harm me. Just to scare me."

"A bomb! Not meant to harm you? How can you say that?"

"Normally I'd be in the back study or in bed by the time the thing went off. And it was set to damage only the front door area. Even if I had been in my little living room, I would have been far enough away that it probably wouldn't have hurt me much. There were some flames at the front door, but no real bomb damage to the rest of the room."

"What do you mean 'bomb damage'?"

"The rest of the place had been totally trashed. I wasn't allowed in long enough to assess what was going on. It may have been someone searching for something. Maybe a VCR, which I don't have. Maybe the death book. Maybe the bomb was to draw attention away from the trashing. But you'd have to be dead not to see the mess."

Dead. Did I say that? Since that book came into my life, I think I had been using that word with increasing frequency. Maybe it *was* cursed.

Her apartment was tiny, all right. One small bedroom, made to seem even smaller by the king-sized bed in there. A tiny living room with a two-cushion couch covered in a damasky gold fabric. An efficiency kitchen with a remarkably large refrigerator. A two thirds bath—no tub.

She was in a nightgown and a demure shiny gold robe, light blue slippers. Hair braided. She said, "I'm exhausted. I got sheets out for you. They're on the couch. But if you wish, you can take the half of the bed I don't sleep on."

A good way to put it. It clarified things perfectly. I chose the bed. She gave me a quick kiss in the air with our cheeks touching and then she took the side near the clock radio. I was next to the little closet door. I kept my undies on, though I usually didn't wear anything to sleep. I did my ablutions and got into bed. She turned out the light and I lay there half expectantly, half too ragged-out to move. I waited.

Then the sun came streaming into the room and I woke up. It was late morning. She was gone, but there was a note telling me to have food (plenty of bagels and cream cheese—no lox—in the fridge) and a shower (plenty of hot water). There was a key for me next to the note. And there was a carnation in a vase with a Post-It: "Smell this. It'll get the scent of fire out of your nostrils. See you for dinner? 6:00? Bye."

Terry Luckombe. Luck. Now what?

NINE

Coster was facing me looking pretty grim. But then, he rarely looked any other way. He said he was in Homicide, but that since I was his case, he was going to stay on it, even though this didn't look like a homicide attempt.

"That's what I thought."

"Someone was either trying to scare you or to injure you. Maybe both. But unless you were right on top of it—like right at the front door, which was unlikely—you wouldn't have been too hurt by that bomb." He called it a bomb. Sounded horrible. I wish he had said 'incendiary device.' I wouldn't have felt in such danger. "We noticed also that the place was ransacked prior to the detonation. Maybe the bomber was trying to take our attention away from that. Not too smart."

"Why?"

"Because bombs have signatures. This one could have been done by any number of people, but we can rule out some of the big guys."

"Who are the big guys?"

"What I mean is that the professionals who specialize in such pyrotechnics would never have done such a simple and crude pipe job like the one used on your place. It didn't even have a timing device on it, except if you call a long fuse a timing device."

"A long fuse? You mean that while I was standing outside talking to Officer Burns, a fuse was burning at my door?"

"That's what it looks like. We found a long trail for it on the grass near your front door and a bit of it in the rubble."

Yikes! What a word to use about my dwelling. I never would have connected anything pertaining to my domicile to the word 'rubble.' It was disgusting and made my stomach churn a bit.

"How long was the fuse? Was the guy there when we were out front?"

"Probably. Though it looks as if he had gotten into your place much earlier. The back door was broken into. Pretty porous security you had there, Mr. Burgess."

"I'd never had trouble there. In two and a half years not a sign of intrusion or even that anyone knew there was an abode back there." 'Abode' sounded better than 'dwelling.' "And Hancock Park is not known for its crime."

"Places that are not *known* for crime are still victims of it." Coster spoke with a deadpan attitude. He said this as if he had said it many times before, with a sort of resigned boredom. As if to say, "How many times do I have to tell people this?! Will they ever learn?"

"So whose signature did you find on this one?"

"Too common and generic a device. Could have been anyone. Even someone wanting us to think he knew little about bombs. So what I said before isn't really too accurate. It could have been a real pro trying to look like an amateur."

"Great! Now what am I supposed to do?" I knew what I wanted to do. I wanted to wring the neck of this bastard with the scare tactics. In fact, I was not too scared. I think I was too angry to be afraid. I was ready to take on this fucker. First I would shoot out his car window.

"Mr. Burgess, do you have any enemies? I know we've asked you this before, but you must think about anyone, anyone at all."

"When I left teaching I had people I would love to have shot. They probably felt the same about me. That's why they deep-sixed me."

"Name names."

"Sam Forester is the first that comes to mind. He led a campaign to discredit me and was successful. But that was seven or eight years ago. And he won. There's nothing more he needed to do to me. He wanted me out and got his way."

"Why did he want you out?"

"I was in his field. He hadn't published in eighteen years; I had published plenty. I was embarrassing him. Also, he wanted me sexually. I wasn't interested."

"Did he proposition you?"

"Yes. He wanted me to accompany him to his club. The Stocks and Bonds Club. Had nothing to do with Wall Street."

"So he has a penchant for pain?"

"Maybe. He had a few henchmen in the department, but they were his pawns. They were harmful drudges, but without minds of their own. I think that's the wrong direction to look."

"Yes, we thought so. We believe the book that you got—that little pamphlet—is involved. If you had had it at your home, and the bomber had torched the whole place, it would have gone up in tatters. This was too carefully placed to want to hurt you or any precious objects in the house."

"And the mess was someone searching?"

"I think so. So putting the book into a bank may have saved it for you."

"I see. Whoever it was has already searched my house and my shop. But not the safe."

Certainly he saw that. "It's a big one. To get in would require a blast big enough to destroy its contents. Or to cut through with a torch would take too many hours. It's the only thing that falls under the rubric of 'security' that you have that is worth anything. But it's breakable. The right man could blow out the dial quickly and not hurt a thing inside. The safe deposit box is as close as you're gonna get to Fort Knox."

"Has anyone ever stolen from Fort Knox?"

"I've never heard of it."

"Well, Officer Coster. I have a notion that someone will soon contact me to make me another offer for my book. And I would think that whoever it is is gonna be quite a suspect."

"We were wondering when you'd hear from Mr. Myers again. He seems a likely candidate for the title of shooting bomber."

"I'll let you know when the call comes. In the meantime, I've got a business to run."

The shop seemed safe. Seemed. That morning the man from Sensible Security showed up. His drawl nearly drove me to call a different company.

"Mister Burgess." It sounded something like "Me Esther Burgess." Why do I have such a prejudice against drawls? That one conjured up watermelons on a lazy afternoon, with flies buzzing around, and chit-lins cracklin' on the stove (if that's what chitlins do, and if stoves are where they do it).

"Mister Burgess. My name's Billy Brinks. Sensible Security. I looked around. You got yourself some security gaps here. We can't lock up anyplace 100%. But we can get to about 95% and then some. But the higher that number, the more you gotta shell out. Security ain't cheap. But neither is trying to recover from theft. Theft not only reduces your assets, it probably also ups yer insurance. How much you willin' to spend on this place?"

Dumb question. If I say three hundred, the bill comes to $299.95. If I say a million, the bill comes to $998,995.00 Only a dolt would answer it. But then, a dolt wouldn't be having his place secured by one of the top companies in the city—recommended by my insurance company. Which, incidentally, was sending an adjustor to the house the next day.

"What kind of security do you recommend for this place?"

"Only the best. That's all we deal in."

Cagey bastard.

"OK. What's the least I could pay to get the kind of security best suited to my business and this building?"

"The least you could pay? No limit upward. Limit downward? You get what you pay for."

"Are you saying that I could pay an endless amount of money and get endless security?"

"Mr. Burgess. Let's put it this way. There's yer generic bars and grates and gates and locks. Then there's yer electronic locks and video cameras that record any movement and any sound. Movement-acti-vated; sound-activated. Then you've got movement detectors, heat detectors, sound detectors, light detectors, shadow detectors, laser lights and visible deterrents, cameras for darkness, cameras for light times, electric beams, bullet-proof glass, bullet-proof walls and doors, electrified ceiling tiles; pressure-sensitive floor coverings; indelible and traceable dyes to spray on yer common intruders, micro-devices implanted in books and onto sheets of paper that can be traced with satellite tracking. So if anything does get out of here, we can find it. Indelible inks; microdots; microstamps; mini-micros with a three-mile range; and infra-red devices the likes of which you'd be boggled to understand. For more money, round-the clock surveillance by armed, fully trained professionals. On-site. For more money, two of them. For more money, three. We can build you a nest inside your walls that is virtually undetectable from outside the walls. You could put a guard in there or a safe or books or yer lunch. Why, I could even . . . ."

Ooh. He was a "why" sayer. I hated why sayers. My ex-in-laws were why sayers. "If'n ya wanna git ta Omaha, why, all y'all gotta do is . . . ." What the hell was that 'why' doing in there?

I settled on one of their White House Packs, safe enough to deter an intruder trying to get into the Presidential Palace of a hostile nation. It was expensive, but my insurance company offered me a rebate with this Pack. And it did offer some serious security: motion-activated cameras for each room; movement detectors that silently sent a signal to a security sentry somewhere close enough by to bring a guard here within seven minutes. There were better locks, better deadbolts, security strips on all windows, a heat detector that could pick up a person's body heat; though why the White House Pack included this I couldn't understand since the movement detectors should have done the trick. I felt safer, but I felt overdressed.

The whole job could be done in two days, and he would start in a week. I would have to learn two different shut-off-and-turn-on-the-alarm codes and carry three extra keys and know how to pray to Mecca.

After days of disruption, and several nights in Terry's big bed—still too big—I felt ready to get back to business. I hadn't turned on my computer in three days. Today I'd have several dozen messages to get through.

The very first was: "I understand you have a copy of the German edition of the *ars moriendi* from 1494. What are you asking for it?"

Bingo! Our first suspect.

Message two: "Please quote your *Ein Buchlein von dem Sterben*. Do you give the standard dealer discount?"

Message three: "Your e-mail about the *Buchlein* was ambiguous. Do you have a copy? If so, is it for sale?

Message four was an announcement about the availability of a dealer's catalog of books on the Mexican Revolution. Amazing! Someone out there who isn't interested in my book.

In fact, there were 77 messages, and seventeen of them were from dealers or private parties (and one library) asking about my *Buchlein*. Book prices, like those of any commodity on the market, are a function of supply and demand. The supply here was short; the demand promised to drive the price of this book into the stratosphere.

The snail mail also brought queries about my German treasure. Oh, Mr. Carl Smith or Rudolf Gens, did you have any idea?

Then a well dressed and elegant young man entered the shop. He walked to me oblivious of everything else around him. He passed the cactus books and the other gardening books. He passed the eighteenth-century shelves with their gorgeous colored, engraved plates. He passed the herbals, including the lovely Girard that I had just acquired. His eyes were fixed on mine, and I knew he was here for The Book.

"Are you the proprietor? Mr. Burgess?"

"Yes. I'm not ready to sell."

"Sell? Do you mean the German *ars moriendi*?"

"Yes. How did you know?"

"How did you know that that's the book I wanted?"

"You just said it before I did."

"But only after you said you refused to sell it."

"Which I still do."

"Refuse?"

"Yes."

Sounded like a Bud and Lou routine. Which book's on first? It takes one man to mend the shutter. Two men? No, one man. Two men? I hadn't heard "Cohen on the Telephone" for probably 35 years, but it had a way of popping into my head with such a conversation as I was having with this Brooks Brothers model.

"What's your name?"

"I'm Sheldon Jones." First it's Mr. Carl Smith. Now it's Jones. Next comes Johnson. "I understand you have . . . ."

"You don't 'understand'; you *know*. Who told you?"

"That's not important."

"It is to me. Who told you, Mr. Johnson?"

He didn't correct me.

"The book is quite valuable, and I would love to add it to my collection."

"What do you collect?"

Asked of a normal collector, this question is a natural. It gives her a chance to open up and brag and schmooze and glory in her holdings. It's an invitation to boast, and exult, and crow. For Mr. What's-his-name here it was a test. He failed.

He fumbled for a moment. Then he said, "I am quite eager to purchase . . . ."

"I heard you before, Mr. Jackson. I want to know what you have in your collection."

"Very valuable books."

"You collect valuable books?"

"Yes," he said with a touch of relief. But I wasn't ready to let this worm off my hook so easily.

"What *subjects* are they?" I said 'subjects' so loudly and slowly that he could not miss the point. He now had to talk about subjects.

"Literature." He was probing.

"Is that all?"

"No. And many other subjects."

"Like what?"

"Mr. Burgess. I'm in a bit of a hurry."

"Mr. Joelson, you have mud on your face. No serious collector comes into a store like mine, offers to buy a very expensive book, says he's in a hurry, and wants to get the transaction over fast. Not for the kind of money we're talking about here."

"And how much is that, Mr. Burgess?"

"How much have you been authorized to pay for it?"

He knew I knew he wasn't here on his own.

"A great deal."

"How much is this great deal?"

"Uh, it's for me, really. I've been looking for this book for a long time, and I would like very much to buy it from you."

"You collect books in the Artis Gilmore tradition?"

"Yes."

"I don't carry sports books, Mr. . . . What did you say your name was?"

"Sheldon Jones."

"Who employs you, Mr. Sheldon?"

"What do you mean?"

"I was told that if you want to avoid answering a question, ask another question. So let me reiterate. Who employs you? Whom are you working for? Who pays your bills? Who supplies your scratch? Can I be any clearer?"

He could see that I was an immovable object or an irresistible force. He was a real amateur. Even I could have conjured up some serious answers. "I collect in the very area of that book. I have had an interest in the subject since my early teens. In fact, I am buying it for my wife as a gift. But as I really want it for my own collection, I tell her I'm buying it for her and then we have it in the collection." Or I could have told a half truth: "I am buying it for a friend who wishes to remain anonymous since he's giving it to a university library. His anonymity is extremely important. It's so important, in fact, that I am really dealing not with him but with an intermediary. I don't know what the book is about. All I know is that I have been authorized to give you a lot of money for it."

But, no. Innocent Mr. Jacobson, here, could only stammer out, "If you are not prepared to, uh, sell, uh, this book at this time, I, uh, I'll see if I can come up with an even more impressive offer. One that you can't refuse."

Original phrase. Good improvisation, airhead. "A more impressive offer? More impressive than what? You haven't mentioned a figure yet."

I shouldn't have said this. It just extended the conversation more, and I was really through with this shallow dandy.

"I could go as high as . . . ."

He paused, thinking. I would usually say that his wheels were turning, but that would have been something of a compliment. His wheels hadn't been greased in decades. In fact, I'm not sure he even had wheels.

"As high as what?"

"I'll get back with you." He tried to sound dignified and businesslike. It came out like Steinbeck's Lenny trying to explain Einstein's relativity. Pathetic. His employer didn't get his money's worth with poor Mr. Johns.

He left with a defeated angle in his shoulders. The suit didn't fit quite so well on his departure.

I sent an email out to the net: "To all who inquired about the *Ein Buchlein von dem Sterben* that I mentioned in an email message a few days ago: My mentioning it did not imply that I owned a copy or had one for sale. I am sorry if I inconvenienced anyone." That wasn't a lie. There really was no such implication in my earlier message. That I did own one was immaterial.

But I was getting curioser and curioser as to what the damn thing said. I could hardly wait to see Terry that night. And not just because of the book.

TEN

Her note had said 6:00. I got there at 5:55. Second floor. The fragrance from within was heavenly. Lightly oiled, softly grilled fennel salad with Greek olives, smoked oysters (oysters!), and lemon juice. Grilled marjoram and turmeric tofu that had been frozen to give it some body—smothered in browned sesame seeds with a hint of tamarind sauce. Slightly curried couscous with sultanas and yellow sun dried tomatoes. Snap peas in dark sesame oil and browned diced onions. Glacéed apples with plenty of cinnamon (you can't put in too much cinnamon; I had it on the best authority) with a cream sauce on the side. And decaf espresso with nutmeg and a hint of cassis. Then cheese with a thinly sliced Chinese pear. I thought of the eating scene in *Tom Jones*. Perhaps the most erotic eating scene I've ever seen in a movie.

She wouldn't let me touch a dish. In fact, completely unlike her (and me), she just let the dishes pile up in the sink.

We sat there stuffed. I hadn't felt this content in the three years since Stacy walked away with her Dr. My own meals had been perfunctory: a quick bite at Crocker's, with Molly's occasional extended narrative on the weather, the salt shaker, or the political climate in Canada. A frozen dinner at home, or a fast bowl of toasted oats with a banana. I had always seen meals as either time-consuming necessities or social occasions. In the last four years, they had become pretty much the former. A social occasion is when you talk to people you want to talk to. I had had little of that in my life lately. This dinner was a pleasant little slice of heaven.

As before, I knew not to speak when I got her I'm-thinking-and-going-to-say-something signals. So I just looked at her face and her hair and her long delicate fingers with the lovely nails. She coughed a little.

"I've been thinking."

"Is that dangerous or what?"

"What," she said.

"What?"

"Well, it's not dangerous, and since you gave me only two choices, it must have been What."

"What have you been thinking about?"

"Well, I love teaching." Pause.

"But."

"But the rest of it sucks. Politics, paper grading, especially in the service courses they force us junior faculty into. Back biting. Back stabbing. Sexist comments from my colleagues. Insensitivity of every kind."

"I learned that the ivory tower was really plastic. It was really a tower of babble."

"Were you sad to leave it?" She seemed particularly interested in this.

"Yes and no. I loved the teaching too—the interaction with the students, the reading and writing and discussing. But I hated all the things you listed and more."

"What more?"

"Specific people, for instance. And the way critics mangled your ideas. You say that A is good and the critic attacks you for not saying that B is bad."

"I've seen plenty of that."

"I guess in some respects the humanities and sciences are the same. Same jealousies, same territoriality, same frustrations."

She thought a moment and said, "I don't know if I want to go on in this world. It does have its benefits. But . . . ."

It was a powerful "But."

"So, what are your plans? You've been thinking."

"I'm not sure. I'd like to get out of teaching, though I like the research and writing. I could still do that."

"Yes." I was in the publish-and-perish cycle myself at one time. When I left it, I felt betrayed by the system and I felt that years of studying were going to waste. I placated myself with the idea that I would continue to do research and publish my findings. But leaving academia meant leaving behind the labs and the grants and the grad assistants.

How could a botanist carry on research about fungus-blocking enzymes when he had no lab and no money? Maybe Terry could pull it off in the humanities.

"All it takes is the books and manuscripts to do the research—you know, a good library nearby—and a little corner with a computer for me to write. That's why I have felt fairly comfortable in this little place."

"I see." And I did. The place was small but tidy and homey. It wasn't quite Laura Ashley, but it wasn't Kmart either. It was sunny and welcoming, not just for shot-up, bombed-out booksellers.

"Would . . .," she hesitated.

"Say it."

"Would you consider taking on a partner?"

Wow. What kind of partner? Before I could say anything she said,

"I've worked in an antiquarian bookshop. I know how to do catalogs, appraisals, sales. I can buy low, sell high. I have a good eye for a good book."

"Whoa. I make enough for me to get by pretty well. Not great, but good. I can't afford a partner. This is a one-person business."

"What about the man who works for you?"

"Dave Daws? Part-time, fill-in, minimal-input assistant."

I could sense something behind all this. And I thought I'd try it out: "You're up for tenure, right?"

She shook her head yes.

"Are you afraid you won't get it?"

Crestfallen she shook again.

"Do you have any back-up plans?"

"Well, you see. I guess . . . I just expected that in academia, where we work by brains and reason, I'd be treated, well, reasonably. I did everything I needed to do to get tenure. I expected to be in this for my career. I never thought . . . ."

"No one does. All the cast-offs from the profession say the same. No back-up plans. No money in the bank. It's not too remunerative being an assistant prof. The first years are the toughest. Low pay, heavy teaching load with all new courses to work up, a sincere dedication to teaching and your students because that's what you think you're here for. No time to do research to the level that you need for the big promo to tenure. Shitty system. My friend Steve Feldman got a Ph.D. in philosophy when I got mine in botany. He's now selling carpets in Florida."

"But, Elliot, I have really been thinking that teaching is not for me. For a few years. Even before the tenure thing came up. I have always been drawn to books—rare books. I worked in it. I'd collect them if I had some money."

"You worked in a bookstore? Which?"

"The George Washington in Cleveland."

Pretty impressive. Run by a famous old bookman, canny, smart, experienced, and sometimes shady, though never caught for anything that I knew of. "What did you do for him?"

"All the things I told you. I studied bibliographical description, so I could do scholarly catalogs for his older books. Collations and accurate binding descriptions and all that. He trusted me enough to go out and buy for him—at least, things that weren't too expensive, like under a couple of thousand dollars."

I'm sure my eyebrows went up. "Why didn't you tell me about this before?"

"It never came up. I wanted to see the book. You wanted to defend it."

"Is that what I was doing?"

"It seemed so. And you had your own *Weltschmerz* to deal with. There was no time. Besides, I was into the looking-good-for-this-person thing. I was a professor. That's what I wanted you to see."

I had been in her bed—bundling—for three nights. I had hardly touched her. There was indeed a bit of distance between us. This was the first time she had shown me something behind the academic façade. I liked her even more.

"I don't think I can afford a partner. Let's let it go for now."

She smiled and reached across the table. I took her hand. The goddam phone rang.

At first, she hesitated. Then she got up and took the call. She frowned and hung up without saying anything after "Hello."

"It was a man's voice. All he said was, 'Tell Mr. Burgess I'll meet him at his shop tomorrow at 10.' Then he hung up."

It was worse than a cold shower. I felt nervous, real nervous. Who would have known to call Terry to get to me? It was almost 9:00; why late at night? Who was it? I guessed. But I had an overlying feeling of something: something had happened at my shop? I asked Terry to ex cuse me. She looked dispirited and anxious.

"Where are you going?"

"I feel I've got to get to my shop. Something's wrong."

"I'm coming with you."

"No; I feel it's dangerous."

"I guess I'm already in danger if someone is out to get you and knows to call me."

We drove in silence. The shop. The new security system. It wasn't to go in till the next day. Shit!

* * *

The lights were off, as they should have been. I opened the front door and reached in to turn on the light. No lights. Shit! I went back to the car and got a flashlight. Or should I wait till the police arrived? I called them before we left the apartment. And Officers Burns and Gracie were behind us. But they were tailers, not in the robbery division or homicide or parking violations. They got out of their vehicle, but they were reluctant to go into the shop. Burns had said, "If you find something wrong, don't go in. Let the police handle it. Don't touch anything." Well, he *was* the goddam police. But he said he had no training in burglaries or break-ins or such stuff. He was there to protect me.

I decided not to wait. Terry and I waded into the darkness, with me seeing in the narrow beam and her hand on my back to follow. It wasn't quite like what I had seen at my bungalow, but it wasn't much better. Most of the books that had been on shelves were not there anymore. Piles on tables were scattered helter-skelter. The glass cases at the left of the front door were empty. They had held some pretty good plate books, which I learned had been scooped out onto the floor behind the cases. The back of the shop was worse. And it had an acrid smell of burnt toast and gasoline—or something. I aimed the beam at the safe. Why was it called a 'safe'? There was a hole the size of a fist in the front of the door where the knob had been. A big punching fist. The doors had been swung open and the safe was empty. Everything that had been in it was either on the floor or in someone else's possession.

I knew that my *Buchlein* wasn't there. So did the intruder. The police arrived a few minutes later, to meet me and Terry outside. I was heartsick and feeling a combination of anger and frustration. I felt capable of vengeance.

"Mr. Burgess?"

"Where the fuck have you been? Aren't you supposed to be guarding me?"

"Yes, sir. Lieutenant Coster told us to."

"So what's going on. Look at this place."

"We are guarding *you*, sir. Not your shop. Not your books."

He sounded insolent and I thought of 'fist' again.

I was too angry to say anything. Now my house was off limits for days because of the police search, and my shop had to be closed for a day or two for the same reason. I felt like Philip Nolan: a man with no country. I felt Terry's hand on my arm. Well, there was a country, wasn't there. She didn't say anything, but she didn't have to. I think she was feeling the way I was. I looked at her and saw the I'll-never-go-hungry-again look on her face. She was really with me in this. Here was one tough partner.

Partner?

We were told to go home after the statements and photographs and guard-postings and assurances that they had "everything in hand." Sure, an open hand. No fist here. I'm gonna kill someone for this.

Back at Terry's place I said, "Listen, this might be the face of the enemy. Maybe that's how this business is destined. You really interested in this?"

She faced me and said with the same firmness that I had heard in her voice on our first phone call: "You want a partner? You've got one. I could kill the person who would treat books like this—who could treat you like this." She hugged me tightly, maybe to comfort both of us. And she looked up at my face with a passion I hadn't seen before in anyone looking at me. Stacy never showed it. I had seen it in the movies, but never this close and warm.

When we kissed it was like an all-over massage, taking much of the tension out of my body, focusing my mind on the contact point of our lips. The soreness in my arm and at the other bruises, which had been hovering in my periphery for days, suddenly disappeared, and all I could feel was the pleasure of a young, firm, warm body next to mine.

I'd like to report that I swept her into my arms and carried her to her—our bed. But I was much too sore for that. We walked there. And we did what I had hoped she wanted as much as I did. Apparently she did. We caressed for a long time, slowly and comfortably, as if we had known each other for years. It was really only a week, but time wasn't the issue. Minds and shared interests and tight muscles were the issues. And tension and release and passion. We slept long after the sun came up.

ELEVEN

We showered together and had a quick coffee-and-toast-and-banana breakfast. I called Coster.

"Your shop is really a mess. I'm terribly sorry."

"Not your fault. You're into murder of people, not destruction of books."

"I thought you were going to get better security."

"He's coming today. The horse has escaped already."

"The place was really easy to get into. Whoever it was went in the same way as last time. Same pane of glass. Same by-pass of your silly little alarm system. Was he there for the book?"

"I can't tell you. But if the m.o. was the same, it was probably the same person."

"That's how we see it."

"I'm guessing that nothing has been taken. He could have taken anything he wanted the first time. Maybe some of the items from the safe were temptations not to be denied."

"When can you get over there?"

"You mean I can go there today?"

"Yes. Sooner the better."

"But my house. I was told not to return for at least two days. Not till I was called."

"The demolition guys take longer on a house. There are more tiny little things for them to sift through. Even an ash the size of a pinhead might carry some telltale information for them. We can go on larger things. The safe was blown by a pro. A small explosive well aimed and exactly the right size and shape. Plastic. Detonated from across the shop somewhere, probably in the front room. Radio activated. Simple and effective. It would probably not have damaged anything inside the safe, and it would not cause a flame for more than a second or two. No threat of fire. Clean. Neat."

If a bomb can ever be called 'clean.' There was nothing clean about any of this. It was really a dirty business, and a darkness emerged from it all. My mood. My fear far outweighed by my anger. The thoughts of retaliation that were strong in me—and in Terry. This was not clean in any way.

"I can be there in a half hour." We had eaten, dressed, done the dishes, and kissed. We were reluctant to part, but Terry had classes to teach and I had a little pile of paper to tidy. Parting was really sweet sorrow.

* * *

Good god! The place was unbelievable! The police had done their searching and dusting for fingerprints (none found, predictably), and had tried to help during their search by placing everything they came upon into piles all over the floor. But the collocation of materials that had been shoved to the floor at one time, and which left fallen stuff next to that which had fallen with it, was now gone. Things from here were piled up with things from there. Somehow, books and papers that I had had in the front of the shop were now mingled with the same kinds of things from the back.

I thought of my wonderful grandfather, who moved a print shop from New York to L.A. in the early '50s. The cretin movers had pied all of his printing types. They must have thought they were doing him a favor by putting it all into one large barrel so that he wouldn't lose any of it. But it was then just a barrel of about 1,000 pounds of lead and iron and antimony. Useless. For the next thirty years, during his spare moments between jobs, my grandpa sorted and distributed the type piece by piece, sort by sort, hoping to recover its use. It was useless. He died with the barrel still half full and with about forty typecases only partly filled with battered type. I still cry when I think about it.

My shop was like a huge barrel of pied books. At least they were bigger than sorts, those tiny leaden soldiers that printed the pages of the books I was now responsible for. I didn't know where to turn, what to do first. There was little room to move since just about every inch of the floor was covered with the things of my livelihood. Someone wanted to hurt me. He succeeded. He probably also wanted to scare me. But the way I felt at that moment, he had failed miserably.

Could I be scared into giving up, selling, parting with the book of death? No!

When Coster arrived he shook my hand and stood compassionately for a moment. "Want some help?"

"No, thanks. This will give me a chance to reacquaint myself with each little treasure I have here. Any ideas who the culprit is?"

"We have the profile. There are some pretty well known safe crackers in town. This could be one of about a dozen. We'll check them out."

"It could also be the work of someone from out of town. He could be from Pawtucket or Pullman or Podunk Center. You could be barking up a blind alley." I loved mixed metaphors.

"Right. But we go from where we are." I disliked muddy clichés like that.

"Could you give me the lists of suspects?"

"No can do. This is police business. You're the victim, not the justice system."

"I thought I might recognize one of the names. Maybe help you narrow down the list. Make your job easier."

I didn't expect him to buy this. If this bomber guy were a pro, he would have been hired to do this job. I wanted to get him and the one who had hired him. Coster thought a moment. I know he knew that the culprit wasn't the one who decided my safe was a goner. I know he knew I wouldn't know anyone on the list. But something in him seemed to understand my vigilante mood, and he said, "I'll have the list faxed to you this afternoon."

"Fine. Thanks."

The rest of the day I spent getting things back onto shelves, making pathways for the security system installers to walk through, and trying to get some sense of order back into my professional life. Funny, but a kind of subtle order had entered my personal life for the first time in years. It was like a pendulum swinging back and forth. Order in business; chaos at home. Chaos in business; order at home. I didn't like the thought. For the analogy with the pendulum made it impossible for me to have order in both places at once. I needed another analogy. Too much to do to think up another one.

* * *

By 6:00 p.m. the next day the shop was practically impregnable. I had called Terry and told her I'd be home late.

Did I say 'home'? Sure sounded good.

"What did they do?"

I told her in outline, with more details to come back at the apartment:

"Decorative grates over all windows, bolted through the walls. New kind of two-pronged deadbolts on front and back door. Sound sensors in front and back. If someone breaks the window, an armed response team will be here within five minutes. Heat detectors over the cash register and where the safe will be. Advice on a new kind of safe. Movement detectors to cover every open inch of the place. If a piece of paper falls off my desk when the alarm is set, response team, five minutes. Surveillance cameras recording everything, covering the front and back rooms. Motion activated. Film-in-the-dark capacity. Five minutes. Noise alarm and silent alarm. Three places where the circuits are activated, all inside. If any one is broken, five minutes. Weight sensor under two area rugs. Invisible cords connecting to the alarm. With a full wireless, remote back-up system. Five minutes. It cost us a fortune, but the stock warrants it. Especially now with The Book."

I had said that it cost *us* a fortune. It sure was easy including her in this mindset.

"While they were working I made major headway through the mess." I told her how the police had helped. I could hear her wince.

I was back at the apartment by seven. I guess I expected her to greet me at the door. She could easily hear me coming down the creaky hall. But when I put my key into the lock, there was no sound on the other side of the door.

I pushed the door and felt a touch of resistance. Not much. But the door didn't swing open as usual. It bumped into something on the other side. My muscles tensed. I felt a twinge in my stomach. I pushed the door open. The lights were dim.

TWELVE

I looked around onto the floor behind the door. There was one of Terry's shoes. It was a spike-heel evening shoe. About four feet beyond it was its mate. Beyond that, dropped into a little pile was a silk blouse, followed a few feet further along by a lovely short skirt I hadn't seen before. It had been laid out showing a high slit up one side. A few feet further along was a see-through camisole. That was followed by a very sexy low-cut bra. Two feet later was a black stocking with a seam up the back. Another led me further into the room toward a garter belt. And then, at the door to the bedroom, a thong bikini. I followed the clues like a good detective. A candle light shone beyond the door. I walked into the trap. And I thought of Sinatra's "Tender Trap." We didn't have dinner till midnight. But I had been feasting all evening.

THIRTEEN

Friday morning I didn't want to get out of bed. We had given up bundling. There was no future in it. It was really a terrible idea in the first place. But I had some kind of meeting at ten at the shop. Terry had a Monday, Wednesday, Friday class at eleven. I ran out feeling no pain, except in my arm, which still smarted, though it was healing rapidly.

I got there just as a Jaguar pulled up down the street and parked. Mr. Edward Myers got out. He wore casual clothes, Jhane Barnes fashions. Casual style, formal expenses. He strode purposefully toward me.

I jumped ahead of him, unlocked the door, went in, pulled out the slip of paper with the new security codes on it, and tapped them into the key pad as he entered. He stopped and looked around at the confusion everywhere. He didn't show any emotion; he didn't react. All he did was say:

"I'm here for the book. What is your price."

I was about to say, "What book?" but that tactic was old. I said, "It's not for sale. I don't know enough about it yet."

"How about $20,000. Cash."

"No. Thanks."

He never asked what had happened to the shop. It was as if he already knew.

I thought I'd take the offensive for the first time. "Your tactics won't work. I'm not selling the book. Least of all to you."

"My tactics? What on earth are you talking about?"

"You know."

"Are you implying that I had something to do with this?" and he gestured to the floor.

"If the shoe fits."

"Nonsense."

"Sense."

He was taken aback. And he probably didn't expect such a response. I guess most people would have sold the book for such a fine profit and gotten the chaos out of their lives. Not me. I had learned to fight when I was denied tenure. I was not about to give up being pushed by this little shit.

He said, "I can't imagine why someone would do this. But who knows, it might happen again." The new security system looked exactly like the old one. Even down to the outside electrical box behind the shop. I wondered if this *could* happen again. I said nothing, but I stared at him with some kind of inscrutable emotional face. That's what I tried for, anyway. I don't know how he took it.

To break the silence I asked, "Who was Gens?"

"An acquaintance."

"Why did he have the book?"

"He was supposed to deliver it to me."

"Who sent it?"

"None of your business. It was mine. I had bought it. Gens stole it."

"How do I know?"

"Know what?" He was getting irritated.

"Who owned it?"

He said gruffly, "It is mine."

"Not now." I was in a taunting mood. It felt good to have some control over him.

He glowered and just turned and strode out. No good bye. No closing formula like "Think it over" or "I'll see you next time." Just out the door.

The tension in the place dropped decibels (if that's how it's measured).

FOURTEEN

It was Saturday morning. We stayed in bed late enough to feel wonderful, but we got up early enough for me to go to the bank (which closed at noon) to fetch the *Buchlein*. It seemed like months since I had seen it. Terry and I drove the few blocks. I ran in, got the book, and got right back into the car. I was sweating, and not from the run.

"Where shall we go?" I asked her.

"Back to my place, of course."

"But the phone call. Someone knows we're together."

That phrase seemed natural, and it gave me a bit of a rush.

"We could go to a motel." She said this seriously, but with a small twinkle.

"Great idea. Which?"

"There's the Oceanside Suites near PCH." The Pacific Coast Highway, number 1, was not far from her apartment. There was a long string of hotels and motels along the shore, catering to surfers, vacationers, old folks out for the sea cure, and whoever else liked the fragrance of salty air. I loved it.

"Oceanside Suites it is," I said.

Terry suggested that I drop her off there then go back to her place to get clothes, tooth brushes, and bathing suits.

"Bathing suits? What I intend to do won't require a bathing suit. First of all, I'm not leaving the book in the room by itself. And I'm not giving it to any bellhop to stick in the hotel safe. That word *safe* doesn't sound safe to me any more. We stay with the book. We call up for room service. I intend to do all my feasting in the room." I looked at her meaningfully and she hugged me warmly. I almost ran off the road.

We got a suite at the end of a long hall—a non-smoking room. Not only for my lungs, but also because I didn't want to expose the *Buchlein* to any foul air. It had lasted over 500 years; I didn't want to contribute to its deterioration.

"This is exciting," Terry said, taking off her blouse.

"It sure is," I said, taking off my shirt.

"I can hardly wait to read this book." Skirt off.

"I'm dying to know what you find in it." Pants off.

By the time she said "I'm sure we'll find wonders between the sheets," we were well beyond reading. At 3:30 I left the room and headed back to the apartment. I got all the stuff we needed and I picked up a pizza on the way back. I kept a keen lookout for followers. Gracie and Burns were there, but no one else seemed to be. They weren't trying to be secretive about being with me. I guess a very visible guard was better than an invisible one.

When I got back to the room, Terry was poring over the pages. I didn't expect to see a wrinkled brow, but there it was.

"What's the matter? You look upset."

"I am. I've only looked at this for a few moments, but it seems that this text . . . ."

"What?"

"I don't exactly know, but there's something wrong with this text. I expected something different from the standard *Ars Moriendi* text. This seems to conform to the true text perfectly."

I sat beside her at the letter-writing table, and I watched her slender fingers holding the book open, turning the pages, making notes on hotel stationery. I watched her exquisite profile and her long wavy hair. And I sensed the sharp intelligence at work. What a treasure.

"Let's look at the book," I said.

"I'm looking at it."

"No; I mean, let's look at it as a book, as a physical object."

She handed it to me. I looked at the paper wrapper. Somewhat smudged with still a hint of the original blue color of the cover paper, though much of the blue had either faded or rubbed away. Neatly handwritten on the cover was the title: "*Ein Buchlein von dem Sterben.*" In the upper right corner of the cover was a handwritten number, "A.III.vii."

She pointed at that and asked, "What's this?"

"Probably some library marking. Press one, shelf three, book 7."

"Press?"

"Yes; it's the old word for a bookshelf. Collectors often gave their books such designations. The most famous, I guess, is the system from the Cotton collection."

"I've heard of it," she said. "It's in the British Library. The *Beowulf* manuscript was in that collection."

"But Robert Cotton didn't number his presses, he named them. After the busts of Roman emperors which were in front of each press. Books designated Cotton, Nero were in the shelves behind the bust of Nero. Books called Cotton, Otho were behind the bust of Marcus Salvius, known as Otho." McRath had taught us about him: Otho was ambitious, but in failure he killed himself.

"There was a Caligula, too." She said it offhandedly, but my flag went up. She saw my reaction. "Did I say something wrong?"

"You said 'Caligula.' That's the name of Myers' bookshop. The s.o.b. who wants to buy this book. The one who threatened me today." I told her about the meeting. When I recounted Caligula's words "it might happen again," Terry shivered a bit—and not just because she wasn't wearing much. That towel looked great on her.

"That was more than a threat. It was intimidation. It was a warning. Did you call Coster?"

"On Saturday? He's hard enough to get during working hours. He's probably incommunicado, sitting in front of a mirror practicing being serious."

We looked back at the book. There were no endpapers. Either they were never there or they were removed ages ago. We could see the sewing threads, which protruded at the spine on the outside of the cover. It was a two-signature pamphlet of only two original pieces of paper, folded into eighths. This made sixteen leaves and thirty two pages. Simple structure.

I held a sheet of the text up to the light. "It's an octavo," I said.

"It looks like it. It's just the right size."

"But size has nothing to do with it."

She smiled at me and said, "Don't brag."

I said, "I'm talking about the book."

"I know," she admitted. "But I thought that all octavos were about this size."

"Many are. But the format of a book has to do with the number of times the original printed sheet has been folded. If you're going to work with me and handle these old books, you'll need to know this."

"Teach me, my master."

I showed her the chainlines in the antique laid paper. They ran vertically. The original open sheet had chainlines running the short dimension top to bottom—vertically. "Fold the sheet once and sew it through the fold and you have a folio. One more fold and another 90-degree turn, you have a quarto; chainlines go horizontally. Another fold and turn, vertical chainlines and an octavo. That's what this is."

She held the book up to the light and saw the chainlines. She learned it instantly. I knew I'd never have to tell her that again.

"There's a watermark here." She pointed to the inner gutter of one of the sheets. "It looks like a star."

I looked. "Right. We can check Briquet."

"Bree Kay? Who's that?"

"Charles-Moise Briquet. The compiler of *Les Filigranes*, one of the great compilations of reproductions of watermarks. If we can find this very star in Briquet, we might be able to localize and date the paper."

"But we know the date of the book: 1494. I can read the numerals."

"If I were to print a book today and put 1900 on the title page, would you think it's from 1900?"

"Of course not. I see. Are you saying that this is a forgery?"

"Not at all. I'm just saying that it is a good candidate for forgery. It's short and scarce and valuable. I took this skeptical tack because you said something was wrong with the pamphlet. Why did you think something was wrong?"

"Not with the pamphlet. With the text. I can't find anything incendiary in the first few leaves. Though I haven't read it all, and my late medieval German is not perfect. I'm going to need a good German dictionary, one that lists earlier forms of words."

The pamphlet wasn't signed; that is, it didn't have any signature marks—letters and numbers—at the bottoms of the pages before the fold.

"Should it be signed?" she asked.

"Not necessarily. The signature marks were to show the binder the order of the signatures. This has only two signatures, so there was no trouble getting them in the correct order."

"What about the pages?"

"Getting the pages into the proper sequence was trivial for an experienced printer like Kachelofen. Or even for a novice printer working on such a short text. And the pamphlet would probably have been put together from a single sheet or two, printed on both sides, folded, bound, and then slit open. No need for signatures."

She looked pensive, taking it all in. "So you see nothing out of the ordinary in this booklet?"

"Not really. But the text seems wrong to you?"

"Yes. I can't see what all the fuss was about if the text were as this text is. Is there some way to test the pamphlet to see if it could be a fake?"

"Sure," I told her; "though I don't think it is."

"It looks genuine enough." She lay the pamphlet on the table and opened it to the center fold of one of the signatures. Very gently she ran her hands over the sheet. "I love the feel of old printing."

"It's one of the glories of the ancient technology: a three-dimensional sheet. The type bit into the paper, probably printed damp, and left its footprint there."

"Footprint? Peculiar image."

After I thought a moment, I agreed. "Yes, the type has feet, where the little jet was once attached when the sort was cast. That jet is broken off and the rough spot where it was attached is filed down so that the type stands squarely on its feet. I guess I should have said that the type leaves its face-print, since it's printed from the face."

"Another odd image," Terry said amused. "Can you have it tested?"

"I have a friend who specializes in testing the ink of early books. Remember, black ink is made partially of lampblack. Burnt stuff, like wood. It's carbon, mixed with linseed or some other oil. It is carbon-dateable. And there is a method of determining what the ink is made of."

"Where is this guy?"

"At the University of Central Delaware." I hadn't spoken to Brad Scharwich in ages, but we had been fairly good friends for many years. He had worked on the inks of early printed books using the cyclotron, and had developed a method of pinpointing the composition of inks much more accurately than anyone else had. And he worked with scientists who could do carbon dating on anything that had carbon in it. Here was a humanist in search of the truth through science. Great mind.

"The only problem is that he lives 3,000 miles from here," I said.

"Why is that a problem? You could go see him. It's a business expense. Charge it."

She was right, of course. But I had to be careful about such expenses. Elliot Burgess' bookstore was doing well, but wasn't to the level of Snoteby's or Christian Brothers yet.

"If you fly stand-by, maybe you can get a good ticket. This isn't a holiday weekend. There should be many flights available. Also, it would be safer having the pamphlet out of L.A. where you won't be able to get it into the safe deposit box till Monday."

"I'm not sure Brad is around."

I pulled up AnyWho on my new smart phone. B-R-A-D S-C-H-A-R-W-I-C-H. Delaware. Bingo. I got a phone number for him and called. The familiar voice, a bit raspy and deep from smoking.

"Brad, Elliot. Elliot Burgess."

"Good God; what brings this pleasure out of the blue?"

"Ink. Can you test some for me?"

"Tell me about it."

I explained who Conrad Kachelofen was, and I described the pamphlet.

"Why do you want to test the ink? You think there's something funny?"

"I'm not sure, but there does seem to be something fishy about the piece."

"Well, Elliot. It's expensive, and it will take a while to set it all up and do the tests. You know, scheduling the machine and working it into my own schedule."

"Could I come tonight?"

"You don't ask much. Sure. Stay with Rita and me. But we eat meat."

He remembered the time he had me over for dinner and served veal, salad with bacon bits, Jell-0, and at least one other unmentionable inedible. "I'll bring my own soybeans."

"You're on. When can you be here?"

"I've got to book a flight. It's really spur-of-the-moment."

"Just call and we can meet you at the airport."

"And I'll be bringing a friend." It just came out—unpremeditated. Terry frowned in curiosity and then looked startled. So did I.

"Any specific kind of friend?"

"The best."

"See ya." I hung up.

Terry said, "Me?"

"Why not? You're in on this. I need your expertise in translating and if you are going to join the firm, you'll need to make the contacts and learn bits and pieces of the trade. This trip is like on-the-job training. It's a business expense. Strictly business, of course."

She was obviously amenable. So was I.

FIFTEEN

We found a red-eye to Philadelphia and were right in presuming that there would be plenty of stand-by seats. It was inexpensive and expeditious, and uncomfortable as all red-eyes. Whoever invented this red-eye should be forced to fly them. Brad met us at 7:45 the next morning.

Terry had called in to have one of her colleagues cover for her in her class, so we didn't need to be back till Wednesday.

Of course, Gracie and Burns were not happy to see us fly beyond their stares. But they were probably relieved that these two vulnerable weirdoes were out of their hair, at least for the time being. I called Coster and told him the plan. He was somewhat surprised and not completely pleased that we had taken the book out of the safe. But now that it was out, it might as well be out of the state, too.

The flight turned out not to be as bad as most red-eyes since we raised the arm between seats and Terry slept with her head on my lap much of the way. I dozed now and then, but the feel of the book in its plastic bag against my chest (inside my shirt) was a deterrent to sleep.

We had breakfast at Brad's, and talked about old times: how so and so was denied his promotion. How so and so put a secret note into so and so's confidential file. How so and so had a mental breakdown at his denial of tenure. The good old days. Lots of laughs.

Brad said, "We can't get into the building till Monday morning. But let's look at the book."

I pulled it out. He went through it with experienced hands and a sharp eye. "Looks good. Nice deep impression with the type. Paper seems right. Typeface. Why do you think it's not genuine?"

"We're not sure it's not genuine. It just seems to be off textually."

Terry explained the Kachelofen controversy and the scarcity issue concerning this pamphlet. Brad said, "A good candidate for forgery. But this looks good. I've looked at hundreds, thousands. The typeface seems right. The impression. Maybe this is a variant, before he printed his incendiary one."

"Or after," Terry added.

Brad had quite a safe in his home. He said he had it built in when he began the cyclotron work. "I couldn't trust anyone at the lab. And there was no place open weekends when I liked to work. If you had given me more notice, I could have done the test tomorrow."

Delaware was beautiful, and I might have been able to enjoy it more had that damn book not been on my mind. It wasn't in my possession, which made me feel uneasy. But probably no one in California besides Coster and his stooges knew where it was. Brad's safe was one of those big heavy jobs with a six-inch-thick door. According to a metal panel on the inside of its door, it was rated to withstand fire for six hours. What fire would burn that long? I always mistrusted such information. It's like the watches that are guaranteed to 200 meters. First of all, probably only 22 people in America could identify 200 meters when they saw them. Second, just about anybody down 200 meters was either dead or not looking at his watch. Third, who the hell was going to test the thing? I could just see someone saying to the watch company, "I took it to only 185 meters and the piece of shit leaked. I want my money back." Or, "The fire lasted only five hours and fifteen minutes and my priceless bonds are charcoal. Pay me!" I'm sure the safe company and the watch company never got returns.

By Monday the façade of joy at reunion with Brad had worn off and I was closing in on a case of basketry. I was jumpy and the more I glanced around, the more Terry and Brad tried to ease my mind. Not possible. So Brad made arrangements to do a cyclotron check that morning—pulling some kind of strings.

Brad described the method with the precision of a surgeon. The cyclotron can determine the composition of the ink without damaging the book at all. By hitting a tiny bit of the ink with a proton beam, one could observe the agitated atoms giving off x-rays for each element in the ink. These rays are gathered and measured by a collector, which can tell parts per million of carbon, lead, copper, and so on. Since most printers mixed up their own inks back in the fifteenth century, the products of one press can often be distinguished from the products of another.

Also, printers didn't always follow an ink recipe to the nth degree. So there would be a variation in composition of inks from one batch to another even in the same print shop. Gutenberg's own inks had lots of copper and lead, which gave his inks a sheen and longevity that is enviable. But the ratio of copper to lead varied, and we can tell from the varying ratios which pages were printed from one batch of ink, which from another.

It took only a couple of minutes for each page we tested. Brad brought us a printout showing the ratios of all the elements in Kachelofen's ink. It was a dull black ink, with no sheen on the page. And it was almost purely carbon and oil, with some copper lead oxide. The carbon derived from wood.

We then went to another lab for a radiocarbon dating of the inks. Though this is an approximate science, it is better than nothing. The dating depends on the half-life of one of the carbon's three isotopes. Isotopes 12C and 13C are stable, but 14C decays slowly, losing half its beta rays every 5700 years. The method is accurate within about 40 years at best.

"Jesus, Brad. I thought you were a Professor of Literature. Who corrupted you?"

"It comes with the territory. I wanted to learn about early printing. Only the scientists could help. The literary scholars, even those studying bibliography and book history, worked by guesswork and supposition."

"Oh, like politicians and doctors!"

"Right. Only, politicians and doctors have something to go on: symptoms. Most literary scholars and bibliographers have never seen a printing press in action; they know essentially nothing about ink or paper or binding materials. Yet they make grandiose pronouncements about printing shop practices that could never have been. Try printing a book by the methods guessed at by the literary scholars and you'd wind up with a pile of crumpled, mangled sheets."

He went on to explain the deterioration of carbon and how, by counting the number of deteriorations per minute, we could approximate the date of anything containing the carbon. "It's not pinpoint accurate, especially since the end of World War II, since the amount of radiocarbon in the atmosphere has skyrocketed with the bomb."

We went to the lab with the mass spectrometer. The results were not definitive, but they suggested that the ink dated from the late fifteenth century, plus or minus about eighty years. Sounded good to me. Terry was relieved but puzzled.

"I just can't explain the feeling that I have that this isn't right," she said over dinner. "Why would Kachelofen print a text that conformed so closely to the approved one? What was the big hullabaloo in the first place if this is the text he published?"

Brad said, "I wouldn't worry about it. You have an incunabulum worth thousands of dollars. You have the only complete text of Kachelofen's volume in existence. And you've had a weekend with me. You didn't even have to eat meat. Why are you upset?"

I think Terry was picking up on my nervousness. She said, "From all historical records, Kachelofen put his head on a chopping block to print this. But there is nothing worth removing his head for. I'm only a few pages into it. But there's no sign of anything heretical. It's got the bits about killing and death and dealing with dead bodies. You've got the way to heaven spelled out here. But it's straight religious stuff. Nothing incendiary."

Rita asked, "Could there have been a frontispiece with some kind of objectionable illustration? You know, a centerfold at the front?"

I said, "Not likely. There would have to be a conjugate leaf on the back, and there is no indication of one. The pamphlet seems complete. The text sure is."

"Is the typeface right?" Terry was looking at the pamphlet intently. "I mean, was this typeface in existence back then?" She may have been thinking about the famous Thomas Wise case in which Wise was caught in his forgeries by having printed using a typeface that was designed and first came into use after the dates on the pamphlets he forged.

"We can go to the NYPL and compare the face in theirs with the types in ours." And we did. The next day we were on a train to the big Granny Smith. Brad had stowed the pamphlet in his safe and insisted we go out to dinner, but I went to a local grocery store and bought a load of good stuff to shove into our faces. I just didn't want to leave Death back in the house by its lonesome. Terry and I kept the book under the mattress while we slept, and while we were awake we hoped the mattress didn't slide back and forth too much.

We got a room at the Renaissance in New York. It was only for a day, so it wouldn't break my bank. I had called Elizabeth Browner at the NYPL to ask if we could visit on Tuesday, and she was in in the morning. She met us in her Rare Book department.

"Nice to meet you, Mr. Burgess. I took the opportunity of paging the Kachelofen *Buchlein* for you. It's on my desk in my office."

Before we got past the security barrier, still out in the entryway to the department, I fished into my shirt and produced our copy of the pamphlet. I unwrapped it and handed it to Browner. Her eyebrows went up. "You were right. It's a nice copy. It's quite beautiful."

I never would have thought of it as that. Intact, maybe. In excellent condition, considering its age. Even impressive, if one considered its probable worth. But not beautiful. Something that possibly nearly got me killed twice was not beautiful.

We signed in, Terry locked her purse into a locker, and we were shown to the reading room. There in a few minutes was the only other known copy of Conrad Kachelofen's *Ein Buchlein von dem Sterben*, staring us in the face. Elizabeth Browner asked if she might sit with us as we compared copies. So three sets of eyes took in two pamphlets that probably hadn't been in the same room together for half a millennium.

The NYPL copy was pretty shabby . Its first two leaves were quite ragged and not all there, except for the inner margin of the second. This meant that pages one through four were not there. Some of the top of leaf 3 (pages 5-6) was also torn away, though only about four lines were missing. The text was then complete through leaves four, five, and six, but leaves seven and eight, that had been conjugate with one and two, were gone.

I took a ruler and laid it across the page from the very first serif on the page to the very last one on the last line. Then I took a second ruler and did the same thing on our copy. Had the pamphlets been of the exact same typesetting, the ruler would have passed through all the letters in successive lines at exactly the same place through each letter.

And I expected to see just that. It seemed to me likely that the pamphlet would have gone through only one printing. But the letters didn't line up.

Terry asked me what I was doing. I showed her how, page after page, the text of the NYPL copy was different from ours. (I was now practically unconsciously thinking in first-person plural pronouns.) She looked on intrigued. And Elizabeth Browner said, "I know that our copy of the pamphlet is fragile, but we have a Hinman Collator, and I can collate a page or two, if you'd like."

The Hinman is a wonderful tool. It was presumably first developed during World War II to study enemy troop movements from the air. An aerial photograph from one day and one from the following day, for instance, were superimposed optically in the Collator. If there were any differences in the formations under scrutiny, they would show up in movement under the binocular eyepiece on the machine. I had used one years ago, and marveled at its precision and at the simplicity of concept. It had been adopted for textual work decades ago. Charleton Hinman used it to compare different volumes of what were ostensibly the same printing of a text. He used it mostly on Shakespeare.

Terry, Elizabeth, and I went into an adjacent room where the Hinman (as it was called) stood. Elizabeth sat down in front of it, opened the glass on the platform on the left, lay her copy of the Kachelofen on it, and closed the glass down over the page. She chose page seven, the first page of full text extant in both copies. Then she put our copy under the glass on the right platform. While looking through the eyepiece, she manipulated the right platform in such a way that both texts superimposed optically through the binoculars. They looked like a single sheet. She then turned the lights on both texts off, and by means of a treadle which she moved with her left knee, she set a pair of blinking lights going, first illuminating the book on the left, then the one on the right. The viewer saw many lines of text under the flashing lights, first left, then right, left, right, left right, leftright. What superimposed perfectly appeared steady and unmoving under the eyepiece. But what was not perfectly superimposed seemed to be moving under the observer's concentrated gaze. That is, if there were an upright lower-case L on the left and a broken one on the right, with a bent-over upright shaft, the

L would look as if it were moving, doing bends at the waist while the platforms lit up alternately. Or if a dot were missing over an I on the left but not missing over the same I on the right, the viewer, seeing first one then the other, would see what looked like a dot appearing and disappearing.

We all took turns. What we saw was not only movement, but chaos. The entire text of every page had been reset. That is, there was movement everywhere. The texts were printed from different settings of type.

But the typeface was correct. Kachelofen had used an early roman type with distinctive slightly slanted serifs. Apparently it was a face designed only for his use, because according to Browner, no other shop seems to have had this type.

"But Kachelofen set most of his books in this. We have his Latin version in the same typeface. It's fairly common. You can see copies all over the country."

I asked Browner if she would have a test done on either the *Buchlein* or on one of Kachelofen's other books. She said she could, but NYPL couldn't pay for it; we'd have to. No problem. I called Brad and he said there was a lab in the city that could do the work. He'd call and set it up. Browner would see to it on Friday. We wanted another cyclotron reading to see how the ink of our pamphlet compared with the ink of the NYPL copy.

The hotel was old and cramped, but comfortable. We didn't need much space. Just the space of a bed and a table, where we ate our room-service slightly cold food. What's wrong with hotels, anyway. Isn't there a way to get food to rooms with some semblance of warmth?

SIXTEEN

Back in L.A. things hadn't changed much. In fact, they hadn't changed at all in my shop, which was only half picked-up when I left. The bungalow was now locked up again, though a good deal worse for wear. A new door had been skillfully put on and painted. But the smell of bomb lingered and I was disinclined to stay there. On the other hand, I didn't feel like getting a different place since I didn't want the bastard who did this to think he scared me away.

Coster had faxed me the list of potential bombers, but of course I didn't recognize any of the names. There were five of them. It was like looking at a class roster for the first time in a new school. No recognition. But that was ok. The list was short enough for me to deal with. I called Coster and asked if they had addresses for any of these fellas. "Only old addresses. I'm not certain they're current. But why do you want to know?"

I had to think fast. "Just wanted to know if they were all still in L.A. You could eliminate any who had moved away or were in prison."

"I'm not as stupid as I look, Mr. Burgess. You know, of course, that I would give you the list of only those still residing in Los Angeles who were not in custody on the night of the bombing. It would have been senseless to tell you the names of those who couldn't possibly have perpetrated this crime."

There was that word again: crime. I was the victim of a crime. I hated it, and I was furious and felt helpless. But not completely.

"Would you give me the addresses?"

"Do you know any of the names?"

What was he doing? Answering a question with another question? That was my tactic.

"What if I did?"

"Don't answer my questions with questions, Mr. Burgess. We need information from you, not riddles."

"No, I don't recognize any of the names. But if I were able to look at their faces, maybe I would recognize one of them." I told him about the gentleman who came to my shop and made me an offer I could refuse. "And there were other customers. And inquiries." I had already amassed more than two dozen email queries about my little book.

"Maybe we could trace some of these. I'll send Officer Pratt down this afternoon."

"I have downloaded each reply. I have their addresses and names—as much as the email contained."

"Good. I may come with Officer Pratt. I need your help, I think."

"Mine? What . . . ?'

"My wife needs a book on gardening. That's your area, isn't it?"

"Botany."

"Same difference."

I hated that phrase. Only an oxymoron would use it. But I didn't want to get into some kind of linguistic nit-pick with him, nor did I feel like explaining the difference between gardening and botany and agriculture and viticulture and citriculture. Gardening! For god's sake.

"I'll help you however I can. Bring some addresses."

"I'll bring photos instead. We don't need no lousy vigilantes running around, Mr. Burgess."

It was the first attempt at humor I had heard from his lips; but it was pronounced with such seriousness that I couldn't tell if he meant it as a joke.

"Great! Come on over."

Coster and Pratt showed up by two thirty, after I had made some headway cleaning up, organizing, dusting off, and categorizing the books and pamphlets that had been strewn everywhere in the shop. I found things that I had misplaced many moons earlier, and I couldn't find a few things that I knew were there before the intrusion. That's what it was. An intrusion. This person had intruded into my life and left a big scar. Another mixed metaphor. My personal space had been breached by an unwanted breacher. My life had been violated, and I was getting madder and madder.

"Mr. Burgess, meet Officer Pratt." Pratt an officer? He was a nerd of a kid, acned and skinny and mussed-haired. He couldn't have been more than twelve or thirteen. I didn't know whether to offer to shake his hand or offer him a zwieback.

"Hello, Officer Pratt," I said. His proffered hand was coldish and moist. But not weak.

"Nice to meet you, Mr. Burgess." A nasally, skinny little pipsqueak of a voice, but spoken with more oomph than I had expected. "I'm here to work with your computer and your email."

While he was talking I noticed that Coster was browsing the stacks. Not too many books back on shelves yet, but piles of books on various topics were here and there and everywhere.

"What do you mean work with me?"

"I'd like to do some little stuff with your computer, if I may. I won't erase any data. You won't even know that I was here. May I?"

Coster looked over and nodded. I said ok and showed him where it was in the back of the shop.

"You've got some books on the floor here, too. Quite a mess."

Such a keen observation. No wonder the local investigation unit put him on their payroll. No one could have missed the mess. In fact, it was pure mess. There wasn't a trace of any organization in the back at all. I was trying to do the front before the customers came in.

"Right you are, Officer Pratt. I had hardly noticed the mess, since there were so many books on the floor."

He ignored or didn't hear me; he was already tapping away on my keyboard.

Coster came over and said, "He's ok. I need a book on succulents. Not your Sunset type book, but one with some authority. My wife is seriously into her succulents."

I couldn't help smiling; in fact, it was all I could do to contain the hilarity of his statement. And I don't even know why I found it funny. I guess with the tension of the bombs, the threats, the messes, and the chaos all around, to learn that this solid straight policeman had a wife seriously into her succulents seemed incongruous and amusing.

"How deep is she into them?"

"Serious deep."

"Example?"

"She is the first one to get through the gate at the Huntington sale every year." The Huntington Library and Gardens had a fat sale of their greenery every spring. Famous for the variety and quality of their plants. "She comes home with a station wagon full of succulents each year. I can't stop her. It's like a disease. It's like she can't help herself. She sees one like the one she already has, but the petals—or whatever you call a succulent leaf—has an infinitesimal hint of pink at the tip. It's different from the one she has. She has to have this one too. I've no clue. Succulents are ok. They can bloom beautifully. And they are fairly easy to keep. We can even go on vacation and they won't die on us if they aren't watered. But, Jesus! where will it end? Now she wants the best book she can get on them. She already has a bunch of pamphlets and books, but she says there is one that she really needs. It's old. And expensive."

"Do you have a title?"

He handed me a slip of paper with an author and title: A.J. van Laren, *Succulents Other than Cacti*. Mrs. Coster had good taste. This was a very expensive book done in two editions, the first virtually unobtainable and the second in only 500 copies. It was printed by the Abbey San Encino Press back in the 1930s. Very collectible press. Very nice book.

"Do you have it?"

"No, but I might be able to find it for you."

"Please do. Her birthday's in a few weeks and I haven't got a thing for her."

I strolled over to watch Officer Pratt hitting the keys on my computer. "Don't you need my password?"

"Not really."

What does that mean? That's another of those phrases that set my teeth on edge. A yes-no question deserves something more definitive than "not really."

"What do you mean?"

"I have your file here." He patted a letter-sized folder filled with papers. "I tried birth dates and addresses, then tried them backwards.

Your password was the last six digits of your Social Security Number in reverse. Simple."

"You could have asked. It might have saved you the trouble."

"I usually don't ask. It's like a little challenge for me. Like a game. I almost always win. And in your case it would have saved me about two minutes. No big deal."

Damn little shit.

"What are you doing?"

"Nothing that you'll notice."

"What does that mean?"

"I've set your computer to transfer all your email to me as well as to you. We can monitor it instantly and thoroughly from the station. You'll never know we're here. You'll have to sign this release." He pulled a piece of paper from the folder and handed it to me.

"How long do you plan to do this? It's quite an invasion of our privacy."

I said "our" again.

"Only till we catch the schmuck who has been bombing you." I liked this directness. No perpetrators or incendiary devices or dwellings.

"But what if I get really personal messages on this?"

"Do you?"

"I asked you a question."

"Think of us like your psychoanalyst: here to help; completely discreet. And we disconnect the moment we have the bomber."

I signed the sheet and handed it to him. He said he'd get a copy of it to me the next day.

Coster came over, holding a book. "I just found this," he said, holding up a copy of *Cacti and other Succulents*, by Ralph Hoffmann and others. "It's about succulents in Santa Barbara. Won't this be good enough for my wife?"

"Not really." I guess it *is* a good answer in some circumstances.

"What does that mean?"

"No."

"Why? It's about succulents in southern California."

"But Santa Barbara is not Los Angeles. It's a good book, but it's from about 1930, so it's not only out of date, it's also out of the area. The microclimate of Santa Barbara, as well as the soil and the local pollutants, are much different from what we have here in L.A. Do you want to spend $125 just to take the chance that you'll disappoint your wife?"

"Not really." It was catching.

"I'll try to find the van Laren book for you."

"Thanks. May I put it down here?"

He indicated one of the dozens of piles that were all over the place.

"Why not?" Of course, it was already part of the rough cut, having been placed in a pile in the front of the shop, but I could always put it back there.

"I'll return it to where I found it."

"Why? I said you could put it here."

"You obviously wanted it in the pile near the front door. Your face muscles say a lot."

I didn't know my face muscles conversed. I must tell them to shut up in the future.

"Here's a present." He handed me a small yellow envelope. I pulled out five little mug shots of potential bombers. Intruding explosive specialists. I looked at the pictures, but they were strangers. There were names on the back of each photo.

"May I keep these?"

"I said they were a present. I don't take presents back."

"Will Gracie and Burns be following me any more?"

"Do you want them to?"

"Instead of asking me another question, why don't you say, 'If you want them to'?"

"If you want me to."

"I do."

"Ok. If you want them to."

"Well," I hesitated. It's not as though I felt much safer with them there. Their presence hadn't stopped the bomber from getting to my two places of activity. On the other hand, some protection—if that's what they were—was better than none at all.

Coster got impatient for an answer. "Well, do you want them to?"

We were back to that.

"No." It was an impulsive answer, but I figured that whoever got to my two places did so despite whatever "protection" the police gave me. These shields were not very good. "You can call them off." Maybe the presence of the guardians up to now would be enough to ward off another attack.

Coster and Pratt (sounded like a comedy team) left, and I spent the rest of the day tidying. By 5:00 p.m. I had a good number of shelves filled with books, some with bent corners, but most in decent condition. Once the first shelves had been emptied, other books were cushioned somewhat by those already on the floor. And I knew that the intruder was not after just any old book. Some pretty valuable books were still there. I was certain that my *Buchlein* was the target.

I closed the shop after arming all the alarms. Barn doors came to mind. I headed home. That is to say, I unconsciously headed toward Santa Monica. Hancock Park was too dangerous and didn't feel like my domicile any more. Terry met me at the door with a kiss. The place smelled of home-baked bread and something else.

"Did you put the book into the safe deposit box?"

"Where else? It's perfectly safe."

I had taken her to the bank and gotten her name and signature onto the card for the boxes. She got the second key, too.

"What smells so good?"

"Dinner," she said, spinning away and marching into the little kitchen. What greeted me was another of her masterpieces: lovely, large, round loaves of sourdough bread, with their heads slit off and their innards removed. They were filled with portabella and shiitake mushroom soup, topped with flaked tarragon. The removed innards had been lightly fried to crisp little browned croutons. The salad had several greens, toasted pine nuts, marinated artichoke hearts, and dried cranberries. The way to a man's heart is what an army travels on.

She told me of her class, and her colleagues who wouldn't look her in the eye, and the shopping she had done for dinner and lots of other domestic kinds of things. I told her about cleaning up.

"We've got to clean up your house, too," she said.

She, too, was using plural pronouns.

"Yes," I said. "I do need a base of operations."

"What's wrong with here?"

"I didn't want to presume." She and I had never talked about any permanent move on my part. As far as I could see, this was still a temporary place to hang my pants till my own place was habitable again. This, mind you, was not what I wanted. But it was sort of the unspoken thing that I had to think, just in case it's what she wanted too.

"I *presumed* we'd live here. Or there. Or somewhere. I mean . . . ."

"I hoped that's what you presumed. Me too."

Her smile was all we needed as a segue for more intimate matters. We didn't do the dishes again.

SEVENTEEN

I got onto the Web and pulled up Webbos Person Find. Then I plugged in the first name on the back of Coster's photos. Armand Grahn. No listing. Anywhere. There were several A. Grahns, but none in California. Could this be an aka?

Name two was just as much of a problem: John Springer. Nine of the thirteen listed for California were in southern California. This was going to take some intelligent narrowing down.

Steven Sonneck. Only one. Great. He probably wouldn't be the guy.

Raymond Chandler. No shit! There were six of them. This guy had possibilities.

And Shirley Dettweiler. The picture was of an old man. At least it looked like a man. I guess back in the early days a guy could be named Shirley. Was that enough to drive him to be a bomber? I got all their phone numbers and addresses.

I also popped into my email and found another five messages asking about my *Buchlein*. All five had about the same message: Do you have a copy for sale? But one was signed by a familiar name, familiar because it was one of the earlier writers. This one was particularly curious. The name was Pinsky. R. Pinsky. I pressed a few keys, pulled up the other messages, and sorted through to Pinsky's earlier one. It said, "Do you have a copy of the book you are querying about? If so, I'd be interested in it." I hadn't answered the earlier messages, waiting for who-knows-what to happen. Pinsky's curiosity got me curious, so I pressed "Reply" and wrote: "Are you interested in buying a copy or is your interest academic?" That was enough to hang as bait.

Then I thought I'd do the same for all the others. Who knows what evil lurks in the hearts of man? and who knows how that evil can be lured out?

But evil lured out into the open can be deadly. Any more deadly than evil hidden in the shadows? I guess the visible foe is easier to fight than the invisible one. And I was spoiling for a fight. I had had a bullet go through my windshield and my arm, a pair of bombs rock my domicile and place of business, a tough guy make me an offer I was happy to refuse, a couple of phone calls that were designed to scare me, and my wits shaken to the point that I was now looking to my ass wherever I went. That was no way to live. You look to your rear too long and someone is going to hit you from the front.

The only good that had come of this book was Terry. She brought new life into me. Not that there was anything wrong with the old life. But the new stuff was exhilarating and intellectual and peaceful. It was nice to be cared for again. It had been too long.

I spent another day cleaning up the store, and by around five the place had some real order to it. Maybe even better than before, because all the stuff that had come in in bits and pieces over the years and had gotten stuck where there was a space for it was now organized into coherent categories and reshelved with like neighbors. I even got several groups of things into some kind of alphabetical order, just right for putting over the Web or in a catalog.

I took a break a few times to make some calls. I started with the Raymond Chandlers. Six of them. I was able to get only one phone to pick up—a woman. When I asked for Mr. Chandler she sounded wary and uncooperative. What did I expect, that she'd say, "Oh, he's out bombing bookstores and won't be back till seven"? I needed a ploy. I told her, "I'm working for a bookstore owner who needs advice about security issues and he's willing to pay for professional expertise." I thought that would be general and unthreatening enough to elicit a return call but provocative enough for him to connect the caller with books. I hoped it wouldn't set off an alarm. I left my phone number and name: Mr. Bucklen. I concluded with, "The information he gives me could be quite valuable, and I'd pay him a good professional wage for it." Let's see where that led.

It was time to go home. The store looked almost ready to open again for business and though I was dusty and sore from stooping and squatting, it was virtuous pain. Time for dinner and a hug and an evening in which I felt at home. I guess I was getting complaisant. Complacency sets a person up for a fall. I wasn't ready for what I found.

EIGHTEEN

O r didn't find. I didn't find Terry. There was no sign of her. There were no clothes on the floor, leading me anywhere. No sign of struggle. No note telling me she'd be back soon or that she was out getting victuals for dinner. Did I say no sign of a struggle? This cloak and dagger stuff was really getting to me. Did I expect a struggle? Was I expecting rough-housing and breakins and bombs too much? Gotta stop thinking this way. It's cutting into my sleep and making me edgy.

But where was Terry? I looked for her purse but didn't see it. Time to worry? I didn't know. She was nowhere. I checked the whole place, which didn't take much time. I looked in the obvious places for notes: the doors, the bathroom mirror, the kitchen table, the refrigerator (too many damn magnets), the bed. Nothing. I checked the answering machine. No messages. Unlike her. It's not as if I can't fend for myself. I'd been doing it for years. But . . . I thought of Professor Higgins.

I was getting agitated. I felt like calling Coster, but there was no sign of any trouble. Maybe she was out getting a treat—a surprise. But she was always home when I got there. I'd spare Coster for now, but what should I do? Did I need to do anything? I expected a phone call, but the beast was silent. I called her office, but I just got ringing. I started feeling mighty worried for some reason. For some reason? The best: she could be in danger. Ever since that damn book came into my life, I felt as if I was moving closer and closer to an edge, and now Terry was with me in it.

If I were writing a book about all this I'd have my hero know just what to do, and then he'd leap into it and catch the scum who . . . . But this wasn't any book. It was my life and I was damn well angry. Scared and angry. That's dangerous—to anyone who got in my way. I remember the feelings I had for Sam Forester, who scuttled my tenure bid. I could have, well, not killed him, but broken a couple of his legs. I'm not a football player, but I am strong, and when I get angry . . . .

I sat down to think. I had a friend who always said, "If you sit down and think about it," and I always thought that was a dumb phrase. I'd say, "Can't I think about it without sitting down?" and she'd miss it altogether and use that trite phrase again and again. It got me sick. But this evening the phrase finally made sense to me. I was so distraught that pacing and looking through the place over and over again was obviously futile and getting me more and more worked up. Sitting was the only answer. I chose a place near the phone, hoping.

Terry had been practically my constant companion since I had moved in. God, I had moved in, hadn't I! We went our separate ways for work, but after work we had just found it natural to be together. It was comfortable and easy. So finding her gone (I love that oxymoron) was a jolt. The book was involved, I was sure. But how? If someone came to the place to get it, she would never have given it or sold it to anyone. She wouldn't just leave with no trace. In the few weeks we had been together I had learned the predictables about her, and that was one of them. I started wondering if the book were safe. Of course it was. It was in the vault and only she and I had keys to that.

Was it still in the vault? Terry's classes always let out plenty earlier than I closed the shop. She could easily have gotten to the bank before it had closed. I hadn't seen the thing in days. It was time to check in on that little trouble-maker. I'd have to look in tomorrow morning. It had to be there. But looking at it would be cathartic, as if my handling it gave me control over it, not it over me and my life. But what to do right now.

I felt the need to call our friendly constable, so I dialed the police station and asked for Coster. He was out. Gone home.

I dialed Coster's home. It was dinnertime. No answer. What the hell does he think he's doing? I'm a taxpayer and he's hired by the city to protect and serve. Well, goddam it, Coster, start serving.

I tried her cell number, but no answer. I got out the school directory and looked up the English Department. No one would be in, but I had to do something. I called several of the numbers of the department's faculty, but as I expected there were no answers. A couple of them had voice mail, but leaving a message would have been futile and might have broached whatever confidence about her private life that Terry had wanted. I called about ten numbers, and on the eleventh I got, "Yeah?" spoken with something of a drawl. Someone who obviously was in no hurry. I wasn't expecting an answer, so I was caught off guard with something to say.

"Uh, I'm calling to speak with Professor Luckombe."

"Yuh got the wrong office."

"Excuse me? Oh, but I called her office and there was no answer."

"Course not. She's not there."

"Who is this?"

"Why d'ya want to know?"

"I'm trying to contact Professor Terry Luckombe. It's rather important."

"You one of her students?"

"No. Just a good friend. Who are you?"

"Tom."

"Tom who? I called the office of Professor Victor Pine."

"He's not here either."

"Why are you in his office?"

"Cleaning."

Mr. Cleaning was sure taciturn, and not very helpful.

"Tom, I'm Elliot Burgess, Terry's friend. She was supposed to meet me tonight, but she's not at home. I am trying to find out where she is."

"Can't say."

Can't or won't?

"Have you seen her?"

"I got here right at five. Her office was one of the first I cleaned up. She wasn't here. But had been."

"How do you know? When?"

"How do I know is that her radio was on. When is I don't know."

"Does she leave her radio on often"

"First time I ever saw. And I been doing this for since before she came."

"Is there any sign of a strug . . . . Is her office tidy as usual?"

"Mr. Whatja say yer name is? No sign of anything. Why the suspicion? You writing a murder mystery?"

"I hope not. Listen, Tom; could I go over there and look at her office. She's just disappeared and I am kinda worried about her."

"What's ta worry?" He asked it tentatively, and either he heard the fright in me or he understood that something was amiss. He was softening a bit.

"I think there's nothing to worry about, but I worry anyway. She's usually pretty reliable, and tonight she was supposed to meet me and she's not here. Maybe she left me a message in the office."

"I'm not supposed to let anyone into the offices. Can't let you in."

Terry's privacy or not, I had to chance it: "I'm not just anyone, Tom. I'm the man who lives with her."

"She did tell me about a man in her life. Yer lucky. She's real nice and pretty."

"The best. I need to find her."

"C'mon over. I'm in the English Building, near the tower. Meet ya at the back. When will ya be here?"

"Twenty-five minutes."

"See ya."

I wrote a quick note, "Terry, I've gone to see you in your office," and I left it on the kitchen table. I hoped Coster wouldn't call while I was gone. But I did leave a message on the answering machine: "We can't come to the phone at present. Please leave a message for one of us: Terry, Elliot, or Tom Clean." I figured Terry would understand that one. And I also gave my mobile number if I wasn't back soon.

I zipped over to the university and saw Terry's car in the parking lot. No sign of anything out of the ordinary there. Tom met me at the loading dock at the back of the English Building.

"How do I know who you are, Mr.?" Tom was suspicious, but not enough to understand the full nature of the criminal mind. If I had been of evil intent, I could have gotten into the chancellor's office had Tom been the guardian of that ivory tower.

"Listen, Tom. I just want to look around. I'm not going to take anything. Stay with me, please. You can watch me."

"Okay, but don't take a thing." If Mr. Clean had been guarding Fort Knox, it would be called Fort Empty by now.

"You can even lead the way, Tom." He liked hearing his name, and he didn't know that I had never seen Terry's office and didn't know where it was. When we got there he took out a master key and opened the door.

"This here's a master key. I can get into any office in the building."

"Impressive, Tom."

He smiled. "Don't touch nothing."

He lapsed into that hick pronunciation, and his double negative invited me to touch any damn thing I wanted. "Tom, you said that when you got here at five Professor Luckombe's office was the first one you cleaned up, Tom. Is that right, Tom?"

"Yep."

"Was there anything in her waste basket?"

"Paper."

Great help. This was going to take some effort. "Where is it?"

"Dumped into my bag."

His bag was a large cloth sack lined with a plastic bag hanging from a wheeling cart that he moved from office to office. It was down the hall two doors at another professor's office. In the twenty-three minutes it took me to get there he hadn't gotten very far. I walked down to it; it was about a quarter full of all kinds of junk, like offers of books from publishers, flyers for desk copies, printouts from computers, obviously rejected for spelling errors or textual changes, downloaded email messages, memos, and the like. I asked him if this bag were empty when he began working.

"You daft? Ya think I'd 'a' started work with a full bag? Only a idiot would do that. In case ya didn't know, my job is to fill this bag, not to distribute this crap into the waste baskets, but to empty them."

"Tom, you certainly know your job. Glad to see you do it so well, Tom. Are you a supervisor? You should be! You could train a whole crew to know what to do here, Tom."

He seemed pleased and smug.

"You bet. I'm good at what I do."

"Undoubtedly, Tom. Now, Tom, would you help me to empty this bag. I'd like to see the first papers you put into it."

"Empty it! I just told ya that my job is to fill it. Don't you learn a thing?"

"Tom, if Professor Luckombe left anything for me here, someone might have trashed it. I just want to see if there is anything for me in the bag, Tom."

I'm not sure he understood, but he stood by while I carefully emptied the bag, getting a bit sticky on a piece of paper that held a piece of cheesy pizza. At the bottom of the bag I found only a few sheets that were from Terry's office, and they were not helpful at all. One was a form letter from a midwestern university telling her that a job she had applied for was filled. Another was an actual personal letter—obviously generated from a form letter, telling her that while she was seriously considered for the position that she wrote about, she was certainly over-qualified in that with all those years of teaching she would have to be hired at the associate level, while the position advertised was only for a beginning-level assistant professor. Painful memories stirred in me, and I understand why this letter was crumpled with emotion. Nothing else there.

Tom was still standing at the door to Terry's office, watching rather amusedly as I picked up all the trash and loaded it back into the bag. I went back to where he was and went into Terry's office for the first time. As I had expected, it was neat, clean, and orderly. If things had been out of place, there was no way for anyone to see. I looked at the papers on her desk. A stack of papers to grade, a memo from the chair announcing a two o'clock Thursday faculty meeting, a calendar showing all her activities for the week. I noticed that the meeting announced in the memo was penciled into the calendar, but also that Terry had written over that in black ink: "2 p.m., shop for Elliot's present." She had reached the same point that I once had: not going to meetings in a department that held no future for her.

One thing stood out: her computer was still on, with that screen-saver of two flexible, vari-colored scrolling and gyrating lines intersecting and waving all over the screen. I looked surreptitiously at Tom, who was looking down the hall for a moment, and I touched the space bar. The purple and blue lines froze, and a little rectangular box appeared in the center of the screen demanding: "Enter Password." To get back into the program she had been working on, I would have needed her code. Not a clue. Where was young Sherlock when I needed him.

"Tom. Does she leave her computer on every night, Tom?"

He glanced back and gave me a puzzled look. "I never saw it on before. But then, I just do the basket and the floor. I don't always look higher than that."

Sad comment. A man who never looked above the level of the world's detritus. Never saw the top of the desk, where intelligence, logic, wit, and meaning existed. Maybe there was meaning for him below that surface. Maybe there was meaning there for me, too.

"You don't remember ever seeing the computer screen lit up?"

"Can't say as I have."

"Do me a favor, Tom. Please don't turn this off."

"Never would. It ain't my job. My job's to clean up. I do it just fine."

"Tom, I am going to say this again. I know you don't touch the stuff on desks. But this you mustn't touch." I took out a twenty and handed it to him. "This, Tom, is for helping me and for making sure that no one else gets into this office."

He was dumbfounded, and at the same time he didn't want to look out of control of the situation. So he stammered a second and then said, "I do good work. I can't tell who is gonna get in here tomorrow. I leave here at 1:30. No one's supposed ta be in here after that. That's the best I'll vouch for. But about this money."

No ellipsis. He never intended to finish the sentence. The bill disappeared into his pocket, and he said, "Thanks."

"You want to see me out, Tom?"

"Oh, uh, sure."

We walked back down the hall, down the few entry steps, and back through the loading dock door.

"Thanks, mister. I'll do what you asked." Which was essentially nothing. But he had to show me he would be earning the twenty I had given him.

I looked into and around Terry's car. No clues.

I drove back to the apartment in Santa Monica. It was already about 8 o'clock. There was no message on the answering machine. I hadn't gotten any calls on my cell. I wasn't hungry. I was restless as hell. I had tried to do something to fill the time, something that could be useful. Now I was at an impasse. I tried Coster again. This time a woman answered, with a very sexy and soft voice. Just a simple "Hello," but it was comfortable and welcoming.

"Please forgive me for calling so late, but is this the residence of Officer Coster?"

"It's not late. We just got in. And yes, Officer Coster is here. Just a moment."

If she was as nice as her voice, Coster was a lucky man. Lucky. Luckombe. I was lucky too, I thought. But where was she!

"Hello. Who's calling."

"Officer Coster, it's Elliot Burgess."

"I'm off duty. What's up. This better be good."

He didn't seem irritated; more long-suffering and curious. I told him about my evening. He seemed unmoved. No, we hadn't had an argument. No, she had never done anything like this before. No, I didn't have a clue as to what might have happened to her. My irritation and fear showed. He said, "Please calm down. There is an answer. What would you like us to do tonight?"

"Maybe there's a message on her computer."

"So?"

"Can we get Sherlock to look into it?"

"Maybe. Tomorrow." It was said with finality. There was nothing to do.

"Mr. Burgess, I understand the feelings you have right now. Some fear. Some frustration at not being able to do anything. Probably a good deal of anger. And certainly impatience. I do understand. What can we do? I want you to know that since we found Mr. Smith dead, we have treated your case as a homicide. Which it is. We take seriously everything that transpires pertaining to you, Ms. Luckombe, and your mysterious book. We have not sat still on this. We are investigating. Investigating." He said this with enough emphasis to get it through to me that my fears were well founded and that he, at least, was an ally. "But you could have waited till tomorrow. My wife and I just got back from a wonderful old French movie, *Diabolique*, and it is our custom to spend a few hours analyzing the motives of the characters, the plot, the action, the camerawork, and so on. You are interrupting my private life. I would appreciate your forbearance in the future. This case is serious, but so is my life. Call me at my office after eight tomorrow morning."

"Sorry. But I . . ."

"Don't apologize. Just go to sleep."

I sat there somewhat stunned. My own last words rang in my ears: "Sorry, but." I absolutely hated that. My ex used to say that to me. "I'm sorry, but . . . ." The "but" completely canceled out the "sorry." I vowed never to do that. I was obviously distraught to have fallen into that pathetic locution.

One last stab: I said to Coster, "Please, just three more minutes." There was a puff and a pause.

Then he said, "This really better be worth it."

"I don't know if it's worth it. This is absolutely uncharacteristic of Terry. I have a terrible feeling about this."

"You've already made that clear."

I retraced some of the facts—for emphasis. "I found her car at her school. And she's always here when I get back. She would have left a note. Called me. Something."

"Did you check your answering machine?"

"No." I looked at the machine; there were two messages on the tape. I told him.

"Maybe one's from her. Call me back."

He knew we had an answering machine, and he knew I couldn't access it while I was talking on the line. "Check them out and call me back," he said with forbearance.

Message one was from a bank, trying to get me to open a VISA account. Message two gave me a jolt. A familiar male voice with a succinct message: "She's safe. We'll let you know what to do. Sit tight." That was all.

I called Coster back. "It's an emergency." I told him of the message. He was silent. "Did you hear me?"

"You said you thought the voice was familiar?"

"I can't place it. But I've heard it before. Maybe Myers. Edward Myers. Caligula Books. I think it was him."

"I've already checked him out. Seems to be a legitimate bookseller. Very rich. He deals in high-end books. Works out of his home in Bel Air."

Coster already knew more about Myers than I did. His card had only a name and phone number, no address. The city was San Francisco, but the number was Los Angeles. I had looked him up on the Personfind website, but it was apparently an unlisted number. I needed an address.

I asked Coster, "What's his address?"

"You sure do ask for lots of addresses."

"I do a good portion of my business mail order." It was a weak answer, but all I could think of at the moment.

"Listen, Mr. Burgess. You are asking for trouble if you go to the homes of bombers or suspects or powerful rich people who desperately want what you alone have. Leave all this to us. We'll check out Mr. Caligula for you." He seemed to say 'Caligula' with some sarcasm.

"Ok, Officer Coster," I said. "But I've got a business to run and a personal life to see to and I *will* find Terry." I tried to sound tough, but I was probably not very convincing.

At first Coster was silent. "You could do yourself some harm. You want a tail? Protection?"

"No. I can handle it." I tried to reinforce my resolve, vocally and internally. I *was* mad. I don't have much of a temper, but when it does come out—when I am really pressed—get out of my way!

"Your call, Mr. Burgess. Someone has shot at you and has set off explosives in your home and store. We don't know where Ms. Luckombe is, but she could be in trouble. So could you. 'To Serve and Protect' it says on our cars. You want us to do these for you, you just ask."

"I will. I'm no hero. I just want Terry back safe."

"How do you know she isn't safe right now?"

"What do you mean? And what about the message on my machine?"

Coster sounded concerned. "It could be serious. It could be diversionary tactics. Where's the book? This seems to be the cause of all this. What did you do with the book?"

"Are you implying that Terry has it? And that she has absconded?" (Do people really use that word?)

"Just a thought."

"It's in our safe deposit box in a locked bank."

"Is your bank open tomorrow?"

"Saturday mornings till noon."

"Check your box. Then if the book is there, call us. If it isn't . . . ."

"If it isn't?"

"Maybe Terry's got it; maybe Caligula has it. Maybe Terry and Caligula are a team."

I didn't believe this. I didn't want to. It did seem to me, when Terry first came along, that she wanted to get her hands on the book pretty insistently. And she convinced me to put it into a box in *her* bank. And she did insist on having a key to the box. But she is too sweet and loving to . . . . I still didn't believe it. I can't say that I loved Terry, but if I didn't, what was it I felt? Trust, for sure. She didn't have the book.

"I feel that I've got to do something tonight."

"Just wait. You said the caller told you she was safe and you would be told what to do. Maybe whoever it is could have killed you, but they wanted the book. Maybe they think they can get it through Ms. Luckombe. Maybe she'll call you and say she's had a flat on the way to a dying aunt. Maybe the call was a hoax."

"Maybe it wasn't. Give me the address."

"Maybe tomorrow."

Too many maybes. I needed something certain, and soon. "I'll wait till tomorrow. Do you work Saturdays?"

"Whenever I have to. I'll be at my home number. Call me by ten. In the meantime, there's nothing to panic about."

"Easy for you to say."

"Good bye, Mr. Burgess."

* * *

I hated being at the mercy of a bully—or of anyone. I had to do something. I called Mr. Caligula's number. A woman picked up the phone on the second ring. In only her "hello" I took in a firm but soft voice, quite sexy. I formed an image: slender, blonde, 5'8", prominent bust, ruby lips, creamy complexion, low-cut dress . . . .

"Hello. My name's Elliot Burgess. I'm calling to speak to Mr. Myers."
"Just a moment."
A moment was three minutes; it was a long time.
The voice came on the line. "Mr. Burgess; what can I do for you?"
"I got your call."
"What call?"
"Where are you?"
That was a pretty stupid question. If he didn't put it onto his card and didn't leave it on the answering machine, I didn't expect him to give it to me now.
"I'm at home."
"At the Bel Air house?" Coster gave me that much.
"How did you know?"
"Friends."
"You must have smart friends."
"Only the best. Can I see you tonight?"
"I'm busy. No time tonight. I'll call you tomorrow. About nine a.m."
I was hung out. I didn't know what to say.
"Are you there, Mr. Burgess?"
"Yes."
"Are you thinking about selling the book?"
"I'm thinking."
"Good. There's nothing to think about. I'll call tomorrow. Everything's ok."
What did he mean by that? It's ok that I am thinking about selling the book? Terry's ok? I'm ok, You're ok? Before I could respond he hung up. I wanted to call back, but there was nothing I could say at this point.
I spent a miserable night tossing, turning, thinking, and twisting. Not the Chubby Checker kind; the St. Sebastian kind. Hell of a way to gain sainthood.

* * *

Morning couldn't come soon enough. I got up early. I turned on the computer and started looking up the other felons who could have bombed my home and store. By five I had addresses and phone numbers for half of them, addresses for another two, and zilch for the rest.

By five fifteen I was dead, distressed beyond measure, and ready for . . . I don't know what. I took a shower, pulled on fresh clothes, and sat down on the bed. Then it was eight thirty. I don't remember sleeping, but I must have. Not much, but enough to be ready to move. And fast. I called Coster's office and got through to him in a moment.

"No word?"

"No. What's the possibility that your computer man . . ."

"He's going to be at Ms. Luckombe's office at noon. Why not go meet him there." Spoken something like a demand.

"No sooner?"

"Be patient, please. We have other cases, you know. He'll be there at noon. So should you."

I called David Daws and asked him to come in early today. I needed him soon, in fact. He was there by nine. I needed to check on my book of death.

The bank opened at nine, and I was the first one through the door. I signed the sheet, and they showed me to the safe deposit boxes. The bank attendant opened the box with her key and mine, and accompanied me to a small room with a small table. I sat down and opened the box. We had wrapped the pamphlet in thin bubble wrap, then put it into a thick padded envelope with a stiff piece of cardboard on either side of it. I pulled out the envelope, felt the stiffness, and looked inside. The two boards were there. The bubble wrap was there. The Book of Death wasn't.

NINETEEN

The quick drive back to my store was in a fog. I was trying to think. Where was the book? Who had it? If Coster was right, Terry and Myers could be laughing at me right now. If I was right, Terry was in trouble. But if Myers (or whoever it was) had her, then they probably had the book too. Then why the message? All they really wanted was the *Buchlein*. They didn't need the *Sterben* part.

Shit. Where was it? Where was Terry?

I called Coster.

"It's gone. The book is not in the safe deposit box."

Coster took a loud breath and let it out. Thinking. "I'll be there at your store in a half hour. Don't go anywhere."

Where was there to go? I called Terry's office. Still no answer. I phoned the English Department. Though it was a Saturday, the phone was answered by a dulcet voice that announced the full name of the institution, followed by, "Department of English, Linguistics, Languages, and Critical Theory. Eugenia Ravenstone speaking. How may I help you?"

Jesus. You could grow old waiting through all that nonsensical palaver. I knew whom I had called. 'Hello' would have been enough.

Ms. Ravin' hadn't seen Assistant Professor Terry Luckombe since yesterday afternoon. I asked about who might have been in yesterday whose office was near hers. The secretary said, "Professor Hanna Rackstraw's office is two doors down the hall from that of Assistant Professor Terry Luckombe. Professor Rackstraw has been in all week. Shall I connect you?"

Need she ask? "Please."

Fifteen seconds later I heard the hoarse smoker's voice of Professor Rackstraw. "What can I do for you?"

An English professor who asks what she *can* do for me? Plenty. What *may* she do was more to the point.

"I'm calling to speak with someone who might have seen Professor Luckombe yesterday."

"Why?" There was an irritated edge to this question. Could this have been the professor out to get Terry? I had to go lightly here.

"I'm a friend. I was supposed to have met her yesterday and she didn't show up for our appointment. I have been unable to locate her at her home or office numbers."

"I don't watch over my colleagues. Can't help you."

Won't help me is more like it.

"Please. Just one more thing. Did you see her yesterday?"

"Yes."

"Did she leave with anyone?"

"You said one more thing; that's two."

"I was speaking metaphorically." I figured an English prof could understand metaphor. "Did you see her leave? Was she alone?"

"No." She was being difficult and I could see this was a fairly blind alley.

"No to what? Did you see her leave?"

"No."

"So you don't know if she left alone?"

"Of course. It follows. Now please; if you're through with the third degree . . . ."

Godddam, lady. You call this the third degree? I was barely past the first degree. I could really grill you if you weren't such a bitch.

"Thanks for your time."

She hung up without another word. I thought of that old saw, "The enemies you know are better than the enemies you don't know." Bullshit. I'd like to kill some of the enemies I knew and take my chances with the new ones.

I got a call from Sherlock. Our pimply computer nerd was on his way to the university and asked if I'd like to meet him there. I told him I was waiting for Coster. He said that Coster would meet us in Terry's office in twenty minutes. I raced past Dave Daws with a curt adios, saying I'd be back when I got back. He said he could take care of the place. Great guy. Reliable. Dull but reliable.

The ride to the university was the pits, partly because the traffic was snarled every which way. Typical L.A. But the worst part of the ride was because of the thoughts running rampant in my head. Terry was the only one who could have taken the book. Why? Why hadn't she told me about it? Where had she put it? Did she still have it?

Where was she? Was she in any trouble? What kind?

Terry and the book. They came into my life at about the same time and both had changed things. Boy, were things changed! Terry was eager to see that damn thing. She was so eager that she suggested that I give her the key to the safe deposit box. Is she in trouble, or did she just take the book? She lived in a pretty modest apartment. She could sure use the money. Would she take it and sell it? She could probably get a lot for it. But she and I . . . . I couldn't believe that she would do anything against me. I felt guilty for having that thought. She was too good to me. Too good? Was she too good to be true?

She could have gotten the book out of the bank any time in the last two weeks. I hadn't gone to the box—hadn't needed to. She had said that she could hide it where no one would find it. Right. Maybe she took it out and hid it somewhere. Another safe deposit box? The apartment? She had said that there was a place in the apartment where she could hide it. I can't believe she would have done that.

I still had to follow up on the bombers. That was on my schedule for today, until Terry disappeared. Now what? Maybe Sherlock would find something.

I got to the university at eleven forty. Sherlock was already tapping away. Coster wasn't there yet. The kid looked up when I came in.

I asked, "How did you get in?"

"Police can get a search warrant quickly. Do you have some vitals on Terry Luckombe?"

I gave him her address, phone number, and social security number. "I tried those already," he said. "More."

Her license plate number: no. I said I didn't know her driver's license number. He said he did. No. I didn't know any of the vitals for her family. He tried them already. The English Department had supplied him with her dossier, and it was full of numbers. He also told me that some programs allow someone to try entering a computer using a password only three times, then the computer shuts down or permanently locks up until a certain set amount of time has passed. This one would have tried that on him, but he anticipated it and overrode it.

"Mr. Burgess, please let me see your driver's license."

"Why?"

"Because I left your file at the station."

A minute later he was in. My birthday. Too simple.

A minute later he pulled up a screen that had only a few letters on it. I stood alarmed. All it said was "CALI."

Coster announced himself with the sound of his footsteps in the hall. I turned, with something of a startled look on my face, and Coster's little smile of greeting faded. He didn't say a thing as he entered the office. The desk was facing the window. He looked over Sherlock's shoulder and saw the four letters.

Pimples said, "California?"

Coster said, "Caligula."

* * *

Coster and I sat in Crocker's Diner. Further searches on Terry's computer turned up nothing that could help us in the present case. There had been essays, chapters for books, a ton of stuff on the *ars moriendi* theme, an outline for a chapter on *Ein Buchlein von dem Sterben*, memos, copies of syllabi, and a cryptic little file called "ten." Pimples thought it was a number, but I figured it was a tenure file. Mr. Computer said he would hack it, but Coster and I told him to forget it—for now. I had seen enough of Terry's pain with respect to the promotion she was being denied. If we needed some fuel later, maybe we would go back to it.

Molly came over. Coster had seen the diner on a couple of his trips to the shop. He wanted to try it. I hadn't told him about Molly.

He looked up innocently and asked, "What's the special today?"

Molly: "Everything we serve is special. You think I'd be so stupid as to say that there is something we serve that ain't special? Well, mister; you got another thought coming."

I was afraid of that.

"The meatloaf is special. The sandwiches are all special. The fish and chips is really special. Nice light batter. You won't find a lighter batter on a little league baseball field. Every darn dessert is special. So's the salads. Why, we have the most special salads you can't imagine. And our pies. Now there's something special. Betty bakes 'em herself. Just try and tell me she don't. We even got special toothpicks. Minty, they are. And not just any mint. Special mint. Why, you couldn't get anything here that ain't special. You want a special drink? We got it. Even the water's special. We put it into a special glass with a twist of lime. You don't like lime? We got special lemons. No seeds. Ever hear of that? Sour as lemons, but no seeds. Now, that's special. You don't like lemon or lime in the water? We put in a special mint leaf, grown in Betty's garden. Special mint. I hope you wasn't implyin' that there are things here that ain't special. Why . . . ."

"No. I just wanted to know what you recommend."

Oh, Mr. Coster. You're just asking for more. The other customers were really enjoying this. The place was silent. Nobody was eating. Just listening.

"What do I recommend? Well, I wouldn't know what to recommend. What do you like? You one of them vegetarians? You'd hate our meatloaf. It's got meat in it. Can't understand anyone not eating meat. It's good for you. God gave us cows so's we could make hamburgers and steaks. Otherwise they don't serve much purpose, do they? You can't take one of 'em into yer house and pet 'em. Cows do taste good."

"No, I . . . ."

"Ok, you don't eat meat. Crazy man. Well, how about one of our special sandwiches. Veggie all the way. Avocados, tomatoes, cheese (any kind you like), sliced black olives, lettuce, homemade mayonnaise, black olive and onion bread. Did I say lettuce? Not that iceberg crap. It's like eating water. No taste. No nutrients. No character." When was the last time anyone had considered the character of lettuce?! "No, sir. We use Boston and romaine. Good for you. Little dirt in it now and then. But that just shows you it's home grown. Betty gets the home grown stuff. It's clean dirt, anyway. Can't hurt ya. And them avocados. Ok, so they're fattening. Lots of oil in 'em. But, so, who cares? A little oil in the diet is good. Juices up yer innards. Keeps ya regular."

I cut her off at this point. I had heard her "regularity" lecture, and just before a meal wasn't quite the right time for it. Least of all a second time.

Five minutes later we finished placing our order.

Coster looked somewhat worn out by then. "What did she say?"

"You don't want to know. Hey, what's going on with Terry?"

Coster said, "I haven't a clue. Pun intended. Unless C A L I is a clue."

"What else can it be?" I was trying to hold back the tension and impatience in my voice. "It looks as if Mr. Myers is deeply involved. It looks as if she was in the middle of something when she needed to leave a clue."

"I'll order a tail put on him."

"Better than the comedic tag teams you had on me?"

"They were there to be conspicuous. This is different. I can have his phone tapped, but it won't help. He's too rich and canny."

"What about Terry? I think she's in trouble."

"So do I." Coster spoke candidly. It surprised me. "The message on the computer monitor. Pretty revealing."

"Have you ever seen Myers' home? The home of Caligula Books?"

"No. I would have expected you to have. You're the book dealer."

"I have never been invited. I don't know anyone in the trade who has. He operates out of his home. Only high-class clients. Only the best books. I don't even know whom he sells to. I can ask around."

"Do. But don't take any of this into your own hands. It looks like dangerous territory. That's where we come in. Understand?"

"Of course. I just want to get Terry back, safe."

"Right." Silence for a few moments. "Have you ever seen the original *Diabolique*?"

"Years ago. I still remember it vividly."

Coster said, "A good deal of the impact of that movie comes from the unexpected. The husband is dead. Drowned in the tub. The lover and wife cart the body down to the swimming hole at the school late at night and dump it in. Then they wait for it to float. They expect it to.

So does the audience. But nothing happens. Then they contrive a way to get the pool to be drained. They do it with a key. Nice touch. They expect that the corpse will be found snagged down under there. So does the audience. No body is found. Expectations thwarted."

"I remember well. We don't expect the dead man's suit to be delivered. We don't expect to see the corpse in the tub at the end." I remember the first time I saw that movie, it was out-Hitchcocking Hitchcock. Filmed in black and white. Why distract with color? "So, Officer Coster, why bring it up?"

"We are now faced with some unexpecteds. The book gone from what seemed to be a secure place. Terry gone when she has been so predictable. Her computer left on, and with a somewhat cryptic message. There is an explanation. We can speculate, but the audience of *Diabolique* speculates based on the clues given them—all visual ones. The husband is dead. His body is in the pool. We are looking at clues that might lead to truths or ones that might lead to falsehoods. Is the book really gone? Is Terry someone's victim?"

"I think that the second is more likely than the first. I can't believe that Terry would have opened the safe deposit box for anyone. She did say that she could hide the book in the apartment where no one could find it. But she wouldn't have tried that if it was safe in the bank."

"Maybe she thought it wasn't safe there. Maybe she was right about hiding it at home."

"Where is she right now?" I knew it was a silly question. Coster hadn't any more idea than I did. But desperation brings out such silliness.

He knew I knew it was a silly question. And he made no gesture or sound in reply.

"I mean . . . ."

"I know what you mean. Elliot, we cannot assume she is safe. At least one attempt has been made on your life. Whether it was intended to kill you or not, a bullet got you. At least one person related to this book of death of yours is dead. Two bombs have rocked your property. And now Terry Luckombe is allied with you. Your safety becomes her safety. Anyone wanting to get at you can do so through her. People know it.

Your life with her is fairly public. We are doing what we can. Los Angeles is a pretty violent city. We don't have the manpower to go after all
criminals, let alone all murderers."

This was cheery talk. I needed to hear it, but I didn't want to. I wanted to shut him up, but the subject matter and the fact that he had used
my first name for the first time kept me sober and attentive.

"What am I supposed to do now?"

"Maybe sell the book. Get it out of your hands."

"As I see it, someone has already done that for me. I told you, it's not
in the bank vault."

"Only Terry Luckombe could have taken it. If it's gone from the
bank then it's in one of two places: in the hands of those who know
where Terry is (which could include herself), or hidden somewhere as
she said—maybe even in her, your own apartment."

"I need to do something. I'll go home and see what I can find."

We parted after a quick sandwich. I went to the store to ask Dave if
he could stay the whole day. He couldn't, but he said he would close at
three thirty. I told him I'd try to get back before then.

There were no messages on the phone machine. I figured that if the
book were in the apartment, Terry would not have hidden it in any of
the obvious places: under mattresses, in clothing drawers, taped to the
undersides of dresser drawers, wrapped securely in several plastic bags
and hung inside toilet tanks, beneath the refrigerator, or stuck somehow behind some wall hanging or piece of furniture. So I checked those
places first. I was right. Not there.

It was a fairly slender pamphlet, but it was thick enough that if it had
been put under the rugs, I would have seen it. I looked under all the
rugs, even the wall-to-wall that was in the living room. Nope.

I checked every cupboard and closet in every room. I looked into the
large oatmeal tin, thinking it could have been rolled up a bit and fit into
that, under all the oatmeal. After cleaning up all the oatmeal, I looked
inside, behind, and under the old wind-up mantle clock. I carefully felt
all along the mattresses—top, bottom, and sides—to see if there were
some opening that the book could have been slid into. I tapped all the
doors to see if they were hollow, but this building was so old that it had
all solid doors. I looked into the medicine chest and tugged on it to see

if it would come out of the wall, but it was a built-in, constructed with the building's original wall tiles. Zilch.

I looked under the two floor lamps, inside the stereo chassis (it was too small, but I looked anyway), and into and around all other appliances. I felt carefully all the floorboards to see if any was loose. The ones that were silent and the ones that creaked were firmly rooted. I checked inside every record album cover, inside and behind and around all books on the shelves, and into every can of every house-cleaning product. The magazines in the magazine rack. The laundry bag. The hanging clothes. The shoes. I felt along all the walls and tapped and tried to pull off the molding at the baseboards and ceilings. Nada. I would have checked in the flue of the fireplace, but despite the mantle, the apartment didn't have one. Who needs a fireplace in southern California?

The more I looked, the more I was convinced that the book was not there. I worked methodically, eliminating one area after another, from the furthest reaches of the little place to the front door. Then I started again, and I went through the whole place a second time. It was suddenly nine thirty. I was famished, scared, angry, discouraged, and I-don't-know-what-else. Whoever had Terry, if someone had her, also had the book. No one who wanted it needed to contact me for it since getting Terry was probably tantamount to owning my *Buchlein*.

What if someone didn't have Terry? Where could she be? Where would she be? If she wanted the book, she had it, and she could be in Luxembourg by now—or well on her way. Would she have done a thing like that? No. And why the mystery of the C A L I on the computer? Was it Caligula? Was Pimples right in thinking she was somewhere in California, Calistoga, or some other Cali- place? I needed answers. I needed to find that damn book. I needed Terry. And at the moment I needed food.

Back to the kitchen. I looked again at the ugly old linoleum. It was tacked down with the same black tar they had used probably forty years ago when the stuff was installed. The cupboards again, this time for food, not for books. I wasn't hungry for anything in particular, and I was so upset that nothing looked good. The refrigerator.

Nothing appealing. Some leftovers: salad, pizza (I had checked the pizza box already), all kinds of jars and storage bottles, milk, yesterday's coffee. I pulled out the pizza box. Only two little slices—anchovy and green pepper. Ketchup and mustard and pickles.

Two part-loaves of bread. Jams and peanut butter. Maple syrup; the real thing. A bowl of left-over fruit salad. I looked into the freezer. Ice cream container, a loaf of Terry's bread, ice cubes, frozen fish, veggie "hamburger" patties, orange juice concentrate.

Concentrate, Elliot.

Left-over tuna salad. Tomatoes. Celery. Goddam it! Where was Terry?

The phone rang. (Just what you'd expect at this point in a murder mystery.) Wrong number. Shit.

The pizza tasted refrigerator-bad, but it filled me enough to let me turn to the computer. Might as well see what came of my fishing expedition with the incendiary device suspects. I flipped it on and pulled up my email. Twenty two messages. Lots of crap from one of Terry's bulletin boards. Item six: "What do you want to know about books?" Some cryptic return address. I am sure that Sherlock had pulled up and scrutinized this one.

I had phoned my message to several bombers. I had gotten no return calls, assuming that anyone who might have wanted to respond would figure my line was tapped. Which it was. No one knew my cell phone number. Only Terry, and she knew not to give it to anyone. One bozo thought he was clever enough to get to me through my email, not assuming that such an avenue might be bugged too, and ignoring the fact that even if it weren't, I could take it to the police anyway. The responder did not leave his name, and his return address looked generic—just a gmail designation. But my own REPLY key was all I needed, theoretically, to get a message back to him. I let fly another hook: "I will pay well for information about a book about the writer STERBEN. What do you know?"

It was well after ten, and I didn't expect an answer that night. So I unplugged and took a quick shower, with the portable phone and my cell on the bathroom sink so I could hear if they rang. At a little after eleven I got a call and I nearly fell down getting to the phone. This time it was Coster.

"Elliot. We have bad news. Your assistant David Daws has been attacked. It's pretty bad." Blunt and cool, but I guess it was the best way to tell me.

I stammered. "Is he alive?"

"Just barely."

"How? When did it happen? I saw him just this afternoon."

"The light in your store was on after dark. We have officers checking the area. He was found about an hour ago. He was hit in the back of the head, maybe with a hammer or metal bar. He was smacked from behind, so he probably never knew it was going to happen."

"In my store?"

"In the back . . . of the store, that is. This time there was no mess. Except for the blood. There was a note."

He stopped, and we were both waiting for the other to speak. I broke the silence with the profound:

"Yeah?"

"Yeah what?" He wanted me to ask, maybe testing me.

"Yeah? so what did the note say?"

"'We have what you want. You have what I want. Let's trade.'"

"That's it? Is it signed? Is there anything else, like how I can get in touch with this 'we'? Where was the note?"

"Calm down. I know you're upset."

Shit. I was upset. Dave was a good friend. Terry was more than that. I was furious.

I said in the most insistent and controlled voice I could muster, "Don't tell me to calm down. I am in full control of my faculties. I'm just pissed beyond belief and I want action." After I had said it, I knew it was stupid. They were doing what they could. "Sorry."

"Don't apologize. We'd like you to come down to the store. We'll have someone there to pick you up in five or ten minutes. Can you make it?"

"Of course. Where's Dave?"

"At Cedars. His wife is there. He was smacked pretty hard. But it looks as if he'll be ok. We just don't know how long."

"Does it really look as if he'll be ok?"

"The doctor said he'd recover. But from the way it looked, he won't be able to tell us anything. Either the trauma would knock any information—memory—out of his head, or he was hit from behind and didn't see anything."

"I'm ready right now. I'll drive over there."

"No!" I had never before heard Coster use this tone of voice. Then back to the Coster tone: "We have a car on the way. We don't want you going out by yourself."

"You're working late," I said.

"Regular hours when I'm doing one of my cases."

"I'll be ready."

Six minutes later they were there—Bud and Lou.

"Nice to see you guys."

All I got from them was a grunt.

This time there was no sign of incendiary devices or intruders.

Coster said, "They knew the book wasn't here. Not a sign of a search. They must have come in while the store was still open. The alarms hadn't been set. We called your company. They keep a computer-generated log of all settings and unsettings of the system."

Coster took me to the back of the store. He pointed to the floor just behind the door to the rear. "He was found here." The blood had stained the area rug and cement. It looked like dark rusty dried stuff on the floor. "He was hit about three thirty, maybe slightly later. We cleaned up most of it." They hadn't done too good a job, I thought. It was a mess, and there was an unpleasant odor of bleach and something else. Coster saw the little grimace on my face as I reacted to the odor and the scene.

"When someone goes through this kind of trauma, there's often a release of bodily materials. He went through some kind of trauma."

"You needn't say any more. I can tell. Why did you want me here?"

"We expect that nothing was taken. That this was a message. That you were supposed to find Daws and the note. You were supposed to be scared into giving up the book. We assume that's what the note refers to. Did you find it?"

"No. I turned the place inside out. I think it's not there."

"Do you want professionals to look? We have guys . . . ."

"No. They won't find it."

"Ok. Call if you change your mind. From now on we will have your place under surveillance. Subtle and good. Not like, what did you call them, Bud and Lou? Don't go anywhere without contacting us. We think your life is in danger."

"Not while I still have the book. Or should I say, Not while they don't have the book. What about Caligula? Do you know where he lives? Can you search his place?"

"He's a very wealthy and secret person. He is also pretty smart. I'm sure he's clean—or, at least a search of his place will turn up nothing."

"He's the likely suspect."

"What about Sam Forester?"

I was surprised that Coster remembered him. "He wanted me out of the school. He wouldn't have anything to do with this business."

Coster looked severe. "He wanted to hurt you. All that has happened to you since that book arrived has hurt you, physically and otherwise."

"He wanted me canned from teaching. He won."

"You told me he wanted to buy some books from you and you thwarted him."

"That was not much revenge. He tried to destroy my life and practically succeeded. I got dumped from the profession I had trained for for years and was fairly successful in. He got my hide."

"You're still walking around in your hide."

"But what has he got to do with my book of death? The note said that I have the book."

"No, all it said was that you have what he wants. Is that independence? Freedom? Books that you wouldn't sell?"

"Ok. Where do we go from here?" I said it with some irony, as if to say that we had nowhere to go.

"What are you willing to give up to get back what he has, whatever it is?"

I couldn't answer that. Would I give up everything for Terry. Probably. But what was "everything"? What was it that I was being asked to give up? Coster said, "I know you can't say anything. We have to wait for another move. Ms. Luckombe is somewhere. So is the book. They will emerge some way or another. We will do what we can to make them emerge the way you want them to. But we'd like to have you around when they do. Don't do anything foolish. Like try to visit a powerful bookseller or confront an old enemy."

He didn't mention locating a bomber. To date the police, trust-worthy as they had been, had been useless. They told me that my business had been rifled. After the fact. They were standing in front of my house when it had gotten blasted. They had told me that my safe had been blown open. After the fact. They had to learn from me that Terry and the book had vanished. They had found Dave Daws after he was attacked, then they called to tell me about it. They were good at report-ing, but reporters go to scenes of crimes after the crimes are committed. I needed to head off some crimes. I needed to stop them.

Whatever the next step was to be, it had to go through me. Whoever wanted me to know that he had what I wanted knew enough that a phone call or email message would have been intercepted. Now even more channels to my head would be observed. The channels to me were guarded by the guardians of peace and justice. I had to keep the channel open to whoever was shitting on my life, but the communication had to come from me.

Coster had said not to contact Forester or Caligula. Naturally that was an invitation, a catalyst . . . .

Coster and his few men left the store. I was driven back to the Santa Monica apartment. No messages were on the goddam phone machine. The computer had a reply to my query "What do you know?" The answer was, "How much?" Answering it would be like carrying on a conference call. I wrote out the address and stuck it into my wallet. I hoped that my secret sharers hadn't followed this conversation too closely. Even if they had, I had to act quickly. The rest of the night was a restless series of nightmares and waking visions of terror and pain, some mine, some others'. I hoped Terry didn't figure into these visions, but I was afraid she did.

TWENTY

I called Shirley Daws the next morning. Her mother answered. I left a message of my deepest respects, and I told her that Dave would be ok. The crying I heard from the other end of the line made me think that my thoughts were not heard; there was too much fear for them to hear my pathetic words.

I then drove over to the store and put a sign up that I'd be closed for a few days. I left the same message on the store's answering machine. I called the university to ask if Hannah Rackstraw were in. She was, so it was over to Terry's office. I needed to talk to Professor Rackstraw, Terry's nemesis. I needed some information, and she was the one to give it.

When I knocked on her partly open door, I got the imperious "Yes?"

"Professor Rackstraw, may I come in?"

"You're the man asking about Terry Luckombe, aren't you?"

"I was. But now she's out of the picture." I didn't know how she was going to take this, but it would never do to let her think she was talking to Terry's ally.

"Out of the picture? What do you mean?"

"Gone. Skipped. And with one of my prize possessions. I'm trying to get it back. Do you have any idea where she is? I'd like to wring her neck."

"Doesn't surprise me. She was untrustworthy. We did the right thing here."

"What do you mean?"

"Denying her promotion. Too arrogant and know-it-all. She offended an untold number."

"She had no friends?"

"A paltry few. Weaver and Marsh and Brothers. Old bastards. Fools. They fell for her looks. We saw through that."

"I'm thinking of taking her to court. I want back what I have coming to me."

"I cannot help you. I have no idea where she is and I could not care less."

This old bitch at least got the idiom correct.

"Sorry to bother you."

"No bother."

Weaver and Marsh and Brothers. I needed to find at least one of them. The English Department office was on the second floor. I found the stairs and in a minute I was facing the Ravin' secretary—Eugenia Ravenstone, who had a nameplate on her desk with her name and title, Department Executive Secretary. I knew the type. Thought the title gave her power. And ironically it did. She had access to every one of the department's files, open and confidential. She could hold up a professor's reimbursement for an expensive trip simply by "forgetting" to put the paperwork through. She could screw up the xeroxing or typing of anyone on the faculty. She had the ear (and often the zipper) of the department chair, and because of this, being her friend was essential if you wanted to get anything done in the department. She was obese, haughty, and ill dressed. Three shades of blue, royal, pale, and turquoise (skirt, blouse, and eye-shadow). No, no, Ms. Ravin'; that will never do. It clashed. And I didn't want to do the same with you. I needed help, not resistance.

"Excuse me. You seem to be in charge. Could you please help me?" Praise; that softens them. Asking for help; that puts them into a position of power—they can help or refuse, at their will. You come begging, and they have you where they want you.

"What do you want?"

"Great earrings! I'm looking for Professor Weaver." Careful, now. If Terry got canned, it's not unlikely that Ms. Ravenstone was in on it. These office managers usually are. And if Weaver were a Terry ally, I have to convince her I'm not one of his friends. "Weaver owes me something, and I'm here to collect." Make it seem he's an adversary. And I still didn't know if Weaver were male or female.

"Before I tell you where he is, I'd like to know who you are?" Weaver is a gent. Good.

None of your goddam business, Ms. Power. "Let's just say a distant acquaintance. Do you know how I can contact him?"

She looked at me with disdain and suspicion, but she had to do her job. "His office is 317. I haven't seen him today, but he could be in. Shall I ring?"

"No, thanks. I'll go up there and see if I can find the bastard."

She smiled. Trouble for Weaver meant pleasure for her. I had known her type in my old botany days. The department chair's spy and hangman. Go hang yourself, Ms. Ravenstone.

Weaver's door was shut. I knocked. "What is it?" A gruff and irritated voice.

"Professor Weaver; may I speak to you please?"

"Who is it?"

"Elliot. Please let me in."

"Elliot who?" as the door came abruptly open.

I was facing a short, slightly overweight, white-haired man with a round, ruddy face. Maybe 65 or 70 years old. A very pleasant and handsome face, but with a sour scowl of impatience and annoyance.

"Who are you? And what do you want? I'm busy."

"May I please come in? I'm a friend of Terry Luckombe."

He practically pulled me into the office and shut the door. "You're taking your life into your hands by admitting that to a stranger in this building."

"You're not a complete stranger. I have it on good authority that you are one of Terry's few allies on this faculty."

"Who told you?"

"Let's just say that Ms. Rackstraw accidentally imparted this information to me. Let's just say that she thinks I am angry at Professor Luckombe. She suddenly became my ally and was willing to reveal your presence to me. You are the one I came to see."

His smile was brief, but it revealed a quick understanding. Some of the irritation drained away. "What may I do for you? Why do you want to see me?"

"How much time have you got?"

"How much do you need?"

I explained who I was and told him of the situation I was in, from the acquisition of *Ein Buchlein* to the present. I told him that I needed to do many things without the knowledge or interference of the police. He squinted in half disapproval. I said that it had nothing to do with anything illegal. All I wanted was to get Terry and my book—but mostly Terry—back. I said that the police had not been able to accomplish a thing and that it was clear that some criminal wanted to operate with me alone. I told him I had a plan, but that I needed a helper; I couldn't do anything at all without the police listening in on everything I did. And I said that that could be dangerous to Terry.

"Why do you tell me this? How do you know you can trust me?"

"I saw you smile when I told you how I had found out you were an ally of Terry. You had to have some kind of courage to stand up against Rackstraw and her ilk in front of this department. Terry told me of her tenure fight. You obviously care for her, or at least respect her. Otherwise the rack lady would not have mentioned you as one of the fools in the department who tried to help her. If you believe me and trust me, then you'll help me, because you know that you'll be helping her."

His eyes narrowed and he sat down, gesturing me to take the other chair.

"It sounds dangerous. One man dead; another unconscious. You shot at. Bombs." He thought for a moment. "What do you want me to do?"

It wasn't an offer. Just probing.

"Help me."

"Evasive answer. I have lived with evasion for nearly three decades in this god-forsaken department. I have colleagues who are worse than toads, festering under rocks, waiting to spit their venom. I was once chair of this department. Now I'm lucky they let me keep my phone. I got tenure 32 years ago. I've published more than most of them combined. They can't do anything to me. So I serve as the department's conscience. I can say anything I please and I can't be touched. So I call them on their illegal actions, their vicious territoriality, their petty power struggles that allow them to lord it over others. I tell you this only to let you know that I am a fighter. I go outside their rules when I want. If you want to do the same, for whatever cause you have, I could help you. But I'm tired of it all. I'm going to retire in a year. All I want to do is get some farm land in Idaho and sit back and relax. Why should I help you?"

Wow. This is much more than I had bargained for. Maybe I should have started with Marsh or Brothers. But here was a great mind still in a fighting mood.

"Because something about Terry Luckombe was worth your fighting for. That's what I'm doing too. I need your help. But not much of it. For now, I'd just like to use your phone and computer. I need a couple of lines—telephone and email—away from the ears and eyes of Johnny Law."

"That's all? I've got no problem with the phone. But I don't have a computer. I tried to get one years ago, but the Raven cut it off." I was amused that he used the same epithet for Ravenstone. "She said that I was too old to learn how to use one, that the department didn't have enough money to buy one for me, and that I would be forbidden to use one of my own here in the office. Would you believe: she said that it would be illegal for me to use university electricity or the Internet or even a computer of my own purchase. She made this up herself, and got Hondo to sign a form backing her on it." Hondo, I learned, was the present, horribly corrupt, chair of the department. "I won't go on about this shit."

"How could they monitor your use of a computer here?"

"The Raven has keys to all the offices. Also, they can monitor Wifi use in all the offices."

"You don't have one at home?"

"Yes, but my manual Underwood is all I have ever used here. I have a computer at home, but I can hardly use it. I don't want to retool now."

"I'll need access to a computer and email. What about Marsh or Brothers?"

"You really did pump old Rackstraw, didn't you?!"

"She was pumpable."

"Celia Brothers has been like a mouse since they tried to deny her use of her office in her semi-retirement. She supported Luckombe and nearly lost everything when she did: her office, her computer, her department vote. She's retired, though she still teaches a class now and then, just enough to keep her office. I'm sure she'll let you use her computer—and her phone, if you wish. But just don't make any long-distance calls. In fact, from her office and mine, you can't. And don't tell her that you'll be operating around the constabulary." He even uses my words. Good man. "She might be scared off. She's old and getting frail, but she's brilliant and clever and kind. Just tell her you are doing a research project that requires your comparing your kind of computer with her kind. If it's in the name of research, she'll help you. If it's to help Terry Luckombe, she'll help you. The best woman you'll ever know. And as for long-distance calls, use my home phone. I get Aadvantage miles."

The two of us went to dinner near the campus, arriving in separate cars. I didn't want my shadows to see us together yet. We talked for a few more hours, and learned about our mutual dislikes of academia, our mutual regrets about academia, and our contentment that soon we would both be out of it. I didn't tell him that I often missed it, but he knew. When we parted, we shook hands in the restaurant, and he went out five minutes before I did.

I went home to an empty apartment, an empty answering machine, and a bunch of email messages devoid of content.

I'm sure Coster didn't like getting reports that I was spending time in "a friend's" home. The next day I couldn't see anyone following me when I drove to work or came home. But I was sure someone was there.

After work I drove over to Abe Weaver's house. He lived alone—a widower—in a lovely old duplex not far from the Farmers Market. He had a simple dinner waiting for me, and we ate it with Celia Brothers, a kindly, erect, sharp woman with blue-white hair, pellucid blue eyes, lots of soft wrinkles around her eyes and mouth, and a soft but firm voice. She was proper, dignified, and elegant. I wasn't sure how much Abe had told her, but without my asking she said, with force and gentleness, "I understand you need to use my computer and maybe even my telephone for some research you are doing. Abe tells me I can trust you. I feel as though I can. He tells me you are Terry Luckombe's friend. She needs friends right now. If you are one, then you can be trusted. I won't ask questions and you needn't explain your work. Here's a key to my office. Don't try to make any long-distance phone calls from there. You can't."

"Thank you," was all I could say.

"You may wonder how I got a spare key. Eugenia Ravenstone hands the keys out sparingly and with an eagle eye. A raven's eye. The key works for my office and the building door. You'll notice it's not stamped 'Do Not Duplicate,' as all university keys must. When they tried to expel me from my office I went to the university key shop. Burt is a friend of mine. He has run that part of the physical plant since I got to the university 34 years ago. I even dated him once. He would do anything for me. Here's proof." And she pointed at the key.

"I'm amazed." And I was. I had tried to get a duplicate key once and was cut off by everyone I asked—the chair, the department coordinator, the secretaries, the physical plant, the local key shop (they claimed that they didn't even have the blanks for that one).

"I hope you don't think ill of me for doing something illicit like this. I was being maltreated by those who were ostensibly my friends. I had to retaliate. A terrible thing to do—retaliate. But I needed to have access to my office and this was the only way I could guarantee it. Abe interceded and I was allowed to keep the office. But I decided to keep the key as a secret way of thumbing my nose at those . . . ."

She didn't have to finish her sentence.

"One more thing: Tom the custodian will be into the office by one a.m. He will not return for the rest of the night. All he does is empty the waste baskets and, on a rare occasion, run a broom across the floor. If you want privacy for a few hours, use the office after one fifteen."

"Thank you."

"Don't thank me. Just help Terry Luckombe."

TWENTY ONE

A nd that's what I aimed to do. After the dinner I went back to the apartment. No messages. I waited till after midnight and drove out to the university. Was I followed? Can't tell. L.A. never sleeps, and there were always cars in front of me and behind me all the way to the campus. Celia Brothers' office was 332, down the hall from Weaver's. It was neat and spare: computer table, desk with two chairs, two free-standing bookshelves, matching file cabinet. Nothing out of place. No messy piles on the desk. A small stack of neatly piled sheets next to the computer. Professor Brothers was writing a book on animals in Renaissance texts. A second stack of photographs and xeroxes of beasts and birds and fish stood next to the first pile.

She had given me her password and it took me no time to boot up and get to email. I entered the address of the person who wanted to know "How much" it was worth to me to find out about *Buchlein*. I entered the following message: "I have cash for answers about *Buchlein*. Meet me . . . ." Where could we meet? If I was followed as assiduously as Coster had implied, then there was nowhere that I could be alone with my suspect. I needed a plan. I erased the message and went home. I had to clear something with Abe Weaver.

Weaver turned out to be quite an accomplice. He had become, from years of dealing with "cretins and slugs," a cynic of the first order. He despised most of his colleagues, many of his grade-oriented students, and the majority of the world's population. His prejudices did not run along racial or religious lines; they were formed from observation of the masses, "worse than sheep, because sheep simply follow without thought, but don't cause much damage; the masses follow with just enough thought to develop neuroses, to screw things up for good people, and to fuck up the world with hatred and illogical thoughts and evil deeds." When he had learned of my own experience in academia, he sympathized, said it was typical and he had seen it over and over in his own institutions, and became an ally willing to do practically anything that upset the powers that be—academic, political, constabulary, or otherwise.

The following morning, from the shop, I called and asked him to join me for lunch at Crocker's Diner. We met and I immediately counseled him to order without making any eye contact with the waitress and without asking any questions. "Select what you want; when the server comes over, just stare at the menu and read out your order. Show no friendliness or hostility. Neutrality here will get you fed in under ten minutes. Inquisitiveness or the least bit of amicability will stretch that to a half hour."

He was perfect. Sober to the point of pure apathy; indifference personified. We were eating in seven minutes.

"Why the lunch?"

"I've got a favor to ask. I need to meet someone—alone. Unobserved." He knew that I was told that I would be under surveillance. Whether I was or not I couldn't tell. If I was, Lou and Bud were doing a good job. I told him, too, that my phone and email—and Terry's email—were not private channels for me. I needed some freedom, some space.

"Does this mean foiling the fuzz? Pedaling past the police?"

"It does."

"Is it dangerous?"

"I'm not sure. Maybe. But I need to do some things on my own. If I call someone and Officer Coster listens in, it could cut off a valuable source of information."

"What do you want me to do?"

"Take my car."

I explained it all to him. He took it in quietly. Then he smiled and said, "I'll prepare you an excellent meal. I hope it's not your last supper."

* * *

The dinner was delicious. It was followed by a quick change in clothes. Though I was much taller than Abe and about thirty pounds lighter, I had worn a bulky overcoat and a visor cap. (I generally looked upon these caps with amusement, but it was necessary tonight.) At about eleven, when the night was as dark as it was to be, Abe slipped out his side door, walked down the driveway, and got into my car. He didn't adjust the rear-view mirror or seat (as I told him not to do), and he quickly had the car gliding down the street in the direction I would have taken to go home.

I waited a few minutes, looking out the slits of the venetian blinds to see if I could discern a follower. It was hard to know, since several cars drove by in the next two minutes. I waited till eleven fifteen, then I exited from Abe's residence by a back door, climbed the short fence between his house and the property that backed up to it, and walked out to the neighboring street. I spotted Abe's Toyota down the block where he said he parked it. I saw no movement anywhere. In a minute I was headed toward the university in a driver's seat pushed so far forward that my chest nearly pressed against the steering wheel. I couldn't see out of the rear-view mirror; it faced far from my angle of vision. But the side mirrors indicated no retinue behind me.

I parked in a lot far from the English building and took a circuitous route to it. I saw no movement anywhere. I entered at the door furthest from Celia Brothers' office, used her key, and took the stairs two at a time to the third floor. No sound. Her office was neat as usual, though I noticed that the picture at the top of the illustrations pile had changed. Celia was working away.

There were two things I had to do. First, I logged in to her email and entered Mr. Chandler's address. I finished my message of the previous night. "I have cash for answers about *Buchlein*. Meet me at Cafe Cappuccino in Santa Monica at eleven p.m. tomorrow (Tuesday)." No telling what this would snag, but it was at least a hook.

Then I pulled out the business card from my pocket:

TWENTY TWO

His card had said "Edward Myers / San Francisco," but the phone number was L.A. When I called I got the same sexy "hello." Great voice.

"It's Elliot Burgess again. Is Mr. Myers there?"

"I'll get him for you."

This time the wait was only a few seconds.

"Mr. Burgess. I had expected this call sooner."

The muscular tone conjured up the muscular body, popping from his Brooks Brothers suit, the steel gray temples, and the powerful hands. Funny that I thought of his hands. I guess they were memorable.

"I'm confirming our date. Your house; five?"

"I'm expecting you." Not a wasted syllable. Rich people can often be blunt, especially tough rich ones. Myers was clearly both, and it was also clear that he liked getting his way—expected to get it. And didn't like being thwarted. All I had over him was a little pamphlet. My little Book of Death. Good god! was that what it was?

There was no telling what I would encounter on this visit, but I didn't feel particularly threatened. I had something he wanted. Maybe he had someone I wanted. If he hurt me, he would not get the thing he coveted so powerfully. But maybe I would be denied the one I craved, too. I cringed thinking about it. But I had to do *something*, and facing Myers—Caligula—seemed to be the thing to do. At the moment I felt that the constabulary and I were both at a standstill. I needed to kick-start something. I hope I didn't get kicked back for my efforts.

I went home, spent a nightmarish night thinking, got up groggily in the morning, and went to the shop. I had to kill hours before my meeting with Myers. I might as well spend them in the shop trying to bring some semblance of order to my life.

* * *

Four fifty five.

The Myers estate—and even that doesn't do it justice—was just like him: massive, powerful, stately, and imperturbable. It was rich and taut and steel-edged and scary. But here I was, facing it and facing god knows what else.

Through the shrubbery surrounding the estate (anything that expensive has to be called an estate) I could see at least three buildings, the main house and what looked like two smaller ones behind. One might be what would in Victorian novels be called the gardener's abode, the other could have been a pool house, but I saw no pool.

It wasn't more than five seconds after I touched the button for the bell that the door opened. I faced—what? Had Myers rejuvenated? Had he shrunk a bit? Had he used Grecian Formula on his sideburns? Whoa!

I hesitantly said, "Hello, I'm . . . ."

"Come in, Mr. Burgess. My dad told me to meet you. I'm Blake."

No question of his genes. Same DNA, same tone of voice, same I-can-beat-the-shit-out-of-you self confidence, and, certainly, the same physique to back that up. Where his pop was a bit stocky, Blake was merely muscular. Dad had the muscles too, no doubt, but they were more visible on his scion.

He took me through an entrance hall the size of the Vatican to a library the size of the Houghton. The books! This was a *library*. I could see not only the typical designer bindings—leather, gold stamping, folios and quartos and octavos—but I could also see that this was not merely a collection of fancy bindings. There were shelves of pamphlets, many in Mylar sleeves, others in their own little clamshell boxes. These were obviously not "for show," since they were rather modest little things. They were interspersed with what were obviously a host of early books, some in their original blue paper wrappers, many in vellum calligraphed on the spine. It didn't look like a working library. I guessed that many were in Latin or early Western languages, and I also guessed that their owner didn't speak a word of Homer or Waltharius or Cædmon or Petrarch or any of those other texts that Aldus and his brethren gave us so many centuries ago.

But it was doubtless the library of a savvy collector and a high-end bookseller. In the few minutes I had waiting for Caligula Senior, I picked out three lovely incunabula, including a magnificent folio of Cassiodorus' Commentary on the Psalms from Octavianus Scotus Medoe, in its original vellum over boards, and with elegant calligraphy on the spine. I was looking at perhaps the most impressive bunch of books I had ever seen.

Where would my little *Büchlein* fit in here? What other treasures would it join, if it made it here in the first place?

Myers and his son and a drop-dead model entered. I could hardly stop staring. My mental image from only her voice was borne out in full view. Taller than I had imagined, maybe close to six feet. And with her stilettos she towered over the other two by several inches. Slender, blonde, creamy, and so forth. I was too stunned to congratulate myself on how accurately I had conjured her up.

Where Myers was graying and mid-fiftyish, Mrs. Caligula (or whoever she was) was half his age—or looked it. I don't know if my mouth was open in wonder, but the look on my face obviously pleased Myers and he smiled for a split second to see the power they all had over me: I was like a captive to these powerful men in their fortress, and I was viscerally captive to . . . .

"Burgess, this is Blake, my son, and Theresa, my wife. Glad to see you."

I shook hands—in fact much of me was shaking, though I'm not sure they saw. Theresa's hands were smooth and slender and quite strong. She shook like a man and pierced my eyes with hers. Blue, of course. Might as well give her the standard heroine features. Hair just below her shoulders and falling undulantly over her clavicles. She looked like a model for Prell. I had the lips wrong, however. Not ruby. Scarlet. The eyes transfixed me. So I was only partly aware of the sleek body, covered with skin-tight slacks—better than Calvin Kleins—and form-fitting turtleneck. Bra or not, her nipples were visible, and that was bad.

"Mr. Burgess?"

I had forgotten where I was for a second.

"May I assume this is not a pleasure visit?"

Geez, man. Look at the pleasure there.

"No. Uh, yes, this is not a pleasure visit. I want to talk about . . . ."

"The book?" Said as a question, but he meant as a statement. I didn't reply, so he said, "Where is it? Did you bring it?"

"Should I have?"

"Of course. You know I want it." He paused. "I want it *back*."

The moment of truth. Anyway, it sounds pretty dramatic to say a thing like that. I didn't know what the truth was and I wasn't sure I could get any truths out of him. I had practiced this for hours: "Where's Terry?"

All three of them reacted with a start. Just a slight flinch, but it was as if I had softly slapped all of them.

"You're looking at her, Mr. Burgess,"

Theresa. Terry. Dumb me.

"You know who I mean. My Terry."

"Mr. Burgess. Elliot. Please. What you are talking about is your personal life. Your pleasure. We have business to attend to first. Let's have dinner."

I was swept into the dining hall. I couldn't say a word. I guess it was a combination of shock, fear, and awe. It was overwhelming.

Then I met Gangsta. He was serving some pretty spiffy edibles, but he looked as if he should be serving time. The clichéd acne scars. The short hair. The fat, sour face and enormous muscles. Central Casting. He spoke softly:

"Dinner will be ready in three minutes, Mr. Myers."

Interesting. He was kowtowing to dad and ostentatiously snubbing Blake. There was a tension between them. I thought Spike was going to shove the son into the fireplace. But all he did was turn his back on the kid and glare a second. A flash of fire—more a little spark—in Blake's eyes. But he carried it off well. He helped Theresa into her seat and took his own. The table could have seated fifteen. We were at the north end. Well, at one end. I have no sense of direction.

I don't remember the dinner. All I remember was the luscious scarlet lips. Postprandially, we repaired (I guess that's what one does postprandially) to the library and sat in stuffed chairs, ourselves stuffed as well.

Gangsta from Central Casting, who had been introduced genteelly as Howard, "our associate," brought us some cordials, and we sat fairly taciturnly for about a minute. A nervous minute for me. All of them, Howie included, were there, and they were apparently waiting for me to say something. So I did.

"Where's Terry. My Terry?"

Daddy answered, in a controlled and subdued voice. "Where is my book?"

Ominous. Threatening. No negotiation here. I didn't know what to say. Re-asking my question would certainly have gotten the same response. The others stared at me, still.

"Mr. Myers. I have lost the woman I love. I don't know where she is. I think you do." No response of any kind, from any of them. "I have also . . . ." I hesitated, not knowing how much to reveal. But it seemed that the point had come at which I could say nothing else. "I have also lost the book."

This got some wrinkles on Myers' otherwise perfect brow. The others looked a bit shocked, and they looked at him, as if for guidance. This was obviously not in their script.

"What do you mean, Mr. Burgess?"

"I don't know where the book is."

"Go on."

"We had it in a safe deposit box."

"I know."

He did? "I went to find it. It's not there."

"I know."

"Do you know because you have it? Because if you do, why this charade?"

"I just know."

So Terry's disappearance and the vanishing book were linked.

"Did you look yourself? You have been at the box? How? Who?"

"Mr. Burgess, I want that book. I will do what I have to to get it."

"And just what is it that you *have to* do?"

"When someone has something I want, and won't give it up, I find ways to get it."

"Are you saying that you don't have the book?"

"Are you saying that *you* don't?"

I hate questions to my questions.

I glared at him. "I guess your asking me that means that you don't."

He glared back, with eyes that I could almost feel. "You are playing with me, Mr. Burgess. I don't like to be played with." He moved in his chair as if about to rush me and pummel me. At least that's what I thought he might do.

"Mr. Myers. I don't have the book." I said it with conviction. "Where is Terry?"

"She's safe."

"How do you know?"

"I know."

"But . . . . Where is she? How can I see her?"

"Where is the *Buchlein*, Mr. Burgess?"

"I don't know!" I shouted it.

"If I were to tell you that you must give me the book or never see your precious Terry again, what would you do?"

"I couldn't give you the book. I don't have it. I've looked everywhere. I don't know where it is."

He thought about this for a moment. "Howard." Casting stood up. Myers nodded and Howie got to my side in a second. The next thing I knew my cheek was burning with pain and the stars were dancing all over the place. When they say "I saw stars," they had no idea what it was to see a whole constellation. I crumpled to the floor, too stunned and in too much pain to move. And sweating and incoherent.

"Enough. Easier than I had thought." Myers's voice was controlled and satisfied.

I don't know how long I was down there, but there was no sound for a while so I looked up. Four faces glaring. Myers with no expression at all. Howard with a little smug grin, very satisfied. Theresa and Junior with a trace of shock and disgust, but also with a sense of you-had-it-coming. No sympathy anywhere.

I staggered up and fell into my chair. I had gotten it on the left cheekbone, and it stung and throbbed. When I spoke, I heard a high-pitched squeal in my left ear and my tongue wasn't quite in control. And my teeth didn't fit together too well.

"What do you want of me? The impossible? I can't give you what I don't have."

Myers penetrated me with his stare. The others looked at him for more instructions. "You don't seem to understand, Mr. Burgess." I still hated that phrase. I did understand; more than he knew. But this time I just let him go on—to tell me what it was that I understood that he thought I didn't.

"You see, I'd kill for that book."

I guess he was right. I didn't really understand *that*. But whom would he kill? Terry? Me? Dave? Smith/Gens?

What does one say to that? Nothing.

"Where is the book?"

"I don't know."

"Mr. Burgess, I'm going to do you a favor. I will let you out of here now. But you shall do *me* a favor. You will return with the book within twenty-four hours."

"Or else?"

"You will see."

That was all. I was sort of ushered to the door, Howie on one side, Blake on the other. I didn't quite fall on my face when I departed, but I did stumble, still reeling from the wayward fist. I drove haltingly away from the house, out of the cul de sac. When I could no longer see the house I pulled over to assess the cheekbone and try to pull myself together. (Weird idiom. I wasn't really apart.) Quite a fine lumpy ugly splotchy thing on my face. How was I going to explain this? To whom? I thought. Maybe Coster would want to know, and "ran into the door" wouldn't do. He would be pissed if he knew where I had been and how I had been tattooed. I'd think of something.

In fact, thinking about it would be a good idea since it would take my mind off the pain, which was considerable. And the ringing in my ear was still tintinnabulating. Hey, guys. I'm a lover, not a fighter. (It's probably the only time in my life I've equated myself with Michael Jackson.)

As I drove back to the office, what I would tell Coster didn't matter too much. I started thinking of other avenues. One thing bothered me. Not once did Myers admit to having Terry. He implied it. He kept using the suggestion as a kind of leverage with me. "We have what you want." Maybe he too doesn't know where Terry is. By letting me go, maybe I would have a chance to find her. What did he mean that he knew the safe deposit box was empty? Had he looked there himself? He never actually said he did.

Myers wanted the book from me. Who else wanted something from me? And what could it be? Was Coster right that Forester might be involved? His ugly face and slippery, unctuous voice kept ringing in my ear. Well, no. The tinnitus from Central Casting was ringing in my ear. But the image of Forester's face kept looming before me, as it had for the six years since he ruined my academic career. Maybe I'd have to check him out.

No way to know if I were followed. Who cares? If it was the fuzz, great. If it was Caligula or his fists, no problem. He let me go. I had at least a day. And then what? I was at a complete loss as to where the book was. I swore it wasn't in the apartment. And it wasn't in the bank. Where else? Terry didn't have a key to the shop, so it's practically impossible that it was there. Terry's car? Not too likely, but maybe the only possible place. I'll check tonight.

Back at the office I attended to the gruesome task of trying to clean up the blood that dripped out of Dave's bump. Not very successfully. Chuck the cheap rug. Get another to cover the stain on the floor. More for my to-do list.

The pain on my face was vying for the fear I felt for Terry and the anger I felt at being practically helpless. Time for more action.

TWENTY THREE

It was about 7:30. I had been to Forester's house about a dozen years earlier, as a brand new assistant professor, but I knew just where it was. In West Hollywood there was a significant community of gays. Forester lived just above Santa Monica Boulevard, in a nice, small house—self contained and easily observed since all the rooms had windows.

I figured a visit unannounced was in order. No time to get his defenses up. I hated his guts. In fact, I hated all of him, not just the guts. Though he had been out of my sight for a few years, the picture of his face kept coming back to me during my nightmares and daymares and morningmares. I couldn't shake his presence. All the years I spent preparing for the academic life. All the classes I taught. All the students whose life I was able to affect. And so forth. Shot to hell by the efforts of a jealous, retaliatory bastard.

Forester was smaller that I was, and clearly intimidated by anyone with physical harm on his mind. The only power he had in the world was over his students (especially the male ones whom he bedded whenever he could) and the junior professors, over whom he had powerful control, what with his long-standing friendships in the department and above at the university, and with the insidious tenure system which rewarded old mediocrity and punished the promising.

On the drive to his place I said to myself, What the hell are you doing? What are you going to do? Are you being a total asshole idiot? And in truth, I didn't really have a plan. What I had was deep fear (some for myself), tremendous frustration, and practically uncontrollable anger at being so in the dark about what was going on. Who was Myers? What did he have over me? Was it Terry? Was Terry somehow in this in ways other than carnal? Did Forester have something to do with this?

Were there any others who might be involved? Who was this Chandler guy whom I was to meet tomorrow evening? Where would I be tomorrow evening? Where was Terry? What was Coster doing? And my little *Buchlein*: where was it? Was it genuine or a forgery? Where did it come from? Would it lead to wealth? to people? to truth? to Death?

All this uncertainty made me angrier and angrier, and I thought that a full frontal attack might not be a bad idea with Forester. If I hit him, maybe I'd learn nothing, but it would sure feel good. And I knew how hitting affected people. My face felt like raw flesh.

On the other hand, I didn't want to do anything that would get me into trouble. Breaking and entering. Battery. Busting in doors or windows. Not in my best interests.

So I parked on the steep incline, walked back the half block (it was a miracle that I had found a place so close in that congested neighborhood), and stood in front of his door for a while. Then I walked surreptitiously around the place—a little one-story bungalow behind an apartment house. His place had probably been the small guest house of a larger mansion that long ago had been torn down for the land. The apartment house there would bring in beaucoup bucks on that spot.

This was not like on tv: no open windows, no open curtains, no basement to slip into (in L.A.? are you kidding!), and no particularly suspicious sound coming from the place. Lights were visible through the curtains. I found a small stone, which I pocketed. Some kind of heroic stuff, eh? I don't know what I was going to do with it, but it seemed like the tv thing to do. Or the stuff of B movies. I was, after all, only a stone's throw (pun intended) from Sunset Boulevard.

I stood again at the front door. Gray. Wood. Brass knocker. And I hesitated. I felt my heartbeat. Not too pleasant, but then again, neither was this encounter going to be. What the hell.

When I rang the doorbell there was a faint sound of some shuffling inside, and then, after about two minutes and another ring, the door opened. Evil incarnate stared out at me. The pounding had made it to my temples, and a faint nausea came over me. We glared at each other for a long time—maybe a couple of seconds, but it seemed like the length of a prison term. I hadn't seen Sam since I had essentially thrown him out of my shop the day he wanted to buy some books from me.

The sight of his face sickened me as it had in my dreams. Only this was ugly flesh staring at me, and I felt anger and vengeance and god-knows-what-else.

He was wearing a robe and was a bit flushed and half jittery, as if I had interrupted something between him and one of his students.

When he saw who it was, he seemed to smile slightly and said, "Elliot. What do you want?"

"I want to talk."

"What about?"

"What do you think?" Maybe that would bring out some information that I didn't know to be probing for: the whereabouts of my companion and my book and my sanity.

"What do you want?"

"You already asked me that."

"Well, I don't really know." Oily bastard.

"What can you tell me about Terry?" It was a dumb question, but I didn't know what else to say. At least it was direct.

"Who is Terry? Is he cute?"

I'm sure he was trying to be cute and to mock me at the same time. I wasn't amused and I shoved myself forward and pushed him into the living room, slamming the door and startling him powerfully. Nervousness, fear, anger, and other reactions showed in his face. He didn't fall down. He then stood quite erect.

There was a small efficient kitchen to my left, a little eating area beside that, and two doors on the back wall leading to what? Quite tidy. Loads of books on the shelves that lined the room.

He said, "Get out of here. I'll call the police."

"What do you think this is, asshole? a movie? People say that in movies. But did you ever notice how few times that gets said in movies and the speakers actually never get to call the police? This is one of those times."

Shit, that was a great comeback. Well, it was pretty stupid, but again, I didn't know where I was going. But I had the upper hand since Sam didn't know either. He didn't know what I was capable of doing. Neither did I.

"I'll ask you once more: Where's Terry?"

He was shaking, but blank-faced. "Who is he? Who is this Terry? I don't know what you are talking about."

"Listen, Sam. A person named Terry is not in my life. And she should be. And someone is responsible. What do you know?"

He seemed to understand the reason for my visit. A muffled noise came from a room behind him. I looked in that direction, and he shifted his weight to block my way to that room.

I didn't say anything, but I made a move in that direction. He tried to block me now, but he was enough smaller that I was able to shove him aside—pretty hard. It felt good. When he fell I strode to the door. He was on my back with a gurgle of anger. Fortunately he held no weapons of any kind. In the movies he would have had a fireplace poker. But this was no movie and it was L.A. where there are precious few fireplaces and fewer pokers. I swung around and bashed him in the chest as hard as I could. It sent him reeling backward and he fell onto the floor, in tears of humiliation and pain. I heard his head knock against a small wood coffee table, but it was no big deal. I wish it had been an anvil. He got to his feet and I kept my eyes on him as I backed to the door. More muffled sounds.

Forester couldn't keep me out. And he didn't head for the phone. I pushed the door open and glanced back to see what was there. Spread-eagled with ropes on the bed, gagged and blindfolded, was one of Sam's boys, probably one of his students. Beside the blindfold, he was wearing only some pubic hair. No wonder Sam didn't want to call the police.

I took another glance back at the b.m.o.c. and then edged sideways to push open the other door. Another bedroom—empty, and a bathroom connecting the two bedrooms. Nobody else. Sam stood between me and the egress. I figured that I had seen enough—enough to satisfy me that he was not the one I should be pursuing and enough that he would not want to have anything more to do with me—with the constabulary or anyone else. To reinforce this, I said as I walked purposefully out,

"The police would like to know something about this. So would the university. Goodbye Sam. Now you can go back and play it again."

TWENTY FOUR

I sat in my car for a moment, partly to let the rage and trembling settle, and partly because I didn't know what to do. A vague idea formed, and as I drove home I knew where I was headed.

As far as I could tell, Caligula was at the center of all this. He wanted the little book, as he had made clear several times. He had the muscle to get what he wanted. And his shadiness in the world I was familiar with made him look like a thug who wouldn't let the law get in his way.

But how to get to him. The best way, I thought, would be full frontal. But I needed Coster to back me on this. Coster once told me he and his men were there to watch my ass. I thought at the time: "To watch my ass get blowed up." The problem with ass watchers is that they are necessarily behind, where the ass is. I needed someone to be beside me or in front of me. But we had nothing concrete to go on, and I wasn't sure Coster would—or even legally could—let me have Lou or Bud for my intended confrontation with Mr. Myers.

And what would Myers do that he hadn't already done? He had me punched out—my face still throbbed where the half-golf-ball puffed up—and he and his thugs and his thuggy family wouldn't let me get close again. And even if I did, why should I expect that there would be a different outcome? No, I had to get Myers alone, in a compromising position, if possible. Without his paid muscles, he was still a powerful figure, but I was no slouch. I'd like to say that I was a boxer in college. Or that my martial arts experience of ten years was sitting dormant. But I never boxed except at a grocery store as a kid. And, as Stacy's departure proved, I was a failure at marital arts (it's all the same no matter how you spell it). I didn't know a judo chop from a tai chi or a chai tea.

I had driven around for a while looking for an angle, a pathway. I needed some coffee. Well, that is what you'd expect of some comic book hero. But I was more a victim of a little pamphlet at the moment, so I drove over to Crocker's to have some hot chocolate. It was by now 9:00 o'clock, and the dinner folks were filtering out like the thin coffee they served. Molly wasn't there. Too bad. I could use a lecture of some kind. I ordered a doughnut with the chocolate. What an outstandingly disgusting repast that was! I hate doughnuts. But isn't that what you're supposed to order when you pop into a diner for a snack? The one I got was pasty, dried out, and so gummy that I needed every bit of the hot chocolate to wash it off my palate. But the grease stuck up there, and . . . . I needn't dwell on this. I had better lucubrations to lucubrate.

Getting Myers alone. The son of a bitch. Getting him alone.

But I *did* once have Myers alone: in my shop. He wanted the book, and he sort of exposed himself for it. Could I get him there again? Probably not alone. He was pretty wary by now, and he must have known that I was at the end of my string. My appearance at his home would have alerted a corpse to my anger and desperation. The only thing I had to lure him in was the book. But I didn't have the book. But he didn't know this. But I did. But it was all I didn't have, and I was going to use it.

* * *

When I got home it was after 10:00 p.m. The apartment still smelled faintly of Terry, and I almost reeled with nostalgia, pain, fatigue, and longing. My face hurt so much it distracted me from the lacerations, the bullet hole, and the shattering ringing in my ears. But over all this was a complex confusion of need to sleep, need to do something about getting Terry (and the book) back, and planning for my next assault. Funny, would that be one on me or one I conducted? Who knew?

I took a long hot shower, averting my lumpy cheek from the attacking water. It felt good to get the sweat of anger and frustration and pain off my body, and I wished I had Terry in there to do my back and other parts.

When I was done, I got my clothes on and went out to the mail box. Was it just in movies that ransom notes were mailed or slipped under doors? I expected phone calls. But the mail beckoned anyway, and I didn't know what I'd find. Phone bill. Solicitation for a VISA card. Titanium! No shit! After gold came Platinum. I never thought that would be superseded. What would be next? White gold platinum titanium diamonds emeralds rubies VISA card, with all of the rights and privileges thereto pertaining (including a usurious interest rate and an obscene yearly fee). I hated these suckers and usually pulled out the postage-paid envelope and sent it back empty. They'd pay postage and handling; I'd get what little satisfaction I could from adding to their work. Tonight I dumped it into the garbage.

Postcard ads for a painter, a roofer, and a local cable company. A blank envelope. This obviously was hand delivered. It made me shake a bit. I dropped everything else and stood there, almost in awe. Should I drop it and let the police check it for fingerprints and lip prints and DNA? I had already handled it, and I wasn't sure, anyway, if you could get prints from paper. I turned it over in my hand and looked at the back. Nothing there. But interestingly, the envelope had been sealed, then sliced open, and then re-sealed with a strip of tape across the slit, almost the full length of the envelope.

Playing Sherlock Holmes, I looked carefully at the tape to see if I could make out a fingerprint where someone held the tape. Nothing.

Something about the envelope. I didn't know what, but there was something about the envelope. My fatigue was completely gone, and my senses were heightened by adrenaline and fear and anticipation. With an X-acto blade I carefully slit the tape, not wanting to disturb the envelope at all. Inside I found a sheet of paper with the simple message: "No book? No Terry!" written in black ink, direct block letters. No one's handwriting. I stared at this for about a minute—seemed like much longer. Then I looked back into the envelope and saw what gave me a jolt: a lock of fine, auburn hair. Looked just like Terry's. Oh shit!

TWENTY FIVE

Was this really Terry's? Was this a warning? I know it seems bizarre, but I had the gruesome thought that at least it wasn't an ear or a part of a finger.

Too late to call Coster. Too late to do practically anything. And the plan I had formed would have to wait till the morning. In utter exhaustion I decided that going to bed was the only thing I could do then. So I fell into bed for a miserable night of half sleep half nightmare. I once read in a Nabokov novel about the term Ephialtes, meaning a nightmare with feverish symptoms, suffered by people who are haunted by the night-hag called Ephialtes. I'm sure that whatever I experienced that night made Effy look like Minnie Mouse.

I was up by six because I was up by five because I was up by four. Another shower didn't help. Coster wasn't in, of course, but I left a message for him. I went back to the envelope. Scrutinized it. It had been sealed then opened. Why? Did whoever sent it put the note in and then open it to add the hair? As an additional warning? But something else caught my attention. The slit along the top wasn't complete. Looking at the envelope from the back, I could see that a sharp edge had been used to open the envelope, but a tiny bit of the flap part was still stuck to the other part where the slit had not gone all the way through the fold. And the connected part was on the right.

I'm right handed. When I slit open an envelope I hold it in my left hand and use the letter opener in my right. So the first part of the cut would slit open the far right part of the folded flap. If that part was uncut, then it looked as if the person cutting the envelope used his left hand. Not much of a clue, but there it was. It's just the kind of thing I might have read about in one of those mystery books I had sold at the beginning of my career. Then again, it could have been opened by anyone, not the original message writer; and it could have been done by a right-handed person who happened to open his envelopes with his left. Pretty thin little clue.

Time to act. I pulled Caligula's card from my wallet and dialed. I got the voice of a serious and disgruntled man. His Hello showed that he was not fully cognizant of the world. I guess 6:45 a.m. calls were not his specialty. I said only: "The book. My shop. Today. One. Alone." I heard a grunt and then I repeated it, with pretty strong emphasis on the last word. I concluded firmly with "Tell him!" and I hung up.

My next stop was Crocker's, at 7:30. I had an appointment.

* * *

The early morning crowd at the diner was always subdued, as if shaking off night cobwebs and girding loins for the day. Coster had indeed followed up on the unnamed person who had answered my query about the little death book. But he said he couldn't trace it since it had been sent from the Fairfax branch of the Public Library. I had gone there to ask about the users of their terminals, but the librarians told me about confidentiality and the fact that they didn't monitor the use of their monitors. (What was the good of calling them that, then?) I told Librarian Marion that I deeply needed information. She seemed to perk up. She was, after all, the reference librarian of the branch. One of my librarian customers once told me that the bottom line for librarians was access: if a patron needs information you supply it. He said that in his Reference course in Lib. School the instructor asked, "If you are approached by a woman who wants to know how much arsenic it takes to kill a 185-pound man, where to get it, and how to administer it, you gotta tell her. Your job is to dispense information, not to question motives."

Armed with this, I approached Marion with a request for information:

"I need to find out something. Are you the Reference Librarian?" (Dumb question: she was sitting under a sign that said "Reference.") She knew it was dumb, but she answered straightforwardly: "Yes."

"I need access to some information." I was laying it on too thickly. I was afraid she'd see through the thickness. But she remained professional.

"What can I do for you?"

"A person who contacted me from here has information I need. Can I leave a note for him? At the computer terminals? I have a little note I could put up on the wall."

"I'm sorry, sir, but we can't do that."

I said that I was offering the other person information and getting it from him. I told her I was a bookseller who needed to know about the value of books—a word I stressed as I subtly gestured about me. I told her I was selling books to academic and public libraries and I didn't want to overcharge them, and this man had information I needed. This seemed to make sense to her. And I said, the note is quite simple and innocuous. I had printed onto a sheet of paper: "Please contact me about the *Büchlein*. It's confidential." And I had my name and Celia Brothers' phone number. It was the only message I could think of that would not be picked up by fuzzy ears.

When Marion agreed to my request, she did it with a touch of hesitation and a stare at me that bespoke some deep secret. I said, "Yes?"

"Well, it's just . . . ."

"Yes?"

"You're the second person to come in here with a request like this one."

"Who was the other?" As if I didn't know.

"He said he was from the Police Department."

"Did you give him any information?"

"Well . . . no."

"Why not?"

"What he said. He said he was from the Police Department and he needed some information about one of our patrons."

"What did you say?"

She thought a second. "Librarians are trained not to give out personal information—circulation information, home phone numbers, and so forth. Even under subpoenas we won't do it. Some of us have gone to jail because we refused to give out such information."

"Really?" I played dumb, though of course I knew all about it. I wanted her to say her piece.

"Oh, yes. He asked directly about information about one of our patrons. I couldn't tell him anything."

"What about me?"

"Mr. Burgess," she said, looking at my card, "You said you wanted to exchange information with someone about books and libraries. You were not asking for private information."

Sometimes your approach, only partially thought out, turns out to have been serendipitously the best possible.

"Miss Marion," I said. She looked puzzled. "Thank you for your professionalism." Her puzzlement turned to a querulous smile and I retreated from the field.

A couple of days later I got the message I was waiting for. The man identified himself as Mr. Smith. (Oh, puh-leez.) We would meet at Betty's at 7:30 a.m.

So here I was.

After several candidates entered, I saw Mr. Smith. Clearly not related to Carl. Tall, wiry, shifty-eyed (well, in that respect he was Carl's cousin), nervous, intent. Well made but seen-better-days clothes: suit, mis-tied tie. Graying hair not perfectly combed, but not bad. He hadn't shaved in a couple of days, though he wasn't seedy. But the thing that stood out most was his posture: tall but he seemed short. He was sort of bent over at the waist and his head was pulled down to his shoulders (or his shoulders were pulled up to his head) as if he was trying to hide.

The wrinkle on his brow and his shifting eye contact told me he was looking for someone he was unfamiliar with. I stood up and beckoned him to the booth at the back of the diner. He wanted to sit with his back to the rest of the customers.

"I'm Elliot Burgess."

He nervously shook my hand and mumbled, "Frank Smith."

We sat looking at one another for a long time—well, not so long, but I guess I'm supposed to say things like that. I wanted him to talk, even though his countenance told me he wanted me to talk.

"Look, I'm not sure . . . ." He stopped.

"Neither am I, Mr. . . . "

"I said I'm Frank Smith."

"Mr. whoeveryouare. Did you answer my request for information about a little book?" I had sent the bombers a question about the dangerous *Buchlein*.

He sat quietly, jittery, looking at me.

I said to him, "Look, Mr. I am a law-abiding private citizen." I put one of my business cards in front of him. "I sell books. I need information about one of them. I need to know what you know." He said nothing. "I need to know why you're here."

"I need money."

Now we're getting somewhere. Real information. What I knew about this Smith had just about tripled in the last few seconds.

"Who doesn't?" I said.

"The only reason I'm here . . .," he said almost trembling. I had to do something to calm him before he lost it. I figured a bit of humor couldn't hurt.

"Are you hungry?" He sure looked hungry. Though anyone that thin *would* look hungry.

I motioned Molly over. This was a gamble, but I had to take it.

"Hi, Elliot. What's yer pleasure."

"Tuna sandwich. But my friend can use a good meal. How's the goulash?"

I knew the goulash had been made yesterday. This was Molly's cue, and was she on stage today!

"Goulash's always fine. You know that. You daft to ask such a thing? But if I was you I wouldn't order that. It's good, mind you, but, hey! it's just not as good as other things. Betty says I should talk up the goulash. But I ain't no liar. It's good. But the pot roast's better. Really better. I mean levels better. Course, if you really want goulash, far be it from me to talk you out of it. I like the goulash. But on a day like today," she said with a piercing eye, "I wouldn't like the goulash as much as the pot roast. You like pot roast, mister?"

Smith didn't have time to reply. He never knew what hit him.

"Why, anyone who likes meat likes pot roast. And that's double for Betty's pot roast. Double, I say. But then again, you got yer veal cutlet and yer ham steak. Both just fine. Finer than the goulash, if you get my drift. But if you want goulash, it's yours. But don't tell me later on that you really wanted pot roast or veal. It'll be too late for that, mister!" A light went on somewhere between the ears: "Hey! You ain't like one of them other friends of Elliot's, are you. A *vegetarian*?"

Smith's half headshake was all she got and it was all she needed to steer the lecture in another direction, but not until she had gotten in the last anti-veggie shot:

"Vegetarians! Don't know a good thing till it bites 'em. No meat! Huh! Stupid plant lovers."

Where to go from here? I just let Molly take her natural course, and she was in pretty good form for so early in the morning.

"So you got yer choice, mister. Goulash, veal, ham, pot roast. Or something else. What else? Well, just look at the damn menu, mister. We got lots of meat. Herds of it. And it all comes with sides like carrots or corn or rice or other vegetables. But ya gotta eat the meat before you waste yer time with the vegetables. Betty don't cook 'em none too long, anyway, and when you eat one of her pieces of cauliflower it practically bites back. Practically raw, it is. Like the carrots and the broccoli. And the zookinny too. Why heat 'em up if you ain't gonna make 'em chewable? When I eats my vegetables, I don't wanna hear 'em crunchin' in my head. Meat don't do that. It lets you alone. But then there's mashed potatoes. They's vegetables, but they're quiet to eat. And the best part is you can slather gravy all over 'em—*meat* gravy. Potatoes is good. Especially the mashed ones. And Betty makes 'em great: little garlic, little pieces of burnt onions—well, not really burnt, but near-burnt; sweet-like—and lots of *meat* gravy. You like meat gravy? It's good. Lots of beef fat and flour and salt. God, mister, you gotta get something with the meat gravy."

Smith was dumbfounded. And disarmed. He was still quite nervous, but he had been relieved of having to do the thinking and fending off pointed questions for a while and a hint of relief showed in his face when Molly retreated from the battlefield. (Smith had ordered the pot roast with mashed potatoes. I couldn't wait till dessert.)

When we were face to face again, he said, "Look. I need money. You seem to have some. Your message . . . ."

"What about my message?"

"The word *Buchlein*."

"Yes?"

He didn't know how to proceed. He was still wary. I said,

"Mr. Smith. First, let me assure you that I am here solely for my own benefit, and not to the detriment of anyone else. If you are nervous about something, I guarantee it will never leave this table. Nothing here is for anyone else's ears. I need to know . . . ."

He cut in, "Not here. It's too public."

All I could think of was Celia Brothers' office. I tore off a corner of the placemat and wrote the location of the office on it for him. He said, "When?"

"Soon. Today? Eleven? In a couple of hours?"

TWENTY SIX

B illy Brinks's office was tidy and spare. Sensible Security was run by a sensible man, he told me. "No mess. No loss," he drawled. (I didn't know that "mess" and "loss" were two-syllable words.)

I had left Smith number 2 in the diner, eating pot roast for breakfast! Molly could sell a plunger to a plumber. My appointment had been for ten, but the Smith meeting broke up early and Jefferson Blvd. wasn't too far, so I got there by nine. The long warehouse looked boring and metal from the outside. Inside, it was exactly the same. Long corridors with no bend in the halls—long vistas of linoleum and institutional gray paint. Doors staggered on either side of the corridor. Sensible was about a third of the way down on the left. I know that Coster's tails were there. But they couldn't know why *I* was there. After all, I was just a client speaking to the one who had installed my security system.

"Mr. Brinks."

"Call me Billy. What happened to your face?"

"An obstreperous door." I think he didn't know one of those words, but he didn't let on.

"Ok, Billy. I need your help."

"When we put in your system, you said the same thing. Gol dern, man, get it right. If you want my help, have me do it all at once. Another meetin' like this, another contract. It'll cost you more the more you come by."

"No. Not that kind of help. I'm going to challenge you." It was like my Librarian Ploy: hit 'em where they are proudest and most responsible.

He squinted like a cowboy facin' west at dusk. He asked cautiously, "What's the challenge?"

"First I gotta tell you a few things."

I explained the little book—how it came and went; the arrival of Terry and the bombs and Coster and gunshots. I didn't tell him about the two Smiths. That might have scotched the deal. I wanted him curious, proud, and in a place to show off, not nervous, scared, or in a place to die.

"When you first looked at my place you said that no place can be made 100% secure. Did you mean that?"

"O' course I did. No place."

"Why do you say that?"

"Well" (sounding like about three syllables as he held onto that vowel), "First off, there's always a chink. Every system in the world can be busted. Even if it takes a bomb to knock it all out, that'll do it."

"What else?"

Another "Well." Waiting through the "wells" was going to challenge my patience. "I guess the final thing [did he say "thang"?] is that someone put it in. So that person knows its weaknesses. Even if six different companies are called in to install separate systems on one place, the system that installer number one put in is as weak as installer number one knows. He knows where it is, how it works, and how to go around it. Now, that ain't always the case since double systems or triple can be put one on top of another by different companies. So in the failure of one, one or maybe two are there as backups and the installers don't know which is where."

"You said that no place is 100% safe."

"I shore did. 'Cuz here's the thing. In this business you gotta instill confidence. You gotta show the client that his place is safe. I mean *safe*. It takes gumption and ego and all them other pride things to convince your clients that they are safe. Anyone in my business ever say, 'Well, that's a pretty good system, but it's got flaws'? I do that since I know what I'm doing. And it's a way for me to avoid getting sued. I say 'Your place can't be entered' and someone enters. My ass is fescue."

"So?"

"Well, most people in this business won't never say such a thing. They say with authority, 'No one's getting in here.' Customers pay big dollars, they want the best. They're told that they got the best. Who's gonna put in a double or triple system? Nobody."

"Nobody?"

"Well" [I do wish he'd stop welling], "Only once did I see that. I did a slam-bang job on a place and when I was doing it I saw the work of one of my buddies in the house too. Big place. Lots of pictures and dishes all around. My buddy's good. Henry. Red-Handed Security Company. He did a good job. But my stuff was better and was more than a back-up. And even my stuff could have been backed up again. Whoever puts in the last back-up system knows all the stuff that comes before. We know where to put what systems: cameras, heat sensors, and on and on. We know the obvious places and the not so obvious places. Let's face it, there are only so many spots in a confined place like a house to put the security. 'Course, you can line every wall and floor of the place with steel. And you can have the best hired guns in the world to guard the shack. But who's to say they won't get greedy."

"So, if I were to ask you to break into a place—just hypothetically—you think you can do it?"

"Easy. Just give me a few hours of scouting out. I can probably even spot the outside signs and know who did the work. We all have our own signatures. Then I could mosey over to Henry's and say, 'Hey, buddy; saw your fine work at the Moneybags house.' Likens to not he'll tell me all about it. I can say, 'Yeah, but did you put the eyebeam behind the mirror?' and he'll know it was just professional chat. No secrets since we're law-abiders."

I then dropped the bomb. (Oh, my god; not more bombs.) "I want to break into a house."

He stared at me. No expression.

Then he said, "What if I tell the police?"

I anticipated this. "Do you have a wife?"

"Girlfriend."

"Do you love her?"

"Pretty Damn." I guessed this was positive.

I reiterated what happened to Terry, whatever that was. I still wasn't sure where she was or in whose hands. "What would you do if you were in my position?"

"Maybe go to the police."

"Done. Nothing. What then?"

"Maybe wait."

"Wait for what? Would you wait?"

He wouldn't answer the first. To the second he said, "No."

"Then what?"

"Listen, Mr. Burgess. This is serious business. I don't do nothing illegal. Clean I am. I got a friend who had a business like mine. Spent one four-year gig in prison. Got out and had to do another business. He wasn't able to be certified any more in this one. Lost everything he had. Me too."

"I'm not asking you to break into any place."

"Then what?"

"Look at a house. Look for its chinks. Tell me how to get in. I'll do the rest. I'm gambling that there is only one system. I'm gambling that I can break it with your knowledge. You take me on as a . . . student. You are just training me to enter the trade. You know of nothing about my intent or my circumstances."

"What if I do?"

"All it does is let me get more information about the woman I love. The one I want to protect." I tried to play on his masculinity with that one.

"It's dangerous. I don't mean for me. I'll just teach you. But for you. If this guy is as careful and bloody as you say he is, then breaking through one system may be leading you into a worse one. You're safe when you're outside. You're in danger inside, no matter how much you broke the system."

"I need information. From you about one thing. All I want is information. Then I can seek professional help." Did I mean Coster and his Cops? I don't know. It was a way of getting through Billy's system.

"And I'll pay you for your services."

"Of course you will. $125 an hour plus expenses."

"You're on."

We shook hands and Billy Brinks promised to get back to me late that night. I gave him Celia's phone number. The plan I worked out with him seemed simple enough, at least from his end. I gave him the address, the go-ahead, and a check. If things went the way I wanted, in 24 hours I'd be out of the woods. Or out of the world.

* * *

Celia's office was once again my haven. Solitude, no tails. If they were there, they were watching my car, but my car was parked outside Weaver's house. Abe's normally garaged car was in the parking lot outside the English Department. At eleven on the money I heard feet in the hall. Two of them. And a moment later Mr. Smith # 2 was sitting across from me, only slightly less nervous, but just as semi-sheveled.

"I want to know your name."

"I told you."

"You lied. One Mr. Smith in this story is enough. And he lied too." And died.

His lucubrations took about 40 seconds. I was in no hurry. I had plenty of time till my one o'clock appointment with the dictator.

Smith shifted. Squirmed. And said, "My name is Simon Johnson."

"Johnson! Johnson! Right!"

"No. It really is."

"I.D." He didn't like being barked at, but he reached into his pocket and pulled out a driver's license. Simon Johnson, address in the Crenshaw district (not a lush abode), height 6'2" (he didn't seem that tall), brown hair, picture of a scared child with wrinkles from the corners of his mouth and on his forehead. For some reason I had a pang of sadness for this man.

"What's your story, Simon?"

"Your email message."

"What about it?"

"You asked in it about a German book."

"What have you got to do with that book? Anything?"

"No, but . . . ."

"Simon, I want some straight answers. You look as if you are in a mood to give them to me." I was trying to grease the skids here. I could be the strong one. He could be the submissive one. Then we'd get somewhere. But I didn't want to push too hard.

"What do you want to know?" He was hesitant, but my forcefulness almost put him at ease. He was relenting to my control.

"What do you know about bombs?"

It practically knocked him over. (I guess I could have said something like it hit him like a bombshell, but that would have been too obvious.)

"How did . . . ? Why do you want to know?"

"Don't answer my question with a question. Tell me about bombs." His reaction told me I was on the right path.

"I've been out of the pen for four years. In for five. I haven't done a thing illegal. I am working mostly as a shoe salesman in a K-Mart, sometimes in the kids' clothing department. Sometimes they have me wash the floors and pick up all the stuff. People who shop there are such slobs."

"Where do you work?"

"The one on Third near Fairfax. It's a mess. Like a third world country sometimes. And minimum wage. I can hardly pay my bus fare back and forth."

"So you need money?"

"Really bad."

"Do you have a family?"

"My wife and two little girls left when I was in jail. Haven't seen or heard from them in six years."

"So what's this about the book?"

"Someone came to me about a three weeks ago." Just after I got the book of death. "Said he wanted me to do some of my old stuff."

"Demolitions?"

"Yeah. I learned it in the Army. Easy to do big or little stuff. I could do anything. A bunker or a pinhead. Just give me the opening and I could do anything."

"Anything?"

"Anything. All I got to do is get in, or out, or even near. I had the best training. Big enough to take out a building. Small enough to take out a pea."

"How about the lock on a safe?"

"A cinch. And with no damage to anything but the lock."

"And a door to an apartment?"

"Sure. I can mess the whole apartment up, with or without a fire, or just the door. Or just a small place in a room."

"When's the last time you did it?"

I was half hoping he would tell me about my little Hancock Park home (what was left of it) or my shop. At least that question mark could be erased.

"Before I was arrested. Maybe nine, ten years ago. Five years in jail and four clean ones since."

"What was the last thing you bombed?"

"A jewelry store. My friend. Friend!" Said with disgust. ". . . got me in. Said the alarms were off. I got to the big safe. Huge mother. I had it open in about two, maybe three minutes. But the alarms weren't off. It took the police only a few minutes to get there and there I was. Alone."

"And the damage?"

"Practically none. But the safe was open. Two quick charges, one on the outside and one inside. Plastic, stuck on just right."

I thought for a moment. This is just the skill I need. But was it for sale?

"Ok, Simon. You mentioned a German book. What's that all about?"

"It's what your ad was about."

"So?"

"So it caught my eye because another person wanted me to get a German book for him. The guy said he wanted me to find it for him and it was probably in a safe. In a bookstore."

"Did you know who owned that store?"

"No."

"Do you know now?"

"No. We never got that far. I told him I was through blowing. I wanted to keep out of prison. He offered me a lot of money. I mean, a ton of money. Like $2,000." The number was right for a ton, but the amount was way off. If he had only known what he was being asked to do, he might have negotiated for more. Pretty sad that that small amount seemed like a bundle to him.

"The guy told me it was just a little book, a German book. I remember it had the words Book Line in the title. Then I saw your message and I wondered if it could be the same one. I left a message from the library. No one could find me that way. But you did."

Good old Marion. Connecting the patrons with the information they need.

"Who was the man who approached you? Where did you meet him?"

"Came and sat at my table at lunch at K-Mart. I don't know who he was. Strong-looking guy with good clothes. Dark glasses. Didn't take them off."

"How old was he?" I remember the two Myerses well, and telling them apart would not be easy.

"Can't say. Anywhere from 30 to 60. Smooth face. Built solid. Couldn't see his eyes."

"How did he know that you were a bomb person?"

"I have no idea. There was a time before I got caught when people knew me and could call me. Not any more. I don't know practically anyone. And no one knows me."

My mind was racing. An idea formed that scared the shit out of me. And I felt that I had to act on it.

"Listen, Simon. I will ask you to do a job for me, and I will pay you well. But it must be completely discreet. No one must know about this. I swear I will pay you well and you will not be in any danger of any kind if you do the job you say you can do."

He looked hesitant and fearful.

"If you can do what you say, you will not break or enter. No one will be hurt. Nothing will be stolen. That is not what I am about on this. And I can almost guarantee that no police will be involved."

He sat there noncommittally. Just looking at me. I waited for a reaction.

"I have to know what it's all about."

"No, you don't. The less you know the better for all of us. I was told that certain bombers . . . ."

I could see him wince a bit. The thought was pretty powerful in him, and the words were too harsh.

". . . certain experts in your former profession" (that was better) "leave their so-called fingerprints on a job. Can you do one that cannot be tied to you?"

"Easy." He was in a more communicative mode when we were talking about what he knew well.

"Explain."

"If all you want is little things, pretty much anyone who knows his stuff would do it the same way. A little explosive placed just right."

"If you can guarantee anonymity—you know, that you won't be identifiable—and I can too, what are the chances that you could be identified?"

"Pretty slim. Depends where it is and how far away I can get in, say, four or five minutes."

"It's a residence."

"Any alleys? Lots of houses? Busy streets?"

"Alleys, yes. Houses and streets, not many. Fairly remote but not far from Sunset Boulevard. Place your car well and you can be on Sunset in a few seconds—under a minute."

"What about my bus?"

Oh, yeah. He took the bus.

"I think you'll be able to get away, lost in the streets behind the house."

"What's it all about?"

He had to know something. Like, why there would be no theft or mutilation of people I'd like to mutilate. So I told him about Terry and Caligula. That was all I needed to tell him. "I think she is in that house. If I can get all the information you need to pop off the alarms—where they are and what kind—can you do it?"

"Easy."

"For $2000 would you do it?"

He didn't like the direction of this, but he squinted and pierced me.

"What do you want me to do?"

* * *

After we talked, and I had laid out my plan (sounds pretty cloak-and-dagger), I reconfirmed with my main man in security. Billy Brinks was ready and willing and able. Simon was already given the scoop and some cash that he said he needed. I asked why and he said, "The less you know about this the better, for both of us." He seemed to know where to get what he needed and how much it would cost. He had the phone number I had given him. And the PIN. (I refuse to make the redundant error of calling it a PIN Number. Even in tense and painful times, when my mind is elsewhere, I am still bothered by my pet peeves.)

Both of them promised efficiency and discretion. They had the afternoon off and the inclination, greased by Mammon. And now, it was

* * *

time for the face off. Bud and Lou were still planted discreetly outside Abe's house. When I called him from Celia's office before leaving, he said they were as hidden as the Empire State Building. I needed to do this on my own.

I got back to my shop at 12:30 and worked on tidying up, since there were still piles and messes all over the place. The blood spot on the floor was horrible to contemplate, but it just made my adrenalin work more. I didn't want to join Dave.

Billy had installed panic buttons in several places in the shop, and I was going to plant myself within reach of the floor-mounted one behind the counter. The constabulary, already on high alert for my place, wouldn't take long to get there if I needed them.

Then I readied my 16-function watch with the laser beam, my exploding chewing gum, and my x-ray glasses . . . . Well, that's what James Bond would have done. I felt as if I could use something like those now. But that put me into the Double O mentality and I grabbed a tiny box cutter—plastic with a small retractable razor blade—and stuck it into my shoe. Was I nuts?! What was I thinking? That I was a double agent? Trained by the Federation to do mind melds and Vulcan Death Grips? No. It was just the only "weapon" that I had.

One o'clock came fast, and so did Caligula, alone. He strode in as if he could afford the place. And he was not happy.

"Ok, Mr. Burgess. No more. I want the book. What was it you wanted me here for?"

"Terry." It was all I could think of saying. I had planned out the conversation, but it took its own direction.

"I just want the book. You can charge me whatever you want—within reason. I'm willing to go to $30,000. No more. And no more stalling."

"Mr. Myers." I was trying to contain my anger. "You skirt issue after issue. Where is Terry? Is she safe? If you want the book . . . ."

"Look, you son of a bitch! You keep talking about this Terry. I have not committed myself about this because if you think I have something you want I'm willing to let you continue to think that I still have it. I want the book. It was mine. It still is. I shouldn't have to pay a cent for it, but it means a lot to me."

Here he was badly making it up. Means a lot to him. So do his hemorrhoids. Probably more than the book. But he had said something that surprised me: he implied that he and Terry were not related in any way.

"How much do you want for it?"

"I want information and I want Terry."

That wasn't too convincing, but it's what I meant.

It was clear that Myers was at the end of his own patience. He reached into his pocket and before I knew it, Howard (Central Casting) was in the shop, at me in a split second (terrible cliché; can you really split seconds?). Before I knew what hit me (another dumb cliché—I knew what hit me) I was on the floor, my head swimming in the familiar stars-and-stripes of Howie's fist. I was held in place by more muscles than anyone ought to have. It was so sudden that I hadn't thought of the panic buttons. My own panic was in place, however, and it was clear that struggle would get me another punch.

"Look, you bastard. Stop fooling with me. Where's my book?"

"I was going to ask you the same question. And where's Terry?" Not a good reply; Myers nodded to muscles and I got another, mercifully lighter, bop on my chin. I hate it when that happens. "Stop!" I gurgled. I was still dazed and it was all I could think to say.

"Mr. Burgess, I don't know what you are talking about." He paused.

Was he talking about Terry or the book? or both?

"Just shut up. Let's go." He stood over me like a tower and pointed at his watch: "Your time is up!"

Howie hoisted me, limp from pain but limper from fear, by my lapels and shoved me out the door of the shop. A limo was waiting. Jesus! this was looking more and more like a B movie. Inside, I was crunched against someone on one side, Casting on the other. Muscles pinned me. I knew some of them belonged to Howard and, turning a bit, caught the face of Blake, half grinning, half scowling, and half being a superior prig. He grabbed my left arm and twisted it to the small of my back, a pretty deft move in the confines of the seat.

The limo pulled away from the curb smoothly and elegantly. Funny how I thought that, with my face and left shoulder burning and my life flashing before someone's face—not mine; I was too scared for anything to flash except my nerve endings.

The ride was tense for me, but eerily subdued for the others. We were undoubtedly going to the Myers mansion. I could see the silent and almost motionless driver ahead of me and Blake and Howie on either side. But I couldn't see Caligula. Blake held my left arm painfully behind me, and muscles pressed me powerfully on the other side. I was in no position, condition, or mood for heroics.

The house was foreboding as we approached. I was in a total funk: frustrated beyond measure in being so helpless and so angry. My anger would need some release. I felt like exploding. Like a bomb. Like an incendiary device.

They hustled me into the library again—symbolic, I thought. My little pamphlet—my little ex-pamphlet—would hardly be seen in this huge collection. I wondered where it was—my little Book of Death.

And then we were all there: Eddie and Blake and Howie and Theresa (how could I forget her name! or her face!) and me. I was scrunched down in a fat armchair—soft leather, good padding, but not very comfortable. At least, not then. My face stung and throbbed, my eyes were not perfectly in focus, and I noticed that once again my teeth did not meet up perfectly. I'd have to see my orthodontist. Overdue.

"No more shit, Mr. Burgess." Howie spoke with more than authority—it was barely restrained anger. "Where's the book?"

Telling him I didn't have it was useless. Whenever I told him the truth in the past, I got hit or bombed (incendiary deviced) or whatever. I had to come up with a plausible lie—or a stalling tactic. But I could hardly think straight.

"I can hardly think straight."

"You better think. Your time's running out."

I thought also that mentioning Terry was just as useless. It never got a clear response from him, and if he was intent on skirting that issue, I had better, too.

"I think I can get the book to you."

"You think? You think that's going to get you out of here? Not yet."
Caligula was playing the emperor, pulling the strings, dealing the cards,
and doing all those other cliché metaphors. "Before you get out of here,
I want to think. Howard and Blake, take him to the blue room."

The blue room, for god's sake! I was blue enough. And black and
blue. And bombed by incendiary devices. And bulleted. And bashed.
What more could he do?

The blue room turned out to be a nice bedroom with—guess
what!—blue linens and wallpaper. It also had barred windows. Typical
of houses in Los Angeles: what the realtors would have called decorative window coverings; what the police would have said were to keep
burglars out; what Myers would have said were to keep prisoners in. It
was pretty impregnable, from either side of the wrought iron, but they
were going to make sure I stayed put. Howie had some rope and did a
real hogtie on me, hands and feet, behind my back. All four limbs immobilized as one. At least the bed was comfortable. Well, nothing was
comfortable hogtied and punched out and with my dignity ruffled. But
it could have been worse.

It was mid-afternoon, but the heavy curtains were pulled and the
room was in shadow. I was facing the window, with the door behind
me. Damn, they had done a good job with these ropes.

One thing gnawed at me. Not once in all of my dealings with daddy
had he tried to use Terry as a bargaining chip. He could have said, 'You
want your honey back? I want my book back.' What did he know? Was
he too cagey? Was he using Terry as a last resort? Where the hell was
Terry?

In my less than liberated situation I heard some pretty heated voices,
though their words ebbed and flowed so that I couldn't quite get the
gist of the rant. Something boiling was going on among these thugs
and their ravishing princess. Theresa. Oh, what a nymph. To have gotten mixed up with . . . .

"Goddam you. I want it." And "Mine." And "Fuck off." And "You
don't know how . . . ." I heard the words, but I could not really tell who
the speakers were. I heard what sounded like "Ambrose," more than
once. It sounded like two bullish voices—probably pop and son Myers

since Theresa's voice wouldn't have had that basso and Howie was hired more for his muscles than for his vocal chords. But the back and forth was interrupted now and then by silence—or by a voice too little to make it to the blue room.

I was miserable. My wrists and ankles hurt from the tight ropes. My face still smarted. And to tell the truth (why would I lie?), even the old bullet wound still smarted. My muscles were starting to ache from being so immobilized. I was sweating and totally miserable. But I repeat myself.

Something. What was it? That conversation in my shop. Myers had said something that I needed to think about. Was it that suggestion that he didn't know what I was talking about with Terry? No. I had already tried, unsuccessfully, to work through that one. What was it?

More raised voices. This time there was banging and bumping, as if there were a fight going on. As if L.A. were having a 6.8. More loud noises. Was that a table that hit a wall? I even heard Theresa's voice for a second. And for a moment Howie's. Then things settled down and I heard footsteps approaching.

I saw the light from the doorway spread on the curtains I was facing. I heard a bull voice, and for a second I didn't know whose it was. It said slowly and menacingly,

"My father says that if you don't tell him where to find the book by ten tonight, you'll never see Terry again. My father doesn't lie."

That was it. The door shut softly. And there I was, helpless, immobile, and with a full bladder. In the haste of the activities of the day, I had neglected to drain my root (as my old college roomie used to say; funny, his name was Myers, too).

It must have been three thirty by now. How was I to reveal anything to anyone when I was alone in the room? I called out. "Hey!" No response of any kind. The room was pretty damn lonely.

Jesus. How many more hours of this?

I was thinking about the meeting in the bookshop. What was it that Myers had said that bothered me? The more I concentrated, the less I could concentrate.

I must have dozed off for a while because I was being shaken, and not with gentle mother's arms. "Burgess! Where's the book?"

"Blake, I'll show you where it is."

"Bullshit! Your time is running out."

"I gotta take a leak."

"Funny! You'll do anything."

"No, I really . . . ."

The punch in my back from the faceless voice told me that the gotta-take-a-leak ploy wasn't going to work.

But Blake did start to shove me forward on the bed. It was not easy for him. I weigh 185 or so. But the next thing I knew I was plopped onto my face over the edge of the bed onto a lovely hardwood floor, probably walnut, nicely polished. Good work. I fell back onto my left side again, with my back against the bed spring, on the wood floor, facing a nice oriental carpet. Probably a Bokhara. Too bad the thing wasn't a few inches closer. I got a fine bump on my forehead, and more stars appeared in my constellation.

Blake opened the door. I could hear the bastard breathing. Pushing me was no lark for him. Small consolation for me. He stood there with the door open and growled.

"In four hours Terry dies."

That was it. I almost didn't hear the door shut, but the light on the curtain, which I could still see, narrowed and disappeared.

I don't know how long I was there, but two things happened. First, I had an accident. I always had trouble micturating in odd positions (not that I had tried it in too many), but after god-knows-how-many hours, it was either have my bladder burst or get some relief. As the old ad asks: How do you spell relief? I don't know, but it starts with a P.

Second, the picture of the bookshop encounter came back to me and I had a flash: the thing that was on my mind was the moment when Myers said my time was up. He pointed to his watch. It was on his right wrist.

TWENTY SEVEN

I hate wetting myself. Water was bad enough.

I hate not being able to do what I need to. I had fought off itches all over my body. Being able to scratch must be one of the most under-rated pleasures of mankind. The pain on my forehead and through my brain was intense. I never slept without a good pillow. This lying on the floor with my head at an unnatural angle was a pisser. Hmmm.

My hands and feet were almost numb—they were at the burning stage. Thinking what to say to the Myers clan hadn't helped relieve the discomfort or brought me to the right response to their inevitable "Where's the book."

What time was it? There was no more light from outside, so it must have been nighttime, sometime. I could still make out a faint glow from under the door, reflected up dimly on the curtain.

Then I heard a fizzing and that small light disappeared. I heard someone shout, and then Howie or Blake busted into the room. It was a heavy man's shoe I heard. The feet clomped to the foot of the bed and someone looked over the edge.

"He's still there." Howie.

In a few seconds the light came on strongly, and with the door open I heard a humming and the curtain lit up.

"Any information for us?" Howie spoke as if he owned the place. "Us?" Not "them?" or "the Myerses?"

"I can tell them where the book is."

"You lying?"

Only on the floor, bastard.

"No."

Howie retreated and closed the door.

In a couple of minutes Blake came in. "What's the news?"

"The book is . . . ."

I had thought of many answers, but none seemed to be the right one.

"The book is in a safe deposit box. I am the only one who can get into it. They need the key and my signature."

Blake stood for a moment over me and then said,

"No way, asshole. Terry's key, with her, opened the box and it wasn't there."

"I moved it to another bank."

"Which?"

"Bank of America on Wilshire."

"There are a few of them on Wilshire. Which one?"

I had no idea. "The one in Beverly Hills." There surely had to be one in Beverly Hills.

Suddenly there was another fizzing sound and an alarm seemed to go off. Howie clumped in. "What's that?" he said.

"Alarm. Someone has broken the perimeter. No problem. There's plenty of back-up. Did they find out what had happened to the lights?"

"Fuckin' squirrel. Found it at the foot of the electric pole, roasted. Chewed right through the wire. Dead son of a bitch."

"Generators seem to be working."

"Right. I'll see if I can find where the alarm was set off." And out he stomped.

All this time I had not seen a human face in hours. I was talking to a hulk with Blake's voice menacingly above me, at the foot of the bed, but out of my line of vision.

"You're lying, Mr. Burgess. There would be no reason in the world to move the book from Santa Monica to Beverly Hills."

Ok, so I was lying. What would you do in my situation?

"I'm telling the truth. I wasn't sure I could trust Terry. I didn't know her well. She wanted to see the book so eagerly that I was suspicious. She is the one who convinced me to put it into a safe box that she had a key to."

He walked around to my feet and I could squint up to see him, the light from the door lighting up the left half of his face. I wanted to punch both halves. Even one half.

He kicked me in the knee, pretty hard. All it did was dull the other pains. I guess I should have thanked him for that.

"It's 9:40 p.m. Terry dies in twenty minutes unless you come up with a better story." Spoken with more seriousness than a nun's confession. With resolve. With barely controlled anger. And with a sense of finality.

"I want you to know that I have killed before. This will be easy."

Another little sound and another bell somewhere. Then another. Central Casting could be heard striding down the hall.

"What's going on?" Blake belched.

"The electricity break seems to have triggered all the alarms: windows, doors, attic, cellar" (my god, a Los Angeles house with a cellar?) "even the lanai and guest house."

"What do you mean 'triggered'?"

"The central panel shows the security system is activated just about everywhere. Shall I call the police?"

"No!" Blake was almost violent in his answer. He shouted it far more maniacally than how a normal person would have said it. "Goddam it. Goddam shit. What's going on?" He bent over me so I could see his face and he fairly yelled, "What's going on?"

I had seen his subdued power in the past. It was subdued no longer.

"Burgess! What's going on?"

I almost felt his breath, and I could smell the wine on it. Probably a Barberra from northern Italy. Early harvest. Could have been better.

"What the shit could I have to do with this, asshole. Look at me."

He stood up, kicked me again in the same knee, and shouted: "Terry dies." The next thing I knew the room was dark and four clomping feet were heading down the hall.

The lanai and the guest house. That must be where Terry was. But how could I get to her? I don't have a way to cut these fuckin' ropes. Oh, shit! I could move my feet just enough to get my left behind my right and wiggle off the shoe. Good thing I wore slip-ons. Shoelaces could have been deadly.

Then I squirmed around so that I could grab the shoe with my left hand. I gripped it with the sole in that hand and the heel facing backwards. I could just manage to get my right hand into it and feel the tiny plastic box cutter. Oh, James Bond would be so proud. Jim! I'd be like a cousin. Jim Bond, look what I did!

It was a terribly awkward angle, but I turned the little tool around between my fingers and dropped the damn thing. I had to scrunch over by raising my nearly numb legs, and I could feel the sucker sliding away from my fingertips. So I wriggled around more than I needed and raised my legs again. This time I could feel the plastic, and I was just able to grip it with my thumb and forefinger. That was just fine for pushing out the blade, but then the blade was facing the wrong way— away from my fingertips. I twisted my hands enough to transfer it to my left hand and rotated it 180 degrees to grip it in such a way that I could cut into the rope.

It was made of a soft nylon, with thousands of tiny threads. Little by little I ran the blade across the rope. In the position I was in, I couldn't even tell which part of the cord I was cutting, but it had to free up something. In five minutes my left wrist snapped loose. I had expected relief, but the pain in my shoulder was burning. I hadn't been able to move for so many hours that the joint felt frozen. (Burning? Frozen? Hmm. Mixed somethingorother.)

At that moment the door sprung open. I was still lying with my back to the bed, so I held my left hand up to the right wrist, the tool inside my right fist. In the darkness I still looked like a sheep ready for the shearing.

Blake's footsteps raised the hair on my neck. The sound of his approach scared me more than anything I had ever experienced. He was on the brink of unhingement. His breathing made it sound as if he had just run a mile.

He reached down and grabbed my jacket lapel and pulled me partly off the floor.

"Fucker." He didn't sound as if he was a happy camper. "Terry's dead. Where's the book? You don't tell me the truth now, you'll be dead too."

"It's in a safe box at the Bank of . . . ."

He dropped me and punched me at the same time. My nose must have done some damage to his hand—he hit me that hard. In fact, he yelled and brought his hand up and rubbed it with his right hand. Son of a bitch. Like father like son.

"I'll be back. I gotta get rid of the body. Don't go anywhere, asshole."
This time I heard the door slam, and then I heard it lock. Oh, what
to do? I opened my hand and felt a little moisture on it where the little
blade had cut my palm. I wasn't going to lose my only means of escape,
so I gripped this thing as if my life depended on it. It probably did.

I also felt sticky ooze on my face. My only comfort (some comfort!)
was that the blood from my nose was getting on his antique Bokhara.

In three or four more minutes my limbs were free, but I could hardly
move. Very slowly I tried to straighten out my legs and arms, but it was
as if they had rusted into place. Where was the WD-40 when I needed it?

When I finally struggled to my feet, I felt the wet pants and the
blood and the bumps and the sore knee (ooh, that one slowed me to a
gimp). The door was locked. As you would expect in a good B movie. I
went to the window and looked through the decorative wrought iron.
Impregnable. The second window likewise. Back to the door. I had to
decide if I wanted to make some kind of shoulder-into-the-door or
shoe-chop-of-the-door move as we see on tv. After all, just about every
time we see it on the tube, the shoulderers or kickers get in in one blow.
That kind of move could have busted my clavicle or scapula and alerted
opposite-side-of-the-door people that someone on the inside was up
and around. Another try at the knob. No good.

My best means of egress seemed to be the fortress windows. The
one on the left looked right out onto the back yard, where I could see
part of the lanai and all of the guest house. But it was quite exposed to
anyone at those dwellings (I thought of the volunteer firemen) or in the
yard. I opened the other window, which was mostly covered over with
a shrub, and expected to hear a bell or chime or other alarm. It was one
of the most welcome silences I had ever heard. But the iron grate was
firmly in place. I thought maybe I could do the Superman thing and
just bend the bars. But when I touched it, though it was setting exactly where it should have over the window, it shivered. I pushed and it
moved. I shoved and it gave way. The nails or screws or whatever holding it in had deteriorated and the whole lovely thing fell to the ground.

Since California has a 12-month growing season, the shrub was in
full shrub, and the leaves covered me well as I swung my legs over the
sill and dropped the few feet to the ground. Now what to do?

I grabbed the iron piece and stuck it up over the window, just where it should have been. A couple of long pins at the top fit into holes in the window frame. It looked good enough to fool a warden. Then I reached up and slid the window down into place.

The yard was lit by beams at the top of two tall poles, but it was dim and tranquil in the yard. Staying in the shadows, I moved against the house to my left, with the guest house across the yard to my right and the lanai directly across from me. Out of the bushes I was in the light, so I moved as quickly and silently as I could. When I got to the corner of the house I heard noises inside. Blake had gone into the blue room and found me gone. (Great idiom.) He looked out the window just as I turned the corner to get out of his vision. He howled, "Howard! He's gotta be in the house. Find him."

On the far side of the house there was a car—it looked like a Jaguar, but even that brand had turned too generic to identify—in a long drive, at the end of which was a garage that I couldn't see till I made the turn. The trunk was open and a dark piece of cloth hung out of it. In low quick strides I made it over there and ducked behind the car—on the opposite side of the house. Then I peeked over the skirt of the car and looked into the trunk. Something was wrapped in the dark cloth. I reached over and touched it. Something soft and stiff. It felt like a body. I heard noises coming from the house, but I *had* to look under the cloth. It was a body, all right. The cloth had been thrown into the trunk and a body dumped on top of it. The corners of the cloth had then been folded over. I felt for the head. Oh, my god! Not . . . .

TWENTY EIGHT

M y heart was racing as I backed away from the car. It's horrible to look into dead eyes that hadn't closed. As I backed toward the bushes that lined the edge of the house, I almost vomited. In the bushes I was invisible, but I was shaking and still in trouble. Blake came running out of the house and toward the car. He looked around and called for Howard, who emerged from the front of the house, the same way Blake had come.

"The bastard's gone. Where the hell . . . ."

"I don't know." This time Howard's voice was powerful and as agitated and commanding as Blake's. "What now?"

Blake stood there. I watched him from behind. I still couldn't see his face, but it was as if the eidetic image of it had frozen on my mental screen: the face staring out blindly from the trunk. My heart was still pounding.

I know that you're supposed to say that your heart is pounding. Well, it was. I could feel it bumping up against all of those things that hearts bump against when they are pounding. And I could hardly catch my breath. I dared not move because I was still in bushes. The blood had caked on my lips and my patella started throbbing. I hadn't noticed it till now. My shoulders still ached, and my wrists burned where the ropes were. But my mind was racing, and I was in a fight-or-flight mode.

Blake shouted, "Get in the car."

In a minute they were backing down the driveway away from the garage. And a few seconds later the car was gone and there was silence. I was still in the bushes, which seemed to be the first protective thing I had encountered since getting knocked over in my shop. I made my way to the back of them and found a brick wall back there. Facing the house, which I could barely see through the bushes, I worked left with the wall at my back. The wall ended about half way across the back of the yard, just adjacent to the lanai. A property behind me was dimly lit in its own glow. But it was pretty far away. These were big lots.

I looked down the wall of the lanai toward the house and could make out a huge swimming pool, the edges of which were raised along a mound of grass, which is why I couldn't see it from the house. No fence around the pool. I thought that was illegal. That's breaking the law! Why, these people should be arrested. (Oops. Have I become a "why" sayer?)

I moved behind the lanai and looked through its rear windows. I couldn't see anything inside, but I figured I had nothing to lose by breaking and entering. What could they do to me? Tie me up and kick me in the knee? Big deal. There was a back door to this pool house. I found a small stone, broke the window over the doorknob, and let myself in. Not much security, but there was little in this place to make secure.

I heard no sounds of an alarm. Looks as if Simon had earned his boodle, and a bonus. But it could be a silent alarm, still alarmed, and I was alarmed to think of this. It made me move quickly, though there wasn't much to see. There were two dressing/bedrooms, one on either side of the little house, each connected to a bathroom. Between these was a huge open room with a kitchen-like area at the back of it, bar and all, and just the front door in the front. (Which is where you'd expect to find a front door.)

The place was empty. Nobody. No bodies.

From the front window I looked across the pool over to the house. There were lights on there, and I saw a shadowy figure pass behind one of the windows on the first floor. I also saw a light go out on the second floor. Was it someone going to bed or leaving the room? Theresa was probably still in there, along with who-knows-how-many-servers—laundresses (an un-PC term, I know, but I never met a professional live-in launderer), butlers (if they still called them that), chefs, and so forth.

Gotta move fast. Out the back door of the lanai and back to bushes separating the properties. Once I was behind the guest house, I made my way to its rear door, which was actually on its far side, just far enough that I was partially screened from view of the house. The guest house was solid brick (a dumb building material for a seismic city), barred windows, well bolted deadbolts on the doors. Built like a little fortress.

I tried the side door and it swung open in a second. I didn't want to spend more time than I needed, but I looked closely at the lock: it lacked a faceplate that would have covered the crack in which the bolts were, and it had a small black charred scar at the wood line around where a faceplate might have once been. I would have gambled that at least one of the wrought-iron window-coverings was loose as well.

There were no lights on. The side door had brought me into a small, beautiful kitchen, bathed in the dark light from outside. Nothing startling there. The door to the kitchen led to a sumptuous living room connected by a half wall to a spacious dining area. More fancy carpets. Crystal chandelier. Lots of built-in cupboards with leaded glass, through which I could see what looked like Flora Danica. Good taste and big bucks. Beyond this was the living room, much larger than the building revealed from the outside. Lots of over-the-top fancy furniture. A half dozen Albrecht Durers on the wall, along with other early engraved pieces, some hand colored. I wish I had time to look. There were many museum pieces here. Too bad I wasn't in the Carl Smith trade.

On the far wall of this room was the front door, flanked by four large windows which faced out onto the yard, with the rear of the main house in view. The light in the lower window was still on, but now so were two others. There was movement there, and I was so scared that I felt one in my guts too.

There was a coat closet beside the front door. Nothing in it but some nice bumbershoots. And a pair of doors on opposite walls. I made it quickly to the first—on my right—and looked in. A tidy bedroom, filled with porcelain and paintings and costly furnishings. Nothing out of place. And still no sign of habitation.

The bedroom had its own bath, also expensively appointed, but empty. I went back into the living room and again looked outside the window. More stirring in the house and the sound of doors opening.

To the other bedroom quickly. Bingo. I saw a body on the bed, motionless. It was a woman, naked, immobile. I could see her long hair and her back and her beautiful skin. Terry's skin. I leapt to the bed and turned her from her side onto her back. She was breathing but totally incoherent. Drugs? I spoke to her softly and shook her firmly but gently. She moaned and turned slightly, but didn't open her eyes. I figured we had to get out of there—fast. Pretty clever! What else was there to do?

I lifted her up and saw that there was a chain on her right ankle, secured by a lock. The other end of the chain ran over the side of the bed and wound around the foot of the bed—an enormous iron thing that came in at heavyweight status. That end of the chain was also snapped together by a similar lock. A cheap but very effective fetter.

There was only one way to get her free: I had to lift the bed to slip the chain off the leg. But it was hernia time. It took both hands and more sweat than one should have to muster up in fifteen seconds just to get the bed off the floor. But then the chain wouldn't slip easily from the leg, which had a metal foot wider than the hole in the locked end of the chain. I dropped the bed.

Did I hear sounds in the yard?

Blake and Howie were presumably off somewhere finding a resting place for poppa. It could have been two hours away or two minutes. There were plenty of woodsy areas here, so they probably didn't have to go far.

I bent over and assessed the situation. I slid the chain down to the bottom of the bed leg, right over the wide foot. Then I stood as best I could on the chain with both feet. In a somewhat awkward position I grabbed the bottom of the bed rail again and yanked up. The chain stayed down, and the foot squeaked and cracked a little. So did my spine. I though I was going to pass out from the stabbing pain. I had to look over my shoulder to see if someone had hit me there with a rod. No one.

A second jerk up and the little foot cracked off and the chain slipped down. The bed slipped out of my moist hands and the leg landed right on top of the chain. One more half lift, this time with my feet planted better—away from the bed frame—and I was able to squish the chain out from under the leg with my right foot. Terry was free.

But she was dead weight. I tried to pick her up under the arms, but she sagged and slipped back onto the bed. Only one thing to do: I wrapped the loose chain around both her ankles, lay her out at the edge of the bed, and rolled her up in the sheet. Damn fitted sheet. It took a moment to get the four corners liberated from the mattress. Pretty soon I had cocooned Terry into the sheet and could lift her. Wow! That hurt my back. I must have torn something lifting the bed.

No time to think of that now. She was over my shoulder in a moment and I was staggering toward the kitchen. Lights went on in the yard behind me as I passed out of the living room. The side door was still ajar and I stumbled out of it as efficiently as I could.

In ten seconds I was in the bushes—*we were*—and retreating into a little copse between the Myers mansion and the neighbor's house. I got my sea legs and was moving pretty efficiently by now, and continued to move away from the house as fast as I could, not knowing where I was going. I heard a man's voice, muffled by the house, but escaping from the open side door. Something like "Not here." And then I heard the unmistakable voice of Theresa, recently widowed, but either unaware of that or unaffected by it. Her voice was strong and unflappable: "Find her."

Of course, I was dying to see what was happening back there, but I was dying even more to get away from a place where I could be dying. For the first time in days I was holding my sweet Terry, but at the moment I didn't think that way. I ducked behind and between one house after another, down the quaint little alleys one finds in Bel Air and Beverly Hills (frequented by many street people, living high off the hogs), and from street to street.

I stopped in shadows, behind trees, and even behind garbage cans, to rest. I was not in the habit of being beaten, being tied up, pissing my pants, being kicked (god! my knee hurt), and toting around a sexy naked comatose woman who was wrapped in a fitted bed sheet. In fact, I couldn't remember the last time I had done this. I was panting with fatigue and sweating with exertion and fear. That smelly sweat that makes you want to back away from people and head for the showers.

The one thing I noticed was that all my movement had been either on the level or down slopes. I must have been nearing Sunset. And then

I was on it. Not far from the northeast corner of UCLA. I don't know how I got there, but I did, and it was late enough that there were few people around.

I remember an Italian movie about a bank heist that goes totally awry and two of the perpetrators get half blown up. They look a fright, covered with black soot and unbelievably torn and tattered clothes from a poorly placed bomb—incendiary device. They are escaping from the scene of the latest blunders, stumbling along, when they see two policemen coming toward them. One of them whispers to the other, "Look dignified." I tried to follow that advice as I stumbled with my sheeted burden toward a well lighted building. It was the University Library. Gotta get away from here. I rounded it, heading west, and came to a narrow pathway with an eating court on one side, bushes on the other. The shrubs were about five feet off the ground and quite dense. But I pushed Terry up into them. Still no response from her. There on the lighted path was a pay phone. My cell was still in my shop. Remarkably, I had my change and my wallet and my watch and my life.

I ordered a cab, but didn't know where I was. I hadn't been at this area of the campus in years. All I knew was the University Library, where I had met with some librarians a few times to sell books to them. But university budgets had dried up for some years, and I had been away for a while.

All I remembered was that the Library School was behind the library, so I told the dispatcher to have us picked up in the little circular lot in front of the School. Terry was moaning slightly in her cocoon, but still completely out of it. I reached up and grabbed the sheet and pulled her down into my arms. Oh, what a thought. She was in my arms again. Life was sweet.

Oh, my back! And my shoulders still ached from their own confinement. And my nose and knees and toes. The only thing that didn't hurt was my left earlobe. There was a stone bench in front of the School, so Terry and I sat down, trying to look dignified. No one could see what was wrapped up in my sheets, but only a few slightly curious people passed. The food service had closed by now, and classes were certainly over for the day. It took about ten minutes before the cab came, and the driver got out to help me with my luggage. He couldn't see the contents of my long white bag, and he couldn't hear the very slight tinkle of the chain since he wasn't listening for it.

I waved him away and made out as if I was carrying a rug or a sculpture or a dead body. Whatever. I got us into the cab and said,

Good god. What was I supposed to say? I didn't want to go back to our apartment. That's where any self-respecting, knee-kicking, son-of-a-bitch murdering thug would expect us. I wasn't sure how long it would be before Terry would be singing or dancing, and I didn't want the cabbie to hear when it began. I had to come up, as well, with a place not too far away. I thought of a hospital, but for some reason that scared me. The logical place would have been UCLA, but I didn't like their hospital, and I didn't want Terry to wake up there. I figured that her life was probably not in danger. Drugs or something to knock her out. She'd be coming to in a while. I just wanted to be in a place away from the world. So I got us into the cab and said,

"Bel Air Hotel." It was close. Expensive, but I could do a night there without having to tighten my belt for more than a month.

The doorman—name tagged Kurt—greeted us, and I jumped out. "My wife got pretty plastered. She's not dressed. I have her in a sheet. No scene? No noise? No reports to your boss?" I held up two twenties, which was probably small change to him.

He looked at me: mashed face covered in blood. Wet pants that were beginning to be rank. Totally disheveled top to toe. Mussed hair.

"Looks like you got plastered too." He was succinct.

"I don't have more than this right now," I said, indicating the Jacksons. But there will be more. Can you get a room? Fast. Quietly? No questions."

"I believe those are quite expensive rooms," he said, with smile. "But for you . . . ."

"I can't thank . . . ."

"Don't say anything," he cut me off. "Just tell me your story later. I am a screenwriter. Need a good story."

You wouldn't believe it if I told you the truth. I thought of Burt Bacharach's "And all the stars that never were / Are parking cars or pumping gas."

"You're on."

"So are you," he said. He lifted Terry as if she were a feather and we found ourselves in a lovely room on the third floor, overlooking money and huge VISA bills and debt and . . . . We were safe.

TWENTY NINE

Coster was furious. "Where the hell are you? Bastard! Don't *ever* pull such a dumb stunt again. We put men on you to protect you. Weaver told us. You shithead. You could have been killed. Goddam it. What did you think you were doing? We are here to help you." Sure. "Where the hell are you."

"You already asked that."

Coster had been alerted late last night that something fishy had gone on. I wasn't in my old bomb shelter, my shop, Terry's and my apartment, or Weaver's house. I wasn't anywhere they could look. Coster had put an APB out on me. (Wowee. Those things really do exist in the real world, not just in Hollywoodland.) Molly hadn't seen me. I learned this later on from a dumbfounded officer who took twenty five minutes getting the "No" out of her.

Myers' house was under surveillance because he was a suspect, but nothing amiss was observed there. I guess the removal of a dead corpse (nice redundancy) in the trunk of a black car late at night is not amiss.

Terry and I had spent a curious night together. We were undressed, but she was still rolling her eyes in a stupor and she still had a chain on her ankle. I had had a long bath, which made me look better but didn't stop the nasal, patellan, or rest-of-body throbbing. I sent my clothes off for de-pissing (chagrined as I was that they were in such a stink), and I lay beside Terry the whole night, looking at her, beautiful, beatific, and beyond understanding. She did, however, wet the bed, which I completely sympathized with.

Coster pounded on the hotel door only a half hour after I had hung up the phone. He stormed into the hotel room in a half-rage. His Who, What, Where, When, Why, and How were perfunctory, and I am sure he already had the answers. His sidekick (is that what detective partners are called? or is that just in old Westerns?) sort of followed his pacing, taking notes, as sidekicks are wont to do in all the media.

Coster's toolmen came along a half hour later to pop the chain from Terry's exposed foot. (The rest of her was sequestered under a fine cotton damask sheet.) And a person employed by the constabulary, but with medical training, arrived to look into her eyes and ears, listen to her heart and stomach (yes, he listened to her guts), and feel her pulse. His pronouncement was that she was drugged. Duh! And she probably would be well in a day or so. In the meantime, try to get her to eat and drink and see if I could get her to walk now and then. She would be mobile in several hours and able to stroll with some support, but she wouldn't remember anything for a few days, which was probably therapeutic. And she might have a colossal headache.

Following Coster's eloquent demands, I told him almost everything I knew, experienced, heard, and felt. He was pretty amused and not a little amazed at the get-away story. I told him that I had busted out of the bars on the window, not explaining how I was able to do this. And I told him about the retreat to the bushes, finding Terry, and all that jazz. "Better than the movies," he said three times. "Sounds like fiction." My thoughts exactly. "Didn't the damn thing in your shoe give you a blister?"

"It was one of those thin things," I told him. "It fit behind my heel to the right side of my Achilles. Never knew it was there. I forgot about it for hours."

"Still sounds like a joke," he said.

When I got to the part of the trunk-of-the-car story, he seemed genuinely surprised. Not used to showing surprise, I thought. It sorta blows his cool.

"You sure it was Myers?"

"Yes."

"Dead?"

"Sure seemed to be. Eyes staring. Not moving. I'd say he was beyond all help."

When he left about an hour later he made a promise to me if I kept a promise to him: round-the-clock protection from him if I didn't try to do anything that he didn't know about. That seemed pretty open to me. I might decide to do some stuff he didn't approve of, but just so long as he knew about it, it would be o.k. I of course didn't interpret my part of the bargain that way to him, but it did cross my mind.

The door shut and Terry and I were together again, in the hush of a lovely room, lights now dim. I took off the plush hotel robe and lay down beside her. Good god, was I sore! It looked as if I had recently had a rhinoplasty (in a way, I had), and my back and shoulders and neck were throbbing. I guess I could have asked the police doctor to give me something for it all, but in the heat of the night (great phrase—perfect for a movie) all I could think about was Terry and sleep.

I lay beside her, beneath the covers, and felt her soft skin beside mine. It was half erotic and half homey and half deeply comforting and half awake and the next morning

THIRTY

the bright sun felt warm and I felt her stir. She was on her back, as she had been all night, shifting slightly, moaning now and then, and making painful grunts every twenty minutes or so.

"Terry?"

"Please let me go," she half mumbled.

"Terry, you're with me. Elliot."

She turned half toward me, eyes fluttering open groggily. "Gotta pee," she murmured.

I helped her to the bathroom and then back to the bed.

"Thank you," she said demurely, trying to cover herself half-heartedly. Back in bed, she slept well after check-out time. I figured a second day at the hotel was worth it.

The phone rang. I jumped. As one is supposed to do in such circumstances. Who besides Coster and the constabulary knew where I was? Would Coster be calling? I guess so.

"Mr. Berglund?"

Berglund? Who the hell . . . .

"Mr. Berglund; it's Kurt."

Oh, yes. I had told them that I was Berglund. Stupid, of course, since they wanted my VISA card and could see the truth. But I had told Kurt Berglund.

"Thanks for your discretion, Kurt."

"All in a night's work. Need anything?"

"Food. No meat. Lots of orange juice. No jello. Disgusting stuff. Muffins. Anything."

When Kurt got to the room, he was in civvies. "I'm off today. But I really dig your situation."

"What do you know about my situation?"

"Well, not too much. You got punched out pretty good. Your woman got snockered or something. You were really scared. And you really stank. Just the kind of stuff I need."

"I thought you were joking about being a writer."

"No way, man. All I need is a good pitch and I'll be out of here."

"A good pitch? How about a curve? I don't have much I can throw your way," I told him.

"Hey, man. Police?! Lots of them. Even now."

I hadn't bothered to look outside the door.

"They aren't dressed like police, and they're just sitting around looking invisible. But you gotta be blind not to see them. What's your gig?"

"My *gig*? Do people really talk like that? Where are you from?"

"Idaho."

"Ok, Kurt. I'll tell you all I can. I am in the Witness Protection Program. I needed a place to hide away. [Sounds like the Beatles.] Yesterday came suddenly. Now I'm out of here, man." (I don't think I said anything like "man" in twenty five years. I'm sure he didn't notice the sarcasm.)

When he left he said, "I know your real name. Where can I find you?"

"Do you read?"

"Sure. And write too. But my last five or six scripts were pretty stinko." (Stinko? Was this word still being used in Idaho?)

"I sell books." I told him where the shop was, and I said I probably wouldn't be there for several days. Then I thought that he had gotten me out of a pickle and I should keep in touch. But not under the eyes or ears of Johnny Law (did I really think *that*? dumb). I said that I had a "regular place" where I could be contacted, and I gave him Celia's office address and number. He caught on quickly.

"See ya," he said as he left, and he dropped a slip of paper on the table beside the door: his name (Kurt Bricker), his address (an apartment in Santa Monica), and his phone number.

Now what to do? Terry was now sitting up in bed, staring at something which I couldn't see. I sat with her and when she felt my weight on the bed she reacted alarmed for a moment. Then she settled down to that stare and said something like, "Elliot. I didn't let them know. Elliot. I didn't." I think that's what she garbled.

I sat stroking her hand. I had called the concierge and had a clothier sent up, with whom I arranged to have a nice set of clothes ready for my lovely friend when she was able to leave this place. The woman who came in knew exactly what was needed—sizes, colors, styles. Was this a common practice at the Bel Air? How many hotels in the world are prepared to help recently saved, naked kidnapees get clothing? This was one class joint.

I once saw a cartoon of two prisoners in total tatters, pinioned, hand, feet, waist, and neck, fifteen feet up a prison wall, with nothing in sight but stone and bars. They couldn't move. One of them says to the other: "Now, here's my plan."

At least he had a plan. What did I have? A bunch of random thoughts, emerging through the pain of a wracked, kicked, stiff body and past a swollen schnoz. So Myers was out of the picture. Did he know about Terry or not? No way to know, but he never did acknowledge that he understood when I mentioned her.

Who would have killed him? His son? Central Casting? His wife? Someone else? Why? Did it have something to do with my book of death.

My *Buchlein von dem Sterben*. I hadn't thought about it in days. But it did seem to have something to do with all this cloak and dagger (was it a dagger?) business. Who wanted it? Myers did, but he was gone. What did Blake know? or Howard? or Theresa? Was it genuine or a forgery? And where the hell was it?

I asked Terry a number of times if she knew, but all the response I could get from her was, "They don't know, Elliot," and that spoken unclearly. I didn't know who "they" was (were?) and I didn't know what it was that they didn't know.

I walked Terry around the room several times, holding on to her as strongly as she held on to me, and I could see her wits beginning to collect. A few more hours. A day. We'll see.

So here's my plan.

It still hadn't formed completely. But I knew that someone would kill for something. I had to figure out who that would be and what was worth killing for. Was it the *Buchlein*? Was it to keep someone quiet? What did Blake have to gain by killing his father? An estate? But what about Theresa, Myers' wife?

One thing was sure, if the plot hinged on the little book, I had to know where it was, or at least I had to let someone think that I knew where it was.

Should I work out a plan with Coster? No. He would want to do it all himself. He was there to serve and protect. I was there to be served and protected.

The day passed and Terry ate well and did her own bathroom numbers and even tried on the new clothes—which, by the way, fit perfectly and which she looked wonderful in. Of course, she looked wonderful in everything, even in the altogether. She soon saw my face with some recognition, and by the second night she knew who I was. She was relieved and clinging and loving, but there was still a hint of terror in her. She looked behind her uncomfortably, she cringed for a second when I touched her, and she backed away when I tried to kiss her. She could hug me for safety, but she had a demon to fight off before she could open up any more than that. It was progress.

The night came on little cat feet, with us still sort of prisoners in the lovely room. When we turned out the light, she lay down in bed, with nothing on, staring at the ceiling for a moment and then she closed her eyes. I watched her with a depth of passion—not the sexual kind (well, not completely)—for about ten minutes. She was still, but not asleep. I could hear a purposefulness in her breathing. As her breaths got shallower, she turned to me and put her left arm around me, and she snuggled close. My right arm went over her thigh and back and my hand rested on her neck, under her soft hair.

She whispered, "Elliot, am I safe?"

I didn't need to reply. My body against hers was her answer.

She responded by hugging me tighter with her arm, and then she said, "Oh, Elliot," and broke into sobs that shook the bed for what seemed like an hour. Before long she was asleep, holding me as a child holds a doll. I was overcome myself, but I cannot say why, and I wet her hair with my tears as I fell asleep.

* * *

We were driven to our apartment the next afternoon, after check-out time, I learned, but I also learned that we were not charged for the extra day. Terry was still a bit tentative and shaky, but she was now talking coherently about whatever came to her mind. She was not ready to talk about her stay with the Myers family, as she made clear to me and Coster, who visited us late that afternoon. "Just wanted to see that you were doing ok," he said, but I could see he wanted to pry whatever he could out of Terry. All she could say was that it was horrible and she couldn't remember anything, but it was horrible.

We were alone again, and I made us a light dinner: a cheese omelet with toast, orange juice, and a piece of old pound cake that was in the refrigerator. We talked about nothing in particular, but that was leading nowhere for me, and I had to make some progress. Was I being impatient?

"So, my love, where have you been?"

"You know where," she said.

"You were in the Myers house?"

"It was a house. I don't know whose it was."

"How did you get there?"

She made a face with pain and fear. I said, "It's ok. I just want you to know that I was worried about you and I'm very happy we are together again. You do know that you're safe again, don't you?"

"Yes."

"I don't want you away from me again. So I should know what happened so that we won't let it happen again."

"I was in my office. I was at the computer. No one else was around. I heard a noise in the hall." She started to look panicky again. I sat beside her and put my arm around her. She half turned to look at me. "I went to the door and looked down the hall. I saw a man. Two of them. One looked like what you said Myers looked like, but younger. I got to my computer but before I knew it, a cloth was put over my head and my hands were pinned behind me. It was terrifying."

"Oh, god. I know it must have been."

"I don't remember too much after that. I was in a car. It was moving. My hands were held tightly. Then I was picked up and carried someplace. Then it was dark. I remember needing to go to the bathroom.

Someone brought me a pot of some kind. I couldn't walk. I could stand
up. That's all."

"Did you eat?"

"I don't remember."

"Did anyone touch you? I mean . . . ."

She reacted for a second with revulsion, and then said, "I don't know.
I don't have any signs."

She was shaken and I didn't want to go on this way.

"Terry, my darling." I pulled her close, and in a whisper I said,
"Where is the book? Our little *Buchlein*?"

"I don't know. I can't remember."

"What do you mean 'remember'? Did you hide it somewhere?"

"I don't remember."

"Terry, did you have the key to the safe deposit box with you?"

"I always did."

"And your checkbook?"

"Yes."

That was all someone needed: the address of the bank and the key.

I was about to ask her more questions, but her body then fairly collapsed into me as if she were completely spent—as if she had come off a
long race and had exhausted all her energy. "I want to go to bed."

"Ok. Let's go."

"Elliot, I don't want to go to sleep. I want to go to bed."

Our lovemaking was tentative at first, with only the lightest touches,
soft, non-committal kisses, hands barely skimming over smooth skin.
We knew there were protectors outside the apartment, but then we
didn't know anything except each other. I felt barriers melting away,
and Terry got more and more animated. At one point she gripped my
neck and said "I need." We both needed. And our needs were satisfied.

* * *

Coster left a warning that we should probably stay in the apartment
for a day or two. He would have food or whatever delivered to us. I
told him I was not in the shut-in mood, and I said that Terry was ok
to be alone now. I needed to get back to my real life as a bookseller. He
relented, as if he had a choice!

At the shop I worked for a while tidying: the books and manuscripts were still pretty much skelter helter, but the act of straightening and aligning and putting things in order seemed to align my brain. I needed to do something other than try to look over my shoulder and be someone's punching bag.

The first thing I could do, related both to my business and my funny business, was to go back to the computer and see what was there: orders from customers? replies about my little book? answers to questions?

I got back to my email; there were all kinds of spams and pop-ups and trash. No, I don't want to get my hands on $30 billion from Nigeria. No, I didn't need ink-jet cartridges for my printer. No, I wasn't interested in penis enlargement.

Then a name popped into my vision: Pinsky. Where had I seen that before? His message said simply:

"My interest is both academic and because I might want to acquire a copy." That was it. R. Pinsky was one of the first ones to answer my original note about the Book of Death. But I hadn't heard from him since.

I hit Reply and typed, "I may have a copy. Please tell me where I can contact you." I left a phone number for him to call: Crocker's. And a time: 5:00 p.m. We had already had enough contact on the e-waves for Coster and his henchmen to know that we were in touch. I didn't want to give them any more information.

Terry answered my call on the first ring. I told her I'd be home about 6 or so. Dinner, chat, curricular activities (they were not extra, they were the main course)—whatever she was interested in. She said, "Come home soon. Safely."

I called Coster and got him in. "What can you tell me about R. Pinsky?"

He was quiet for a second longer than he needed to be. Then he said cautiously, "Who is R. Pinsky?"

I responded, "You answered my question with a question. I was asking you about someone you already told me about. Was your question rhetorical?"

Another pause. "We identified him as one of the people who could have bombed your places."

"I know that. But I asked what you know about him?"

"Why do you want to know?"

"Why not?" We could both play this game.

Coster could see that I wasn't going to give him any information without his giving me some first.

"Rapel Pinsky. He was recently released from prison. Known as a person who knows something about explosives. But he denies that he ever did anything illegal. He served only about three months. What we had was inconclusive and his lawyer convinced the powers that be that he was not the one who did the crime."

"What was the crime?"

"Cashing stolen checks. Acquiring them in the first place by blasting his way into the home of a local banker."

"Why was he released?'

"Mr. Burgess, you don't need to know any of this. He is out of the picture. Flew off to Poland two days ago."

"Out of the country doesn't mean out of the picture," I said. "Some of the shit I've faced recently took place more than two days ago."

"We're taking care of things."

"I know you are." Did he hear my sarcasm? "Why was he released?"

"There was no proof that he had set the bomb. It was a pretty generic device. Well done. But it could have been done by anyone."

"Was it a bank?"

"No, a house. A pretty secure one at that."

"Doesn't sound like it. What was missing from the place?"

"The banker was fuzzy about it. But some of his checks were cashed a couple of days later. Big sums. They seemed to have his signature on them, but the banker says he never signed such checks."

"Is Pinsky dangerous?"

"Why do you ask?"

"Why not?" I swore that I'd never give a straight answer to his question of my question.

"Do you think he is any danger to you?'

"Is he dangerous?"

"Ok, Mr. Burgess. Obviously you don't like my answering your questions with questions. It's an old tactic that often works."

"Not on me. Is he dangerous?"

"It depends."

"Ok, Officer Coster. That's just about on par with a question. Depends on what?"

"We incarcerated him on the suspicion of having used explosives to gain entrance to a domicile he had no right to be in."

"What you are trying to say is he was arrested for bombing his way into someone else's house."

"You could put it that way."

"So could you."

Pause. "If he was really the one to bomb his way into someone else's house" (now you're catching on, officer) "then he could be dangerous. But we don't know if he actually did it."

"And the checks?"

"We are pretty sure he is the one who cashed them."

"Pretty sure?"

"He was identified by a teller at another bank. But he has no really outstanding characteristics: mustache, scars, warts, hairstyle. His lawyer made a case that it was mistaken identity, and even with a bank camera, we couldn't tell clearly enough to be sure."

"So he's out?"

"On his way to Poland. He has Polish and German family there."

"How do you know where he's going?"

Coster didn't like to have his statements—especially ones about what he knew as an expert cop—questioned. "We know!" he fairly shouted.

"The way you knew that I was no longer in Weaver's house."

This stopped him flat.

I figured I'd fill the uncomfortable silence.

"What has happened to Blake Myers?"

"We're looking for him. Nothing yet. He's pretty conspicuous. We'll find him soon."

"And his body guard, a guy named Howard?"

"Howard Blanding; he's probably with Blake."

"And Theresa?"

"We have questioned her. She says she was asleep the night you were there. She says she knows nothing about the events of that night."

"Did she know where her husband was?"

"She said she didn't know, but it was not unusual for him to disappear for a day or two on the trail of some books."

"Did you mention what I saw in the car?"

"Of course not."

I felt like the detective. I know that Coster knew that I had come closer to some truths than he had been able to, but the frustrating thing for me (for both of us) was that I didn't know what the truths were. Who planted incendiary devices in my place of domicile and my place of employment? Who killed Smith/Gens? Who bashed Dave? Who killed Myers? (Or, indeed, was he really dead? Did I really see his body, or was it wishful thinking?) Where was the little book? What had really happened to Terry? What's the truth about Theresa? Where were Blake and Howie? Who was Pinsky?

Pinsky. I hadn't really told Coster anything about him. He had said that Pinsky was out of the picture. Maybe for Coster. Not for me. This was another lead I didn't want the police to mess up.

Five o'clock. I was at the phone in Crocker's. The phone rings. It's a goddamn wrong number. A woman asking for a bagel bakery. No shit! Ten after. Another call. "Mr. Burgess. I'm Pinsky." Cultivated and self-assured voice. No fuss.

"I can't talk to you now. Take this number and call me there early tomorrow morning—7:30." Celia's number was still off limits to the fuzz, I believed.

The rest of the restless day I had no rest. Tidying, thinking, planning. I could hardly wait till the morning. But in the meantime, I could hardly wait till I got home. I ran to the Ralphs on Sunset and picked up some flowers. I ran to the Beverly Center and got some See's Candies. And then I ran home to get some flowers and sweets of my own. I waved to Bud and Lou on the way in—whoever they were. And I was greeted by one of the warmest, most powerful hugs I have ever felt. Terry had made a simple dinner: homemade pizza with shrimp, anchovies, artichoke hearts, black olives, sun-dried tomatoes, and three kinds of cheese. She said that she loved having her tax money go for getting her food-delivery service. She brushed the edges of the crust with dark sesame oil, and she topped the whole thing off with delicious basil leaves. We feasted the whole night.

THIRTY ONE

The phone helped me shake off some of the cobwebs. (Silly image.) Pinsky's strong voice—definitely not calling from Poland: "Hello. Do you have the book?"

Pretty blunt. "Which one are you referring to" I responded, in my most innocent voice.

"Please, Mr. Burgess. Just tell me where the book is. You don't have much time."

What did he mean by this? Was this a threat? A prediction? A warning? "If you are referring to the little German book, Mr. Pinsky, you should know where it is." What else could I have said? It's in my trunk. The car's parked on Melrose near Stanley? I won't be able to get over there till tomorrow afternoon?

I could tell this was going to be a standoff conversation. I said, "Let's meet." We agreed: Celia's office, noon. I think Coster's men were all over me, but at least they didn't have an ear in the office. Pinsky knew the campus and said he could come from an angle that would leave him unseen.

He was six feet, 200 pounds, mid-fiftyish. Mid-brownish hair. No wrinkles. No warts. No distinguishing characteristics. Except maybe his hands, which were strong and delicate. Fine fingers emerging from muscular palms. I didn't hear him approach, but suddenly he was in the office.

"Let's discuss the book." Here was no nonsense personified. He didn't take the time to greet me. But his presence was imposing. He was no taller that I, but he seemed to hulk over me like a *presence*.

"Let's get to know each other," I said. "I'm Elliot Burgess. I own the *Buchlein*."

"You have possession of it. It is really mine."

"How so?"

"I can't give you the story. It's mine. I want it back."

"You can't give me the story. I can't give you the book." It was ambiguous. Of course, he didn't know that I meant it literally.

He looked at me, with a hint of menace. He thought. I was obviously not going to budge.

"What must I do to get my book back?"

"Have you thought of explosives?"

This got no reaction from him.

"Have you tried kidnapping?" Still a statue. "Breaking and entering?" The Thinker. "What will you do, Rapel?" He seemed surprised that I knew his name.

"I am a professional. I do to perfection what I must to survive."

"And just what is it that you do to perfection?"

"I acquire and market books."

"You say the *Buchlein* was yours."

"Is."

"Ok, is. Where did you get it?"

"I don't reveal my sources. All I can tell you is that I owned it legitimately and it was practically stolen from me."

"What do you mean 'practically'?"

His eyes narrowed as he weighed his answer. "Myers paid me for it. He gave me nothing. It's worth a fortune, but he threatened me with . . . . I had to sell it to him for nothing."

"What would you do to get even with him?" Was this too obvious?

"I'd kill the bastard. It took me years to come up with it."

"So you killed him?"

He looked puzzled. "What? Of course I . . . . Is he dead? Who . . . ."

His response seemed genuine enough. But there were all kinds of con men out there. For all I knew he leveled Myers himself. I figured I'd wait till he spoke again. Silence is mightier than the pen.

"Do you have my book?" It was all he could think about. I saw him tense up. I felt an alarm rising. Here was danger. I felt that the wrong answer could be my last answer. (That sounds pretty dramatic, but it's how I felt.) If I told him the truth—that I didn't know where it was—

he would probably believe me as much as (and treat me the same way as) Myers and clan. If I said Yes, he might treat me worse.

"I'm in an awkward position," I said. "The book is in my possession, but I can't get my hands on it."

"What does that mean? I know it's not in a bank vault."

"How do you know that?"

It was more information than he had intended to give me, but now he needed to explain. "Myers told me."

"Told you what?"

"That it wasn't in a bank vault."

"How did he know?"

"I don't know how he knew. He just did."

"And you trusted him? Someone who had stolen you blind? Someone you could kill?"

"It's what he told me. Why should I not believe him?" He spoke uncertainly. I couldn't tell if it was because he was lying or because he was trying to work out an answer that would sound plausible.

"Because he had already swindled you."

"Look!" I felt the danger rise again. "I just want my book back."

"I don't want to get into a circular discussion." I was getting peeved, too, and I guess a little counter-steam might show him I'm no punching bag—a fact belied by my nose and other visible parts. "I can't put my hands on the book now. That's it! You want it? You'll have to wait. And you'll have to pay."

He was taken aback at my pugnacity. Well, it was more like impugnacity. But he didn't know it. "How much?"

"Millions, for god's sake." I didn't really have a figure; I was speaking metaphorically.

"It's worth it."

"What do you mean?"

"The church . . . ." Then he shut up.

"What about the church?"

"I know who I can sell it to."

(It should be "whom," you ignorosis.)

A good deal of the dignity had ebbed from his voice. He could see he had no control over this situation, and he seemed to be reverting to punk. (And not the pierced kind.) The strength was still there, but not the resolve. He knew there was nothing he could do. Even punching me out wasn't going to get him his precious book.

I told him that I would keep in touch, but I needed touching points. He wrote out a phone number. I asked for an address. He looked wary. "What for?" he asked.

"My phones and email are . . . being observed. If I want to get in touch, I can write you. A couple of snail-mail days won't hurt our business. He added his address to the sheet. Then he backed away to leave. "You know you're being tailed?"

"Of course. They're my friends."

"Not mine."

"Why?"

"You don't need to know."

"Does it have anything to do with incendiary devices?"

It was like dropping an egg.

"I don't know what you're . . . ."

"Of course you do. I'm not as dumb as I look." It was a phrase I used to use as a joke, until one day Stacy the ex said, "Thank god" to that and I had let it go ever since. It just seemed to leap out now.

"What do you know?"

I told him about the banker and the checks. He was silent.

"You know too goddamn much."

"I know just enough," I answered. But I thought that I could sure use a bunch more knowledge.

"I didn't have anything to do with that," he almost shouted.

"Someone did."

He now knew that I knew something "secret" about him and he seemed fearful that I was going to call my friends in the parking lot. "I'll get back to you" was all he could say—as a way of departing and a way of trying to maintain some dignity and control over a situation that was degrading to him and pretty much out of his control.

When he left, all I could do was feel relieved. It was as if a falling boulder had missed me. As if I had been pulled out of a flood.

The church. I made a call to an old friend of mine. I'd see him in a few hours.

* * *

Father Eric Bernstein—yes, that was his name, from old Lutheran and Catholic stock—met me in the rectory of the church. We had met at an antiquarian book fair at the Century Hilton many years earlier, and in the intervening years he had become a good customer of mine, specializing in books on—believe it or not—church history. Also, wasps. Not too many books on that subject, but he had most of them. Once we got past the prelims—talk about his life and mine, books, and politics—we got down to business (or up to business; I never understood why business had to be down somewhere).

"So, Elliot, what's the reason for this visit? Ready to convert?" This was one of his long-standing jokes. Not too likely since I came from a long line of pretty serious pagans.

"Maybe later. I'm too busy being an infidel right now."

"Ok. Later. I'll hold you to that."

"Eric, I need some information."

"About wasps?"

"No, not even about Catholics."

"Not very funny. What can I do for you?"

"It's about books. One book."

"But you're the antiquarian. I'm just a pathetic little collector. What can I tell you?"

"I have a book that maybe you can tell me something about. I know a good deal about some aspects of it, but I need another angle."

He nodded and squinted in anticipation.

"It's called *Ein Buchlein von dem Sterben*." The recognition in his eyes told me that I didn't have to fill him in much about this pamphlet.

"The German text? Not too common. I know the genre, of course. In fact, in a way, that's my job right now: preparing people for death. Though, of course, we don't approach it that way. We tell our parishioners that we are preparing them for eternal life, 'the life everlasting.' It's sort of a euphemistic way of looking at their own mortality."

Eric Bernstein was never much of a believer, I thought. We had talked religion for years and he never seemed to take the cloth too seriously. To call what he did euphemistic was typical of him.

"Everyone fears death. That's practically the basis of Catholicism—of all religions. The art-of-death texts served two functions. They helped people feel less afraid of dying. And since the texts were promulgated by the church, it made people feel indebted to the church. Look at all those magnificent cathedrals. All built on fear of dying. These *Ars Moriendi* preachers could wring a stone out of blood with the fear they instilled in people who didn't give to the church to have their souls saved."

"I see you're familiar with the genre. But what do you know about the publishing tradition?"

"Listen, Elliot. How long have I been buying church history books from you? You know, I even read them. Amazing! A collector who reads his books."

"Amazing!" I echoed.

"There were plenty of editions in Latin. Naturally. The church could retain complete control of the texts—and therefore the audience—that way. It was an economic thing. In the Middle Ages most of the laity couldn't read, anyway. But by the time printing was around, mid-fifteenth century, readership was growing. That's why printing flourished."

"Of course."

"Oh, I forgot: you're the book man. I can't help getting into my sermonizing mode."

"So what about the printing history of these texts?"

"As I said, most of the texts were in Latin. Control and all that. But by the 1480s, some printers were putting out the texts in their native languages. It had a mixed impact on the church. On one hand the church fathers could not oppose the publication of their teachings. After all, the first book ever printed *was* a bible. On the surface of it, they would have encouraged such publications. But in fact, there was a suspicion in the church that two things might happen. First, that people would begin to rely on the books themselves and essentially cut out the middle man. Priests feared they would lose control, which they did. That they would lose income. Which they did."

"Every man his own path to salvation."

"So to speak."

"What was the second thing?"

"There was also a fear that these books could get into the hands of unscrupulous mountebanks, unable to read Latin, but able to pass themselves off as preachers. There were still huge masses of illiterate, all waiting to be saved."

"Guys like Chaucer's Pardoner," I said. Scoundrel who passed off pig bones as religious relics.

"Exactly. And they were right. Pardoners and their kin sprang up all over Europe. But another, less common but nonetheless alarming, thing happened. In a very few instances, printers who were violently opposed to the church . . . ."

"I can't imagine *anyone* being opposed to the *church*."

"Your sarcasm, Elliot, is going down in my book."

"I'm worried."

"These printers saw the *Ars Moriendi* texts as a potential weapon against the church. If the church advocated a particular kind of behavior, spiritual and clean-living and so forth, the printers could publish what appeared to be an honest religious pamphlet, but it would contain totally blasphemous materials."

"Like what?"

"Well, on the simplest level, the texts would start off with the standard ploy of telling the readers that they would be totally prepared for death if they read the text. But soon the message would evolve into what was essentially a diatribe against the church."

"I can't imagine . . . ."

"That doesn't even merit a reply, you heathen."

"What could be so blasphemous? Telling people that their priests were on the take?"

"That's an odd way to put it. But not on the wrong track since 'on the take' implies that they were out for the money. And who knows, maybe they were, to an extent."

"After all, it takes a big budget to keep up a church. Washing all those stained glass windows, mopping those cold marble floors, dusting off the gold statues."

"Ok, it *was* an expense keeping up the churches."

"But also," I quickly added, "feeding all those fat monks and friars. Food wasn't cheap. And they would have needed new belts every year or two. That would mean having to slaughter a fatted calf now and then."

He ignored my sarcasm, pretty much the way he had ignored it for years.

"So, specifically, what would these texts contain?"

"They would start off straight. Then things moved downward."

I remember Terry saying that something was wrong with the text. That it started out too religiously. We were both expecting some fireworks right up front.

"After the negative picture drawn of the priests and the church—with its greed and endless hunger—the pamphlets would parody the genuine *Ars Moriendi* texts by having sections on the seven deadly sins, but showing how the church and its priests were performing these sins. Interestingly, in the very middles of some of these pamphlets, there would be a section of what seemed to be a perfectly moral, honest-to-god *Ars Moriendi* preaching. It made sense. The printers might start off with serious-looking text, and even end with it. And a genuine religious passage in the middle would make it possible for them to lambaste the church even more in the incendiary passages that abutted the rest of the text. Also, if the shops were raided by the church 'police,' the printers could have these serious passages, set in type, with proof sheets of the unobjectionable text, available for inspection."

"Clever bastards!" I could see that Eric was not happy with my interjections, but all this religious talk required occasional interjections of levity. It kept me sane.

"There was another reason that the text had serious matter up front and at the end. Sometimes the church censors would rush into a shop and grab various publications that were available for sale. They might look quickly at each, and if the first pages looked ok, they would go on to the next volume. The shops often contained many books and they would have taken a good deal of time to get through. For centuries the Vatican cataloged its own holdings, mostly their manuscripts, by the first sentences in the text. They obviously put a good deal of store in openings."

"I know about this," I said. "It has caused untold numbers of important manuscripts to be buried for centuries since they would have been obscured by opening matter that had nothing to do with the subject matter of the manuscripts themselves. So the pamphlets would have had spiritual materials at the extremities?"

"But around all the serious passages, things would really go downhill. If the church preached abstinence, these parodies . . . ."

"Parodies? I think of a parody as something that makes you laugh, something amusing."

"They *were* amusing to those who published them. It was their way of getting back at an institution that bled the people dry, taxed everyone, even tried to hold the secular royalty in their bonds."

"Ok, so 'if the church preached abstinence'?"

"Then the pamphlets would call for licentiousness, debauchery of the most vulgar kind. And some of these texts were pretty explicit: fornicating with children and relatives and animals."

"Even *I* draw the line somewhere."

"I'm glad to see that. You do have a spark of decency in you. Some day you'll come to me on your knees to be converted."

"If I'm on my knees it will be because I dropped one of my contact lenses. So how common were these pamphlets?"

"Not very. In fact, we don't know since the church suppressed them with a vigilance greater than that of the Marys at the tomb. Among the readers of the day, many were educated in the church or by private tutors who had church educations. Not too many people visiting the bookshops would have been as irreverent as you are. The church essentially had a spy network blanketing all the literate countries of the West."

The chair I had been sitting in had been in shadow when we began talking, but the shifting sun had lighted my shoulder and face, and I had to move. Was this some kind of sign? Silly thought.

Father Bernstein shifted his chair so that he could face me again. He continued sermonizing. "The church understood the danger that these pamphlets posed, so they assiduously sought them out and destroyed them. And they were powerful enough to get the perpetrators into some pretty hot water. Fines, imprisonments, placement into stocks in some countries, beatings, and—possibly worst of all—the destruction of the printing shops."

"What about excommunication?"

"They threatened that aplenty, but to people producing these sacrile-gious texts that wasn't much of a threat."

"So, where are all these texts today?"

"As I said, the church got most of them. The church, after all, can be a pretty potent enemy. If they didn't scare the printers up front enough to stop the production of the pamphlets, they got them at the oth-er end. Fines, book burnings. Only a handful of these original pam-phlets survive, and they are pretty well sequestered in church libraries. Even public or academic institutions and private libraries—so far as we know—don't have more than a few of them. And most of *them* are incomplete. Pages torn out, charred remains."

I couldn't help saying, "Pathetic little reminders of the power and authoritarianism of a totalitarian church."

"That's pretty strong. But perfectly accurate."

"If one of these things surfaces, what is it worth?"

"So this is the reason for your visit, my son."

"I'm speaking purely hypothetically."

"Of course. So let me answer hypothetically. Elliot hypothetically acquires what hypothetically is a hypothetical *Ars Moriendi* pamphlet from some hypothetical source."

"Enough of the hypotheticals."

"Sure. If it is genuine, it could be extremely valuable."

"Why do you say 'if it is genuine'?"

"Because these things are so sought after—like a holy grail for some collectors (I'd love to have one in my library) . . . ."

"Of course you would."

"For historical and research purposes only, naturally. It would fit per-fectly into my church history collection."

"Right!"

Ignoring my sarcasm, he continued, "They are so sought after that many copies have come on the market that are pretty obvious forger-ies."

"I can see why people would want to forge such a thing. They are short and easier to fake than a whole book. They are scarce and in de-mand."

"It's something like the 'Oath of a Free Man.'" Father Bernstein knew of Marc Hoffmann's attempt to pass off as genuine his forgery of the first printing of this Oath, no copies of which are known to survive. He almost got away with it. "Not only are they short, but the demand is pretty high. Supply and demand. For one that is genuine there could be a bidding war that could reach the stratosphere."

"Hundreds of thousands?"

"I don't know the market as well as you do. But let's look at Harvard with its billions in endowments. The Vatican with its . . . ."

He saw my smirk. "It's just what we were talking about, isn't it?"

"Yes," he admitted. "The Vatican would probably want it for more than one reason: to add it to their collection of religious texts (regardless of how irreligious it was) and to keep it from prying eyes. Then there is Texas with its oil money."

"Some of the wells are dry," I said.

"For some things, wells can be revitalized. Maybe the Mormon Church, which would want something that discredits a rival religion. But also, the Mormons are true scholars, and it would not be inappropriate for them to have such a thing in their possession. I can think of a couple of other institutions that would want it and could survive a serious bidding war."

"And I can think of some pretty well heeled private collectors or other institutions. Bill Gates. The Getty."

"Sure," he said. "The possibilities are great."

"Anyway," I said, "it would take only two bidders."

There was a lull, but not one that was relaxed or vacant. Father Eric sat forward in a conspiratorial pose and asked,

"Do you have one?"

"One what?"

"You answer me with a question?"

"Isn't that your style too?" I asked.

"Shouldn't it be?"

"Why do you ask that?"

"What? About your questioning style or about the book?"

I got serious. "I may have a copy."

"'May'?"

"Another question? Well, since you are my Father Confessor, and I know that there is such a thing as Father Confessor-client privilege, I know I can keep you discreet about this."

"Of course." He said this seriously but with a sense of curiosity that bordered on one of the seven deadly sins. I'm not sure which one. Maybe having something to do with a neighbor's wife?

"Father Confessor Bernstein. I sort of have a pamphlet, in German, that has what looks like a genuine title page, genuine fifteenth-century paper, typeface of the appropriate date, and so forth." I described the item to him and mentioned the tests that analyzed the inks and dated the paper to the right era. I also told him how the thing had vanished.

"Has someone from the church been involved?" he asked.

"Not that I know of." Gens, Myers, Dave—all victims of the Book of Death—and Blake and Howie and Theresa and Rapel Pinsky. Terry Luckombe. Even (or especially) Elliot Burgess. None seemed to be religious in any way. Maybe some were religious about money or power.

I had what I needed. The pamphlet could be my retirement in luxury. I rose to go. Father Bernstein grabbed my outstretched hand and said, "This has been . . . illuminating and pleasant. Do let me know what happens."

I said I would.

He closed with, "Dear Elliot, a blessing upon your head. Or, more importantly, on your nose." He always did try to get the last dig.

* * *

It was afternoon. My time in the shop had been productive. I had gotten a few orders, filled some older ones (when I could locate the books), and worked my emails down to nothing.

Coster had called to report that Howard Blanding and Blake were in custody. But he didn't know for how long. They were playing totally innocent. Kidnapping? Assault? The whereabouts of Edward Myers? They knew nothing. They did seem mildly surprised that daddy was gone. He was probably "off on business." (What a trite line.) It wasn't unusual. He'd be back in a day or so, they were sure.

I asked if I should file some formal papers, but Coster said that there was no way I could prove that they had done anything to me. Myers' disappearance was not yet old enough to raise any curiosity, especially since his whole family were taking it so coolly.

Charlie Chan would have employed Number One Son to infiltrate the gardener's crew to get information. But Number One would have messed it up. And I had no sons. And I wouldn't even have known what to do with one.

The gardener. I'm sure Myers had one. What would he know? (Sexist of me. The gardener could have been Olivia or Melanie.) No, that was a silly line. There was no gardener residence at the Myers place. In that neighborhood the landscapes were usually attended to by Mexican gardeners who came in once or twice a week—during the day. I'm starting to think like a real Hollywood detective.

If I could only get the book to emerge, I might be able to rekindle some activity. Back home, I was greeted by an even warmer and hungrier kiss and hug, and a superlative dinner. Terry was back at the stove. Cooking was therapy. I guess for both of us.

In bed I began reading *Lady Chatterly's Lover* to her, and we fell asleep spooned and cozy.

THIRTY TWO

When I called the next morning, Kurt was groggy. It was already 9, and I figured he'd be awake by then.

"Sorry I woke you."

"It's ok, man. I had to get up to answer the phone anyway."

That wasn't too original, but it meant that he wasn't totally pissed at me.

I told him to meet me "at the regular place." I was still being accompanied to the university, but as far as I knew Celia's office and phone were untapped.

He got there at noon, well dressed, smoothly shaven, looking ready for anything.

"What did you want to see me for?"

"Maybe I can help you with a plot."

"Hot Damn! Great!"

"Where do you get these expressions from? Hot Damn?!"

"My dad says it all the time. I guess it's in my blood."

"What does your dad do?"

"I like to call him an engineer. He owns a car dealership, Belcher Motors."

"Sounds like the motors could use a repairman. Belcher?"

"It's my real name. I figured I'd never make it in Hollywood with a name like Gideon Belcher."

I tried to stifle a laugh. I wasn't too successful.

"See what I mean? Would you buy a script from Gideon Belcher?"

"Probably not."

"So what's the gig?"

We discussed the gig. I wanted him to go to Rapel's place and see what he could find out. I didn't know what that might be. But Pinsky and Terry were the only two people I knew who had something to do with the book with whom I still had some approachability. I could handle Terry. I needed a neutral party to case Rapel's joint. (I'm really starting to talk like a dime-novel detective. Should I have said 'gumshoe'?)

"Don't do anything dumb. Pinsky could be dangerous. He could probably flatten you with a single roundhouse."

"Hey, man. I'm strong. I picked up your friend with one hand, practically. And I'm not dumb. I have a Master's in drama from Colorado State. Minor in psychology. I figured that I'd need psychology to make my writing more believable and human."

I warned him again, but he insisted, "But I have two other traits that serve me well: fear and speed. I am fast. I haven't seen this Rapel guy, but I am pretty sure I can outrun him."

"Can you outrun bullets?"

"That's where the fear comes in. I like living a lot. I don't take chances. When I saw you and the missus, that was a pretty safe chance."

"And thanks again. I don't know what I would have done."

"Give me a dynamite plot. That's all I want from you. And it sounds as if you have one abrewing."

"Did you say 'abrewing'? Dad?"

"Yeah. I know enough to keep that kind of thing out of my scripts, but I can't stop it from coming out of my mouth. Instinct."

"Like the instinct to live?"

It didn't require an answer. With this final warning he took his leave. (Left! Took his leave, indeed.)

* * *

The plan was for me to lure Mr. Pinsky from his place and hope that Kurt could find a way to get in there and scout around. I phoned the Pinsky residence but got nothing but ringing. I don't know why I had expected him to be in in the early afternoon. This was a pretty stupid plan, though it sounded rather dagger-and-cloak clever at the time of its birth. What if Pinsky were out but was back there by the time Kurt got there? Kurt said that he would ring the bell. I asked what he would do if Pinsky opened the door. He said that he started out in drama as an actor and had had several improv classes. He could improvise, he said.

"Excuse me, sir. I'm looking for donations for the boy's club. They are a worthy group, sir. And hard-working chaps."

"*Don't* say 'chaps,' Kurt. Anything but that."

"Of course," he said. "My boys are in the process of helping to build an orphanage . . . ."

"Jesus! An orphanage?! Let it go."

"Of course," he said. "My boys are raising money to help them get to the Hayworth Terrace Rest Home to keep the old folks company."

"Jesus! You gotta be kidding. He'll plug you right there."

"Of course. Then I can say, I'm trying to raise some money to take the boys on a camping trip."

"To where?"

"Uh, San Clemente."

"Why there?"

"It's the first place that came to mind."

"San Clemente is the first place that you thought of? Are you sane? What's there?"

"A friend of mine told me that when he was a kid he went camping in San Clemente. If Pinsky is a foreigner, he won't know the difference."

"One thing, Kurt. You better knock on some other doors, too. If he sees you just go to his place . . . ."

"Of course."

And so it went. The little rehearsal took only a few minutes, but I had to admit, Kurt could deliver a line seriously and earnestly. I might have forked over a bunch of bucks for his boys.

Back to the shop, all three of us. I even decided to make some serious contact again with my servers and protectors.

"Hi, Bud and Lou."

Bud poked his head out of the passenger side window. "I love being called Bud. Reminds me of my childhood. What's up professor?"

"Just wanted to make contact. You've been chasing me for a few days. I wanted to thank you and tell you that it's ok not to chase me anymore."

They did make me feel safe, but they were also stifling.

"Thanks for the thanks, but we're just doing our duty."

That sounded canned. "Then how about going off duty?"

"Not till eight. Then it's Chuck and Ignatz."

"Ignatz?"

"That's his name. It's worse than a boy name Sue, if you ask me."

It was time to talk to Coster again.

"We will take the tails off when we feel you are safe. Besides, it's part of an investigation. If someone wants to get to you, we want to be there. You'll feel better. So will we. It won't be for long."

"How do you know?"

"I think we are on to some information about Blake. We have questioned him and his step-mother several times and their stories don't quite superimpose."

"Like how?"

"She claims the house was peaceful that night. Blake says there was quite a fight. She says she went to bed at eleven. Blake says the fight was at about ten thirty. She says that all the alarms were in place while Blake says that there were some problems with them. He talks about a squirrel nibbling through some wire somewhere. But things were restored by the morning."

By the morning! Billy and Kurt had done such a number that I doubt that the system would be up for several days.

"We also found some mud on the car's tires, mud that doesn't come from anywhere that they would normally be driving. We have a soil database, which we are checking."

"Soil?"

"Yes. The database is amazing. We have gathered information about trace elements in soil all over the state. We can tell if you've been driving at Big Sur or Mount Waterman. We can even narrow down sand from beaches north to south, though not with perfect certainty since the shore sands change a lot."

"What does Blake know about all this? And Theresa?"

"They know we're pretty serious. But since they have shown no panic about Myers' disappearance, we can't operate on only your words."

"You don't believe me? Kidnapping? Bodies?"

"We believe you. We just can't do anything about it for a few more days. The Myerses know we want to speak with Edward when he returns. If he's not back in a few days, or if they don't have any information where to find him, we can kick this into gear."

This was going nowhere, so I closed up shop and went home. And, oh, my! what a reception!

THIRTY THREE

Terry was at the kitchen table reading the Book of Death.

I stood there dumbfounded. Then I said, "I'm home. My god! Where did that come from?"

She had been so engrossed that she hadn't heard me enter. Then she jumped up and hugged me.

"Where?" I fairly shouted.

"I told you I could hide it so no one could find it."

"Where?" I sounded like a defective record with a needle skip.

"Have some toast," she said.

"I'm not hungry. Not now. Tell me."

"The toast," she said. It was one of her beautiful sourdoughs, a large round loaf. The one I had seen in the freezer?

"Yes. I baked the bread; when it had cooled I wrapped the pamphlet in Saran Wrap, slipped it into a slit in the loaf, sort of sealed the loaf with a touch of water at the slit, and froze it. It was literally in deep freeze. Couldn't hurt the book. And fooled everyone."

"When did you remember where it was?"

"I dreamt about it after you left this morning. It was a pretty vivid dream."

"I should say so! You dreamed it back into existence."

"I thawed it slowly. I didn't want any condensation to form. It looks as good as new."

"Not bad for something over 500 years old."

She had been engrossed in the text for two hours and had made only scant progress.

"I checked out the structure and paper and typeface again. It sure looks good."

"What about the text?" I told her what our Father Confessor explained about the opening and closing pages of the text, and the fact that even in the middle there was likely to be some pretty serious pages.

"That's what was bothering me," she said. "I knew that this was supposed to have a pretty incendiary text. But I saw nothing. I'm still in the opening pages. My German isn't too bad, and fifteenth-century German is closer to modern German than the equivalent for English. But the typeface and the archaic forms . . . and my dictionary is in fraktur. It isn't easy to get through this."

"Just keep at it. I'll make dinner."

"Corn flakes. It's quick and easy. And it won't take too much time to eat."

She was really into this, and it was a joy to see her back from the depths.

At midnight she was still going strong, with me at her side. And by two a.m. we were almost done. The text was only thirty two pages, and we got that roughly translated. We'd need some help with several words and a couple of sentences. Even Internet dictionaries didn't help us much. And then there were the marginal marks. Someone had been marking up the text, for what purpose? We couldn't tell. This would be even more challenging since the notes were in a scrawl—in an early form of an unfamiliar language—and we could make out barely a word or even a letter for many of the notes. The signature, Frithof von Escher, and the note on the last leaf were barely legible. We were out of our depths here. But when we had the pamphlet examined in Delaware, the marginal inks seemed to date from the fifteenth century.

We slept soundly, but with German words leapfrogging in my head all night, superimposed over a blotch of scrawly scrawls and half-legible type.

I felt that some of the secret to this pamphlet lay in the marginalia, but I wasn't sure, and I wasn't sure we could ever get this deciphered. It could be like the Voynich Manuscript, baffling scholars for a century. It was found in 1912, and the best scholars, cryptographers, and computers in the world have been unable to crack its code. I hoped our *Buchlein* would not prove to be so impenetrable.

Terry and I showered together and then had more cereal. We were eager to get back to the pamphlet, but to do what? We had a translation of what was a bizarre and explosive text. But there was really little more we could make out of the piece.

My first impulse was to call a professor of Old German at UCLA. But I didn't know any, nor did I know if there was one there—or anywhere in the city. Then we had to decide how to make the text available to someone, and who that someone might be. A university linguist seemed the logical choice, but how would she see it? In our place? It would obviously take hours to read, both to correct our translation and to work on the marginalia and other manuscript additions.

The person could work from a photocopy, but we didn't have a copier, and I wouldn't feel too comfortable sticking it in a backpack and strolling over to Kinko's. Also, now that the thing had surfaced, I felt especially nervous. Like sitting on a keg of TNT. We decided to call Coster and get his advice. Not that we liked asking for it, but he could tighten up the security and ease some of our misgivings engendered by ownership of such a powerful piece.

And what a piece it was! The opening pages did what Confessor said they would: they were straight *Ars Moriendi* text. They started with the standard statements:

> In the days of our lives, Death is a matter of daily remembrance. Our Lord gives and takes away. In our bed as infant we are made of earth, formed in the image of God. In our bed as youth, we help to form our image of God. In our bed at sundown we return to our God. We come from the heavens and we enter the world clean, despite Adam's stain. When we leave the world, our deepest desire is to return to the heavens, equally unstained. The hopes and fears of the living shall be assuaged by the rewards and support of the hereafter, in heavenly bliss, but only if we merit such a passage through our Good Deeds and Clean Spirit. Though the plague attack us, though old age weaken us, though enemies assail us, though the ultimate enemy, the Devil, seduce us, though the evils of the world draw us down, there is a path through the world and the flesh, a path to the Heavenly Glory. Death need not be our enemy. Death may bring us to the Holy Seat, quelling anger,

suppressing covetousness, foiling envy, stifling gluttony, combating lust, avoiding pride, and defeating sloth.

In our waxing and our waning, the light rises and the light falls. Our Lord is our light. In our passage there is a moment when things move toward death. This is a movement, a waning, that has its own rhythm. An altered form of existence beckons us, the Devil tempts us, but the Lord guides us.

The book went on like this for about 2½ pages. This section concludes with the exhortation:

Heed, you believers. Listen to the falling off of the music, to the last chord. In this falling off lies the paradox, for this leads to life in all its fullness. It leads to a life of spiritual satisfaction. It leads to a sense of completion in the cosmos. It leads to the fruit of our goodness—or the nettles of our sins. Death is the fruit of life. It allows our souls to ripen into the empyrean, approaching the heavenly Rose, bearing reward in all of its living potential. Death will make us grow. Death will inspire us—breathe life into us. It will bring us to the heavenly glory.

But your way, oh, Pilgrim, is fraught with danger. The pitfalls of sin, the chasms of despair, the succubi of temptation await you. They wait for your moment of weakness. They threaten your very soul if you stray from the path of righteousness. You could be protected by angels or tortured by demons.

Read this book, sinner, and learn the Way. Learn to meet Death with your soul shriven of its evil. Learn to emerge from the shadows of the flesh into the light of your Redeemer. Learn to resist all temptation. To struggle successfully against vice. To be made whole.

Life is nothing but a dance, from parturition to interment. It is signaled by constant change in the physical realm, leading to a realm of permanence, either in Heaven or in the Inferno. The corporeal body contains Death. But it also contains seeds for life everlasting. The flesh is the container. The flesh will transmogrify to airy nothing, but the soul will remain. Good and evil, reward and punishment, are at stake.

Heed, oh reader, the Way. Follow the paths of our teachings and you will survive. Live well, remember Death, say your prayers, reflect and meditate, mortify your flesh, practice self-flagellation. We shall show you the way.

There is a printer's fleuron here in the text, and the new section begins with advice.

The flesh must be mortified. Approach your enemies with their own mortification. Who are your enemies?

At this point the pamphlet really takes off. It mentions the lower prelates, how they treat people falsely. It moves up to deacons, priests, bishops, archbishops, cardinals, and, ultimately, the Pope. For each level in the hierarchy, the crimes of these sinners are spelled out, from the thievery of the priests to the conspiratoriality of the bishops, to the egocentricity and abuse of power of the archbishops, to the plotting and greed of the cardinals, to the ultimate evil of the Pope himself. Explicit passages about fornication, gluttony, sodomy, homosexuality, murder, evisceration, eye gouging, dismemberment, and the like leapt off the pages.

It read like the worst of a Holocaust history, like the worst one could imagine of de Sade, like one's worst nightmares. It was so appalling that one could see why the church would want to suppress it. Even enemies of the church would have been revolted by the depictions of depravity, the explicit record of a truly immoral, evil people.

But near the middle of the pamphlet, about on page eighteen, the text took a 180. There was a sentence that said something like:

Follow my words. Believe what I say, though you know me not. I must remain in the shadow, for to expose myself in the truths I am revealing would be death to the one who has revealed it, as I have done here. I do not fear the consequences. No one can assail me since I know too much about the evildoers.

This, I recalled, was on the first page of the New York Public Library copy—the end of one of the objectionable passages before the doctrinal text kicked in. In the following pages, the subject was the church itself.

> Our Mother church shall be our guide. We shall be suckled and nurtured within its sacred walls. We shall be given the model of its beatific splendor. We shall be led down its aisles of purity, cleanliness, honesty, beauty, sanctification, and piety. We shall see the beatification that the church offers. Its Trinity of faith, hope, and charity shall be made available to us. We shall learn of Eros, Agape, and Caritas—fleshly, brotherly, and divine love.

And so forth, for about four pages. Where did all this come from? After having been almost sickened by the vulgar passage, this came out of nowhere, and we read it with doubt about its honesty.

One thing bothered us, however. The translation that Terry and I (mostly Terry) came up with was crude. Many words were not in our dictionary or online, and we had to try to work them out from context and etymology. Some of the sentences were simply untranslatable to us, and we had to write down the gist of them as best as we could figure. But the plan of the pamphlet was quite clear, just as Father Bernstein had said: clean stuff, bad stuff, clean stuff, so far. We were surely headed into another section of bad stuff, and sure enough, it began with a fairly unsubtle transition:

> We can be guided, in our passage down the right path, in our preparation for death, by the uncomplaining Jesus who on the Cross asked "Why hast thou forsaken me?" The reason, dear reader, is obvious. God will forsake even his own living flesh. God will forsake you. Jesus died in total despair, and his soul rots in Hell.

Wow! The next few pages trashed the church, god, Jesus, and just about every doctrine that the church promulgates. Caritas, the love of god and the love of all things for the sake of god, is a joke, a conniving way to make people subservient to the church and its corrupt clergy. The Trinity was a triply powerful way to fool people into fearing their pastors. Free Will was not a Divine commandment to keep oneself holy; it was a way to justify the evil deeds of the church's ministers. And so on.

This last was a segue into the notion of Free Will. For mankind, there are past, present, and future. For god there is only one tense. All of history is known by god at one moment, so all time is just present time for god. That means that at any given moment, god knows what is in store for you in the future. And god's foreknowledge makes it impossible for anyone to change what is already foreordained. It makes it impossible for us to do anything that would alter what our sealed fate already has in store for us. So we might as well go out and do whatever we want.

The next section then told people what they should do. If they need provisions, go to the church. It is their labors that have provided for the church. The goods of the church belong to the people. Take what you can. It's yours already. Beset by the importunings of god's messengers? Do away with the importunings by doing away with the messengers. Does this sanction murder? It is not murder, it is self protection. Would you kill someone to protect your life and that of your family? Then kill, no matter who it is who is the focus of your murderous acts. God gave you life to protect your life. Protect it from anyone who is out to diminish your life in any way. If a minister of the church wants to take away anything you own—and even warns you that your soul is in his hands if you don't give something to the church—then that person is attacking you and diminishing your ability to live. Defend yourself.

The book went on in this vein for several more pages. Then it moved on to the ways people could defend themselves. It advocated murder of various kinds: poisoning, stabbing, suffocating, drawing and quartering, and so forth. And if the church has tortured you with its gluttony and threats and greed, you should retaliate in kind. Starve your priest to death. With a large band of fellow-sufferers, waylay your bishops or deacons and beat them to death, the way they try to beat you into submission.

The pamphlet then shifts: At the bottom of what would be page 28 we are given the last piece of advice. The bible talks about an eye for an eye. If the priest tries to take what is yours, it is as if he believes you to be blind to his thievery. You may take his eyes out. On the top of page 29, we see,

> So the church can deal with you in many ways and you should answer in kind. You should prepare your body, your mind, and your spirit for the final journey. The church can be your salvation. It will always have its doors open to you. For those who believe, the church will be a bulwark of strength. For those who come to the church on their knees, the church will raise them up. For those

who enter hungry, the church will feed them. For those who enter spiritually depleted, the church will buoy them up and bring them to the gates of paradise. For those who come to the church soiled by the sins of the flesh, the church will cleanse their spirits and make them ready for the life in paradise that is due them.

The final statement in the pamphlet was. "Follow the good advice in this *Buchlein* and you will meet your reward."

Terry and I were struck dumb. When we had looked at the New York Public Library copy, all we saw were the middle pages. Nothing was amiss there. But here, in all its gory, was the true *Buchlein*, a text not seen for perhaps 500 years.

We looked at each other in disbelief. We tried to talk about it, but for the first hour we could only sit there and ruminate about the kind of mind that would put something like this together.

Finally Terry said, "Do you think the Vatican would want to get its hands on this?"

"Many places would."

She then asked, "How much is it worth?"

I gave her the standard answer that any antiquarian gives to that question: "Whatever anyone is willing to give for it."

"How about one's life?"

"Maybe."

THIRTY FOUR

Kurt reported back the next morning. I was sitting in Celia Brothers' office.

"Too bad I had to go to work at the hotel, cause I think I was onto something. He lives in a little apartment on the second floor. When I got there no one seemed to be home. I did the thing about knocking on doors around the place, but since he wasn't in, that did no good, and I can't do that again. But I think I could sell about a dozen Britannicas."

I hadn't thought of Pinsky's not being there. I had written a defective detective script.

"I waited for a while after knocking on his door to see what kind of response I would get. No response at all."

"How long did you wait?"

"At least three minutes, and then I knocked a couple more times."

"How did you get in?"

"Jesus! There was a door at the top of the rear steps, and the back door was not locked. I just walked in. Doesn't surprise me since there's really nothing there to steal. No tv or stereo or cd player. Nothing fancy like jewelry or coins. It's an inexpensive neighborhood, but nicely kept up, with lots of people walking around. It's not far from Ladera Park, and with the nice weather . . . ."

The weather was always *nice* in L.A.

". . . there were plenty of pedestrians. I'm sure no one saw me enter the house. The back was pretty concealed."

I asked, "What did you mean that you might have been onto something?"

"I can't tell you what it was. I just saw things there I didn't expect to see. So it seemed that something was sort of wrong, or different, or, well, suspicious."

"Are you the naturally suspicious type?"

"Not suspicious, just curious. And when I see something I don't expect to see, I always try to figure out how it got there or what it is doing there."

"What did you see?"

"A small saw. Some really old, dilapidated furniture, or what was left of it."

"What do you mean?"

"There were the remains of a couple of very old chairs, which were certainly in horrible condition when they were brought in there. But the legs had been sawed off. The seats were still there, all groaty and split and almost crumbly. Pretty disgusting. It seemed odd to have this in the kitchen."

"Anything else?"

"Yes. He had cooking oil—a big container of it. It looked like cooking oil."

"What's so unusual about that? Maybe he likes French fries."

"But usually you keep your bottles of oil in the cupboard. This one was on a counter—set up like a work bench—and the rest of the counter was perfectly clean. In fact, the whole place was. That's why I was surprised to see such a broken down chair there, under the counter."

"What else?"

"Some art tools—an X-acto knife, a long ruler, some sheets of paper, neatly stacked up on the table."

"What was on it?"

"Nothing. Just plain white paper. A couple of pencils. Oh, yeah. There was a little dish. It looked like a soy sauce dish. It was empty. I thought that was a funny thing to have out."

"Did you get into any of the other rooms?"

"It's just a one-bedroom, and it took only a couple of seconds to see that there was nothing to steal there. He had a tidy, well made bed and a dresser with nothing on it. It was a clean room. I looked into a few of the drawers of the dresser, but they contained only carefully folded clothes. I didn't see a thing worth noting in there."

"Was there a desk?"

"A small one with three little drawers on one side and a big one in the middle. They were also neat and not worth mentioning."

"What was in the drawers?"

"More paper. Wite-Out. Paper clips. Erasers. What would you expect to find in a desk? There was also some thread and a couple of needles, like for mending pants. Only slightly bigger. And there was a long thin thing that looked like a letter opener, but it had no handle. Looked like plastic. And one other thing: a little round magnifying glass—the kind that you stand up on a table top and look down through. The whole place looked as if it had just been cleaned and tidied and scrubbed. Nothing out of place. Kitchen stuff all neatly tucked into the cupboards—except for one little iron pot. If I lived like that I'd die from terminal cleanliness."

"What else?"

"Books everywhere, but neat. There were three large bookshelves on one wall, a free-standing one beside one of the armchairs, and a built-in shelf beside one of the side windows. Big books and little ones. Old and new. Falling apart. Some with paper covers. Some little skinny notebooks and such. Thousands, maybe."

"How long were you in there?"

"About ten minutes. There just wasn't anything to see. And my shift at the hotel started at six and I needed to get dressed and over there. So I didn't have any more time than that. But I sure didn't need any more."

"What can I tell you? You did a great job. Thanks very much. I know you don't want anything but a story, but right now I can't give you a thing."

"It doesn't sound as if I earned anything. But it was great. Like being a detective—a P.I. I loved it. Like, my hair was sort of standing up on my neck. I had a vision that I'd get caught. I'd do it again."

"You may have to. We'll see. Thanks very much."

"No prob, man." And he was out of there.

* * *

I phoned Elizabeth Browner at NYPL. "Remember me?"

"Of course. You're the one with the Kachelofen *Buchlein von dem Sterben*. Do you still have it?"

"Why do you ask?"

"The Library would be interested in acquiring it. I've talked to some folks here and to some of our richer donors. We might be able to make you a substantial offer."

"What is so appealing about this book?"

"You seem to have the only complete Kachelofen Book of Death from the incunabula period. If it is as incendiary as it purports to be— you know, it was not only banned, but copies were assiduously burned and Kachelofen was imprisoned for it. It could have a text that scholars have speculated about for eons, but they have never seen."

"And you believe that my copy is genuine?"

"It sure looked like it. Of course, we'd have to do some of your tests over again and get some experts to look at it, but if it is what it says it is, we are really interested. Do you still have it?"

"Yes. But for now it's not for sale."

"I hear the hesitation, and I know there are others out there . . . ." She paused, looking for the best way to say she wanted it and didn't want any competition. "We can probably offer you quite a lot of money for it. It would save you from having to get a bidding war going."

"That's one way to put it. Who would bid for it?"

"Oh, Mr. Burgess, you know I couldn't say. But you know the answer to that already. It's your profession."

"I'll sleep on it."

"Why did you call?"

"Well, basically to see if you were still interested. I guess you've answered that question." I had sent her results of all the tests we had had done on our copy. So I asked, "What were the results of the testing you did on your copy of the Kachelofen pamphlet."

"The paper was just like yours. The ink—well, it was the same as yours in its make-up, but with different proportions."

"Different ink? All that suggests is that the two were printed at different times. We did see a complete resetting. So it's not unlikely that some time after the printing of the first of our *Buchlein*s, by the second printing Kachelofen had new ink made up."

"Certainly," she said. "And the typeface was the same, no doubt of that. On the basis of our tests, your Kachelofen is as genuine as mine is."

"I'd like to ask you one more favor. Can you tell me whom we can go to for more authentication?"

"For the text the best is Hans Sachsen at Wisconsin."

Sachsen. The name was familiar.

"For the item itself, any number of people," I said.

"It's sounding good. By the way, Mr. Burgess, have you read the text?"

"A colleague of mine and I have translated it."

"Is it . . . blasphemous?"

"You could say that."

"Wonderful."

"What's so wonderful about a blasphemous text?"

"It's just that for centuries this text has been lost and word was that it was pretty strong, heretical. No one could prove it without seeing the text. Now we can."

"I'm not sure who 'we' is . . . are. I'm not sure I want to show this to the world in case it is a forgery."

"Do you think it could be?"

"Anything's possible," I said. "Besides, the text is, as you said, pretty blasphemous. I'd hate to foist upon the world a text with this kind of power unless I knew it was authentic."

"If you have doubts, maybe you could bring it back here and we could have our own experts look at it. We'd pay your way. And your assistant's, of course."

Terry my assistant? Never thought of her that way.

"The thing is," I explained, "I don't want too many people looking at such a horrific text."

"Is it that bad?"

"I believe so."

"Wonderful."

"Or 'terrible'; depends on your perspective."

"Please do think about our offer. We are quite serious."

"I'm thinking. I'll get back to you."

Her last admonition was another insistence that we give the New York Public right of first refusal. I made no promises, but said I'd keep in touch.

Hans Sachsen? Where had I heard that name? I checked my fattening folder of information about the Book and soon found the name. He had answered one of my first emails, way back when, about the book. I found the printout; he had asked, "Is this a joke? Why do you want to know?" I used the Brothers computer to get to Google to get to the University of Wisconsin site to get to the faculty and staff listing to get to Sachsen. I never expected him to answer on the first ring. And he didn't. Nor on the second or fourth. I left a voice mail message for him, hoping to provoke a return call: "Call me, please, about the *Buchlein von dem Sterben*." I'm sure I didn't need more than that. I left him times that I expected to be in Celia's office, when I'd be at the shop, and when at home, with numbers for all. I figured that anything he and I said was not privileged. I didn't care if Coster and his constabulary crew knew about the book or my gathering information about it.

Next call: Billy Brinks. "Wow, Billy. You did a great job."

"We aim to please."

"Do send me an invoice. I can't tell you how important it was that you did your job so well."

"I'm sure I saved your life." Little did he know. "I'll think about what to charge you. Gotta tell you: that was really fun." Jeez, he and script-writer Kurt were having fun on this. How come I wasn't? "It's like a test to see how on top of my profession I am. I hope I passed the test."

"With flying shrapnel. Did you have any problems?"

"Waal" [well, it sounded like that], "Not really. That was a good job someone did on that house. But really nothing special. All the predictables. Right down to the sensors on the iron window grates. With a good pair of field glasses, I could make them out from sixty yards away. Subtle, but there. I knew what to look for."

"It will have been worth whatever you charge. But do keep the cost down to a million."

"We'll see. It was so much fun I'm thinking of sending *you* money for the entertainment value."

"Whatever. Just remember that this is lawyer/client privilege."

"What are you talking about? I never did anything for you. You're daft, man."

He said "man." Has he been talking to Kurt? "Anything you saw worth mentioning? Anything unusual?"

"I can't really say. There were the windows and doors and . . . ."

"No, I meant activities, people, events?"

"I was there for about an hour and a half. Going around. Scrutinizing." Pretty big word for him. "Just the regular comings and goings."

"Who?"

"I didn't know any of them. A woman, a few men—three or four—and some who were servants, like a gardener, who left for the day, a maid who does windows, but who leaves about 3:30."

"You said 'three or four.' Were there three or four?"

"Mmm. I remember three for sure. Maybe there was a fourth. Someone who went in by himself. Not with the others."

"Did he come out by himself?"

"Not while I was there."

The mysterious visitor. "What did he look like?"

"I wasn't looking at people. I was looking at a security system. Didn't look at his face. But he must have been 5'10' or six feet. That's all I can tell you."

"What was he wearing?"

"Clothes."

"What?"

"I'm telling you he wasn't naked. That's all I remember."

"Anything else?"

"I can't think of a thing."

"Thanks for your work. Send me an invoice."

"In time, Mr. Burgess."

You'd better do it while I'm still alive, I thought.

Time to go home.

THIRTY FIVE

Terry and I had a simple dinner: barbecued tofu and peas, toast, and Greek yogurt with cucumbers. We were feeling close to the pre-abduction days, but still not quite. I was still a bit tentative with her since I didn't want to invade her space (sounds like '60's pop psychology) and she was obviously not completely comfortable with whatever would be a demon for her for who-knows-how-long.

Her lovemaking was particularly strong. She clung to me more powerfully than ever before. She snuggled and curled up and pressed her body to mine all night. It was wonderful and sad and comforting and frightening. She was now part of me and I think she felt the same. I was furious that she had suffered such trauma. It made me feel almost murderous, but my fury had no outlet. So I converted it into the softest tenderness I could muster up, and our time together was rich and satisfying. Beyond the chaos and death that the little *Buchlein* had brought into my life, it had brought Terry. And for that I was deeply grateful.

With Coster and Bud and Lou (and their cousins) in the picture, we figured the pamphlet was safe enough, though we did hide it—silly as it may seem—under our mattress. Really dumb? Maybe it would have been so obvious that someone wouldn't even think of looking there. Not that we expected anyone to get in. We could barely get out, what with armed bodies at the gates.

My next stop was Celia's office again. Before I left I called Abe Weaver, who said, "Let's have lunch before you go anywhere." He said he had some information for me.

We met at Sushi Mac on Third. Cheap, delicious sushi. Noisy. Crowded. And anonymous.

He didn't waste a moment:

"You've got to use another office. Celia's has been compromised."

"How do you know?"

"Celia went in there and saw some intrusions. Not very subtle, if you ask me."

"What kind?"

"Art on the wall shifted. Something about the phone. Not much, but she doesn't miss a thing. I have another place for you. By the time the police figure out you have taken up new residence, I'll have another place for you."

"Thank you. Why are you doing this?"

"I like you. Anyone who deals in books has a head start in *my* book. Do you need any other help?"

I thought a moment. God! that unagi was delicious. "I'll let you know. Not right now."

Abe knew a professor at the rival school across town, someone who trusted him blindly. When we parted, I had two more keys in my pocket, one for a building, one for an office. And I had a plastic mirror-hanging parking pass and directions to the appropriate lot. Garth Brooks sings of friends in low places. I felt I had friends in new places, and I felt honored.

I found myself in the office of Joyce Dennis, History Department. She had pictures of family on her desk, and a cat. In fact, there were more pictures of the cat than there were of family. We knew who was in charge. There was also a note on a Post-It on the phone: "Welcome. The place is yours." There were instructions how to use the phone for local and other calls, how to pick up messages from the office and away from it, and so forth. "Just use it!" was the last sentence on the note, which was signed "JD." A lawyer? No, just someone willing to bend the law for a friend of a friend.

I had to do *something*. So I called Hans Sachsen at Wisconsin. This time he was in. "I just got back from a trip to Germany," he said. "I got your messages, surrounded by dozens of others. I have your number. I was going to call you today."

I gave him the new number, JD's. I could hear the curiosity in his voice, along with more than a hint of foreign (presumably German) accent.

"Your original email mentioned *Ein Buchlein von dem Sterben*."

"Yes," I said. "You responded, 'Is this a joke?' Why did you ask that?"

"The German text is pretty scarce. There are many Latin versions of it. But to see someone asking about a German text is pretty rare. In fact, it's the first time I have seen such a message in my whole career."

He sounded old enough that his "whole career" could have been substantial. I told him about the pamphlet. He was astounded that it had surfaced. I didn't tell him of its contents, but I didn't need to.

"If you have a complete Kachelofen printing, it is unique. I don't know what it contains—nobody does—but I'd love to see it. Have you read it?"

"Some. What would you think it contains?"

He told me about the rumors that had been circulating for centuries. Kachelofen imprisoned and fined. Copies destroyed. And the rest that Terry and Browner had told me.

I said, "We have had the pamphlet scrutinized by paper experts, people who know typefaces, ink analysts, and booksellers whose instinct about such things is generally unerring. Could you tell me if you thought the text is genuine?"

"What do you mean?" he asked.

I told him about the Thomas Wise forgeries, how Wise was caught on some of his pamphlets on the basis of the text. "What I'd like you to do is read the text and tell me if you think it could be authentic. Would it be the right vocabulary? The correct use of idiom? Could there be any anachronism in the wording or imagery? By analyzing the language and the content, could you tell me if such a text could have been produced in 1494?"

"With about eighty five percent certainty, I could. But I should mention that if I could authenticate it as appropriate to its era, that would mean that I *knew* what was appropriate. Which means, additionally, that I could possibly produce something like this myself. What I'm saying is, even the least suspicious, most authentic-looking text could still be a modern fabrication."

"Added to the other corroborations we have, such authentication might bring us closer to the truth about the piece." We may never know for sure if the pamphlet were genuine, but we could add up all we knew about it. The less information that suggested it was false, the more authentic the pamphlet was likely to be.

Sachsen gave me a fax number and I promised to get a copy of the text to him in a few days. But I told him of Terry and her research. He had heard of her. I said that I wouldn't send the whole text since Terry was preparing a publication on it. He said he would not want to scoop a colleague. Sure! I knew academia well enough . . . . At any rate, he said that the pleasure of seeing the text for the first time—maybe for the first time in five hundred years—would be enough for him.

In all the dealings I had had with this Book of Death since it had come into my life, I had not a single clue of its provenance. Where did it come from? Who had owned it? How did Gens get it? From whom? Gens had said that he had gotten it in a box at the Pasadena flea market. No way. But since anything in the world might turn up there, it was as good a cover as he could find. I needed to find out more.

I needed to talk to Pinsky again. He obviously knew more than our previous conversation revealed. I called him and got him on the fourth ring. He sounded nervous when he heard my voice, and he asked if I would be *alone*. He didn't want any company.

I told him, "The police think you're out of town."

"I know."

"Even after our discussion, they still think that."

He paused. "Thank you."

"Meet me at Canter's on Fairfax. 2:30. I'll buy you the fattest pastrami sandwich you ever saw. Seeded rye. Best caraway seeds in the west. Even the mustard is good."

This didn't disarm him as much as I had hoped. There was still nervousness and hesitation in his voice. "Alone?"

"Guaranteed."

* * *

Canter's wasn't too busy. They saved their crowds for dinnertime and after midnight. Sun-glassed Pinsky got there five minutes late. He was probably there earlier, but he manifested himself at 2:35. We got a table in the back of the original part of the restaurant, under the silly plastic ceiling with leaves and branches and sky. I didn't like it when they put it in thirty five years ago, and I still didn't.

We ordered from our hundred-year-old waitress (oops, serving person) and then sat staring at one another for a couple of minutes.

"Why do you want the police to think you are out of the country?"

"I don't need them in my life right now."

"Right now? What's going on right now?"

"My business."

"How did you pull it off?"

"I have a cousin who looks like me."

"He now has your passport and driver's license."

"You don't need to know. Why the lunch?"

"I need information."

He sure didn't look as if he were in an information-sharing mood. "About what?"

Pretty dumb question. Not about the underwear he had on.

"Please, Mr. Pinsky. No belligerence. You know what I want to know. Please talk."

He said, "Why? What good will it do me?"

I said, "You want the *Buchlein*. I have it. You'll never see it unless I have some information from you. Even if I get the information, you may never see it. But guaranteed you won't unless I get some facts from you."

He looked uncomfortable and he shifted his eyes around the place to see if we had company. No one was near enough to hear us.

"How do I know you're not working with the police right now?"

I told him that they had been more hindrance than help, that I needed to operate without their knowing, that I was able to contact him through private lines that they had no access to, and that if he didn't believe me, he should consider that he was strutting freely in the world right now. I told him that the business of the book was mine, not the police's. And I told him that I could be counted on for discretion, but only if I got what I was after.

He was visibly nervous being there, especially since he knew that the fuzz were in my life. But he said, "What do you want to know?"

"Where did you get the book."

"I *won't* tell you that." That was flat. I could see there was no use pursuing that line of questioning.

"Who was Gens?"

He seemed surprised for a second that I knew of smelly Smith. "A friend."

"What kind of friend?"

"A *friend* friend. What's it to you?"

"Did you know he's dead?"

Rapel couldn't suppress his shock. "What happened? Was he killed?"

"I don't know the details. I'm not sure the police do, either. It looked as if he had been tied and tortured."

Pinsky was upset at this. "I trusted him."

I had expected something more personal. "I will miss him." "He was a good friend."

"What do you mean by that? That you trusted him?"

He hesitated, as if weighing what he would tell me. "He's the one who stole my book."

"How did he get his hands on it?"

"I gave it to him to deliver."

"To Myers."

Pinsky could see that I knew more than he had given me credit for. "Yes."

"Why did you give it to him? Why use him as a delivery boy?"

"He had helped me in the past. I thought I could trust him."

"Where did you get the pamphlet?"

He got angry. "I *told* you that's not your business."

"I need to know."

"No you don't. You're not getting anything from me."

"Do you know where it's from? Who had it before you?"

He just glowered.

"Why do you want it back?"

"It's mine."

"Not if you sold it to Myers."

"I told you, he gave me nothing for it. I know I can sell it for a bundle more than he gave me for it."

"Sell it to whom?"

"You know."

"What do I know?"

"Libraries. The church."

"Booksellers."

"Myers offered me a lot of money. Then he must've found out something about me. I was in jail for a few months. Let off. They had nothing on me. Myers said he could tell them about me. He said he would keep quiet if I sold him the book. He sent me a check for a pittance with a note that more would be sent when he got the book. I got the check and called Gens. He took the book and I called Myers to tell him it was on its way over."

"That's when Gens disappeared."

"Yes. I didn't hear from Myers for a couple of days, so I called him. He said he was still waiting for the book. I didn't believe him. I waited another day and called him back. He said he still didn't have the pamphlet. Then he started accusing me of stealing from him. I told him I still had the check. He could put a stop on it. He said he already did. The son of a bitch had stopped payment on it before it even reached me. He was going to take the book and leave me dry."

"You never got a cent for the book? So you killed him."

"What are you talking about? I never killed anyone."

He didn't seem to be as surprised about this as he had been about Gens's death. "He deserved to die," he said.

"Do you know who killed him?"

"No."

"Or Gens?"

"Maybe Myers. He wanted that book viciously. He would kill for it, I think."

"So would you."

He didn't like that. But he didn't deny it. There was a power in this man, suppressed but just beneath a surface. I was still wary of him.

"Ok, Mr. Burgess. I want my book." He said this menacingly.

"I'm not sure I have anything to give you," I answered.

I could see anger rising. "I came here to make a deal with you. I came here to talk. I want the book back. There's no telling what I'm going to do."

"Is this a threat? It sounds like it."

"Take it for what you want to. You have something of mine. I want it back."

Everyone wants this thing. In fact, he might have had a point. If it was really his and it was stolen by Gens, then it might have been considered Pinsky's by a court of law. But would Pinsky do well in a court? Not likely. He was a bomber with some police record. He would not want to go near a court. The only other option for him looked like taking the pamphlet by force, a prospect I was not congenial with.

"For now," I said, "the pamphlet is safe. Behind locked doors. In a bank. Behind a squad of police. *Inaccessible.*"

He hadn't touched his sandwich. He had ordered corned beef.

He rose, glaring at me. "I *will* get it back."

Then he was gone.

I didn't know how he planned to get it back, but I was unnerved by the determination in his voice. How did he plan to do it? When? Who would be hurt?

I didn't want to use my cell. Coster was probably listening. At Canter's some of the tables used to have phones. These were now gone so I went to the second floor lounge to phone Kurt Bricker. "I have another little job for you. It could be dangerous."

"I love it. What do you want me to do?"

"The same as before. I've been thinking: just because the place is neat and tidy doesn't mean that there is nothing there that I'd want. You've got to look again. Maybe for a notebook or a bunch of tools. Anything. There *must* be something there. You said something of a bunch of pamphlets on a shelf. Can you look through them?"

"You're on," he shouted. "I've got time later today and also tomorrow morning. I'll get back to you asap" (he said it as if it were a word). His voice disappeared.

Back to my table. They hadn't cleared it since there were still two uneaten sandwiches on it. And there was a visitor.

"What the hell are you doing?" Coster was perturbed.

"Eating an egg salad sandwich."

He wasn't amused. "Who was that person with you?"

"A guy I just met."

"What's his name?"

"Doctor / patient privilege," I explained, making it clear his questions would yield little.

"You went across town this morning."

"So did Lou and Bud."

"Elliot." I was surprised he used my first name. "People are dead over your book. You could be, too. No more hi-jinks. You've gotta go through us."

"No disrespect, Officer Coster," I said. "But going through you has turned up nothing."

"We have Blake Myers and Howard Blanding in custody. We are questioning Theresa Myers. We think we know where Myers the dad is. And we know that someone has been doing strange things to the Myers house. Any idea who?"

"What kind of strange things?"

Coster picked up the corned beef sandwich. "This for me?" He took a fat juicy bite, in the process pulling out a mass of meat, some small pieces dangling out of his mouth on strings of fat. "Mmmm. Good" came out of the bite. He chewed for a long time, as corned beef from Canter's requires. After his third swallow (one bite, three swallows— what fine fat sandwiches you get here), he said, still chewing on the leftovers in his mouth, "You know what I mean. You told us you escaped from Myers' house. You didn't tell me you had the place torched."

"What?" I played as dumb as I could, but I guess I must have shown a hint of a smile or something. Whatever emerged from my battered face, he saw it.

"As you know," he said deliberately, "someone destroyed the entire security system on the whole property. Don't know how anyone could have done that. What do you know about it?"

"As much as you do" (and a damn sight more).

He eyed me with suspicion, but then he said, "Not that I care. Myers has been a shady figure in L.A. for a long time."

"How so?"

"He doesn't fall into my division; but I hear about books and antiquities that he sells. Where he gets them is anyone's guess. They seem to be smuggled out of countries in Europe and Asia. I was called in a few times concerning these things since people suspected to be involved with him wound up in my jurisdiction."

"Dead?"

"Quite."

"Can you tie him to Dave Daws or Rudolf Gens?"

"No, but then we could *never* tie him to anyone. It's the same pattern: a valuable item, something goes wrong in its delivery, a body or two appears. Sometimes there are bombs, sometimes it's poison, sometimes it's some kind of torture and beating. Gens was a good example."

"Why didn't you tell me about it?"

"At the time we first spoke of Myers, there was nothing to talk about. No bodies or maybe a body that had nothing to do with him."

"My book, the store, Dave, Terry, me. There are some connections that implicate Myers. You could have said something."

"I guess we should have. Now I'm here to tell you: no more detective work! No more! Now, who was that person I just saw you with?"

"He was the guy who gave you his sandwich" (which Coster had done serious damage to).

It was useless and Coster knew it. "Call me. You're not out of the woods." Great cliché: the woods possibly saved Terry's and my lives.

"Explain."

"No need to."

He was right. I knew that there were still people out there wanting what I had. I knew that I still had it. I knew that people had been killed for what I had. What Terry and I had. I wanted to protect her by telling her to go live with a distant relative (distant in distance, not in genealogy), but she refused. And I understood: she needed to be with me, fighting the nightmares and feeling safe. What a joke! Safe in the eye of the storm. Well, that's not a bad place to be: you can see in the eye of a storm. And the storm doesn't harm you when you are at the eye. But getting out of the storm means going through it. I hoped we made it through.

I knew I was safer with Coster informed, but I also felt that Coster informed meant Coster at my elbow. Which meant that I had no room to maneuver. I wanted revenge for Dave and Terry. I was bursting with pent-up anger. And I had no outlet. Someone was responsible. Someone needed to have his nose flattened (other than me), and I needed to do the flattening. I couldn't let Coster get too close, so I couldn't give him whatever information I had that would open things up for me.

But open what? I didn't know. I needed a plan.

"Officer, could you do me a big favor?"

"Depends." (Did he wear those things?)

"I need to get a few copies of the little book."

His eyes widened. "You have it?!"

"Yes. It was well hidden."

"Where?"

"Lawyer / client . . . ."

"Shit! Tell me!"

"Let's just say that it was on ice for a while."

This didn't seem to register, but he was curious about other things. "Why do you want copies?"

I told him about Hans Sachsen and the need to authenticate the text. It seemed reasonable to him.

"I'll have a hundred-man escort take it to our labs."

"No way!" I said. "I don't want it disappearing into any constabulary vault. Terry and I are working on it. We need to study it, physically and intellectually. We need the original. Sachsen only needs to see several pages of the text. We want to keep it in our possession."

This calmed him and he said he would have the pamphlet picked up whenever I wanted. I said the pamphlet stayed with me—and me with it. I wanted to take it to Kinko's. "There's one on Wilshire near Crescent. I know it well. It's easy to guard. Only two doors, front and back, and the machines are in clear view from both doors. Just a quick in and out." I thought of the burger chain and then I thought of Terry. Shame on me.

I drove back to the apartment with an entourage of unmarked police cars. There must have been ten of them. Quite inconspicuous. People kept looking for the hearse. I felt as if I were in it.

It went like an aborted marriage: it came off without a hitch. Back in the apartment, Terry and I settled down to a nice private evening, with ears and eyes everywhere: at the doors and windows, on the phones, on the roof, in the cellar (well, we didn't really have one; this *was* L.A., after all), and everywhere an ear or an eye would fit inconspicuously. Terry had accompanied us to the Kinko's, from which we had additionally faxed a copy of several pages of the text to Sachsen. I loved Kinko's, a full-service store. I still can't understand how their well trained staff can be congenial despite their minimal salaries.

We had needed food for the cupboards, so Lou or Bud or one or two of their cousins had taken Terry to Trader Joe's. She wanted to go to the one on Santa Monica near Poinsettia. We had a belt-breaker of a dinner, with Joe's Coho salmon and corn the centerpieces, Trader Jose's tortilla chips and dips, and one of their frozen fruit pies for dessert. I loved cheese cake, but the Joe version had gelatin in it, and vegetarians stay away from rendered dead-animal feet and bones.

The snuggling and cuddling weren't as clingy and insistent, but they were there to our satisfaction. I felt that Terry was slowly backing away from the trauma, which was healthy, and that our caresses and kisses were less fiery and obsessive, which was also good. We made love twice that night. It had been years of sexual drought, and now I loved the flood.

THIRTY SIX

We woke to the phone. Jeez, it was only 6:55. Who . . . .

"Mr. Burgess, it's Hans Sachsen. I hope I'm not waking you."

"No, I had to get up to answer the phone anyway." Kurt taught me that one.

"I'm sorry. But this is important."

"I would assume so," I muttered. The cobwebs were still there.

"Have you got a few minutes?"

"I guess so. I'm not due into my shop for three hours. What do you know?"

"I got your fax last night, and I went to work right away. The language is pretty clear. It's my native tongue, after all, and the language hasn't changed as much in the last five hundred years as English has in that time."

"So?" I was now fully alert.

"I think this thing is genuine. I've never seen anything like it."

I had sent him the opening pages, which of course didn't surprise him, and then I faxed a bit more than half of the heretical ones, taken from the areas of the pamphlet where they appeared. The final leaves were also unremarkable, so I sent them as well.

"It's even better—or worse—than I could have imagined." Funny, he came up with the same assessment as we had. "The language is pure fifteenth century. The spelling, the dialect, the idioms, and so forth. Well, spelling wasn't too fixed by then, but what is there does fit. It's the sentiment that is so . . . outrageous. I can see why Kachelofen was treated so severely. This is pure molten lava."

Do they have active volcanoes in Germany? Or in Wisconsin?

"Is there any chance that this could be faked?"

"Of course, there is always a chance. As I told you on the phone, I guess I could have come up with something like this. Though I think my own vivid imagination could have never produced some of the pictures you sent. It's outrageous."

"You already said that."

"I mean, it's truly outrageous."

"How about the sentiment? Is it believable? I mean, for its era?"

"Undoubtedly. At the time there was a strong uprising against the Catholic church—I should say 'the church,' since it was *the* church. Protesting sects, rabid fundamental groups, theologians of all stripes were questioning the dogma of the church. They would do anything to discredit it. The Reformation was under way. People at all levels of society were fed up with the strictures of their religion. Wasn't a religion supposed to ease their burden? Well, the church seemed to be working exactly in the opposite direction."

"Who would have written this?"

"It could have been anyone: someone educated in the monasteries, and that includes many people. Someone educated in one of the public schools or universities. Someone in the court. Authors, students, even some artists who were highly educated. It sounds like the language of a person of the cloth, but since churchgoers would have been exposed to the sermons of the middle ages most of their lives, they knew the vocabulary, the grammar, logic, and rhetoric. They studied the Trivium, these three branches of learning, from early on in their education. A solid basic education, an exposure to the scriptures and sermons, an understanding of theological doctrine, and a knowledge of the workings of the church, mixed with a fanaticism against the current oppressive religion—these are the ingredients of this pamphlet."

"Who else beside you would know all this?"

"Ask Dr. Luckombe. She would know it. So would any scholar of the German Middle Ages. Especially ones schooled in the history, religion, and language of the time. There must be hundreds of us all over the world."

"So, you're saying textually it could be genuine, but you're not sure. It could have been written five hundred years ago or five hundred hours ago. You think it's the kind of thing that could have been written, but you've never seen anything like it before. Where does that leave us?"

"Well, one more thing. You sent a copy of the last leaf, with the signature. It had a signature on it that you said looked like Frithof von Escher. It was Eschen. Frithof von Eschen. His name indicates that his family originally came from Liechtenstein."

"Who was he? Anyone you met?"

"It wasn't too hard to find him. He's mentioned in several histories and reference books. He was a landgrave in a village west and slightly north of Leipzig, Halle. From the end of the thirteenth to the fifteenth century the city was a member of the Hanseatic League. By 1544 it had fully accepted the Reformation. By the time the pamphlet was written, von Eschen was already making a name for himself as a heretic—at least according to the Catholic church. He was fairly well known for his outspoken criticism of the church. He was tortured and hanged, but not until he had gathered to him a pretty vocal band of followers."

"Are there any examples of his signature around?"

"Not that I know of. I don't know any more than my sources reveal, and they talk more about his rabble-rousing than about anything he wrote. No way of knowing right now. Many of these religious fanatics did their damage on soap boxes, not in print. But he was probably not the author. He probably owned it."

"Of course," I acknowledged. "There's no way to know who the author was and no way to ascertain that the signature is genuine?"

"No more than for the rest of the pamphlet. But it sure looks good. Even the marginal annotations, obviously written by a sympathizer of the text. Someone would have to know the calligraphic style of fifteenth-century Germany. And someone did. I can't say when it was signed, however."

I guess this left me only partially whelmed. It looked genuine but maybe wasn't. The paper, ink, and type evidence said it could be genuine, and probably was. The text said it probably was. But these were only probablys.

"Dr. Sachsen. Why would anyone do a thing like this, either then or now?"

"Then, for many reasons: to discredit a corrupt church. For revenge. To roil up the people. To sell pamphlets. Kachelofen himself might have written it. After all, he stood to make a lot of money if he sold lots of these."

"And now?"

"Now. Well, you're a bookseller. If this thing were genuine, what would it be worth?"

"I was going to ask you."

"I don't know. But if you could prove its authenticity, you could have a bidding war going on for it."

War sounds right. With guns and bombs and enemies and hostages.

"Any last words?"

"All I can say is, thank you for letting me in on this. I won't use it. But I sure would like to see the whole text and I'd love to know if it was authentic."

"Me too."

Terry was naturally awake and listening to my end of the conversation. I told her what Sachsen said. She was impressed but not surprised. "It's no more than I told you," she said.

"We needed a second opinion. You're a doctor. You should know that."

We talked strategy, but we were at a standstill. The people to contact were Blake and Howie, who were in custody, and Pinsky, who knew something but wouldn't squeal. Anyone else? Coster, but he was holding his cards as closely as I was. Sometimes when you can't think of an avenue, one opens up for you.

It was Abe Weaver on the phone. "Elliot, have you seen or heard from Celia?"

"No. I haven't been in her office for two days, now. Why?"

"She didn't show up to a faculty meeting—and she hasn't missed one in more than twenty years. There's no answer at her home or office. I drove over to her place. Her car is there, but she doesn't answer the door. I'm worried."

"Me too." And I was. There was no reason to believe that the police were the only ones tailing me to Dr. Brothers' office. If someone thought she might know anything about me or the book, she could be in danger.

"Abe, I'm calling the police."

"I already did, to find out if they knew anything. They said nothing and that it was too early to report someone missing. They said wait another day."

"I'll call the constable. Sit tight."

Coster had been apprised of Weaver's call. He too showed concern. "We'll send someone over to her home with a search warrant. That way we can enter the house if no one comes to the door. It'll take a few hours, but in an emergency . . . . And this looks like one. We knew we weren't the only ones following you around."

"Why didn't you say something?"

"We were there to protect you. We couldn't concentrate on all the people you came into contact with."

"I saw her only once, long ago."

"But you were in her office every day. It wouldn't take much to connect you to her. Or her to you." He paused. Then he added, "I want you to know that Blake Myers and his driver are back home. We had nothing to hold them on. They denied your story. We couldn't keep them here. You should have heard the threats their lawyer made."

"I can imagine." What a scary notion: two homicidal people out there angry at me for implicating them in crimes that they actually committed.

"We of course were not intimidated by their threats."

"Of course."

"We'll keep an eye on them. You and Ms. Luckombe are safe."

"From them. But what if there's someone else?" I thought of Pinsky. Where was he? What would he do? I knew what he was capable of, and that scared me.

"What do you mean 'someone else'? What do you know?"

I didn't feel like giving up my last trump. "Nothing. I just hypothesized."

"We don't need hypotheses."

"I guess you are still monitoring my phone."

"Yes. I just got a report of your conversation with Professor Weaver. We won't wait another day. Sit tight." I wondered if he heard me say the same thing to Weaver. I was not sitting tight. I was sitting nervous. I wasn't sitting pretty. I was a sitting duck. And I didn't feel like sitting around. I kissed Terry and went toward Celia's office. I still had the keys.

I could find nothing amiss in her office, though she herself saw something. What was it? There were no clues, no messages, no nothing. In a murder mystery there would have been a hair or fingernail or scrap of paper or a pad on which someone had scribbled a number which could be seen by rubbing a pencil on the blank sheet that was left when the top sheet had been taken away. I couldn't see hairs or nails or pads. So much for the murder mystery angle. I thought I'd call Coster to ask him if he would also get a warrant to scour Celia's office.

Coster took the phone from some drawling flunky at his office. "What is it now?"

"Did you plan to look into Dr. Brothers' office, too?"

"Of course."

"I guess I didn't need to ask. All I had to do was call someone and suggest it and you would have thought of it."

"Why?"

"Don't be naïve. You're listening to everything. I'm bugged."

"Yes, we've heard everything you have said on your home phone and on your email."

"What! What about this office?"

"What office? Where are you?"

"You don't know?"

There was a pause. "Of course, I know. You are at the university. Probably in Dr. Celia Brothers' office."

"What do you mean 'probably'? You should know for sure."

"And why is that?"

"You've got everything bugged. You probably have the toilets in the mayor's house bugged."

"No. We don't have that office bugged. Why are you so sure?"

I told him what Weaver had told me.

There was another one of Coster's patented pauses. "We didn't need any special permissions to listen in on your life. You gave them to us. We would need permission to listen in on a phone in someone else's life, even if you were using it."

"So if Dr. Brothers' office is bugged, someone has piles of information from here. And it's not you?"

"No."

"And I don't even know who knows what." I couldn't remember all the calls I had made on that phone. Or even the conversations I had had. Right here there should be bunches of speculation of who could have bugged the phone. But we all knew.

Coster wasn't pleased, either at me or at himself. Within an hour he had mobilized a small force with photos of Celia (gotten from Weaver) and with papers to have access to her home, her bank accounts, her office, her computers, and even her hairdresser's information. What was going on?

I didn't know, but I didn't want to be there when the office was raided. I was out of there in a flash.

* * *

Back in my shop I had time to ruminate: Was the office really bugged? I guess Coster would let me know soon enough. If so, who had done it? When? What did someone know? And more to the point: what did this mean about Terry's and my safety? And our book?

I figured that with the increased protection, Terry and I were somewhat safe. Also, with Blake and Howard recently arrested, they would be cautious, for a while at least, about entering my sphere. And Rapel Pinsky wouldn't want to become too public since he did his best to convince the powers that be (I hate that phrase) that he was in Poland.

This reckoning had two effects on me: first, a slight sense of relief that the people who, it seemed, could do the worst to me, and who had a reason to, were probably going to retreat from the fray. But second, it made me antsy. I am a person of action. I hate sitting around waiting for the other sword of Damocles to fall. I hate having my dander raised, my sense of injustice and the need for vengeance aroused, and not being able to do anything about it. I needed what the pop-psychologists call closure. (It's what follows openure and manure.) Unless there was someone else pulling the strings here, all I could see was a long drought with my suspects. I had to stir up the hornet's nest. I had to get this train out of the station. (I could set a record for conflicting metaphors.)

What could I do to spur some action? The one catalyst that I had was the *Buchlein* itself. It opened eyes. It elicited visits and emails and phone calls. It was like waving a flag at a bull. But what to do with it?

Harry Luben. As much as I questioned his sales tactics—expensive books to rich clients—I had to admit that he was one brilliant bookman. He knew everyone he needed to know, from sources to customers. He had the best stock in the city. He had practically unparalleled experience. If you needed a Gutenberg leaf, call Harry. If he didn't have it, he could get it. Connections like nobody else's. I felt pretty small beside him and I wasn't even sure he knew who I was.

Near my worktable I keep lots of reference tools. I pulled out the directory of the American Booksellers of Old and Rare Books (ABORB) and paged to Luben. The phone was passed off to him.

"Luben here."

"Hi, I'm Elliot Burgess."

"Elliot! Good to hear from you! Why the pleasure of this call?"

No fuss, no muss. He made you feel good and he didn't waste time.

"I have a pretty spectacular book to sell. If you have a client, we could split the proceeds."

I could have called any number of libraries or private collectors. But that way the transaction would never be made public. I needed publicity. Harry knew everyone. He'd want to ask others about provenance and authenticity and values—though on an item like this, if he knew his printing history (which he did), he wouldn't need to go further than his own reference library to know that this was a winner.

"Why come to me?"

He knew, but he was fishing for a compliment. "I can't think of anyone with more connections."

"If it's the *Buchlein von dem Sterben*, I can sell it easily. But you know that the Huntington, the British Library, the Library of Congress, Texas, Berkeley, the Vatican, any number of libraries would snap this up. Why me?"

"Libraries generally have limited budgets. I thought you might know of private parties whose budgets are bigger."

This seemed to satisfy him. He asked, "What do you know about this little pamphlet?"

I told him about the cyclotron and the typeface and the paper and Dr. Sachsen's appraisal of the text. I didn't mention Caligula, Blake, Howie, Gens, Pinsky, Theresa, Terry, Coster, Bud and Lou, or bombs. If he didn't already know, he didn't need to know.

"Can you bring it to my shop today or tomorrow?"

"I'd rather not. Why don't you come to my place tomorrow morning. Say nine o'clock. I have hired a couple of bodies to watch the place, so don't be alarmed if you see thugs guarding the door."

"Really?" Said more in sarcasm than as a question. "I'll be there at nine. Ta." Click.

"Ta?" Did he really say that? I might need a chaperone when he gets there.

Next the Internet. I put out a message on the Out of the Library website: "*Ein Buchlein von dem Sterben*, Leipzig: Kachelofen, 1494. Excellent condition. Text complete. Price on request." Followed by my contact points. This could get some response.

I thought of eBay, but I figured not too many people shop for million-dollar pamphlets on eBay. I left a voice mail message for Hans Sachsen that I was in the process of marketing my gem. I said nothing more. If he was interested, he'd call. Then the word might go out in the scholarly world. And I considered calling the two other owners of the pamphlet, Pinsky and Myers frere. But I figured direct, full frontal assault on them would not serve any more purpose than having them find out about this sale from other sources.

Some of the bait was now dangling.

I sat for a moment deciding which pile of books to deal with next— the shop still looked something like the aftermath of a college-departed teen. The phone jingled.

"Mr. Burgess? It's Kurt."

"Kurt. What's up?"

"I'm back here. I think I found something. I'm not sure. It's not too big and it's pretty inconspicuous, but it may be what you were looking for."

"You went back to Pinsky's place?"

"Yes. I had to do some pretty nifty dancing to get in."

"What do you mean?"

"Lots of people on the street. I felt as if they were all looking at me. Probably not, but I felt creepy. I still do. It's kinda creepy here."

"Naturally."

"I took a clipboard with me with a pad on it. It looked sort of official, businesslike. I knocked on the door a few times, like before. No one came out. If he had I was going to tell him I was doing research on the garbage service in the neighborhood. I had already gotten some statements from neighbors."

"So?"

"The place is empty. And the back door was still unlocked."

"What did you find?"

"A pamphlet. I've got it here."

"Where did you find it?"

"On a bookshelf. It looked like nothing special and was thin enough to be practically hidden."

"Did anyone see you?"

"I don't think . . . ."

There was a funny muffled banging sound immediately followed by what sounded like a fast exhale, and then nothing.

"Kurt?" I called a few more times, and then I heard the phone hang up.

The hair on my neck did its thing again. Something was really wrong. Where was he? Simple. I called Coster's office and got him in. "Coster, what can you tell me about the source of a call to my shop?"

"We can tell you where it came from. Why?"

"How soon after the call can you tell?"

"If the call was a minute or so long, maybe in a moment. If the call was shorter, maybe not at all."

I had been on the phone for just about a minute with Kurt. "I just got a call from Kurt Bricker. Know who he is?"

"Tell me."

I told him, "A friend. Interested in the *Buchlein*."

He said, "Wait a minute."

In two minutes he was back at the phone. "The call came from an address in Inglewood. But it could have come from anywhere if it was on a cell phone. What's up? What does Bricker have to do with all this?"

"Probably nothing." Again, I didn't want the police to know too much. Call it silly, but I felt that I could make more progress on my own than if I were burdened with the L.A. constabulary.

"Call me if there's something." He said it firmly, with an edge of irritation.

"You know I will." I did my Boy Scout best on that one.

"Right!"

* * *

I knew I was not alone in my drive to Pinsky's place. I had carried his little slip of paper in my wallet since his first visit. The apartment was not hard to find. I pulled up to the curb, and since it was a narrow residential street with little to obscure anyone's vision, I clearly saw the police park behind me down the block. I didn't know what I would find, but I sort of knew what I would find.

It was a good neighborhood, but the place was in an interior courtyard, on the second floor of one of those ugly stucco tract apartment buildings from the '50s. Faded yellow, chipping paint. Smell of garlic cooking somewhere. Iron rails and banisters. A couple of scruffy trees. Dirt where there was supposed to be grass. The door to the place was open an inch. I walked up to it slowly and stopped just outside. I listened. No sound. I could actually feel my heart bumping, and, though seriously intent on my business there, I felt my nose throb to my heart's rhythm. That sucker still hurt. I reached up with my right hand to touch the door.

"You can't do that!" came wailing from beneath me—in a child's voice. Another child, older, "Yes I can." "Can't." "Can."

There was the sound of a tussle and then the smaller voice crying and threatening to tell. Kids always say "I'm gonna tell." Whom are they gonna tell?

The distraction caused my arm to drop and my knees to bend a bit. The fight or flight reaction. I felt the acrid sweat in my armpit and my heart beat went up another notch. Another ten seconds at the door. My arm went up again.

When I pushed, the door swung open enough for me to go in with some room to spare, but it snagged on something behind it that kept it from opening more. I didn't need to go inside to see the horror.

It was as if a raging bull had been set loose in the place. There were shelves and things and wall hangings, but everything was on the floor. Everything. Paintings, books, dishes, kitchen utensils, clothing, pillows, cushions, broken things. Everything. And amidst the ruins was the body of my playwright. Good, god, what a mess. I recognized his hair, though the back of his head had been smashed. He was lying on his stomach, his head turned to the left onto his right cheek. He was breathing, but faintly. And motionless.

A bookshelf had partially fallen on him, and he and the floor were littered with books and pamphlets and magazines. But the real mess came not from that little shelf.

Someone had been looking for something. Dumb statement. Of course. The mess throughout the place made it look as if someone hadn't found what he was looking for, so he kept looking. Piles of papers and stuff filled the floor; it was what had stopped the door as I entered. The place seemed to consist of only a single room—small kitchen area on one side, opened sofa bed on the other. Even the bed had been torn apart.

My instincts were fighting each other. Stay and you can be the hero and find the clue that solves the case. Your powers of deduction and acuity will let you see the *thing* that the intruder missed. The other side of my brain said, get the hell out of there. If the attacker didn't find *it*, why do you think you will? And if he did, then it's not there for you to find.

That sounded sensible. Also the place smelled funny and the search through the rubble could have taken hours. And I was feeling sick and smelly myself. And I got the hell out of there. I knew I couldn't help Kurt—not the way he was. Someone could.

So, back on the street, I ran to the police and told them to get up to apartment 7 Now. (It was great to have the cavalry there when you needed them.) One of them ran up and the other told me to stay with him. It wasn't Bud and Lou. In less than two minutes a call had been sent through to Coster's office. We were to wait there until Coster himself came. That took about twenty minutes, though it seemed like twenty three minutes.

In fact, three cars showed up—one an ambulance. Kurt was still alive and being carried out on a wheeled stretcher thing. The next thing I knew I was answering questions in Coster's office.

The debriefing, such as it was, was not too long. I told him of Kurt's offer to help and that Kurt had called to tell me he had found something."

"We know."

Coster had to sound as if he were on top of all this stuff. Sure, he knew. But only from the phone call that his fellows and I heard.

"What was he looking for?"

"I don't know."

"Don't play games." Coster was really irritated.

"I'm not. I had told him that I thought there must be *something* there."

"Where's there? You mean, where was he looking?" I'm sure Coster had no notion of Pinsky's involvement yet.

"At the home of someone who wanted the pamphlet," I said.

"Related to Myers?"

What good would it do not to tell him at this point?

"I'm not sure. It's Pinsky."

Coster tried to look cool, but he was stunned by this and he couldn't hide that. "Pinsky's in Poland."

"Then someone else who looks like him, answers to that name, and lives in his place."

"How do you know what Pinsky looks like?"

"The photos you gave me way back when—when we were looking for someone who might have incendiaried my house and shop."

"You remembered what he looked like from those photos?"

"Not exactly. But I do know what he looks like: I've talked with him, in person."

"You sure it was him?" Coster needed to ask questions to show he was in charge. These were pretty dumb questions.

"Are you sure it wasn't?"

And there we were again, at a circular, questioning conversation. Twenty more minutes of that was all Coster needed to see that I had nothing to tell him. At least, nothing more he would get out of me. I drove home with my escorts and waved bye to them as I let myself into the apartment.

* * *

When Terry heard me come in she ran to me, kissed me warmly, but then pulled away.

"Ugh. You smell."

"I love your tender, erotic greetings."

"No, Elliot. I mean you smell. Where have you been? Get out of those clothes."

"Sounds great."

"No. Take a shower. I'll dump your stuff into a plastic bag and get it into the hamper. Where have you been?"

Over one of her scrumptious dinners I told her about my day. Shock, pity, terror, all these and more showed in her responses.

She told me that she had called the university to ask for an emergency leave. They said she had to ask in writing. She wanted a couple of months to rebuild, she said.

That night it was just cuddling. But it was the best cuddling one can imagine.

At breakfast we tried to gather what we knew about everything to see where that might take us.

"Where do you think Celia Brothers is?"

"I can only imagine," I said.

"Whoever killed Gens and smashed Dave and probably killed Myers shows that killing is not an issue. The booklet seems to be the key."

"Yes. And it makes me nervous to have it here."

"We're protected." When she said this, I could hear the emphasis on protection, which she still needed. "But, you're right. We have to get it out of here."

I thought for a moment. "On the other hand, anyone looking for it would *never* expect to find it here. Back in a vault someplace, maybe. In the possession of the police. But here? No way. I think it's safe. But are we?"

It had occurred to me that someone wanting the pamphlet but being denied it long enough might just get vengeful and try to take us out. Of course, I didn't mention this to Terry.

In movies you often have a peaceful scene grossly interrupted by trauma:

The phone rang.

Coster: "We have bad news, Mr. Burgess. We have found Celia Brothers. She had been beaten up and dumped in a gully in the hills above Sunset—not far from Coldwater Canyon. She's at the UCLA hospital. She'll recover. But for someone that frail, it was pretty bad."

"What . . . ."

"She is still incoherent. We don't know anything more than I told you. Someone found her. She had crawled into the street and had fainted. She's tough."

"It was my fault."

"In a sense." I didn't want him to agree with me. "It almost certainly had something to do with your book."

Gens, Dave, Kurt, now Celia. All of this violence. No one would ever want to meet me again. I was the kiss of *Sterben*.

I needed to change the subject. My sadness for that kind, sweet, brilliant woman was overwhelming. "Tell me about Kurt."

"He was smashed from behind by some kind of blunt object."

In a murder mystery it would have been a poker. But not in L.A.

"He had been unconscious for whatever time it took for you to get over there. We have the time of the call and the time when he stopped speaking. It was pretty precise."

"And in the apartment?"

"As you saw, it was trashed. He mentioned a pamphlet."

"Yes," I said. "I thought of that. Someone might have thought he was talking about *the* pamphlet. He said something about having it there with him. Someone might have thought that what he had could be found easily. It didn't look like a big place."

"It was an efficiency. Everything that its resident owned, probably, was in that room."

"What did you find?" I didn't really expect him to have found anything important or startling. If the trasher had found what he was looking for, it would not have been there. If he hadn't, it would have been buried under such a mass of mangled detritus that it would not have been recognizable as something important—worth killing for.

"Nothing out of the ordinary. We found piles and piles of jumbled papers, some books, pamphlets, cd's, blank paper, and the rest."

He had said 'pamphlets.' "Could I go over there to see?"

"We've had the place blanketed with security and searchers since yesterday. I don't think there's anything for you to see that we haven't already seen."

I may be looking for things they weren't seeking. "Could I go? I mean, I feel responsible. It's the least I can do. Maybe I can find something . . . ."

"Ok. See if you can come up with something. But you'll be accompanied by a couple of eagle-eyes."

"I don't intend to take anything."

"I wasn't suggesting that you were."

"Well, I wasn't." I tried to sound offended, and it would have been genuine if I had really not intended to take anything. But who knows what I might find?

Terry was shocked to learn of these developments. She said she was thinking we should just get rid of the pamphlet and move to another state. But we both knew we couldn't get out of this till we knew more: who, what, where, when, why, and how.

I met two policemen, one fat and sweaty, one mesomorph with a silly mustache, at the apartment. Going in gave my stomach a churn, but I couldn't do any inspection from outside. There was no Kurt, but there was blood on the carpet where his head had lain, and there were piles of papers, half neatly stacked all over the room. It's hard to believe that such a pile of materials could have been in drawers and shelves and on tables. There didn't seem to have been room for it all.

I knew that I was looking for what Kurt had called a pamphlet, but what did it look like? How big was it? Where was it? And what did it contain? I'll spare the details of a half-hour search. I found what I think he was talking about, about 4" x 6", stapled into a black cover. It was in a large and totally sloppy pile of *Variety* and other magazines, notebooks, sketch books, and loose papers. I saw it there, but I didn't want to call attention to it. I grabbed a *Time* magazine and shielded it from sight with my body. The two officers were carelessly watching me, getting bored, and fidgeting as if to say Let's get out of here. Enough, already!

I turned my back to the pamphlet, putting the *Time* behind me. One of my acquaintances said, "What do you have there?"

"Nothing of importance."

"Ok. It's important to us. Let's see it."

"It's really nothing. Just a magazine."

"You're not to take anything out of here. You know that."

"I'm not taking anything."

"Then let's see what you are holding."

He was standing across the room, so I carelessly (carefully) tossed the *Time* to him just out of his reach. They both turned to watch it. I had used an exaggerated motion in my toss, and down I went, right onto my derriere. Right onto the pamphlet I wanted. Their eyes went from the *Time* back to me in an instant, and they both saw me flop. They laughed derisively, and then they both turned to pick up the magazine. I got up red-faced and one pamphlet heavier. It was small enough that I could quickly slip it into my inner blazer pocket in a swift move, and then pretend that that arm had shot across my body to rub the other arm, as if I had hurt it when I fell.

The whole operation took less than five seconds. But we were satisfied. I knew why they were; they didn't know why I was.

"C'mon; let's go."

"No," I said firmly. "Just a few more minutes." I didn't want them to connect my willingness to leave with the instantaneous hiatus in their surveillance of me. I poked around purposefully for another ten minutes, complaining of my sore left arm. But even I couldn't play this game any longer, and I reluctantly left the field with them.

They followed me home, as per their regular routine, and I went in to see Terry as painfully as I could make it look.

* * *

"Elliot!" I hadn't seen Terry this animated in days. I had just walked through the door and Terry was in front of me. "You got a call. Someone wants to see you right now!"

I could see and hear that this was not merely excitement; it was anxiety. Though we had discussed our Book of Death since her ordeal, it was always with a sense of nervousness on her part. She had recalled that during her time at the Myers place, she had heard voices demanding "Where is it? Where is the Book?" many times. She said that she didn't remember telling anyone anything. All she could remember was saying "I don't know" over and over. In her constant stupor she also remembers some kind of threat about me if she didn't tell them where the book was. And when she told me this, she shuddered.

"Tell me about the phone call."

I knew the fuzz knew of this call. I wanted to know as much as they did.

"It was a muffled voice, but it reminded me of one of the voices I heard at that awful place." She didn't say "the Myers house" partly because the place gave her the creeps and partly because she wasn't sure where she had been.

"Can you tell me whose it was?"

"No. I didn't know then. So I can't tell you whose it was. And I'm not sure anyway."

"What did he say?"

"'I know we're not alone on the phone. Tell Mr. Burgess I must see him now. He knows the address.' That's all I heard. Oh, but there was one more thing. He said, 'NOW—OR ELSE,' really loud and demanding."

Or else what? "That's all?"

"Well, there was some talking in the background for a few seconds and I heard the word 'bomb.' It really scared me."

I thought a moment. The police would know about the call. They would surmise that it was from Myers or Pinsky. Who else's address did I know? And Pinsky was out of the picture since Terry had never heard his voice. But did Coster know this? Probably not. Coster would not know that Terry had never heard Pinsky's voice and would certainly not know that she thought she recognized a voice on the phone. It had to be coming from the Myers residence.

I felt that I needed to follow up on this immediately. To begin with, I felt sure that Simon Johnson was not the original bomber, which would mean that another incendiary fellow out there, at least once under the employ of Caligula Books, *was* still strutting his stuff. Was it planted or a piece of "good" fortune that Terry heard that word? It made no difference.

Also, Coster and his crew may not know who made the call if it were made from a pay phone or somewhere else. Which was likely since Myers and friends would know that the line was tapped. This meant that they knew of the call, but not of its source.

Now, if I went to Coster with this, he would back me off and take charge. But there was nothing to take charge of. He might have heard the call, but he wouldn't have known whom it came from. Further, there was nothing he could do even if he figured out it came from Myers. Blake could simply deny it, if the call hadn't been traced to his phone.

"Terry, how long did the phone call take?"

"It couldn't have been more than ten seconds."

So Coster probably didn't know. I sat down onto the couch for a few minutes, Terry at my side, holding my arm. But my mind was far away. I needed to face Myers myself. I didn't know what would come of it, but Terry would know and if I disappeared for a while, without checking in to her, she could call the cops and tell them where I was. I figured that Blake and Howie and Theresa wouldn't dare to attack me again, knowing (or at least thinking) that I was being closely tailed by the police. I needed to make them think that.

My first act was to dial Pinsky's place. Remarkably, I got him in. Quickly I said, "Pinsky, I'll be there as you wish. Eight tonight. Stay put." Then I hung up. He hadn't had a chance to say anything. Now Coster knew whom that call was from. That's where the militia were headed.

Then I called Abe Weaver. "Abe, I need to talk with you. Can you come over to my house?"

Abe said, "I can be there in twenty minutes. You in the Santa Monica place?"

"Yes. Come for dinner, about six thirty. And please bring your cell phone." I had seen one beside his couch when I was there.

Terry said, "What are you up to?"

I couldn't tell her the whole truth. "I need to confront him." She knew I meant Blake. "I need to get him off our backs. I think I can do that if I make a deal with him. I will sell the book and give him a substantial percentage of the take. He could get a half million from it, maybe more."

"That sounds ridiculous. He is crazy and murderous. He sounds unstable. He could have killed you . . . and me." She said it with trepidation. "I won't let you go."

"Terry," I said, in the softest and most reassuring tone I could muster up, "The man is driven almost exclusively by money. He wants money. He knows that we own the book and he has no legal right to it."

"How do you know that?"

"He would certainly have gone through legal channels by now if he thought he could prove ownership. Presuming that Edward Myers is dead. A fat chunk of the sale of something he doesn't own would be better than being out to dry."

"But he's dangerous."

"I don't think so by now. He will believe I'm not alone on this visit. He will see that I am there to offer him something better than what he can otherwise hope to get."

What I didn't tell Terry was that I was roiling with vengeance. It had been growing in me since the fist in the face, or even before when Poppa Caligula presumed he could push me around. Every time I opened my mouth, my nose hurt. The bullet hole was still healing. The pain in my wrists, shoulders, and neck had settled in as if for the long haul.

Every step I took hurt my patella. And my home and business had been ransacked and bombed and raped.

Worst of all, Dave and Celia and Kurt were in hospitals and Terry had been brutally traumatized. Someone had to pay. And I knew who it was. Whether it was Caligula or the son and his gorilla, someone had to be punished for all the havoc wrought on my life.

I don't like to fight. But pushed against a wall, get out of my way! All the simmering frustration of defeat and being pushed around and told what I could and couldn't do, should and shouldn't do, of the last few weeks were driving me mad—angry mad. I was against the wall.

I had only a vague plan of what I would do when I got to Myers's place. Maybe it had to do with trying to get some information out of him. Whose pamphlet was it, really? Is it genuine? If so, where did it come from? If not, who did it? Who killed Edward? Who attacked Dave and Kurt and Celia? And Gens? Why? Maybe I could barter some of the profits of the pamphlet for information. Maybe I could get something on them that would . . . . Not a chance. They were too cagey and self-protective. Just the ropes on me and the chain on Terry indicated that.

But though I didn't know exactly what I wanted to do there, I felt somewhat safe. I did believe that they wouldn't come at me again. That would be pretty stupid since I was accompanied by police (they would believe) and I would not place myself into their clutches without having some kind of foolproof protection (they would believe). I hadn't yet figured out what that protection would be. But I felt the necessity to confront these demons to exorcise them.

When Weaver arrived I explained my tactics. Wearing my well known blazer, he was to take my car and drive away. This would pull the guards off. I would take his car and head out to Myers's house. After about ten minutes of driving, he was to stop, get out, and ask why he was being followed. The tails would see they were onto the wrong man and would let him be.

"Just where is it you are going?" He asked with a tone of mere curiosity, but I could hear more in his nonverbal cues.

"Why do you want to know?"

"All this cloak, dagger, and death stuff. You haven't kept me up to speed. Where does it all stand? Who are the perpetrators? What have they done?"

I told him about Dave and the other victims, not mentioning Celia, but I needn't have said a thing.

"Does Celia's being beaten up figure into all this?"

"I believe it does." What could I say? He was too canny for any issue-skirting.

"What proof do you have?"

I filled him in on my and Terry's adventures at *chez* Myers, leading up to Kurt's and Celia's attacks. We were silent a moment. Then he said:

"I have loved her for many years." It was confessional, therapeutic, and probably the first time he ever uttered it. And it was something I already suspected.

"I thought you might," I said soberly.

"No, you don't understand. She and I joined that faculty over forty years ago. We were the two young kids on the block, so we had a pact between us as cohorts with a common enemy. Her work and mine were good enough to get us tenure, but we saw one after another of the poor assistant professors being shafted and murdered by our colleagues. We became very close friends. Very close."

"Weren't you and she married?"

"Yes, my sweet wife was simple enough to be unaffected by the snakes in the department and loving enough to take care of me like a prince. And Celia's husband was a good man, lost to lung cancer when he was in his forties. My wife lived about ten years beyond that, and since then Celia and I . . . ."

He couldn't speak any more.

"Abe, I am deeply sorry. And I am sorry that I involved you both in this affair."

"We were all in it together. You were, after all, one of those poor assistant professors. You were one of ours."

I said, "It looks as if Celia will be ok."

"Yes," he said wistfully. "Thank heaven."

We had a simple dinner and talked about academia and Celia and being safe and being unsafe. Eventually Abe asked again.

"Where are you going? To people who may have . . . ."

"Yes. But I think I'm safe." I told him why. He agreed that it would be a form of suicide for the bad guys to come at me again.

"Where is the house?"

I gave him the address. "It's such a beautiful house, in such a lovely setting, you'd never know what evil lurks inside."

"Sounds like academia," he said.

* * *

Using Weaver's cell phone so that we wouldn't be eavesdropped on, I called Blake Myers. His intermediary got the message to him. When he took the line I said, "We will be there tonight at eight."

"Who's 'we'?"

"You know who is on the line. I'm not alone. I want to talk. Is it safe?"

Dumb question. What's he going to say: "Come on over and we'll punch out your schnoz again. It felt so good the first time."

"Just come."

"Is it safe?"

I guess one dumb question unanswered needed to be asked again.

"What do you think?"

"I have a full report written out. I am being followed by the city's best. They know where I'm going and who is here. They expect me to reappear in a half hour from your house. I won't be wired for sound. Whatever we speak about is confidential. I need some information."

"Where are you calling from?" Blake had a right to be suspicious.

"Someone's cell phone. It's private."

"What information do you need?"

I couldn't tell him that I was there to look around for weak spots. In him; in the house. Anywhere. I needed to do some incendiaring. I was near the end of my fuse.

"I'll see you at eight."

That was the end of the call.

Weaver told me to hold onto his cell phone; he had another. My raised eyebrows expressed my amazement. He added, "I have a computer, a DVD, a Walkman, and hand-held calendar/phone directory/ and message center. I even have a pager, though I have never used it.

And I have all kinds of other stuff for my protection—things I still haven't used, but you never know. So why the surprise at two cell phones?"

"Who uses the second unit?"

"I do. When the battery of one runs low, I use the second."

"How often do you use your cell phone?"

"I used it two weeks ago. I was reading on the couch and wanted to make a call. It was close; the regular phone was across the room."

"How many calls do you get on these phones?"

"Well . . . so far not too many."

"Two different cell phone lines and few calls?"

"Since Celia's been in the hospital, none. She was the only one who knew the numbers, and she used them maybe twice. She usually got me at the home number."

"You've received only two calls on the two phones since you got them?"

"Uh, yes. But you never know."

"Who has the numbers?"

"No one that I know of. The phones are for me to call out on. Not for anyone to reach me."

"Great. So if we needed to talk privately, we could do so on the two phones?"

"Yes."

"Do you have both of them with you?"

"Of course. What's the use of having cell phones if you don't carry them with you?"

We went over our plan. I told him that when he shook his tail, he should call me. I took one of the phones. He said that he had each phone number programmed into the other phone, and he showed me how to use the auto-dial for the other unit. I thought of something, rummaged in the drawer of a desk, pulled out a pack of cards, and took off.

Our apartment was about a twenty-minute drive from the Myers mansion. At seven fifteen Abe took my blazer, squeezed into it, grabbed my car keys, and took off. We parked the car in the front, as usual, and sure enough, the fuzz took off after him. I went out the back way and took an alley to where I had told Weaver to park his car. In a few minutes I was taillessly motoring to Bel Air.

In the heat of the planning stage—which was pretty chaotic and exuberant—I felt I had things all worked out. This was a reconnaissance trip. Raymond Chandler would have said I was out to case the joint. Things seemed pretty clear when I was sitting with Terry and Weaver.

But with the drone of the motor and nothing else around to distract me, I had the time to see what a stupid mission this was. I had to do *something*, but this was increasingly feeling like the charge of the dark brigade: into the valley of death. All for the Book of Death. Was I going boldly into the jaws of death, into the mouth of Hell? I kept trying to formulate what I would do and what I should say. And also, what might happen if my dumb half-plan didn't go the way I half-planned it. Would I come out of this . . . .

There was the cul de sac. There was the house. There was my fate.

THIRTY SEVEN

To see the house was already to be seen. Though I was a couple of minutes early, it made no sense to stay in the car. There was a huge lawn with a circular drive to the front door, and another drive to the left of that that went back to the garage—the path on which I had found the car with the body. No other car seemed to accompany me, and I felt nervous about that. The folks in the house could see me, do doubt. If they saw no other vehicle, what would they think?

I had to do something to give the impression that I was not alone. I took out the cell phone and dialed Terry, just so that I could be seen in contact with the outside world. She answered in a second.

"God, Elliot. I'm worried. I haven't heard from you."

"Did you expect to?"

"No. Well, we hadn't talked about it. But I was hoping."

"I'm calling just to tell you I'm ok. I'm in front of the house, and I'm going in soon."

"Be careful." It's what I expected to hear. This was no time for some sarcastic reply. She was scared, and so was I.

"I love you, Terry."

"I love you and need you, Elliot."

That was it.

There were lights on everywhere. As I approached the front door the goose bumps probably raised my clothes several inches from my body.

I didn't need to ring the bell. As I stepped onto the stoop, the door opened. Howard, menacing Howard, was there, not looking happy, and not looking inviting. In fact, he didn't invite me in. All he did was step aside. I didn't want to walk in and have him at my back. I stepped forward a foot and motioned for him to go ahead of me. He backed up and gave me room to get in, with him still in front of me. I shut the door so that he wouldn't have to go behind me to do it. And with him a couple of paces ahead, we walked into the library. I knew this room.

I reflected that I also knew part of the floor of another room in this house, and a section of a lovely Bokhara carpet. I was not feeling like a hero, but I was emboldened by my anger. To keep this going, I kept thinking of being tied up and kicked; of finding Terry chained to a bed; of smelling the smoke and the acrid ashes near all my books. I thought again and again of Dave and Kurt and Celia. I was near boiling. But the valve held for now.

Howard went out of the room behind me, which gave me the willies, but he walked discreetly far enough away that I felt only eighty nine percent threatened. I stood facing Blake, who seemed calm but crazed. He didn't move or speak. He just looked at me, I guess waiting for me to speak.

In about a minute—which in such silence was interminably long—Howie returned. "I saw headlights."

I don't know what he saw, but it was sort of like the cavalry not quite coming over the hill, but knowing that they were there.

"Howard." Blake looked at him and then at me and then he nodded.

Howard approached, and I backed perceptibly away.

"Mr. Burgess. You said that you were not wired. You never said that you wouldn't be armed. And maybe you're wired, too. Howard knows about these things. He won't hurt you."

It's ok to pet the rottweiler and the pit bull, kid. They won't hurt you.

I still backed away.

"Give Howard your jacket."

It sounded reasonable enough. Since I could have been dead meat at any time.

I was really sweating and starting to feel musky. And I'm not sure, but I think I was shaking a bit. But it was not from fear. I noticed that I was feeling almost giddy, bold, lightheaded, invulnerable. Well, not quite. But I wasn't scared. I had gained entrance into their inner sanctum and they didn't know what to make of it. It was as if I had *them* on the defense, and I loved it.

I handed Muscles the coat. He felt it here and checked it there. He pulled out the deck of cards.

"What's this?" It was the size, I suppose, of a battery pack for a listening/recording device.

"Cards."

He carefully opened the box. Cards. He looked puzzled and then put them back into the pocket.

"Now you," Blake said.

I did feel less intimidated, almost reckless.

"Sure." I raised my hands.

I guess Howard had seen all them gangsta pitchers, 'cause he patted me down the way they do in Hollywood. I expected to hear him say, "He's clean."

He looked up at Blake and said, "He's clean."

Son of a bitch! He learned his lines good.

I put the jacket on again and stood there, waiting, watching the two faces face me.

"What!" Blake practically yelled it at me.

"'What' what?"

"No games. Why are you here?"

"I need some answers."

"What makes you think I have them?" I had expected him to use the plural pronoun, because I couldn't conceive Blake to be quite smart enough to be heavily involved in all this by himself. Mean and stupid and dangerous, yes. But there was a gulf between him and the book— its contents, its look and feel, its existence—that made me wonder what his connection to it could possibly be. And Terry's kidnapping was certainly related to the book.

"I think you have many answers."

"Like to what?"

"How about, 'Who owns the Book of Death'?"

"I do."

"Why?"

"Because it's mine."

"C'mon, Blake," I said, with some condescension. Was it dangerous to take this tone? "Do you really believe you own it?"

"My dad did. I am his heir."

"Where is your dad?"

Oops. He had to backtrack. By suggesting that he was the heir, he was admitting that poppa was in a position to bequeath.

He tried to sound controlled and indignant, but his "I don't know" was unconvincing.

"Don't know? It's a wise child who knows where his father is." I'm sure the allusion went over his head.

"He goes on buying trips. This is not unusual." A line he has rehearsed many a time.

"Where is he now?"

"I don't know."

"He claims the book was his. Why does he claim that?"

"He said he paid lots for it. It was his."

"Whom did he pay?"

"I don't know." This time I heard the glitch in his voice.

"Tell me."

"I don't know. But Pinsky was involved in getting it. I think he stole it."

"From whom?"

"I don't know."

This was leading to someplace that Blake didn't know about. So I shifted gears.

"Who broke into my shop and blasted my safe?"

"I don't know."

"Look, Blake." I showed him how perturbed I was. "You don't answer my questions, you haven't a ghost of a chance to get the book back. I *mean* it. Answer me!"

"A guy named Sonneck. I don't know his first name. I told my father I could get the book back. He laughed at me. He always did. He never trusted me."

"How did you find this guy Sonneck?"

"It wasn't hard. I found out."

"How?"

"There's a database."

No shit! A database for people who bomb bookstores for hire?

"A what?!"

"I went to the library."

"Which."

"LAPL."

The great old L.A. Public Library, known for its three famous fires and its spectacular collection. But also priding itself on its great service to the community, like Reference. Ask the Reference Librarian a question and you got an answer.

"What did you ask for?"

Blake looked proud. "I told him I was writing a novel and I needed some real names of bombers. And I wanted to know if there was such a thing as a listing on the Web of such people. It didn't take him long to find it."

So in effect, the taxpayers of Los Angeles had a hand in blowing up my shop and blowing the door off my house.

"Where is this Sonneck?"

Blake paused again, as if looking for the right way to frame his lie. "I don't know."

"Original! Blake. I want to know where he is."

"We paid him and he disappeared. It's been weeks. We didn't need his services anymore."

"You call blasting my home and shop 'services'?"

"We needed to scare you. We told him not to damage anything. He said he could do that."

"Of course, you didn't want anything damaged. It had nothing to do with courtesy to me. It was because you didn't want to damage the pamphlet."

"That too," he said, trying to look as if he had done a decent act. The bastard.

"What did your father say when you didn't get the pamphlet back?"

"He was pretty mad. He told me that my method was dumb. He said his method was better."

"And what was that?"

"He said he used two tactics: fear and money. He thought he could scare you into giving it up, especially if you were to get a lot of money for it."

"What's a lot of money?"

"He said something like fifty thousand."

"Is that a lot?"

"To us it is."

"What do you mean. Look at this place."

"Non-liquid assets. We need the money. We could sell the book for a lot."

"What's a lot?"

"A million, my dad said."

"Why do you need it?"

"We've got a few debts."

"Whose?"

Blake obviously felt uncomfortable with this. He said nothing.

"That's my answer, Blake. Where did you get these debts?"

Again silence. My feet were hurting, and my knee. And my nose.

"May we sit down?"

Blake seemed relieved that he didn't have to answer the last question. I sat on a couch across from their chairs. My back was still to the door of the room, which was a bit of comfort. There was a door behind them, too, leading to somewhere in the rest of the house. And a window to their left, my right. One of the windows I had looked in on one of my informal visits. The curtain was open and I could see the lights from the property's periphery—the ones that flooded me with fear on the night of my escape. These thoughts made me even bolder.

"Blake! I don't give a shit what the problems of your family are. They don't mean a flying fuck to me. I just want some facts. No one else needs to know about them. The debts?"

"I got into some trouble with . . . a deal that didn't work right. Buying and selling bonds. And with gambling." That said it all. Even William Bennett, the *Book of Virtues* schmuck—who should now write the *Book of Vices*—had a gambling problem.

"What did the Book of Death mean to you?"

"Nothing. Well, except that we could pay off the debts."

Howie from Central Casting was shifting uncomfortably in his seat by now. He obviously didn't like how much information was emerging.

"And your father's role in this?"

"He was the one who owned the book. He was going to sell it and clean up. He was really pissed when he found out about my . . . problem."

"I guess so."

"I thought he was going to kill me. He never took much interest in me and the only time I saw him was when I was in trouble at school. He was really a shitty father."

"Who grabbed Terry?"

Again he knew he was in trouble with the facts. "I really needed to get the pamphlet back. We never intended to hurt her. We didn't hurt her."

"She was drugged, stripped, and chained."

"We never hurt her. We wanted her drugged so she wouldn't be able to recognize us or the house. We took her clothes so she wouldn't run away. And we used the chain for the same reason."

"She was out of her wits."

"We couldn't help it. We had to do it."

I was really on the verge of explosion, with the images just delineated and the stupidity and callousness of these punks.

"We thought you'd come here. And you did."

"What did you expect to gain?"

"The book, of course."

"Why did you imprison me?"

"To scare you some more."

"And hurt me?"

"We were going to let you both go. But we thought that pain and fear would get you to give us the book."

I sat there, thinking. Long enough for Blake to get in a question.

"How did you get out of here?"

"Sonneck's cousin."

"What?"

"I'm Superman."

"What?"

"I'm asking. You're answering. Who killed Gens?"

"Who is Gens?"

"Called himself Smith."

"He wasn't supposed to die." Then Blake realized what he had just said. He had admitted to something that was death-worthy.

"Why?"

"He took the book. We thought we could get it back from him. But he said he didn't have it. My father was furious."

"Who did it?"

He didn't' reply.

"Where did you do it, Blake?"

"I wasn't alone."

Another admission. This was getting productive.

"Who else?"

"Listen, Burgess." Howard spoke with power and finality. "Enough! Why are you here?"

"Not enough. I want more information. What's it to you? You're the hired muscles, right?"

Howard Blanding didn't like to be put into the shadow that way.

"I am a friend of the family. I help out when they need me."

"Don't tell me there's no monetary angle for you."

"None of your goddam business. I help out. They need me, I help out."

Pleonasm was his strong suit.

"Who else, Blake?"

"It was Sonneck. But he's gone. I don't know where he is."

"What did you do?"

I already saw what they had done, but I wanted to hear about it.. To reinforce the level of the scum I was dealing with. Maybe also to justify the vengeance that I hoped to wreak.

"We worked him over." Nice phrase, right out of B movies. "He wouldn't tell us anything except that he sold the book to you."

"What else did you expect to get out of him?"

"I guess that was all."

So the sons of bitches, in their anger at redolent Smith, killed him.

"Why did he have the book? Where did he get it from?"

"I don't know."

"Bull shit!"

"My father hired him to pick it up from someone and deliver it here."

"From whom?"

"I don't know. Maybe someone named Pinsky, maybe someone else."

"Who was he?"

"I don't know. Someone my father knew. I think he had done things for my father. I don't know what."

That was now a dead end. "What about David Daws?"

"Who's that?"

"The man who worked in my store?"

"What happened to him?"

"As if you don't know."

"I don't."

He was being stupid, canny, or ignorant. But his body language, his non-verbal skills, were pretty readable, and I felt that he didn't really know about Dave. I thought he didn't need me to tell him stuff that he didn't already know. I tried a last time.

"Daws worked for me. He might have known where the book was."

"I didn't know about him."

"And Celia Brothers?"

"She was the old lady from the school? You were in her office. You must have talked to her about the book. We figured she knew about it, where it was."

"Why did you beat her up?"

These words were like a slap in the kisser.

"She wouldn't tell us anything."

"She couldn't. She didn't know about the book. I was just borrowing her office."

"No, I mean, she wouldn't tell us a thing. About the book, about you, about anything. She just refused to talk. She really pissed us off. It was as if she had secrets and she could hold that over us."

"Why brutalize her?"

"She knew what we looked like. She didn't cooperate. We couldn't let her go until we scared her pretty deep."

I figured I'd go the rest of the way in the encyclopedia of crime:

"Who smashed Kurt Bricker?"

"Who was Kurt Bricker?"

Again he sounded truly in the dark. "He visited me a few times. Why did you think he knew anything about the book?"

"I don't know who he is."

I stared.

"*I don't goddam know who he is,*" he yelled. He was angry, now and he stood up menacingly. I stood up, too. So did Howard.

"So you're a gambler." I pulled out the deck of cards. "What if I tell you I'll share the profits from the sale of the book if you just lay off my life?"

He didn't answer. Didn't know what to make of this.

"I'll cut the deck. If you get a red card, you get fifty percent. If you get a black card, you get nothing."

"I should get it all," he shouted.

"You don't have the book. You can't prove that it's yours. I am offering you a deal because I want you out of my life. You want to cut the cards?"

I lobbed the deck toward his face, gently, and he snagged it—with his left hand. A southpaw, just like his daddy. I thought of the envelope. I thought of the "No Book? No Terry" note. It had been in an envelope opened by a left-handed kidnapper. I had assumed it had been daddy. But daddy's little boy had just incriminated himself for the last time with me, and my ire was up.

"I told you all this because you'll never be able to tell anyone else," he said with an edge of insanity. It sounded like another potboiler, but he was dead serious. "If you're dead, I'll get the book. You have only been in the way."

He reached into his pocket and pulled out a pistol and aimed it at me. I froze—not that I was in the middle of a sprint or anything. He then said, "Ok, Howard."

Shee-it. Howard came at me. Things happened fast. Things blurred.

I had a flash of my older brother telling me, when he was about ten and I was seven, if you want to hurt someone, hit him either on the bridge of the nose or in the neck. I had never used this, but I had thought about it for decades. My brother might have saved my life.

My first move was instinctive: I crouched in the fight/flight position and stepped back a tad to my left. Howard was on me with a snarl. I saw movement in the room behind him. I think Blake was getting into a position to shoot me. Howard's fist caught my left shoulder. From my crouch I lunged upward as fast as I could, my right fist powered at his adam's apple. It felt weird. It hurt me, but it also felt soft and giving and solid and gushy and disgusting.

I knew I would get only one punch, but, God! Dennis. Thanks for the boxing lesson. I was in a total tizzy, my mind whirling. Fighting was not my thing. I'm a lover, not a fighter. Hadn't I heard that before!

In another second I heard very loud noises. In a fog I watched Central Casting fall backward, and in the same fog I heard more loud noises and simultaneously felt something burning on my left side. I fell back as if pushed and hit the floor askew; I heard glass shattering—or something like that—and out of my periphery I saw Blake swing around, then fall. Noises. My own yelling. A horrible noisy gurgling sound from on the floor near me. Howard was writhing in a small pool of blood near his head. The pool widened and I saw spatters of blood here and there and on his chin and cheeks and he was clutching his throat and then he just writhed for a moment and the gurgling got deeper and thicker and then he was still. I saw Blake on his side, still clutching the gun, but barely moving, breathing scratchingly. I thought I heard a door slam.

I didn't know what had happened, but I did know I was bleeding from my left side, at my ribs. And it hurt. So badly that I couldn't feel my sore nose anymore. Or my patella. Just the sticky powerful sharp burning on my left side.

Lying on the floor didn't seem too productive, and getting up didn't seem too dangerous since my nemeses were lying on the floor seemingly unable to rise. I painfully rolled onto my right side, the way my yoga teacher taught me, and pushed my torso into a sitting position. Ow! Other than my moaning, it was quiet in the room—the sound of rough breathing from Blake, no movement elsewhere. I sat there looking from Blake to Howard to Blake. I was in too much pain to stand up, but at least I knew that I was still alive and that whatever was hurting and causing the bleeding, I wasn't going to die in that horrible place.

"Elliot."

God! in my stupor and the shock engulfing me, I thought I heard my name.

"Elliot." It came from the window.

"I've called the police." Abe's distant voice.

I turned and saw his face between the bars, looking in as I had.

"Let me in. The front door is locked. Are you ok?"

"Does it look as if I'm ok? I'm bleeding. I think I don't have any intact ribs on my left side. I'm on the floor with what look like a bloody corpse and his friend. I'm in a strange house where I was once tied up and kicked. Does it look as if I'm ok?"

I staggered to the front door. Abe came in and reached out to steady me, hands on my upper arms. He got me right where Howard did, on my left shoulder. That hurt. In fact, I think my *shoes* didn't hurt. We bumped along to a couch and I sat down. Abe gingerly walked over to Blake and kicked the gun from his left hand. Blake was either unaware or too injured to move.

"What happened, Abe?"

"I'm not sure. I saw it through the window. You got a good chop at that guy. He went down fast. Mighty punch."

"No, just well placed."

"Then I saw the other young guy spin around and then fall down. There were lots of noises, like gun shots."

"I thought I heard glass."

"I saw the fight start so I broke the window. I thought I could distract them."

I was trying to think through the agony. "Get out of here, Abe. I can handle it."

"Here's your car key. Give me mine. And my phone."

These were in left-hand pockets, and it was excruciating to pull them out.

Then he was gone. He said he had called the police. I figured it would have to come out in some way or another. I might as well just sit there. Which I did, slumping back into the soft bloodied leather. Sinking into the couch. Sinking.

THIRTY EIGHT

The folks at the hospital took their x-rays and did their bandaging. My clothes were a mess, but I wasn't. I had been grazed by a bullet that actually seemed to have skidded off one of my ribs. Amazingly, nothing was broken but my skin and my spirit.

I was still sitting in the emergency room, five hours later. It was nearly three a.m. Coster showed up. "Asshole!"

"Hi, Doctor Coster." I had doctors on my mind.

"That was a pathetic stunt, with some old man taking your car."

Some old man. Maybe they didn't know it was Weaver.

I recounted again the scene, the actions, and what I could remember of the coda. I didn't mention my swipe at Howard or Abe's having been there. Coster said that he had been called after nine and that he had sped to the Myers house. Something mighty peculiar was going on. Lots of photos had been taken, lots of examinations by lots of experts. Lots of theories. He wanted lots of answers.

I told him again that in the heat of battle, I was not too cognizant of details. There was Howard's lunge and his punch. The burning in my side. The vision of Howard or something behind Howard as Howie slumped back. Other movement. Sounds of—were they gunshots?—and glass and gurgling and much more that I couldn't remember except through the haze of pain and falling and dizziness.

"What did you find?" I had to ask him something because I didn't want any more questions coming at me.

"Blake: shot twice. Once in his left arm, once in the back of his chest. It collapsed one of his lungs, but it missed his heart by a couple of inches. He's upstairs." We were again at UCLA's famous hospital, the one nearest the Myers home.

"And Howie?" I asked.

"Howard Blanding. We are running a check on him. It might have been an alias."

"What happened to him?" as if I didn't know.

"This is weird. He drowned."

"What!"

"It seems he had esophageal varices . . . ."

"Come again."

"Esophageal varices. It's like varicose veins in the throat. They sometimes bulge, especially with people who have been heavy smokers. They can be harmless or fatal if one of them bursts."

"What can cause them to burst?"

"Anything or nothing. Sometimes they just go. If Howard lunged at you, that could have been enough to cause the dam to break."

"Then what?"

"The bleeding can be pretty profuse. I'll skip the details. He tries to breathe. That's what caused the spatters of blood. But his exhales that spray alternate with his inhales, which suck the blood into his lungs. It can take only a few minutes, but he essentially drowns in his own blood. It looks as if Blanding did himself in."

"What else?"

"There was a broken window. It looks as if it had been broken from the outside, but there's no way of knowing. If there was someone out there, there's no trace now."

"On tv they get boot prints."

"This isn't tv, Mr. Burgess."

At this point I had to listen to about six and a half minutes of abuse for the stupidity of my actions. Not worth mentioning. I expected it, and I was glad to get only six and a half minutes. When the storm settled, I said,

"You said that Blake was shot twice? By whom?"

"We don't know yet. It's funny. We'll have to seek the bullet from his arm. It went somewhere in the room. The one from the back got him pretty square. We're trying to figure out how he could have been hit from two different directions, if there were only one gunner."

"Could he have twisted around?"

"I guess so. But it would have been pretty awkward. He was hit in the left arm, which was facing the window. This might have gotten him to slue around so that his back was facing the window, too. That would explain why both bullets came from the window. But it is unusual for someone to turn so neatly at a ninety degree angle under such circumstances."

"If there were a second person?"

"We're not too sure of this either. If there were and the two bullets came almost simultaneously from two different directions—the window and from behind him—then maybe."

"I did think I saw something moving in that part of the room. But I assumed it was Blake getting a better angle to shoot me."

"He got a pretty good angle. He essentially missed your heart by about five inches."

"How do you know I was hit by his bullet?"

"We found it and we found the smoking gun with his prints on it not far from his hand."

"Howard was a smoker. Blake's gun was smoking. Don't they know that's playing with fire? Someone could get hurt."

Not much humor, but it was the best I could come up with then.

"Now, Elliot. There's something that I will ask you. And I need the goddam truth. No shit! The truth."

"Sounds ominous. What?"

"What did you learn from your little visit? I mean, *what did you learn?*"

"About what?"

"Don't give me that shit. I don't want a question. I want answers. Plural!"

I figured there was nothing to hide about some things. I told him that Blake essentially confessed to killing Gens and kidnapping and attacking Celia. That he had taken Terry. That he seemed to know nothing about Dave Daws and Kurt Bricker. That he confessed to hiring someone to set the bombs. Called him Sonneck. That he was deep in debt because of what he called buying and selling bonds and gambling. And that he was sitting on a house full of "non-liquid assets," he called them. "He doesn't seem to know much about the provenance of the book. He just says that he owns it. But the more he says it, the more it is wishful thinking, not pure conviction."

Coster was taking mental notes. He let all this sink in for a moment. Then he said,

"There's another problem, Elliot."

I could see that this was a question of a different kind.

"Someone had your car. He was stopped. Actually, he stopped and flagged our car down. They saw they had an old man, not you. We don't know why he did this."

"Fascinating." I felt like Mr. Spock, but my eyebrow wouldn't go up the way Spock's did.

"When our men found you in the Myers house, your car was parked at the end of the circle. How did it get there?"

"Are they sure they were following the right car?"

"They're not as stupid as you take them to be."

Wanna bet?

"And how did you get to the Myers house?"

"I'm sure you can figure it out. It's too many for me." Pretty lame answer. But Coster could see that that was all he would hear of it from me. That session was over.

* * *

Terry was relieved to have me home, but was in tears when she saw the shirt and pants and blazer and bandage and even my slightly swollen hand. Even an adam's apple packs a wallop if hit hard enough. The two big knuckles on my right hand were bruised and puffy. (Nobody had gotten me in the feet yet. That was good.) Her crying was mostly in fright, and I tried to make light of my situation and my adventures, but there was no making light of the pain I was in, which was pretty clear. I took a couple of the pills I was given at the hospital and drifted off till . . . .

I think it was noon when I felt some movement. I didn't want to feel anything. But nature called and while I was up I thought I'd sit down and see if I could get down some poached eggs which Terry fixed me, along with rye toast and sesame oil and a banana. I didn't feel much like eating, but there it was.

Terry said, "I spoke to Officer Coster. He questioned Theresa about the events, but she said she was at a spa. Coster told me everything he knew; now he wants to talk to you. He said he was frustrated with you. So am I."

"So am I," I said. My frustration had to do with the questions I still had unanswered. I said to Terry, "Who shot Cock Robin?"

"What?"

"Who shot Blake?"

We discussed the possibilities. Maybe it was the person who sold the book to Myers. Maybe it was Theresa, though she said she was out last night—at a spa in Beverly Hills. She always goes there and spends at least two days getting cleansed. The spa corroborated this. She had been there since yesterday morning. And her treatments had ended at five, when she had a watercress and celery dinner, and had retired.

"That says nothing. She was only a five- or ten-minute drive from Bel Air."

"Right, Terry. But her motive? To shoot her step-son, even if she were his age?"

"So who else could it have been?"

"Pinsky."

"Why do you say that? His name hasn't come up in all of this shooting stuff."

"But his name did come up in my conversation with Blake. He said 'Maybe Pinsky,' nothing definitive. But it's the only name we have that goes with the case."

"His motives? What is his connection to all this?"

I ruminated while I masticated. Multi-tasking. Quite a chore for someone in my condition. "Maybe he thought *he* owned the book. Everyone else seems to have thought that." Then I added, after more chewing: "We still don't know if the *Buchlein* is genuine."

"It sure looks like it."

"That's the trouble. It looks too good."

"But, Elliot. The paper, the type, the binding thread, the text—everything seems correct. Even the carbon dating and the ink."

"Ok. What do we do with it? I'm a little reluctant to get rid of it until all this Book of Death stuff is taken care of. I want to know where the pamphlet came from. I want to know if it's genuine. And I want to know who killed Myers. And who hit Kurt and Dave."

"What can we get for it?"

The question that has been echoing ever since Mr. Redolent entered my shop.

"I think there could be some serious bidding for it. I think some pretty high rollers would want to grab it. Like the Vatican and the Getty and the Huntington. Well, the Huntington does have some budget constraints. But they also have some sugar daddies. And what about Texas? Harvard? The thing could net over a million. The text alone is worth it."

Terry pondered the possibilities. "For a million dollars we could be out of here and in some comfortable, safe town, selling books and being happy."

"I'd be happy no matter where we are, if we're together. I like my shop. I'd like to stay in L.A. And I don't want to get rid of the book yet."

The problem was, what were we to do at this point? Then Coster called:

"The bullet that hit Blake in the arm flattened out and we can't do any ballistic tests on it. And it was almost the same weight as the one in his chest. No way of knowing how many assailants there were. But I do have a piece of news. Howard Blanding *was* an alias. His real name was . . . ."

"Sonneck?" It leapt to my lips.

"What! How did you know? Steven Sonneck."

"He was on that list you gave me eons ago. The bombers."

"How did you know it was him?"

"No pun intended: process of elimination. Ok, pun intended."

"You never said anything to us."

"Why should I have? It was pure speculation."

"Ok, Holmes. Then speculate about who shot Blake."

"Hey, Coster. That's your job. My job is books. Yours is murder."

"We're working on it. The only name we have is Theresa Myers. But she seems to be out of it."

"She was at the spa? Are you sure she was there all night?"

"No. We have no way to know one way or the other. She seems weepy, but it looks like alligator tears."

"Nice turn of phrase, Officer." He had been around me too much.

"We have no witnesses. No clues that make any sense yet. Nothing."

"Did she own a gun?"

"We don't know yet, but we're checking into it. The gun that Blake had was unknown. Not registered or anything."

"Has she ever taken classes in shooting?" I was trying everything.

"From the distance the shooter was from Blake, he didn't need shooting lessons. Two feet. Maybe less."

We hit an impasse. What more questions were there to ask? Where do we go from here?

Coster rang off with: "You've been lucky, Mr. Burgess. Foolhardy and lucky. No more shenanigans. Stay home or go to your business. But leave the rest to us."

Terry and I discussed the case all day and very gingerly made love half the night. Mostly with me flat on my back and drugged half way to the land of Nod. It was sweet pain and I wanted it to go on and on, but I fell asleep after our climactic moments

* * *

and I woke in delirium through the night and into the morning. I could be all dramatic and talk about my dreams of chasing and being chased, of fighting and running, of being naked and immobilized on a table like a patient, and so forth. But there were no dreams.

Lying around did no good. I needed something to focus on, and the book business, which had languished long enough, was where I needed to be.

It took another three weeks for me to get my shop completely in order. I even had a professional crew come in and get the blood stain off the floor. I was putting my cheaper books onto the Web again, and working on a catalog of pretty exciting high-end books.

The throbbing ebbed and my nose looked something like a nose again. My patella was still sore, but I could walk without a limp. And I was able to take deep breaths again as the pain in my rib subsided. I would say that life was back to normal, but I didn't even know what normal was. For the longest time, normal was crisis. And that seemed the mode to be in. Without Blake and Edward and Howie hounding me, the book business seemed a bit dull.

Dave Daws was now home, recuperating, his wife relieved but still teary and fearful. Kurt was in a coma, and all the doctors could say was that if and when the swelling went down . . . . No prognosis yet. Celia was still in the hospital, doing "as well as can be expected." She had identified her attackers as Blake and Howard. She also said that they had demanded to know things from her—which she didn't reveal—and had said nothing at all about themselves. We learned nothing new from her adventure. Still questions lingered. But it was getting back to routine, and I was itchy for closure.

Then Coster called.

"We think we found Myers."

"Alive or dead?"

"Quite dead."

"Where was he?"

"In a ravine in the hills behind Bel Air. There was a hasty grave, but it was effective since the body was thrown into a gully and covered with dirt and then with branches. There's plenty of dirt and stuff in the hills up there."

"Are you sure it's him?"

"Well, he is pretty desiccated and all that."

"Any idea how he died or who did it?"

He said, "Not yet."

"Pretty disgusting job you have there, Officer."

"All in a day's work." Back to the clichés.

"All's well that ends well," was all I could say.

"Yup," was all he could answer.

"Nothing else to report?"

"Nope."

"Me neither."

"If you hear of anything, or think of anything, call us. We're here to serve."

"Nice to hear from you," and a bunch of other trite pleasantries. End of call.

Then the phone call came—the one I was anticipating.

A woman's voice. "Do you still have the Book of Death?"

"Who are you?"

I knew, of course.

"You know, of course."

"Yes, I know."

I hadn't seen Theresa Myers in weeks, but her vision passed by my head often, waking or sleeping. One of the most gorgeous women in Los Angeles. In a mansion in Bel Air. Widowed so young. Poor thing.

"Well, do you?"

"Know who this is?"

"No. Do you still have the book?"

"The book is safe." And it was. It was in a safe deposit box in a bank near Coster's station. Not that putting it closer to him made it any safer. It was a good bank with what looked like pretty decent security: which these days means that they had a guard who was under seventy five, not grossly overweight, and who looked as if he could run a block or two.

"I want it," she said matter-of-factly.

"I own it."

"I need it." Still no emotion in her voice.

"Why do you need it?"

"I need the money."

I felt awkward talking about this on the phone. She must have known that Coster was still listening in.

"Can I meet you for lunch? Today?" I thought it might be fun to sit at a table with this lady. And I didn't want anything we said to be heard by anyone else.

"When and where?" She seemed nervous but willing.

"Crocker's Diner, one o'clock." I gave her the address. "I'll have Molly save us the back table." It's the one I always use for trysts with lovely maidens and potential bombers.

Terry and I tried to figure out what information we needed from Theresa, but nothing specific came to mind.

Terry said, "You can't outright ask her about her finances, can you?"

"I don't see why not. She said she needs the money. She brought it up."

"And you can't say, 'who killed your husband and shot your step-son?'"

"Right. Coster suspected her or someone else in her house, but ob-servation for weeks now has not yielded anything suspicious. And her spa story seems to be holding up."

"But anyone can see that there was plenty of time to be out of the spa, then back to the house, and back to the spa while all the shootings and stuff took place."

"No way to prove a thing."

"But if she *was* at the house, would she be able to kill someone?"

Terry was thinking the same way I—and also as Coster—would. Sus-pects, motives, opportunities, willingness, ability.

"Let's see what I can find out."

* * *

Theresa Myers and I got to Crocker's at the same time. The bereaving widow was dressed to kill—in a manner of speaking: dark sun glasses, low-cut skin-tight knit on top, short skirt on the bottom, Chanel shoes, about three inches high, sheer hose over those perfect legs, and a small Louis Vuitton bag. At least they were mourning-black.

Molly had saved us the rear table, as I had asked. I took the seat look-ing out. Not that I didn't want someone from the front door sneaking up on me. It's just that I didn't want anyone sneaking up on me.

"Thank you for meeting me." She sounded more demure than her outfit would have led one to believe she could be. There was a tone of "pity me" in her voice. She took off her glasses.

My god! There was a complexion that millions would die for. I'd have to get the name of her spa.

"Let's eat," I said. I was hungry for many things. Mostly for informa-tion. But I thought a meal would ease things along.

Before I could issue my standard warning, Molly had descended. "Howdy, Elliot."

"Hi, Molly." I could have saved us the misery if I had had a chance to know what Ms. Myers wanted. It was too late. Molly was obviously quite curious about my tryst. She had practically followed us to the table, eyes glued to the black ahead of her.

Theresa said, "What do you recommend?" Oops. There goes ten minutes.

"Depends what you want. You—"; she looked closely at Theresa, bending a bit to get their faces level. "You, you probably don't want no meat. It's got grease. Your skin can't take such a thing. Grease. And your body. Too thin. I'd give you meat to put some flesh on you. But then your skin would be no good. You look like you eat healthy. Elliot here brings in all his vegetarian friends. Damn fools. Meat's good. But not for you. But Betty has some meat that don't have too much grease. And I can tell her to drain all the grease off. That way you can get your meat and not the grease and your skin will keep up its fine look. Got something new on the menu. You'll love it. Just right for you. It's a salad. But not just any salad. It's a special salad."

I loved the way she pronounced the vowels in "special." And I knew she loved the way she pronounced them. That's why "special" was one of her favorite words. Here they come.

"This here salad's got real special lettuce." (Oh, no. It was the salad lecture.) "Romaine and Boston. And Betty's added butter, too. Not grease butter; butter lettuce. It don't taste like butter, honey. And it won't hurt your skin. But that's not all. It's got them real special salty olives. With the pits. I like the kind of olives they grow with no pits. Easier to eat. You don't have to look around for a place to spit the pit. Them pitless olives are more dainty." (A word I never expected to hear from Molly.) "But these salty one, they taste like alum or something. Betty tells me people like them. I don't. I hate the pits. Betty calls this a salad nice ways. You can have it really nice ways. It's got egg on it. Not plain egg. You can get Sam and Ella from them. Whoever Sam and Ella are. Betty says she don't want nobody getting Sam and Ella from her food. So she cooks the eggs till they're hard. I hate hard eggs. If god wanted us to eat hard eggs, he woulda given us hot chickens."

One never knew what to expect from Molly. I had vowed to record her someday, but I never had my recorder on me when I ate there.

"Salad's also got tomatoes. Not them waxy plastic things you get in the market. No sir. Why, Betty gets 'em from a farmers market. You can even taste these tomatoes. And little round potatoes. Don't taste like anything but potatoes. Betty says we gotta have 'em. Why would anybody grow them little potatoes, anyway? Takes the same trouble to grow a big one, and then you got a nice big one. Them little ones don't amount to much. But Betty puts 'em in there. Got to, she says. I told her she could take a big one and just chunk it up. But she says, No. So you got your little round potatoes, honey. And green beans or 'sparagus—whatever is in season or comes cheaper. I like them. There's also some of them capers. Little things that look like dried up peas and don't taste half as good. And the worst part of all, you get a couple of anchovies. Horrible stuff. Dead, bony, little salty fish. God didn't want us to eat such things. But he did put 'em into the ocean. That's why they're so salty. But Betty says some people eat 'em. I don't. Nasty little buggers. But Betty says if folks don't eat 'em, screw them. A nice ways salad's gotta have 'em, she says."

I tried to interrupt, but Molly was on a roll.

"You, honey. Why, you should have one of these nice ways salads. They're nice, just like their name. But if I was you, I'd put the dressing on the side. It's a dressing with grease. I can tell you like how you look. Too skinny for me. But if you wanna stay that way, don't eat too much of the dressing. Grease. It'll make you fat and wreck your skin. Look at me! I'm livin' proof." (And she was. Way too much grease.)

She took one of her short breaths, indicating that she was still holding forth. But I grabbed the mike. "Two salads, Molly. Nice ways salads."

She was disappointed. She was having a good time looking Theresa over, and she wasn't quite through with her speech. My counter-attack put her into a reluctant retreat.

Theresa looked relieved. I said, "I hope a salad is ok with you. If you want, we can change it. But it might mean another sermon."

"I hate anchovies, too. But I can eat around them."

"Ok, Mrs. Myers. Why are we here?"

"You asked me to lunch."

"You called and asked to be asked to lunch."

I'm sure she was trying to be winning, but with her it was a losing game.

"I need the book."

"Why?"

"I told you. I need the money."

My look made words unnecessary.

"No. I really do. There's nothing for me."

"Your husband is one of the most famous high-rolling booksellers around. How can you need money?"

"It was all in stocks. In the last three years he lost about eighty five percent of his portfolio."

"The books must be worth a fortune."

"You mean what you saw in our house? They're all on consignment. We didn't own most of them. That room . . . ."

The room of blood and pain and death . . . .

". . . was filled with one huge library of a rich collector. He wanted us to sell the whole collection. We got rid of our own books to make room. Our books looked good, but they were nothing."

"There had to be a nest egg. It takes money to live in a house like that."

"That wasn't living. It was enduring. Besides, Blake . . ."; she shook her head with a little shudder. "It was so awful." There seemed to be real emotion here.

"What about Blake?"

"He had run up some pretty big debts. We were trying to figure out a way to pay them off."

"Sell the house. It's worth millions."

"The bank owns it. We've been in it for about five years. There's no equity in it yet."

For some reason I didn't feel sorry for this poor pretty waif.

"What do you want me to do?" I said.

"You could offer me the same deal you offered Blake. A percentage of the sale of the book."

"Why would I do that? It's mine. You don't have a ghost of an interest in it."

"Things could be really bad for us if you don't help me."

"What do you mean 'us'?" She had lost her husband and her step-son was in jail, waiting to be tried for his crimes—Gens, Celia, who knows what else. Who would "us" be?

"You know: us." And she looked deeply at me, leaning forward enough for me to feel the heat.

"Is this a threat?"

"No. Your Terry and you are pretty safe for now. But . . . ."

Pregnant pause.

"But what?" I was getting testy.

The salads were delivered. There was silence until Molly withdrew.

"But what?"

"I like you," she said. "You have guts. You're smart. I'd hate to see . . . ."

"You are not unlike your late husband, are you Mrs. Myers?"

"He's dead. There is no similarity between us."

She said this with a chill in her voice that made me shiver. Fainting flower? More like a Venus flytrap.

We sat for about two minutes. No talk. Just eye contact. It was a really long time. She showed no traces of any emotion, and she was waiting for me to say something brilliant. I was waiting for her to finish her two sentences.

"Think it over, Mr. Burgess," she said. Then she stood up, spun around, and walked away. Even from the back she was more delicious than a nice ways salad.

* * *

"Coster called." That was the first thing that Terry told me after she had hugged and kissed me when I got back—with two fresh, plastic-packed nice ways salads for our dinner.

"What about?"

"He didn't say. He wants you to call him back."

I did. When he heard my voice he said, "How was the lunch?"

"I know you're listening to me all the time. But couldn't you be more subtle about it?"

"I need to know. We located Howard Blanding's place. You know, Steven Sonneck."

"So?"

"It was full of all kinds of stuff for making bombs—big ones, little ones, ones that go onto safes and doorknobs. And he *was* involved with the Myers family."

"That seems to answer that question," I said, "But who shot Blake? And who bumped Dave Daws and Kurt Bricker?"

"No reason to assume it wasn't Sonneck. He had an interest. He knew about them."

I said, "He knew about Dave, of course, since Dave worked for me. But what did he know about Kurt?"

"Kurt was attacked at Pinsky's place. He didn't have to know anything about Kurt to find him there and smash his skull."

"Or Pinsky could have done it. It was, after all, his place. And what would Sonneck be doing at Pinsky's place?"

"Elliot, we believe that Pinsky is in Poland."

"Whatever!"

"And he would surely not have left Kurt there, unconscious, and ransacked his own place."

"Unless he was trying to make you think he was in Poland."

Coster said, "We thought of that. It's not logical. It's not likely."

"But you can't rule it out. Look, Dr. Coster. Let me say this again. I think Pinsky is still here in L.A. I think I met him. I think he is just as much a suspect as anyone else. If you try to place all the blame on Sonneck, and Sonneck is dead, then you have no one to be looking for. No suspects. No one to think is out there and dangerous. That means leaving me and Terry alone."

"We thought of that." Yes, you thought of all of that, didn't you!

"Not that Terry and I wouldn't mind some privacy. I mean, when I call her from the shop, I would like to say things to her that are not for the ears of your spies."

"We don't have spies."

"And we don't necessarily like being followed wherever we go. Your guys are pretty pathetic if they are trying to do it indiscreetly. And if they aren't, they are even more pathetic. It's like watching Buster Keaton running away from a whole police force."

"No jokes, Elliot. We are here to serve and protect. We're protecting you."

"From whom?"

"We don't know right now, but we have suspicions."

"Want to share them with me?" I could see this was running in a loop.

"Not right now. Soon enough."

"What's soon enough to you? Days? Weeks? Centuries?"

"I understand how you feel, Mr. Burgess . . . ."

"I doubt it. How does your nose or your patella feel? How are you healing from the gunshot wounds? How is your mate dealing with her kidnapping and my own traumas?"

He was silent.

"What the hell are your suspicions?"

"Ok. Maybe we do suspect Pinsky. But we must find out where he is."

"Who else?"

"Maybe someone who is owed a lot of money by the Myers family."

"Organized crime?"

"Possibly."

"Would they kill people who cannot repay debts from the grave?"

"It may have gone beyond that by now. Vendetta. We just don't know yet."

I loved hearing that word "yet" again. It implied that the infallible constabulary would get their man someday. Maybe, but with whose help?

"Officer, please keep me in your loop. It's my life."

"You bet." I don't bet. I don't gamble, despite the deal I offered Blake. Blake. I needed some information that Coster *might* hand over.

"How's Blake doing?"

"You know. He's in jail. He was arraigned and he'll be tried in a couple of months. No bail. He's pretty sullen. Won't talk to anyone."

"Anyone?"

"Nope. He can't get phone calls. Won't accept any visitors. Won't read anything sent to him. He's like on a deserted island. Total clam."

"Is it fear?" I asked.

"Maybe that and humiliation that he got caught. Also, he said something about being a target for the people he owed money to. Since that speech, he's been 100% incommunicado."

"Too bad for him," I said. "But it's probably better for the rest of the world."

"Sure." Coster paused. I heard the intake of his breath, indicating that he had more to say. "How are you and the missus? I mean, you and Terry?"

"As well as can be expected." I'd been around doctors too much. "Thanks for asking." We hung up.

I liked Coster, but I couldn't help thinking of him as only half-efficient. I felt I could get further on my own than with his assistance. Our call ended amicably, but there was still some hesitation on both parts. For Coster, I know he wasn't feeling too proud of his contributions in this case so far, especially since someone was still out there with an itchy trigger finger. For me, I felt the same kind of nervousness knowing that there was someone out there with an itchy trigger-finger. I also wanted to know who it was and I wanted to know more about our little book.

I told Terry all about the call. Then I said, "I have been replaying my conversation with Theresa Myers. She said something that bothered me—set off an alarm."

"At what point in your conversation?"

"It was near the end. We were talking about . . . whether I would sell the book and share the profits. I've got it! She said that she wanted me to make the same deal with her as I offered Blake—that he could cut the cards and if he got red I'd split the profits. How could she have known that? I said it only once, to two people, one of whom was dead in a few minutes and the other who hasn't talked to anyone in weeks. They haven't told anyone."

"Wasn't Abe there?"

"Hmmm." I couldn't believe that he was involved with the Myers clan. But I needed to talk with him.

I called him. I heard a glum and world-weary Hello.

"Abe, it's Elliot."

"Hi. How are you doing?"

"I'm healing. Pretty well, actually. I've gotta ask you something. But not on the phone. Can I come over?"

"Any time. Want to bring Terry over here for dinner? I'd love to see her again."

"What time?"

"Seven thirty. I'm a good cook."

"See ya."

* * *

The place smelled like garlic, which can be good—especially if you're not the only one eating it. But it was pork chops. I forgot to tell Abe of our eating habits. When he served it up, it smelled fine, but we ate the potatoes and bread and asparagus. White ones. Delicious. He was embarrassed. "I guess I should have asked about diets."

"No problem. You make great bread."

He had greeted us with a warm handshake for me and a bear hug for Terry. We ate a fine meal around the pork chops.

After dinner we sat in Abe's comfortable living room. It was now appropriate to ask,

"Abe, why were you at the Myers house?"

"I knew you'd ask me eventually. I thought of many answers, but I guess the truth is the best. That way, I won't have to remember a lie later on."

Then he sat still for a few minutes. No one felt like talking.

"You told me where you were going. And I knew why. You didn't seem to have thought out your attack, or whatever it was. It seemed to me a foolhardy and rash visit. I feel . . . ."

He was searching for the right words.

"You were once in the position of one of my best friends. Herman was a very bright and sweet young professor. I won't give you the details. You'll both understand them, anyway. I was sort of like a father to him, though neither of us would have ever put it that way. He was denied tenure. Politics. Meanness. Jealousy. All kinds of manure. I felt that in you, Elliot, there was a touch of Herman. I anticipate that you too, Terry, will understand the position that I was in. I tried to save Herm, but he disappeared into the world. We never saw him again. Maybe he died. I have felt horribly guilty for many years about that. I should have been able to protect him. I didn't do it. And I see you—both of you—as sort of my way of undoing what I attribute to my own lethargy in the past."

"What about Celia?"

"I was getting to that. When Celia and I found ourselves with deceased mates and no kids in the nest, we renewed a friendship that went back more than forty five years. She was my companion in thinking and talking, in discussing movies and books. She and I could sit in a room without speaking and . . . ."

He paused and knew he didn't have to finish that thought.

"We lived in our own homes because we both always lived in our own homes. But there was a symbiosis between us. When she was beaten up . . . ."

"I understand, Abe." I tried to tell him, but he didn't need to hear anything.

"When Herm was killed off, figuratively or literally, by the department, I found a level of anger in me that I thought I never had. It was fury. It took total control of my brain. But the frustrating thing was, there was no outlet. No one took responsibility for anything, though, of course, I knew who was to blame. I couldn't do a thing. I had to watch character assassination and maybe corporal assassination, too. I could almost kill, but I couldn't do such a thing. For many reasons.

"Since then, when I see good people being badly treated, I feel I owe them some protection."

"Were you at Myers's house to protect me?"

"I am not sure. I was there. That's all I can say. I knew where you'd be. I understood the situation. And I knew that I couldn't hurt by being there."

"What did you do?"

"I saw you go in. I had pulled up into the dead-end street and stopped the car at the end of it."

"Howard did say he thought he saw another car out there. They thought I had been tailed by the police. They couldn't know that I had shaken them. Your presence there . . . ."

"So they thought I was the cavalry?"

"I think so. But that didn't stop them."

"No, they acted as if no one was there. I stood at the window, watching. I could tell that you seemed to have the upper hand for a while. I could read your body language. But then things turned fast. I saw the big hulk run at you."

"Scared the be-jeevers out of me." (Where had that phrase come from?)

"Me too. And when I saw the other guy pull out a gun and aim it at you, I had to do something, so I broke the window."

"Why?"

He paused a while.

"Maybe to distract their attention. Give you some time to do something to protect yourself."

"Was that all, Abe?"

He knew what I knew.

"That was almost all."

"How many times have you shot a gun?"

"At a target, many times. At a person, only once. One pull of the trigger. That's all. It sickened me. But for some strange reason it made me feel powerful, useful. It was as if I was committing a completely justifiable crime."

"You pulled the trigger once. You got one perfect hit."

"He was holding the gun in his left hand—right where I could see it. I aimed at his upper arm. But I think he shot a split second before I did. Maybe at the same time. I saw that you were hit, and I was squeezing the trigger a second time when he went down. He had been standing just inside the far door, and I saw it open. Someone from there shot him from pretty close up. I couldn't see who it was. He never came into the room. The door shut and I looked back into the room. The man I shot was practically flat on his face, not going anywhere, and the guy who attacked you was falling back, reeling as if he had been hit square on the jaw by a wrecking ball."

"Not quite."

"I never saw what happened to him. Did you hit him?"

"Abe, I was just trying to protect myself."

"I watched for a couple of minutes. It was ghastly when the blood . . . ."

"Yes. Horrifying," I said.

"When things had settled—you know, when there seemed to be no more danger to you in there, and you were still moving and the big guy wasn't and the other guy was barely rolling around on the floor—I called out. You let me in and you know the rest. I didn't kill anyone, did I?"

"No. Blake Myers had a wound in his left arm and a bullet, in his back. He's still alive. In jail. Howard Blanding died from a smoking problem. Not a smoking gun."

Abe looked tired and relieved. "I'm glad I told you. And I'm glad I didn't kill anyone. And I'm glad you are safe. I hated having to keep that in."

"Well, if it means anything to you, Abe, you saved my life." And after a pause I added, "And you wrought vengeance on the people who attacked Celia."

He shuddered a bit at that. "I thought so."

The three of us sat still for ten minutes or more. It was as if a stiff muscle was taking that much time to loosen up. A few cars passed outside. There was no wind. In fact, as is usual in Los Angeles, there was no weather at all. Inside or out. Terry was beside me on the couch. She had grabbed my arm at the beginning of Abe's story, and she was gripping me strongly at the end. I could see she was near tears. I put my arm around her and held her.

"Coffee?" he finally said.

"Decaf," we said in unison.

And that was that.

THIRTY NINE

The bomb had really busted things up. Holy be-jeevers.

Terry's and my apartment was just about totaled. It had happened only minutes before we got there, and flames and smoke and dust were all over the place. Sirens. Firefolks. Police. The place was a mob scene. Noise that must have rivaled the sound of the bomb. It was not a simple fire. A huge hole had been blasted out of the building near one of the windows. All the materials from the walls were knocked out to the curb. Something went off inside. If we had been home only five minutes earlier . . . . If we hadn't gone to Abe's for dinner and confession. . . .

We were in shock. (No shit!)

And we couldn't get close to the place. The fire people, who had arrived just seconds before we did, pushed everyone back. There were screams from inside. Terry's second-floor apartment was the target, but there were people below and on either side. People from the apartments beside hers were out on a small balcony, readying to jump or whatever. Two people in pajamas came tumbling out of the window beneath her place. Others were streaming out of the front door.

You know the rest.

An hour later we were in Coster's office.

"What did you do now?"

I said, "We went out to dinner."

"I know. To see Abraham Weaver." I forgot that he knew every step I took, every bathroom break. "Did you leave the apartment knowing anything like this could happen?"

"Jesus! No. If we had known, we would've called you. Let neighbors know. Called the FBI."

"What happened at Weaver's?"

"We watched him eat pork chops."

"Please! You always have sarcastic answers. You're always skirting the issue. What do I have to do to get you to answer a question straight?"

"I guess say what you just did."

"I needn't repeat the question."

I certainly wasn't going to implicate Weaver in anything. I said, "We had a pleasant dinner and we talked. We talked about Celia and the mess that Terry and I are in. We discussed suspects—same way you and I have, Officer."

"Please call me Detective."

"Right, Doctor. We speculated. We came up with no answers."

"What did he know about the events in Myers's home?"

"Only what I told him. He was concerned. Terry and I remind him of a young colleague he once had who disappeared, maybe died. He wants to protect us."

"Ok. Tonight at your place. Who would have done this?"

"Your guess is as good as mine. Maybe the person who shot Blake. And killed Blake's father. This person has killed so many times he wouldn't be any worse off if he offed a couple of others. What do *you* know?"

"We didn't have anyone there. We pulled them a week ago."

"What! You never told us."

"Did you need to know?"

"Son of a bitch."

"Besides, with you away from the place, we had you covered at Weaver's."

"I'm comforted. What else?"

"Someone threw a bomb into the apartment from the grass in front. It went off practically on impact. It seems to have been a simple pipe bomb. Any dumb shit kid could have rigged it up. It was pretty powerful. We were able to contain the fire, and only the four apartments were seriously damaged: yours, the two around you, and the one beneath. No one was hurt. But this was different from the ones at your bungalow and store. Those were localized to damage only a small area. This one could have killed you both. Quickly."

"That's a mercy," I said. "Anything survive?"

"Only the living room was badly damaged. The bedroom was a bit soaked with the firemen's work, but clothing and furniture and stuff is safe. We're going to lock up the place for a few days. You can get what you want from there when we are done making sure it's safe to get in."

"Any idea who did this?" Another stupid question. If he knew he wouldn't be talking to us this way. And he already said that any kid . . . . He knew he didn't have to answer me.

Terry said, "What are we going to do now?"

"Mr. Burgess's place is still there. Furnished. With most of his things still there. We have been watching it."

Great! They watch the empty place and let our live-in abode alone for a bomber to pipe the place. Or a piper to bomb the place.

Terry pulled me over and whispered, "Tell him about Theresa?"

Why not.

I told him about Theresa. That she knew of the deal I said I would cut with Blake and that only someone who was there could have known about it. She *had* to be there.

"We know that she could have. She had the opportunity. But what motive?"

"Maybe she heard I would be there and she wanted a piece of my punishment. Maybe she was after someone or something else. Maybe she left her nail file behind and needed it that night."

Coster said, "We thought of that." (Here we go again.) "But she has an alibi that is unbreakable, and there is nothing anywhere suggesting that she has any kind of violence in her background. No arrests. No driving tickets. No jaywalking. Just a beauty queen from Montebello." (I could see why.) "Squeaky clean."

"She told me that she knew about the family debts. Did Blake or his pop have a big life insurance policy?"

How trite can this get? Well, it's possible. Coster said soberly,

"We thought of that. Nothing we can find. No claims have been filed. There were no domestic violence reports. Neighbors said she and her doting husband seemed happy together. They played tennis together. She usually won. She seems to have had no motive."

"Then what was she doing in the house when Blake shot at me?"

"We don't know and there is no way to prove that she was really there."

"*I* know it. Now you do, too."

"Hearsay. How can you prove it? She will deny that she asked you for the same deal you offered Blake. She will say she was having her beauty sleep at the spa. We wouldn't have a case. Even if she said outright that she was there and heard your conversation, there is no way to prove that she shot anyone. It could have been someone else. Someone was, after all, at the window."

He was right. She was untouchable. At least for now.

Terry said, "Is there a way I could get to her? I mean, she probably doesn't know what I look like. She would suspect any man, let alone Elliot, who approached her. Maybe I could get some information from her. Incriminating information."

"*We* sure can't," Coster said. "But it would be too dangerous. If we were to use that ploy, it would be with an officer. It doesn't work too well. Too many tv shows that have that method on them. Besides, you were sort of a guest in his home. She may well have seen you."

I said, "Constable Coster."

"Detective."

"Whatever. Have you made any progress on Pinsky?"

"No. We still think he's in Poland. But he's not completely ruled out."

"Of what?"

"Of all these crimes."

Glad to see he was coming over to my side on this.

He'd have to be a perfect idiot not to.

And Coster wasn't perfect.

* * *

"I've gotta find Pinsky."

It was the next morning. We had spent a nervous and exhausted night in the little Hancock Park bungalow. We clung to each other the whole night, both of us in a stupor of fatigue, disbelief, fear, and need. She seemed to need my body as close to hers as I needed hers close to mine. We didn't make love, but we made something infinitely more passionate and binding.

"I like this place," she said. "Why Pinsky?"

"We're at a stone wall with Theresa. Pinsky must be involved." A bolt hit me: "Pinsky! Kurt was attacked in Pinsky's place. He was there to find a notebook. He found something, and I had it in my blazer pocket. The one that got bloodied when I was shot. It's gotta be there. I don't know what's in it, but maybe it will answer some questions." This whole story, from Gens to the last bomb, was a chronicle of questions. There were always more of them than answers. "What did you do with the coat?"

"I put it into a plastic bag. It stank and was really ugly. I mean, bloody. It's on the floor of the closet."

With any luck the plastic kept it from fire-water.

"I've got to get it. Be back in a few minutes."

I drove over to the Trader Joe's on La Brea and Third to get food for our "new home" and to make a call. I got Abe at home.

"One last favor? Maybe two? I need to contact someone. Probably by email is safest. And it's gotta be confidential."

"So your email is taboo and mine isn't?"

"You got it."

"Whenever." As usual. He was more than a prince. "What else?"

"I'm not sure how to explain this, but . . ." I explained the thing about the booklet.

"You want it back? How can I help?"

"I'm stuck like flypaper to folks from the constabulary. Or they're stuck to me. Same effect. I need to get the thing. Soon."

"Who knows you have it? Other than Terry?"

"I don't know. When Kurt was bashed at Pinsky's place, the whole shebang was gutted. Stuff all over the place. Pinsky himself would not have done that. He would have known exactly where the pamphlet was—either in his apartment or on Kurt. He wouldn't have needed to make such a gross search. It had to be someone else. But not finding it, the other person may have believed it didn't exist. And I think no one would know that I got in there and got it. The only ones who were in there when I was were the police. And I'm sure that even they didn't know I got it."

"I'll see what I can do."

"Don't endanger yourself, Abe."

"It's not in my nature."

"May I come over at noon?"

"Any time."

That was all.

When I got back from the market, we ate toast and coffee. It was already after eleven. Though we slept only a short time, we hadn't gotten home till well after midnight, and we had stayed in bed till after ten.

"I'm off."

"Come back!"

"You're here. You know I will."

I got to Abe's and when he opened the door he handed me a wrapped sandwich and guided me to his car. "What's going on?"

"Nothing. You have been tailed enough to my place that I don't feel confident that my computer and phone line are private any more. Here's my second cell phone number. Use it from now on."

We drove for about twenty minutes to a modest house near Western—St. Andrews Place. Nice old neighborhood, gone to seed, and the seeds were beginning to sprout again. In ten years you couldn't touch a place here for under six hundred thousand. I filled Abe in on the latest incendiary device.

A middle-aged man—maybe forty-five or so—answered the door. Short and thin and hollow-eyed; wiry; with a strong grip and a comfortable smile. He was neatly dressed, even with a tie, in Los Angeles. Must be from Boston. He gave me an Any-friend-of-Abe's-is-a-friend-of-mine welcome. His little apartment was dark, with heavy curtains over the windows, but it was immaculately clean and beautifully laid out, with fine furniture and lamps, and all the other trappings of refinement: candles in silver sticks on the table, Frank Lloyd Wright clock on the wall to go with his other Mission style designs.

Abe introduced him as Philip Bonnie, a former student who had been Abe's fix-it man for nearly thirty years. What was it that Abe thought he could fix for me?

Abe said, "Philip, my friend Elliot needs something. It's in an apartment that has been bombed and nearly gutted. It was a bomb to kill. The place is still under surveillance."

"But presumably not under lock and key," Philip said.

I told him what to look for and where to find it: the coat in the plastic bag. He never asked any questions. He knew what he had to do and he took it on with no curiosity. "Don't you want to know what you are looking for? Why I want the coat?"

"No. The less I know the better. All I need to know you have told me. It's enough."

I ahem-ed. Then I said, "As for . . . ."

"I don't want anything for my help. I'm doing this for Professor Weaver." It sounded funny to see a man in his forties call Abe by his honorific. "I owe him."

"You owe me nothing, Philip. But I know I can trust you. That's why we're here."

"You'll also want to use my phone and computer. Yours are off limits right now. Correct?"

"Yes," I said. "Thanks very much."

He set me up at the computer in a back bedroom and returned to the living room to speak with Abe. The bait worked once before. No reason to assume it wouldn't work again. I put out a message on the old standby lists: ABAA, ABORB, and OUT OF THE LIBRARY. I had been selling my cheaper books on the Web over LINK'N, a database of millions of titles, subscribed to by thousands of people wanting to sell books. This would not only expose my item to millions of buyers, but it would make it searchable on the Web. I'd have a worldwide clientele.

The message: "I'm ready to sell *Ein Buchlein von dem Sterben.*" I figured I didn't need more than that. I wondered if Coster would be surfing for the title. But I guess it wouldn't matter. He would know that something had to give with the book.

I wasn't sure I really wanted to sell. Probably not. But I needed to contact someone, and with Myers out of the chase, I didn't know whom I was dealing with. If I did get some calls, I had to decide what I'd ask for it. If it went to auction, we could get big players facing off. But then, it could go too low, and the auction house would take its chunk. What I thought I'd do is tell callers that no price had been set, but that it would be in seven figures. I'm sure that wouldn't chase some potential buyers away. Maybe I'd even have a silent auction.

My work was done at Bonnie's place. I figured a day at the office would not be as profitable as a day at Terry's and my place. I went home to the Hancock Park bungalow and spent the afternoon with Terry. Rewarding. Delightful. Orgasmic. What more could one ask for?

Then Coster called. He got right to the point:

"We found out that there was a two-million-dollar life insurance policy on Edward Myers."

"In whose name?"

"It looks like just his only heir: Theresa."

"Did he take it out?"

"We can't find out. It may not be possible to learn this."

"How did you find out?

I could hear Coster smile smugly. "We have our ways."

"That's almost like answering my question with another question. Not satisfactory. How did you find out?"

"We had probable cause. Lots of evidence pointed her way. So we were able to get a search warrant of the house. We accidentally blundered onto a check book on a desk. It had a record in it in which we found checks written to an insurance company. We got a subpoena for the company, and there it was."

"Did Myers know about it?

"Of course. The insured has to sign the policy, even if he or she doesn't pay for it."

"So we have a motive?" I asked.

"I guess so," he said, "but not much of one. Just because there was a policy does not mean the beneficiaries killed him. They cannot really be connected with the crime through the policy."

"You said there's only one heir?" I asked.

"Yes. Just Theresa."

I wondered why there was no one else. Wasn't there anyone else in his life? Pinsky? Other heirs? "Were there any creditors?"

"He wasn't in debt. But his son was. To a high tune."

"So I heard." Coster was just confirming to me what I had heard from Blake in his library and from Theresa in Crocker's. I said,

"As you know, Blake told me. So did Theresa Myers."

"When you met her for lunch at the diner with the mouth of a waitress?"

"Yes. She said that Blake had big debts—probably gambling—and that the family had lost most of their savings in the stock market."

"Damn fools."

"Why?" I asked. "Everyone who had money in the market lost. And not all of them are fools."

"I had plenty in the market, and I did ok. Not great, but ok."

"What stocks did you have?"

"Only necessities, things that will keep selling: water, fertilizer, clothing—low-end clothing—toilet paper . . . ."

I had heard enough. We rang off with a "keep us informed" from both directions.

Terry and I spent the rest of the day lolling around, snuggling, listening to blue grass. (One damn fine genre, though totally unappreciated in L.A. You ask for blue grass in L.A. and they guide you over to blues. Damn fools. I'm surprised they don't send me to the gardening section. In L.A. it's all new metal, punk age, hippity hop, and jazzrap, with some oldies but goodies thrown in. And to these children "oldies" means early '90s. That's not old. That's just bad. Way bad.)

* * *

I logged on to the computer the next morning at about eight, and Bonanza! Word had been circulating about the *Buchlein* for some time now, as it will among members of any fraternity. Booksellers all over the place, including Germany and Holland, Italy and Australia, sent queries. So did libraries: the Huntington; University of Texas's Humanities Research Center; the New York Public; the Getty; and—holy Rosary, Batman—the Vatican. The British Museum and the Bibliothèque Nationale also sent notes. The basic message was: Who is the printer? What is the date? Is it complete? Is it the full German text? And—not surprisingly—How much?

The message from the Vatican Library, in immaculate English, explained why the Vatican was the *only* place that booklet should be. Father Bernstein had been blabbing to the Pope or someone. The Huntington said that there was no better home in the country for such an important item. The Getty said it was probably the only institution which could afford to pay what it was worth. The BL said it would fill a significant gap in their research collection. (Of course, it would. Every research collection—every damn collection—in the world had this gap to fill. Maybe I should sell it to an orthodontist.) The Bibliothèque Nationale, in fairly halting English, said that even though the city on the title page was Leipzig, it was probably really printed in France and that the volume should never have made it out of the country. They wanted it repatriated.

There were a few private collectors who answered, as well. Manuel Richards of New York, famous for his magnificent collection of incunabula and other high spots. Theodore Rockstein, in Philadelphia, who could afford just about anything under a billion. I didn't hear from anyone with a Microsoft address, though this probably meant that Bill Gates hadn't yet heard about the little Book. If he had, he'd probably want it. But there were no responses from anyone with a Caligula pedigree.

At the end of the barrage of queries was another message that gave me the chills. It said, "If you sell that book, you are dead meat." Then the phone jingled and I jumped. It was—you guessed it—Officer Dr. Coster.

"We see the message, Elliot. It was sent from a public library computer in Inglewood. There's no way of knowing who sent it."

"Officer . . . ."

"Detective."

"Yes. Coster. I like being live meat. This dead meat just isn't for vegetarians. How safe am I?"

"As safe as we can make you. This could be a crank."

"Not too likely. Would a random crank see the offer of the *Buchlein* and go out of his way to send me such a message? Pretty unlikely. What can you do? What are you doing?"

"At the moment we can't do any more than we already are: covering your movements and contacts and quarters. We are looking for Pinsky, but we believe he is in Poland. There is no record of his having returned."

"What proof do you have that he went there?"

"I told you. He got on a plane."

Pinsky had told me that his cousin, who looked like him, got on the plane for him. I wasn't sure I wanted to share this with Coster. But I asked:

"Is it possible that someone who looked like him could have used his passport to leave the country?"

"It's unlikely, but possible. This kind of nonsense could land him in even more trouble if it came to light. He's in enough trouble already."

"But it's possible?"

"Possible, but unlikely."

"You're repeating yourself, Mr. Coster."

"So are you, Mr. Burgess. I already answered that question."

He got me there. No denying it.

"So who sent this last threat?"

"We don't know yet." There's that "yet" again. It's in his blood.

"That does Terry and me no good. An incendiary device made its way into our living quarters at a time when we could have been there. There was no effort to pinpoint the explosion to a safe or a doorknob. It was meant to kill. What did you do to prevent that? Ok, it's a rhetorical question since you didn't prevent it, which means that you didn't do anything. To prevent it."

He was listening. I could hear a disgruntled expression on his face.

"I'll tell you, Dr. Coster, we're not happy."

"We have added personnel to your home and business, both when you are there and when you are away. We are listening in on your calls and monitoring your email. We have been able to listen . . . ."

"You mean you could hear Abe Weaver's phone?"

"Yes. You were spending time there. We wanted to cover you as much as we could. But you must help us. You keep going off to have meetings at people's houses and to use other people's computers. What do you expect when you evade us like that?"

"Big brother is watching," I said. "It gets pretty oppressive."

"Better to be oppressed than dead."

He got me again on that one. We concluded with promises on all sides. I'll keep in touch. You'll keep in touch. Like a game of tag. But I didn't like being *it*. I didn't want a tag on my toe.

Again Terry and I spent a quiet evening on the couch, thinking and discussing things. I told her what Coster had said and said that I still didn't think he was helping.

"With him there, all he's doing is either chasing away the person we need to get close to, or making that person be more aggressive in getting to us."

"I feel safer with them out there," she said. "Look what's happened to us! Bombed, kidnapped, beaten up, shot at. And I don't want to lose you."

She said it with deep honesty and pathos and then hugged me tightly. All I could do was whisper "Amen."

* * *

The morning started auspiciously. There was a rap on the door at eight. I was sipping some decaf with soy milk (so keyed up that I didn't need any caffeine) and could see out the window of the kitchen that the messenger had been inspected by the inspectors outside. He was cleared to knock.

"What can I do for you?" (I know it should be "*may* do for you," but that sounds pedantic. Far be it from me to sound pedantic.)

"I have an envelope for you."

"Where do I sign?"

"No signature is necessary." What! In the movies . . . .

"Who sent it?"

"I don't know. I just deliver."

"Whom do you work for?"

"Universal Product Senders. We're based in Inglewood. We're really not universal. It's our owner. He wants everybody to think we can compete. For local things we can. We have twelve messengers like me."

"Would he be able to tell who sent this?"

"Prob'ly not. Anyone can come in, give us cash, and have a letter delivered anywhere. It's expensive."

I wondered why he added this tidbit. "How much for an envelope like this?"

"A hundred and twenty five. Cashier's check or cash. Boss gets most of it. But we give good service. The owner even has a car for each of us. A Kia."

That's the Korean car that thinks it's cute with the capital A with no crossbar in it. If those were Greek letters, it would spell KIL. Dumb name for a car. Stupid typography.

I gave him a $10 tip. Cruddy little job.

Terry came out of the bathroom, smelling of a Dove bar. Not the ice cream; the soap that claims it has a third skin cream in it. That always seemed dumb to me. The idea of soap is to get the oil off your skin; the cream is oil. It's as if the two ingredients cancel each other out. Besides, these bars melt away in water like melting ice. You get only about three baths out of one bar, and you feel slimy when you use it. What a waste.

But she smelled good anyway.

I showed her the envelope. We knew instinctively what it was about.

The note, printed in simple block letters on a 3 x 5 card, said:

"I have money and answers. You want them both. Meet me at the ferris wheel in Santa Monica. Come alone or else. Tonight. 8."

"How can I come alone when I'm attached to two officers at all times? Can I use the Weaver ploy again. I don't think so."

"Elliot, you can't be thinking about doing this." Terry was quite upset.

"What are my options?"

"Call Coster. Or I will."

"Coster has been a hindrance. He has learned nothing of importance except what I have told him. He hasn't protected us from being bombed or kidnapped. He's got a poor track record."

"But you keep doing things without his knowledge. You evade him and do things that get you into trouble."

"Terry, this is coming to a head. If Coster's face appears in this, nothing will happen. Someone will back away. And we're back to where we are now: with someone willing and able to bomb us out of existence roaming around just waiting for an opportunity. Coster and his fellows won't be there always. This guy can go dormant for months and then come back with a bazooka. I don't want to live under that shadow until then. I've gotta do something. We've been waiting for this opportunity. I have to go."

"You don't even know who it is you're meeting."

"Whoever it is, he'll know me. He knows where we live. He certainly knows what we look like. Do you want to walk down the street thinking that anyone around you could stab you at any moment? Or shoot you from a passing car? I don't."

"I'm scared." And she really was. I could feel it in her.

"I am too. But I'm angry and frustrated. That doesn't bode well for the ones making me feel this way."

"What are you going to do?"

"To begin with, you're going on a little excursion this evening. To the Beverly Center. We need something at the mall."

"What?"

"We need you to split the spies in half. If there's only one car out there, it has to follow whoever is out. If there are two, I can slip away from one more easily than from two."

"It's crazy. You are putting yourself in danger."

"The note said 'alone,' not 'unarmed.'"

"What weapon do you have? I don't like this."

"So far in this conversation everything you have said has been to oppose this idea. If you have a better idea—and calling Coster is not one—then tell me. If you don't, then think positively with me."

She was silent for a moment. "We have a small paring knife that will fit into your coat pocket. And you can wear several layers of heavy clothes. If someone wants to harm you, a gun would make too much noise. The person is more likely to go at you with a blade of some sort."

This was more like it. God, she was wonderful.

"You have a leather jacket. It's pretty thick. You can hide a knife in it. Or a rock. And it will go over a leather vest and a few sweaters. Nobody will notice since you have to dress warmly at the beach at night."

"I also have an L.L. Bean jacket with lots of pockets. I can fill them with books."

"But what if he attacks you in another way?"

"Like what? And we don't even know if an attack is what is planned for me."

"Why else would someone want to see you alone? At night? In such a crowded place? It's dangerous."

I said, "He wants to negotiate. There's no way to do it by phone or email. No other private way to get to me. The note said he had money."

"I don't trust the note. It can be as much of a lure to you as your message about the availability of the book was to him."

Neither of us really knew what to expect, but we agreed that it was an opportunity I couldn't let pass.

"How will you shake the tail if there is one?"

"I'm going to have a party."

"What?"

"Just leave it to me."

To test things, I told Terry I'd drive to the shop and she would go out in her car to anywhere—a drug store, a shoe store, anywhere. She drove away after lunch and I saw a car follow her—pretty obvious. Maybe that's what they wanted—to be seen. I made my phone calls, and then I headed to the store, and sure enough, I was accompanied by Bud and Lou or their buddies. If a third party was still there to protect the house, I couldn't tell. Things were rolling.

When we met back at the house at four, as we planned, we embraced, recounted what we had seen and done, and went over the plan for the night. Terry arranged my wardrobe, I screwed my courage to the sticking point. (That requires a comment, as usual, but I'm in no mood to come up with one now. My life could be on the line.)

* * *

At six thirty Abe arrived, wearing the most generic clothing one can imagine, and a visor cap. A few minutes later his student Philip Bonnie came, in the same habit. In a few minutes my security team leader, Billy Brinks, showed up. Nice visor cap. Nice black sweater. And after him was my friendly bomber-for-hire, Simon Johnson. Lovely little baseball cap, Simon.

For good measure, I had Abe invite another friend, a retired professor—Shane Harvey—who liked the idea of a party, especially one, as Abe told him, that had an air of mystery to it. He too wore the uniform.

I had them all park in the long drive, between the glow of light thrown off by the lamp posts. It really wasn't very dark there, but it was dim enough to obscure facial features in the shadows.

By seven we had had snacks and coffee. By seven fifteen we had gotten our plan worked out. And by seven twenty five we went into action.

One at a time, someone left the house, took a car, and drove away. And you can bet that no one took the same car he arrived in. Except me. And I was the third to leave. I figured with Terry gone, we were down to one or two tails. That would mean the first two cars to take off would pull whatever spies were left. It was a harebrained idea. There was no way to suppose that this would work. That they didn't have a way to identify the drivers. That they couldn't get backups. That's why we did this in quick succession: not to give them time to replenish the vehicles of the cavalcade.

When I pulled out in Shawn's car—he was so new to the scene that I assumed I could increase the odds of not being followed if I took a vehicle that the fuzz weren't familiar with—I headed east. I saw no one in the mirror. I made several turns onto residential streets. First over by Western Avenue (I know it says West, but it's east of Hancock Park), then back to Highland, then onto Rosewood to La Brea, and so forth. No one in sight except different cars everywhere I went.

Much of the L.A. commuter traffic had made it to their destinations, so I figured Wilshire would be a good street to take to the beach.

I found a parking lot on PCH (Pacific Coast Highway—pretty obvious name) and walked toward the ferris wheel. Lots of walkers around, not unusual for that area of Santa Monica. It's an area of hopping night life. The place was mildly mobbed, mostly be teenagers out to hang out. I strode down the wooden walk, past the tee shirt shop and the tourist trinket shop and the video arcade—noisy! Kids in there will be wearing hearing aids by the time they're thirty. The old ferris wheel, which looked magical from a distance, with its undulating lights, looked pretty seedy and creepy from nearby.

I saw no one, though, of course, I was surrounded by people. Kids, old folks out for a stroll in the bracing air, lots of ring-toss and knock-over-the-milk-bottle people, silly-bowling-game people, and others at all the arcade games that I used to hunger to play as a kid, but for some reason shied away from when my parents let me have a quarter or two.

It was a couple of minutes after eight when I got there. The air was cold, but the smells of candy and the old wooden sidewalk and people and cheap greasy hot dogs (Molly wouldn't approve) and the occasional street person down-on-his-luck and a hint of salt air made the place intermittently too warm and too chill. It was redolent of my childhood and made me long for the baseball-at-the-park-in-our-family-match-ing-red-plaid-shirts days. And for the pony ride at La Cienega and Beverly. And for the ugly Baldwin Hills bobbing birds—the oil pumps that had been working for more than a half century.

I looked out above the seedy buildings and saw the night sky. No stars. (In L.A. they don't have stars in the sky, only on the screen and in the sidewalks.) What a place! The pier. Santa Monica. L.A. City of the angels—and a few devils.

The pressure on my back could have been anything. I had so many layers of clothes on that I couldn't tell if it was a gun or a knife or a finger or a newspaper.

"Don't turn around."

I didn't have to.

"Hello, Rapel."

"How did you know?"

"I don't forget voices." Or bullets or bombs or fists.

"Let's take a walk."

"Where to?"

"The arcade."

Whoa! It was way too noisy there. Not only could we not hear one another, we would also not be heard, and we would be swallowed up by the anonymity of the mob of kids, shooting, punching, driving, dancing. The dancing machine made you try to follow a pattern of foot movements at break-neck speed. Break-neck. Bad image at this moment. The dancers would try to look cool and nonchalant, but there was a frenetic level to this game that belied their exteriors. I didn't want to be near such a high pitch of tension. I was tense enough.

"Not there. I won't go."

"What choice do you have?"

"I *won't* go." And I didn't budge.

"Ok. Let's take a ride, then." He pushed me toward the ticket booth and reached a fistful of ones over my shoulder. "Buy two tickets for the wheel."

I did.

There was a short line. We were in our gondola in a couple of minutes, me first, on the left.

When we ascended, I turned to face him. He had a knife that looked big enough to kill a moose. It was pressed against my right ribs. Not on the side with the bullet wound. And the point was firmly against me. I couldn't imagine that that blade would be hindered by a mere twenty layers of leather and Kevlar—that aramid fiber that you hear about in crime shows. I wasn't wearing one of those vests. But even if I were, the knife was in my ribs, where the vest wouldn't do any good. (Notice in the movies the bad guys always aim at the torsos of the good guys. Dumb. They're not wearing the bulletproof stuff on their heads.)

"Ok, Pinsky. Let's talk."

"Burgess. You don't have much choice here. I'll talk. I want the book. Your *Buchlein von dem Sterben. My Buchlein.*" The emphasis on 'my' was no typo. "I don't care how you get it to me. I *will* get it."

"What's to make me?"

"I have taken steps. There are bombs. I am good at these, as you know."

"Are you the one who bombed my shop?"

"Of course."

"And my house?"

"Yes. Nice jobs, right?"

"What's nice about a bomb."

"They can be beautiful. My bombs are beautiful."

"And my apartment?"

"What are you talking about?"

"My Santa Monica apartment?"

"I didn't do it. When?"

"You should know."

"I don't." He said this with some testiness.

"Someone blasted the place with a pipe bomb, thrown from the outside."

"Not my style. It's too messy. People could get hurt."

"As if that ever stopped you." I felt the knife press against my side.

We had reached the top of the arc. From up there I could see mobs of people below, the ocean, dark and mysterious, with the skitter of a light now and then from a distant boat. It was cold.

"Who shot at me when I first got the book?"

"I don't know. Maybe Myers. Or his son. I don't know."

"Who attacked Dave Daws?"

"Who is Dave Daws?"

"The man who worked for me in the shop?"

His pause told me that he knew.

"I didn't do it."

"That doesn't answer my question."

We were spinning now, as in free flight. The gondola swayed and made me feel queasy. Or was it the predicament?

I said, "Who bopped Kurt Bricker?"

"I don't know a Kurt Bricker."

"You hit him over the head."

"No! I didn't. Shut up. I got you here to tell you this. I can kill you and your honey any time. The people who are 'protecting' you"—he said it with derision—"don't know what they are up against. My training is the best. I can kill you. I can kill your woman. Any time. And I will. But I don't want to have to do this. I want the book."

"Why?" Another one of my dumb questions.

"I need what it can bring me. Money. Lots of it."

"Where did it come from?"

"No one needs to know."

"Is it genuine?"

"Of course, it's genuine. It's real. You have felt it and seen it and read it. It's real."

"But is it *genuine*? Is it authentic? Is it a forgery?"

"Who cares?"

"I do. Lots of people do."

He seemed to be at a point of relishing this. "You will never know the truth. It doesn't matter. It's how the world judges it. I say it's genuine. Everyone says it's genuine. So it is."

"That doesn't answer my question."

"It's all the answer you need. And all you'll get."

"Who owned it before I bought it?"

"I guess Myers, but it wasn't really fair. He didn't pay enough for it."

"He paid with his life."

"That lying, cheating shithead. Of course he did."

"So you killed him?"

Another revealing pause.

"He was in the way. He deserved what he got."

"Why did you do it?"

"I wasn't alone."

"Blake?"

"Yes."

"Why?"

He said, "We were told there was an insurance policy that would make getting the book back unnecessary. We needed money. For Blake. For me."

"Why for you?"

"We had plans. But we needed money."

"Who is 'we'?"

Silence again.

"Here's my deal. You get the book to me, one way or another, and I won't kill you and your lady."

"Absolutely not."

"You get that book to me or your lady dies. Then you."

"How can you do it? I'm covered by the fuzz everywhere. I can't even brush my teeth without the police frisking my toothbrush first."

"They can be slipped. You're here with me, aren't you? No one followed you. I know. You're alone."

"What if I sell the book? Then we can split the profits."

"*No!*" That was as adamant a 'no' as I have ever heard.

"Why would I do this for you?" I asked.

"You're doing it for yourself. And your lady."

"So I give you the book. What then?"

"You'll never see me again. I'm out of your life forever."

"What can you possibly do with it?"

"I know where I can sell it. For lots of money."

We were on our second revolution and I was on the edge of nausea. Fear? The movement of the gondola. The ferris wheel kept stopping to pick up people and each time we rocked back and forth. I think there were a couple of things I would rather have been doing right then.

"I won't give it to you. I won't sell it to you. I need more answers and I am not afraid of you."

"What answers?"

"Dave Daws. Kurt Bricker. The bomb in our apartment? Who shot Blake? Answers!"

"I can't answer them."

"Can't or won't?"

"I don't know anything about Daws or Bricker or the bomb."

"But you know about Blake?"

"I *want* the book. You *will* give it to me."

His agitation was more than obvious, especially as he started to push the knife into my side. The clothing held. For now.

"Ok, Burgess. I don't need you to get the book. Your lady will give it to me." He said this with ice and malice. With a finality that made me shiver more than the cold air did. "I will kill you. It's no problem. I have killed before. Many times. You are just more dead meat." I now knew whom the email message had come from.

"How can you kill me? You're with me here. Anyone can see."

"In this crowd. No problem. I jump out when the ride is done and I'm invisible."

"Why kill me?"

"When your lady hears about it, she'll be so scared she'll piss and want to get the book out of her possession fast. I can get it from her. If it takes six months, no problem. She'll live in hell those months. The police will think she's safe. They'll back off. Or if I can't get to her, I'll just kill her. I have infallible ways."

"With bombs?"

"Just one. It's all I need. In fact, it's already in place. On her car. I can detonate it from ten thousand miles away. I can monitor her movements and wait till she's in the car. I can kill when I want."

He waited for my reaction. But I didn't know how to react. I was numb, from the conversation and from the chill air.

"My last offer. If you get it for me, I can have it sooner. That's what I want. But I can wait. You get it to me now and have your life back; or she gives it to me later and maybe gets her life back. Your choice. Tell me where it is and how you'll get it to me."

I hesitated. He didn't like that and pressed the knife deeper. It felt as if it was already piercing my clothes, and it hurt.

I felt the kitchen knife in my left pocket. In the confines of the gondola there was no movement that I could have made that he wouldn't see. "My nose is running. I gotta get a tissue."

"Get it!"

We were three-quarters of the way around, sitting there, rocking gently, waiting for the next party to enter the bottom gondola, a couple of seats ahead of us. We had been sitting like that for a few minutes. I wanted to wait till we were in movement again, maybe to distract him. There was no time to wait.

I slipped my hand into the pocket. The knife handle was placed just right. I pulled my hand slowly up, coming out of my pocket. Pinsky glared at me, suspiciously.

"Blow your goddam nose. Then you're dead." He was angry and I could see he was serious. Murderous. With nothing to lose.

"Now!" He yelled.

In a quick move, I pulled back and twisted my body, my right side sluing around toward the seat, my left side swinging out away from it. It took a split second. The movement freed up my left hand and twisted his knife at an angle. It pierced my leather jacket and the point was stuck in such a way that my movement angled his knife backward. He was stunned. The look on his face was half shock, half rage. He shoved his hand forward, and I felt the knife come through the clothes and a sharp pain near the back of my ribs. My left hand was now flying, and I slashed him on the face. He screamed and pulled the knife out, raising his hand to strike. There was an explosion, maybe two. There was a frenzy of wrath on his face, but he didn't strike. He screamed and the knife fell on our laps. There were voices, yelling, screaming. You know the rest.

FORTY

Once again in a hospital. But this time it wasn't too bad. I had loaded the pockets of my Bean jacket with paperbacks: Sue Grafton, Sara Paretsky, Miss Marple. Pinsky's knife had been near my ribs, but the twisting movement got the books partly between me and the knife. I had a scrape, but no broken bones, no real piercing, and no time off for bad behavior.

Coster said, "You're a damn fool."

"But I lived to tell about it."

"No thanks to you."

"Where did you guys come from? I didn't see any horses. I didn't hear the bugles."

"We were in the two cars in front of you and the two behind."

"Who told you where I'd be? Where I went?"

"You did. Sort of."

"What did I say?"

"Ms. Luckombe filled your clothes with devices. Your outer and inner jackets had homing devices and little microphones. When you were practicing splitting up our followers, she came straight to me."

"I told her to go to the mall."

"Maybe she heard you say 'them all.'" (He sounded like me.) "Maybe she figured we were them all."

"Funny."

He said in a really smug way: "We were there to protect and serve. In fact, we were there an hour before you were. And we protected."

"I can't say that I'm not grateful. In fact, thank you very much." I said this with as little sarcasm as I could muster, considering whom I was talking to. After all, he did stop the fight in mid stab. Who knows where it would have ended up. "What happened to Pinsky?"

"He's in Poland."

"No dumb answers. Where's Pinsky?"

"Which one? The Rapel who flew off to Poland? He's in Poland. The Pinsky who was trying to turn you into schwarma?" I gagged when I smelled that thin-sliced beef spinning on a kabob in Middle Eastern restaurants. And I didn't feel less nauseated when I was compared to it. "That was Viktor Pinsky. The other Pinsky's cousin."

"There are two Pinskys?" I was genuinely surprised.

"This one looked like Rapel, and they both had the same training as young men. They were both good at explosives. They were in the Army together. Same unit. We didn't know of this one until tonight. He was going under the name of Koralcik, Alex Koralcik."

"Whose apartment was Kurt attacked in?"

"This guy's. But he swears he had nothing to do with it. He says he went back to his place late at night, found it surrounded by police, and ducked away. Says he hasn't returned."

"What was he afraid of?"

"Mainly, I think, the fact that he is here illegally. His visa ran out months ago. But also he seems to be afraid to be sent back to Poland. Something about 'being wanted.'"

"Where is he now?"

"L.A. General. He's in deep trouble. We have a confession from him on tape. Well, half a confession. But if we tell him he'll have to give us the whole story or we'll send him back in irons to Poland . . . ."

"What happened? Is he in any danger?"

"Don't congratulate yourself. We shot his right arm. And he has a pretty bad cut on his face. The right side will never look like his face again. But there is nothing fatal about his wound. His pride and his ego are more damaged. To think that he was beaten by an amateur like you."

I resented that. So I said, "I resent that."

"You *are* an amateur. Look at the mess you were in. If it weren't for Ms. Luckombe . . . ." He knew he needn't finish that.

"What are you going to do with Pinsky . . . ? You know, Koralcik?"

"Hold him till we know what we can do with him. His confession about Myers was pretty sketchy. We'll either get a confession out of him or send him home. Either way, it looks like he'll be out of society a good long time."

I still needed some answers. "He told me he didn't bash Dave or Kurt."

"Dave we don't know about. Kurt? That would have been a cinch. He comes home, finds a stranger in his place, and knocks him on the head. Kurt was hit from behind."

"With what?"

"That's been bothering us. The blow wasn't from a sharp object of any kind, like a stick or bat. It looks as if it was from a large blunt object. And there was some water on the floor and on his clothes. We're working on it." His standard pose.

"And Dave?"

"We already discussed this. Remember, it could have been a tire iron or bat or heavy rock."

I had called Terry from the hospital and when I got home she flew to me and held on for dear love. I said, "Terry, thank you . . .," but she kissed me and wouldn't let me finish.

* * *

"The numbers are dropping." Weaver and Terry and I were at lunch at the wonderful Sushi Roku on Third. Superb nigiri and maki, in a dark and intimate setting. We felt we needed something quiet and enclosed. My knife scratch of two days earlier was not quite behind me (it was, after all, on my side), but it was settling down to an annoying itch.

It was Sunday. On the day of the split-up party, Abe's friend had retrieved the Pinsky notebook in the bloody jacket in the plastic bag in the water-soaked closet in the bombed-out apartment in Santa Monica. He wouldn't say how he had gotten it. "The less you know the better," was all he'd offer. He gave it to me that afternoon, and I had Terry run it over to the bank to stash it with the *Buchlein*. I had glanced into it, but then, in the haste of the day, left it for the future.

We'd get to the bank to fetch the Pinsky notebook the next day.

"The numbers are dropping," Weaver had said. "We are now down to only one person still at large."

We had gone over it: I was bombed twice by Viktor; Karl Smith, alias Gens, was done in by Blake and Howard; Myers probably killed by Viktor, with Blake and maybe Howard as accomplices; Blake and Howard were responsible for what had happened to Celia (who was now home and back to her writing). Viktor could have assaulted Kurt but no one knew and he denied it. No one knew who battered Dave or shot Blake. And the two Pinskys were out of it, one in Poland, one in prison.

I was curious to know what was in Viktor's pamphlet. We'd get it soon. But we needed to come out of the woods. We could see the light at the end of the tunnel. We were coming to the end of our rope. Things were unraveling. We were about to see the light. Things were dawning on us. And I was going to be arrested by the cliché police.

Terry said, "We're down to Theresa Myers. What do we know?"

We rehashed the whole thing: her interests, her opportunities, her motives. The whole shebang. (What the hell is a shebang, anyway?)

I said, "We have to draw her out."

Abe: "What's her weakest point?"

Terry: "Money."

Elliot: "Maybe some man."

This brought their attention. I said, "Money is one thing, and I'm not ruling it out. But what if there is a man involved? Could she have done these deeds herself? Attacking Dave and Kurt, for example? Even trying to get rid of Blake?"

Abe: "She could have."

Terry: "But she's a woman. Not very strong."

Abe: "It doesn't take much strength to smash someone over the head or to pull a trigger."

Elliot: "Why would she be in my shop? Well, to get the book. And she could have come armed, to take the book by force, if need be."

Terry: "Why would she be at Pinsky's—I mean Koralcik's?"

"If Elliot is right, it could have been a tryst." Abe was attacking a bowl of edamame. "Or it could have been because she was after what Elliot wanted and Kurt found."

"The pamphlet." I could hardly wait to read it.

"Back to my question," Abe said. "Her weak points."

I said, "The pamphlet, which represents money; and maybe a man."
"Or a woman," Terry added.
Another wrinkle. Too many wrinkles in this case. We needed Botox.
"I think I may know how to get to her. The pamphlet, of course. But also money, which is what the pamphlet represents to her." I was on the verge of a plan. "We'll tell her that the *Buchlein* is a forgery. That we know who did it. That we are ready to expose the person. And that she may be implicated. Who knows what that will elicit from her."
And so we did.
In fact, the note I wrote was even sneakier. It said:

Dear Ms. Myers,
    I have come to the end of my rope. [Watch out; more cliché fuzz.] It is time to reveal the truth. And you know what that truth is.
    I don't want to go to the police. They don't know too much at this point, and it is better for both of us if that remains the case.
    There have been bombings and killings. You know a good deal about these.
    There is a pamphlet that I have determined is forged. You know about this, too. It is worth practically nothing. Anyone foolish enough to try to sell it would not only be risking his professional standing, he might also be risking legal action.
    On top of being forged, it is stolen. You know about this, as well. I have proof. If that proof comes out, you could be in trouble as an accessory after the fact. You and your husband, and possibly others in your circle, knew of the pamphlet, knew its origins, and knew its ownership. The pamphlet was stolen by someone you or your family hired, and it came to me by accident. I now possess stolen property, so I don't want this affair to be made public. That is why I am writing you in confidence.
    I don't want the *Buchlein von dem Sterben* in my possession. I could be implicated in crimes I didn't commit. It could destroy me professionally. I could be arrested for knowingly holding stolen property. I would rather burn the thing than run the risk of being caught with it in my hands.

In fact, I almost burned it. But since you were the previous owner—albeit that it was in your hands illegally—I thought I owed you the courtesy of discussing its fate.

Let me repeat: I have seen things. I have heard things. I have been in your house, and I know things. My revealing them could blow this thing open in both of our faces. I do not want to destroy myself, and you in the process.

We must talk. I will burn the book in a week if I don't hear from you.

Sincerely,
Elliot Burgess

I called Universal Product Senders, and our little delivery man showed up in less than an hour.

"Nice to see you again," I said.

"Same here," he replied. "I guess you liked our work."

I handed him the letter and a hundred-and-thirty-five in cash. He counted it out (mostly twenties from the cash machine) and smiled when he passed one-twenty-five. "It'll be there in under an hour."

Once again, the bait was cast.

* * *

Terry and I spent a fine couple of hours sitting, reading, and listening to Flatt and Scruggs. Lester and Earl—boy could they pick it!

All of this, dear reader, I want you to know, was under the auspices of L.A.'s finest. Coster convinced me that even a sexy, young, innocent-looking thing could pull a trigger and wield a tire iron.

But on the same visit from Coster on which we obedient folks cleared this plan with him, we learned that Viktor was no longer. He had gotten into a fight at the jail, charging the guards and threatening them with big injuries. The guards said he was almost suicidal. He yelled that he would not rot in jail, and he would not go to Poland. He'd rather die than face either of those fates. In his fury he yelled, "I have nothing to lose. Kill me or I'll kill you," and he charged. He had been at a hearing and was being brought back to his cell. He was shackled and cuffed, but still strong and agile. He was hit by bullets from two guns just as he got to the throat of one of the guards. Killed instantly. And there goes one more source of information.

I reminded Coster, "Viktor said that he had rigged bombs into our cars and home."

"He was trying to scare you. We have gone over everything carefully. There are no bombs."

This was only a partial relief. I guess I had to learn to trust Coster and his crew. They weren't all that bad. They *were* the cavalry coming over the ferris wheel, after all.

That morning I had gone back to my e-mail to find a few more queries about the *Buchlein*. Some high rollers. There was a Rosenthal, offering to broker it for me. There was a New York dealer offering me a half million, cash, on the spot. There were follow-up messages from the Getty, the NYPL, and the Vatican. And there was an impassioned message from Brigham Young Univ. concluding: "Please do not sell it without giving us the last bid."

All the messages contained something about "if proven authentic," "if we judge this not to be a forgery," or "on conclusion of certain tests that we wish to subject it to." Damn Doubting Thomases. (Was that Danny Thomas? Marlo Thomas?) But I knew this was reasonable. For that kind of money they would want to test each letter and leaf.

We had decided that if we were going to sell the *Buchlein*, we'd try to get at least a million and a half; and we'd do it with a silent auction—all the bidding done on the Web. As each bid came in we'd post it. But two things intervened. First, the timing had to be right. We didn't want to do anything until the final answers were answered. Who killed so and so? Are all the wrongdoers now getting their just due? And second, we had to feel reasonably certain that we were selling the genuine object.

Back at the house we found a message on the machine. "I got your note. Please call." It was a very sexy voice, but with an edge of irritation to it. Or was it fear?

I used Abe's cell phone—his second one.

"Theresa Myers? It's Elliot Burgess. Again."

"Can I talk?"

"Yes. I'm on a cell phone."

"Where can we meet?"

"How about in the same diner where you learned about nice salads?"

"It's Sunday. Are they open?"

"Yes, and Molly—our sermoneer—will be there."

"Oh. What should I do?"

I said, "Just don't look at her, and order quickly when she approaches."

"When should I be there?"

"How about two? Most of the late lunchers are gone."

"I'll be there."

Coster was listening. It's even easier to trace a cell phone than it is a regular one. He said, "Don't do anything dumb. You won't be alone."

"I like being live meat."

It was set.

* * *

This was Sunday. The day of churchgoing and atonement. Of preparing oneself for a cleaner life. For asking for forgiveness for one's sins, and for vowing not to continue making them. This was the day which, by its intrinsic nature, was designed to put people into the very mood that the *ars moriendi* books taught. The Book of Death. The Book about Dying. The Book to guide one to the paths of righteousness in the temporal realm. My little *Buchlein* had probably gotten a bunch of people to their makers prematurely. It lay peacefully in a bank and a few people now lay peacefully in their graves because of it. All for a little, unassuming pamphlet—thirty two pages of heresy. What a tangled world it was.

* * *

Hot on the heels of the Vatican's second message was a third. For these guys to be working on Sunday was extraordinary. What has this church come to!

Cardinal Uccello wrote: "If the pamphlet that you have is genuine, we are able to offer you $1.5 million for it." My song, exactly. "We wish to send two of our bibliographers to your city. The tests could take a week or two, maybe more. But please let us acquire this from you. It is extremely important."

A similar message came from the Getty. "We are able to offer you quite a substantial sum for the *Buchlein von dem Sterben*. In fact, we can probably outbid any other prospective buyer. We have a special fund for special acquisitions. Your *Buchlein* falls under that rubric. We have a Conservation Lab at our new building." You better believe it! It was about six years in the building, that monstrous white castle on the hill. Not far from UCLA. Rising majestically above the world's biggest parking lot: the 405—one of the most heavily traveled highways in the country.

Word has it that when the massive white structure was in the planning, the architects looked the world over for the right stone. They found a quarry in Italy. They bought the whole quarry. If they could do that, they could damn well outbid anyone else for the Book.

Outbid. That's quite a notion. But I didn't want this to become too much of a bidding contest. There is something frenetic and tentative about sales at auction. We had had enough freneticism in our lives. We wanted a swift and tranquil conclusion to this. Tranquil. A word I hadn't needed to use in months.

There were stirrings in the book world, and we started getting calls. A sale would not be the problem. Choosing whom to sell to would.

* * *

Once again Molly showed us to the back table. Her eyes were popping out, looking over Theresa Myers, who was even more revealingly dressed than she had been on our earlier date. Possibly braless, or with one of those no-bra-line type things that just keep you from sagging or jiggling too much. A mini-skirt just longer than a micro-mini. No visible panty line. Legs . . . . Well, you get the picture.

We did the prelims: Thanks for meeting me again. How are you? Nice weather. Great body you have there. You know: the regular.

Molly came over and Theresa looked down at the menu and said, "A nice ways salad, please."

"You gonna eat it this time, honey?"

"Yes." No eye contact.

"Lentil loaf with no gravy on the potatoes. And two glasses of water, one with no ice. Thanks, Molly."

She was frustrated, but she knew when to retreat. Which she promptly did, with long lectures bottled up and no outlet for them.

She got right to the point. "I want the pamphlet. Even if it's not real. But it is."

"How do you know?"

"My husband said so. He was a great book dealer. He wouldn't make a mistake on such a thing."

"You got my note. You know my feelings. And you know that I know a lot."

"What did you see when you were in my house?"

Wow. She wasn't sure of what I knew. This was progress.

I needed to empty my bladder. I think I was pretty nervous. I excused myself and took off back toward the center of the diner, where there were two tiny rooms for visitors' relief. One had a picture of a hamburger on the door. The other one showed a salad. You had to guess which was the men's and which the women's.

When I got out I saw Molly waddling from our table back to where I was standing. The water in the two glasses was still swaying. She really took up the aisle, and when I tried to get past, she whispered, "Mr. Burgess. Did you know that Barbie over there has a gun?"

I said, "Thanks, Molly" as I squished past.

Forewarned is forearmed. But I was two-armed and unarmed. I'd better be careful.

When I sat down, Theresa started up immediately.

"I need to know what you know. Your note was ambiguous."

And intentionally so. "When Blake was shooting at me, I saw the person behind him." What I didn't say was that I saw *who* that person was. Her silence and the way she glanced down spoke buckets. (Can one speak buckets?) I was in the speculation mood, so I forged ahead. "You were there."

Again she said nothing. I wanted this to sink in, to make her sweat. So I remained silent.

"I want you to know that I saved your life." She said this with what sounded like an excuse in her voice.

"Did you shoot him to save my life?"

"I saved your life. Don't ask why."

"Did you shoot him because he was in debt up to his eyes?"

"My motive is not important. You are alive. You should thank me for that."

When she said this, she reached across the table and touched my hand. "I saved you. You owe me much. And I can offer so much." This came out with a come-hither smile totally out of character for the conversation or the circumstances. I pulled back.

"We can make a lot of money with the book, Elliot. Then we can go anywhere we want. Can't you see the offer I am making?" And she took my hand again.

This was someone used to using her wiles and getting her way.

I pulled back more and said, "I'm not interested."

A blow to her pride, but I'm sure not unexpected.

"I know more."

"What?"

"You know who smashed Dave Daws. In my shop."

Another blind stab.

"The book was there. I wanted it. He was in the way."

"If it had been me there? Would I have been in your way?"

"I needed the book. I still do."

"Would you have killed me for it? There in the shop?"

Molly's timing was impeccable, as usual. My lentil loaf looked just right, and there were a few green beans and a particularly generous pile of mashed potatoes—sans gravy—filling the rest of the plate.

The nice ways salad looked good, too.

Molly retreated, though not until she had hovered over the table and got her eyes filled with Theresa's cleft. It was pretty bizarre.

"Would you have killed me?"

Without hesitation: "If necessary." There was now an edge to her voice. As if she had grown big muscles and was pushing back.

"How did you do it?"

"I walked into the shop. He was standing by the desk, looking down at a book. He half looked up, saw me; probably not my face; and then looked down again. I had a pipe in my purse. It took only a second to get behind him. He never knew."

"His wife and family know."

"He didn't die."

"How do you know?"

"I called the hospital. I know he's still alive."

"Why were you carrying a pipe?"

"I thought I might need it."

"To get the book?"

"I didn't know. It was just instinct to take it with me."

"Not premeditated crime?"

She was quiet a moment. "I needed that book." She was now turning pugnacious. As if her need justified her crime.

"Then Kurt Bricker. Why did you smash him?"

"Who is Kurt Bricker?"

"He was in Pinsky's apartment."

She sat back a bit in her seat, thinking.

"The police weren't the only ones listening in on your phone. We heard the guy say he thought he had the pamphlet. He said he was at Pinsky's apartment. I was out in the car and got a call telling me about this. I was already in Inglewood, a block from the apartment. I thought that Pinsky must have gotten the pamphlet back from you. I was headed over there. I was only about a minute away when I got the call. Whoever was there couldn't have been there more than a couple of minutes before I got there."

"What did you find?"

"Some guy with his back to me. The door was locked, but I had a key. I heard him say that he had a pamphlet there. I had to move quickly. I had a vase of flowers with me."

"Why?"

"I was bringing them . . . ." She choked up a bit. Then came back strongly. "When I opened the door the guy was talking, I guess on a phone. He didn't hear me. I hit him with the vase. Hard. He fell over and fell against a free-standing bookshelf. That fell over and everything spilled out onto him."

"Go on."

"I didn't know what the pamphlet looked like, but Edward had described it to me. I didn't see anything like it. It had to be there. I searched everywhere. I was desperate."

"Obviously. You almost killed for it. That's a sign of desperation." I was trying to draw her out even more. "Did you find it?"

"No."

Something she had said popped up. "Why did you have a key?"

No answer.

"Why were you carrying flowers?"

A fire came into her eyes.

"Viktor is dead."

My god. There it was. Not the money—though that certainly played into it. It was Viktor. Pinsky. Mr. Korlacik.

"What about your husband?"

"That son of a bitch. He was broke. He was self-absorbed. Never looked at me. Treated me like one of his shitty books. Viktor was . . . ."

She stopped.

"Why Blake?"

"Edward made him the heir. Once Edward was dead, if the book came back, Blake would have gotten it."

"Who killed Edward?"

"Blake and Howard. They hated him too. They were greedy. Edward threw his weight around and tried to buy everything he wanted. He bought me. But he was awful. As a husband, as a lover, and as a father."

"What about Viktor?"

That was a dumb thing to bring up. I had already seen her get emotional when she was thinking about him.

"Viktor and I . . . . You killed him. You did it! It's your fault. You deserve to die."

"No . . . ."

Before I could finish the sentence her hand was at her purse. It took about a second. And it took me just under a second to grab my plate and fling it. It was like the Three Stooges: mashed potatoes all over her face. The gun was out, now, but I was sliding right, off my seat. In another second the gun blasted and there was a shattery splat behind me and a strong hand grabbed Theresa's. The whole thing took about three seconds. The officer from the table behind was serving and protecting. Thank god.

Molly was there in a trice. "I had 'em put extra potatoes on your plate. Ya never know. Ya just never know. Shot a hole in the wall. She's a bad shot. But I guess folks with potatoes in their faces can't aim too good. Extra potatoes. Not them little ones. Waste of time, them little ones. I had 'em put . . . ."

"Please step aside," the officer said. He had wrestled Theresa to an uncomfortable position in the booth and had gotten handcuffs on her. He was proud, she was totally pissed. And she looked quite funny, with the potatoes all over her face and prominent chest. Though at the moment I wasn't thinking about how funny she looked. My heart was racing. I couldn't even think of the brilliant mashed-potato defense that I had just exhibited. I owed Molly a hug. Or something. Maybe a pacifier. No. I'll think of the perfect thank-you for her.

Things were really turning in my favor: someone shot at me and *missed*. This could be the start of something big. Or was this just an aberration in the natural course of the planets? I like aberration. Thank god for aberration. And for L.A.'s finest.

* * *

Abe and Terry were at the house. So was Coster. It didn't take him long to get there. And I knew the humble pie was coming:

"You see, Elliot. Trust us. You should have trusted us from the beginning."

"Right." I think my sarcasm was back. But so was a sense of relief, and I want it placed on the record that I heartily thanked Dr. Coster and shook his hand. I guess relief from such stress makes a body do things he wouldn't normally do.

"We have enough on her . . . ."

Coster of course was proud of his stratagem of having me wear another little microphone. Shit. Anyone watching Ironside or Columbo or Mattlock or Hawaii Five O would know of that trick. No big deal.

"She gave us plenty of information. Now you can rest easy, Elliot." Spoken boastfully, taking all the credit where only a tenth of it was due. I didn't care. I was still alive and so was Terry. And it's true: a good deal of the pressure was off.

Abe had brought over some wine. He said champagne hurt his stomach. But wine was the right thing for celebration. He said, "I believe our questions are finally answered."

"Except one," I said. "What is the story of our *Buchlein von dem Sterben*? Where is it from? Who really owns it? Other than Elliot and Terry. Is it genuine? What should we do with it?"

Terry said, "Elliot, I have a daring idea. Let's not read Pinsky's notebook until we have decided what to do with the pamphlet. Until it has been evaluated by the best scholars these libraries can dredge up. We don't know what's in the notebook. But it might be fun to savor the ownership and the limelight and see how these places curry our favor. We might never have an opportunity like this one again."

"Splendid," Abe said. "Sort of like karezza."

"I wouldn't go that far," I said. "After all, when you hear of the benefits of such delayed pleasure, it makes you want to shoot the guy who first thought of it. Who wants to delay pleasure. I sure don't."

"I can vouch for that." Terry was pretty much back to her old self. The weight of the unknown had been lifted. At least, the weight of the part of the unknown that could have been fatal.

So we sat back and watched the offers come in and planned how we would spend our fortune. It was better than trying to figure out where the next bomb was coming from.

FORTY ONE

When the folks from the Vatican arrived we were ready for them. They were dressed in immaculate suits (Hart, Schaffner, and Marx?) with really beautiful ties (from Japan?). And their English was elegant, Britishy, and almost correct.

In my shop, with a couple of armed guards at the door (we figured we could afford Brinks now), and with our new employee looking on, we showed them the cyclotron and carbon-dating reports and the *Buchlein*. They had brought a few pamphlets of their own: a couple of Kachelofen pieces from the same year and the years around it, a few copies of the *Buchlein von dem Sterben* in the 1502 and 1505 printings, and a clutch of other pieces. They spent half a day going over the materials, and at one point I heard their reaction to the text: a sort of murmur of surprise and disapproval and shock. I don't speak Italian, but I could tell that they were not happy with the text they were looking at.

On the other hand, it was obvious that they were impressed with the pamphlet. They handled it gingerly, looking at the paper, checking out and making a drawing of the watermark, feeling the impression of the type (whatever there was left), smelling it, copying out a couple of passages—though I told them they couldn't do more than a few lines—and generally taking in the experience of being in the presence of something extraordinary.

They stood, told us they had seen enough, said they would go back to the Pope (right!) and consult, promised to get back to us in three weeks, and took their leave. Their parting words: "Don't sell this to anyone else until you have heard from us." It was said with kindly deference, but also with a firmness that hinted that we would be facing some of their friends if they heard the book was sold to someone else.

When they walked out of the shop our new employee stood amazed and querulous. Angel Giote, whose ancestors were possibly related to the two who had just departed, came on board a week earlier, answering an ad for a slot in the rare book world. We needed a replacement for Dave, who had recovered enough to say he'd never come back. We advertised and were quickly blessed with an Angel.

Angel, from Kittyhawk, was a lovely twenty-something, smart as a whip-welt, educated at Smith College, where she had been exposed to the Pioneer Valley book arts community, and where she had picked up plenty of knowledge, lore, and vocabulary of the rare book trade. She was perfect—in more ways than one—to fill in for Dave Daws. She had plenty to learn, but she was a fast learner and easy on the eyes.

We had told her of the *Buchlein von dem Sterben* (her German was pretty good and though the text was particularly difficult, she was able to understand its gist—which she read from the Xeroxed copy we showed her), and we also told her a small bit of what we had endured to acquire and hold on to it. She was, however, not quite prepared for the dignity and majesty of the visitors to the shop who wanted to see the booklet.

"Are they going to buy it?" she asked.

"We're not sure we want to sell it. But if we do, they are some of our more promising customers."

"How much is it?"

I told her about the silent auction that was on. The highest bidder, and so on. I told Angel—brilliant, beautiful, and delightful—that she would monitor the incoming bids and post them on our website. I added that there would be a few other suitors arriving in their tuxes and ties. The fact that bidding increments were to be a hundred thousand dollars added to the thrill—for all of us.

Having the silent auction was conducting a sale without going through the regular auction channels. But what the heck, I had the goods, the buyers could bid through me directly, and the auction places wouldn't extract their rigged fees. After all, if the book went through Snoteby's or Christian Brothers or Butterfield Eight, the buyers would have to pay about an extra fifteen percent or more to the auction house as buyer's premium, and the seller would have to give up a chunk to the auctioneers too. Besides, with all the corruption that had come to light in the last few years about these miserable businesses, I was disinclined to use their usurious services. My own bidding war was easy enough to set up. The availability of the *Buchlein* had been gossip for months, and now it was an open topic of conversation. Just like after the discovery of Poe's *Tamerlaine*. There would be no shortage of interest.

And sure enough, we were visited, with equal aplomb and dignity and flourish, by representatives from the New York Public Library (including Elizabeth Browner herself), the Huntington Library, the Getty, the Bibliothèque Nationale, the Bodleian, and other countries. Harry Luben sent over two scientists and a bibliographer. And by golly, Bill Gates sent in a team of five.

The intensity of activity in the shop, the scheduling of the visitors, and the overall level of excitement made life fun again, at a time when wounds and pierced skin and bashed noses were getting back to normal.

Between sessions of suitors, all of whom demanded right of first refusal, Angel pointed out that while I was at lunch that day someone had come in with a book for an appraisal. She had told her that the boss was out to lunch and that she could leave the book for a few days and speak with me when I had had a chance to do the evaluation. It turned out to be a huge, massive, leather-bound bible in poor condition. One of those nineteenth-century volumes with thick boards covered in sculptured leather, lots of gold stamping, edges gilt, and reeking of attic. It suffered from red rot—flaking, smearing, messy leather—and it weighed in at about fifteen pounds. It would be worth about a dollar a pound.

Angel knew that few of these were worth anything intrinsically. Their value lay more in the sentiment than in the book. But the woman insisted that the shop owner see it, so Angel took it in. I left it on a corner of my desk, waiting for its owner's return.

The whole visitation period took about three weeks. The shop was back in order. Things were put where they belonged. We found fewer shards of glass each day—memories of more traumatic times. The flow of orders from the Web was slow but steady. And life was good. We had regular Friday evening dinners with Abe and twice-a-week lunches at Crocker's. (Molly loved the Take-A-Diva chocolates I gave her, along with a splendid new apron that said "kiss the waitress," the talk of the diner for years to come—all thanks to her snoopy eyes and loose tongue, which I promised not to make fun of for at least three weeks.)

Life at home was peaceful and pleasurable. The summer session had begun and Terry had no teaching to do till the fall. But she wasn't sure she wanted to return to the ivory towers. After all, ivory was now illegal.

Precisely three weeks after the Vatican visitation we got another offer of 1,347,822 Euros. It took a quick phone call and a few seconds with a calculator to figure one point six million dollars. But the message that followed was unambiguous: "This is a firm offer. We wish to be the future owners of *Buchlein von dem Sterben*. We are prepared to transfer to your account this amount today. We trust that you are satisfied with this offer. If you are not, please contact us at the following phone number."

Our first offer. It was pretty exhilarating. And it made us nervous. I had never had anything like this kind of infusion in my whole life—probably not with all of my previous business combined.

My next task was to notify the other potential customers what the situation was. My message:

"In its silent auction, Elliot Burgess Books has a recent bid of one point six million dollars for its 1494 *Buchlein von dem Sterben*" (it sounded as if I had other bids for the same title, other dates) "printed by Conrad Kachelofen in Leipzig. Other bids are encouraged. Bids will be posted as they are made. Bidding increments are $100,000. The auction will conclude on July 14."

I figured Bastille Day (also Terry's birthday) would be symbolic of the War and Peace that this booklet had brought into my life. It also left five weeks of bidding, enough for bidders to raise the money, not enough for it to drag out too long. The world was good.

We received tenders from several libraries, with a flurry after the opening bid was announced. Then slowly, one or two a week, they came in. Things hit the two point four million level and started to slow down.

I was excited. But Angel was ecstatic. She told me over and over again how she loved being in the rare book business. What a lucky thing it was for her to have been hired by Elliot Burgess Books, and how she was thinking of going into this forever. I had to remind her that we didn't have a book like the *Buchlein* every day. Or every month. Or every decade. This brilliant, enterprising, energetic young lady, however, would not have enthusiasm dampened by some old fart, and maintained her level of fevered excitement throughout the bidding. All I could say was that Elliot Burgess Books had been totally blessed by Angel's presence. She was a gem.

Late on a Friday, the first week in July, just before Angel left the shop, she recorded a bid of two million five hundred thousand. The Vatican was still "interested." And thank goodness, so were two other bidders, the Getty and Bill Gates. Very promising. Angel left the shop agog, almost reluctant to go. And normally I would shut up about five, but today I thought I'd stay a bit longer to see what kind of response we'd get from the next bid.

I waved goodbye to Angel, who had become like a member of the family by now, and walked back to my desk, ruminating what I would do with the proceeds of Carl Smith's "expensive" book. When he had said that "one is expensive," he had no idea what he was talking about. I recalled the whole story, from purchase to bidding, and pondered whether it had all been worth the effort. The final assessment: Terry had entered my life because of this book. I had acquired a pearl without price, and I was eternally grateful to Smith/Gens for the service he had done for me.

I got to my desk, coming out of this reverie, and I heard an unfamiliar voice behind me: "Don't turn around." It was spoken with finality and power, and it gave me a shiver. But our natural instinct when we hear a noise that attracts our attention is to turn to see what caused it. I began turning and heard what sounded like a hoarse cry:

"I said 'Don't turn around.' I meant it. Freeze!"

I froze. "Who are you?"

"Never mind. You are Burgess."

No question in the pronunciation. A simple fact.

"You killed my cousin."

"Your cousin?!" It had to be Pinsky. The real Pinsky.

"I killed no one. Your cousin committed suicide. In prison. I had nothing to do with it." I was scared and sweating, and I could smell the fear on my body. I hadn't felt like this for months, and I didn't like it. I was also angry. Once again I was being told what to do by people, a person, who had my bodily harm in his control. "What do you want?"

"Viktor was my cousin. He was more—he was a brother. He saved my life. He loved me. He was the only one I had in the world."

"I had nothing to do with his . . . ." I shouldn't have begun the sentence that way. The obvious words to complete it would have been "death," or "demise," or "suicide"—all reminders to Rapel Pinsky that he no longer had in his life the one who loved him.

"You did! You got him arrested."

"He was trying to kill me. He stabbed me. I have a scar." I started to turn.

"*Don't turn,*" he yelled. "I don't care about your fuckin' scar. I don't want to look at you. I'm going to kill you. It's the vendetta. Your meddling in our life caused Viktor's death. I must get even."

"Wait." I didn't know what else to say. This was, I admit, pretty inelegant, but what does one say at such a time? "Are you Rapel Pinsky?"

"You know I am."

"Why did Viktor use the name Alex Koralcik?"

"He was hiding. We had . . . ."

"What?"

"None of your business." He was agitated.

"What difference does it make?" I asked. "Why did he use your name?"

"I didn't know that he had. It was ok. He was closer than a brother."

"He was trying to kill me."

"You had him walk into a trap."

"No, I didn't," I said with force. "I didn't know the police were there."

"Bullshit."

"They followed me. I didn't know they were there." Then I thought I could get his guard down a bit by asking him, "How did you hear about all this? Where were you?"

"I was in Poland. My family was notified of my cousin's death. They said he killed himself. Viktor wouldn't do that. Unless he was forced to do it. His honor . . . ."

"I didn't have anything to do with it," I said again, this time almost yelling.

What was I to do? Did Pinsky have a weapon? What was he planning?

"Why are you here?" I said this with false bravado.

"I am going to kill you."

"How?"

"I have a gun. It will be easy. I will shoot you and get out. I am still in Poland."

I could hear him shifting to his left, beside the large bookshelf opposite my desk. I needed to do something.

"Do you want the book?"

"I don't know about the book. Viktor told me something about a book. He said it was his. His child. He wanted it back. He didn't tell me about it."

"I have a book. I bought it from someone. Viktor said it was his, but I bought it."

"I know nothing about it. I don't need to hear about a book. But I want to look you in the face. Don't turn! When I am about to shoot you, I want to see the fear in your eyes."

I heard him shifting another foot or two. What to do?

I saw the bible at the corner of my desk, right at my crotch. I grabbed it and swirled around in a flash, with the bible held in both hands in front of me. There was a piercing sound—another gunshot. God! Enough of them! I felt the impact through the pages and for a half second I reeled, then I lunged, tossing the book with both hands at Pinsky's face. Pinsky's face. It was Viktor. Unbelievable. Viktor was dead. Viktor was wreaking vengeance. From the grave? From Poland.

The bible barely left my hands by the time it hit Pinsky's face. He had been only a couple of feet behind me, and I gave it the best shove I could. It caught his face in dead center and I heard another bang. He reeled back under the weight of the word of god. If you ever thought god's word didn't carry a punch, you should have seen Rapel falling backwards, crashing into the huge shelf behind him. It was filled with massive books, all unprocessed. The shelf reeled back a couple of inches, dislodging books from the top, which shifted the weight of the whole cabinet forward, and the shelf toppled forward, with a rain of folios and quartos crashing down on Pinsky's head. The last thing I saw before he disappeared under a shower of books and the giant slab of shelf was a startled, angry face, hands going backward to try to steady himself in his fall. The gun banging to the floor—just where Dave Daws had landed.

Unbelievably stupid of me! To have such a huge shelf, loaded with lethal books, not bolted to the wall. In the earthquake capital of the universe.

I heard some loud grunts and moans from under the pile, and then silence. My desk was covered with broken and banged-up volumes, and the phone on it was on the floor behind the desk somewhere, buried. I looked through the pile of books on gardening and thought that a good gardener would be needed to dig Rapel Pinsky from the good earth.

I pulled out my cell phone. This time I called 911. After what seemed like an inordinate amount of time and explaining and urgency, I got the responder to say that someone would be over in a few minutes. I called Coster, who was on a lunch break, but he had a pager and he would get back to me in a minute.

Two minutes later I was talking to him. And three minutes later I heard a siren. I could see Rapel's hand, which fluttered a bit, weakly. I was afraid to touch it, so I didn't. By then I had run back and unearthed (unbooked) his gun and, with a dust rag, picked it up and put it where he wouldn't see it, in a cabinet in the back of the shop.

The next two hours were a blur. I remember police arriving, pulling guns, calling for back-ups, yelling to everyone and no one in particular, and making quite a ruckus. They saw Viktor's hand, felt it, got a pulse, and began the urgent excavation, with me restrained at a distance, but yelling not to damage the goods.

They began shoving books aside—despite my loud protestations that they were doing more damage. In fact, at one point I even had the temerity to shove one of the gorillas aside, when he didn't heed my protestations. He fell over, stumbling on books, and he looked up at me with fire in his eyes. Civilians don't do that to police officers. I could see getting handcuffed and shoved into the Black Mariah because I had assaulted an officer.

His blue-clad mates froze for a moment, in awe, deciding in a flash either to come to the rescue of one of their brothers or to break out in laughter, which latter they did with gusto. It was clear by this time that Pinsky was no threat, and the tension of the scene needed some comic relief. A Keystone Kop on his keester was what we needed. He rose with a menace, but when he saw the reaction of his mates, his steam disappeared. There was a moment of sanity here, and I was able to guide these folks in the proper way to pick up a book. They saw the usefulness of this, and the rest of the pick-up—really the big Pinsky dig—was reckful (as opposed to reckless) and compassionate to the old tomes that had taken a dive to save their owner. It didn't hurt that I yelled, "These books are worth thousands. If you damage them I'll sue." They became gentle and almost meticulous then, and the extraction of Pinsky didn't take an additional toll.

Viktor Pinsky looked ashen and hollow. He was alive, but his face looked as if he were at peace. I guess being crushed under books isn't so bad, after all. All in the business of the Book of Death.

Coster arrived and I told him the story. I led him to the gun, which he partially unwrapped, scrutinized, smelled, and rewrapped.

"You're always getting into trouble, Burgess."

"That's all you can say?"

"That's all I need to say."

"But if you guys knew where Pinsky was in the first place, I wouldn't have been in any trouble. It's your fault."

"Bullshit!" This was a defensive reaction, more instinct than wisdom. Then he said, "Yeah, you're right. Sorry."

I could hardly believe my ears. Well, my ears don't lie. I could hardly believe the words from Coster's mouth.

I hunted up the saving grace, how sweet the tome. There was a bullet hole right through the middle, as if Pinsky had aimed at the dead center of the book. And the bullet went in perpendicularly. I had picked it up with both hands, cover up, so I had hit Pinsky with the bottom of the volume. The bullet had made its way religiously through the New

Testament and stopped in Leviticus, at 24.17: "And he that killeth any man shall surely be put to death." Hmm. Pretty contrived? No, that's where the damn bullet stopped. In my Book of Life.

The bible had a family genealogy in it, and with any luck, the bullet didn't go through any of its owner's relatives. What would I tell her? That the good book had saved my life? She might take this as the admission of a fundamentalist. Better use another line. That a stray bullet from a street gang gunfight made its way . . . ? No. That would be dumb. I'd just have to make up something. I decided on "I got shot at while I was holding your precious book. It stopped the bullet. I will compensate you." How much didn't matter by then. I could afford anything. I thought.

FORTY TWO

(the number of lines of text on most pages of the Gutenberg Bible—
the first book ever printed from movable type)

I don't even know what 'normal' means any more. I was going to say that by July 14 life had returned to normal. But there was nothing normal about a shop receiving bids and phone calls from all over the place. Reporters had heard of the book and the attack. Great news fodder. This is not the kind of publicity I sought. But it brought people by the hordes into the shop and sales were brisk.

The *Buchlein* price had stalled out at two point nine million dollars. With only about two hours to go on the bidding, and the bidders fully aware of it, there was likely to be a final bid or two, and then things would come to an end. The Getty, the Vatican, and Bill Gates were still in the picture.

It was five thirty and we were closing the bidding at eight. Terry had come to the shop for the last supper—before doomsday. She brought with her Viktor's pamphlet. The envelope it was in still had my blood on it, and I thought of all kinds of symbolic things to say about it. Let's skip it.

This time we were in Nobu Matsuhisa, the best restaurant in L.A. The traffic on La Cienega was slow (as it is everywhere in L.A.—no such thing as *rush* hour there), and we were in a slow and lazy mood. We figured we could afford such an indulgence and the sushi and sashimi and unagi and uni and nigiri and ubi and other strange-sounding things ending in *I* are truly delicious there. We relished the meal—top notch! and sat back sipping on cool sake (someone once said if you are drinking warm sake, it's inferior). We enjoyed the orange slices and snuggled side by side, letting the mood settle.

At the right moment, Terry pulled out the notebook. It had gotten somewhat crumpled but was nonetheless perfectly legible. And we read with astonished eyes what Viktor Pinsky had so meticulously recorded.

There were several pages, each with an all caps header, and each with short paragraphs and short lists and checked-off items. Everything was written in the neat European script one would have expected from someone whose apartment was immaculate. The first leaf was blank. The second recorded:

PAPER:
Johann von Paltz
Das buchelein Wirt genant die himelische Funtgrube.
f°
Leipzig, Conrad Kachelofen, ca. 1495[?]
Goff: J-387

Large endsheets.
Copy at Berkeley. ✓
Copy at BN ✓

Leaf three had:

TEXT: NYPL ✓

Leaf four:

INK
Chair from Stillwell Antiques, London ✓
Linseed oil
Copper lead oxide—Murdochite ✓

Leaf five:

TYPE
NYPL copy ✓
Scanner
Photopolymer ✓
Mounting stock

Leaf six:

PRESS
Mainz museum

Leaves seven through eleven contained notes pertaining to travel arrangements, to San Francisco, Paris, Warsaw, Lodz, New York, Los Angeles, Köln, and other cities. Full airlines information was given, with record locators. This was followed by a haphazard expense account, listing a few things: chair 400 Euros, tickets, press use.

Other notes on later pages: "Use lampblack sparingly. Mostly Murdochite." "Mohawk for proofs—same weight." "Pavel Nov. 13." "Myers Nov. 17."

We read in silence, and I could see Terry's head shaking left to right. She didn't understand it all, but she knew what it meant.

"Elliot. What is this?"

"It's a recipe for deceit," I said. "It's a formula for forgery."

I explained.

"The paper in our *Buchlein* could come from another Kachelofen volume, printed in 1495 or so. It was a folio. That's what the F with the little zero above it means. That means it was a large volume. If someone stole the endsheets, most librarians wouldn't notice. They'd be concerned about the textblock, where all the printing is.

"Also, the other *Buchlein* that is listed here is large enough to supply a good deal of paper for a small pamphlet. Two endsheets from two copies of the book would yield enough paper of the right date and with the right watermark for our little Book of Death."

"I understand what 'Text' means, but what about ink?"

"When we visited Brad Scharwich in Delaware he told us of the cyclotron examination of Gutenberg's ink. We know that ink makers used lampblack and other ingredients. The Kachelofen ink was made of the right stuff. And the furniture from the antique shop in London could have been used to make the lampblack. It would give a carbon dating to the right era. Kurt said he found a piece of a chair in Pinsky's apartment."

Terry was shaking her head in disbelief. So was I.

"What about type?" she asked.

"I told her about the Mormon forger who photocopied a typeface contemporary to a document he was duplicating and scanned the text into a computer. Though the Mormon forger used a more primitive method, all he'd needed to do was use his computer to pull out words or even single letters, and compose a text on the computer in the right typeface—one that dated to the era of the item he was forging. And for our text, if it was forged, it could have been done from the very typeface that Kachelofen had in his shop. The final product could be assembled on a screen, with perfect alignment of letters, as would be necessary for printing from moveable type, and printed out on a plastic sheet. This could be placed over a photosensitive polymer sheet and exposed to light. The result would be a three-dimensional, relief, image of the text. This would then be mounted on what our pamphlet calls 'mounting stock' and put into a press. It would print the way real metal type would, and leave impressions in the sheet as type would."

"And Mainz?"

"It looks as if Viktor knew someone with a press in Mainz. There is a Gutenberg Museum there at which people can print some of their own projects. He could have found any number of places in the U.S., but he may have thought it would have seemed too dangerous to have anyone here know about the pamphlet."

"So our *Buchlein* is a forgery?"

"It looks like it, but I can't swear to it. All we have in this notebook is a recipe. We have no proof that Viktor did any of this. Even if we can show that he traveled to the places the notebook talks about, even if we can learn that copies of the 1495 Kachelofen books lack their endsheets, and even if we can prove that the chair he bought from Stillwell's in London was from the end of the fifteenth century, there is no way to know if he carried out the whole project that he maps out in the notebook."

"So the pamphlet could be genuine?"

"Yes. Our copy could be the real thing and the information in the notebook just tells us that Pinsky was planning to make some copies."

"But it could be fake?"

"Absolutely. There is the matter of the text. Where did it come from? Could Viktor have fabricated that too? I don't know anything about his education, but that would have to have come from someone pretty well versed in the religious controversies of the late Medieval period—the terminology, the language, the typography, the personalities, the church, and so forth. And the calligraphy. Did Pinsky know all this? Or did he copy this from some source? The text looks good enough, linguistically and textually and typographically, that all the experts believe it's genuine. We've got nearly three million dollars riding on it."

"What do you think, Elliot?"

"I plead ignorance. I feel like an agnostic. I just don't know."

There was a long pause. Terry slid her chair even closer to mine and I felt her shoulder and arm on me. It was indeed peaceful. If nothing else ever came out of this Book of Death . . . .

I felt her hand on my thigh—not in an arousing way, but in a way that said, "We are together. We are happy."

"What do we do?"

"I don't know."

"We should go back and see if there is a last bid."

"We should go home and sleep on it."

She turned to me, swiveled in her chair, and put her arms around me. I encircled her in mine. She looked up into my eyes and I felt her breath as her lips approached mine. The *Buchlein* would have to wait.